Cody cou
to have h

"I'm sorry," she whispered.

"I'm not." Cody had never been one to beat around the bush. "Not in the least," he added.

Heat radiated from where her hands were touching him, warming him in ways he couldn't understand but didn't question. She tensed her fingers as if to pull away, but if that was her intention, she didn't follow through.

Once more his gaze sought her mouth. Never had it looked more inviting than it did at that moment.

It seemed only natural to kiss her. Hell, he'd been thinking about doing exactly that for hours, but now that the opportunity presented itself, he hesitated. It was as if an inborn defense mechanism flashed a warning through his system. Kiss Christy Manning and you'll never be the same again, it seemed to be saying.

But the words of caution counted for nothing. Cody couldn't have stopped himself if he'd wanted to. Whatever came after, whatever life held for him, whatever the cost, he was going to kiss this woman.

Debbie Macomber is a #1 *New York Times* bestselling author and a leading voice in women's fiction worldwide. Her work has appeared on every major bestseller list, with more than 170 million copies in print, and she is a multiple award winner. The Hallmark Channel based a television series on Debbie's popular Cedar Cove books. For more information, visit her website, debbiemacomber.com.

Lee Tobin McClain is the *New York Times* bestselling author of emotional small-town romances featuring flawed characters who find healing through friendship, faith and family. Lee grew up in Ohio and now lives in Western Pennsylvania, where she enjoys hiking with her goofy goldendoodle, visiting writer friends and admiring her daughter's mastery of the latest TikTok dances. Learn more about her books at leetobinmcclain.com.

THE SHERIFF
TAKES A WIFE

#1 *NEW YORK TIMES* BESTSELLING AUTHOR
DEBBIE MACOMBER

BESTSELLING AUTHOR COLLECTION

If you purchased this book without a cover you should be aware that this book is stolen property. It was reported as "unsold and destroyed" to the publisher, and neither the author nor the publisher has received any payment for this "stripped book."

 Harlequin®
BESTSELLING
AUTHOR
COLLECTION

Recycling programs
for this product may
not exist in your area.

ISBN-13: 978-1-335-46356-2

The Sheriff Takes a Wife
First published in 1990. This edition published in 2025.
Copyright © 1990 by Debbie Macomber

The Soldier's Redemption
First published in 2018. This edition published in 2025.
Copyright © 2018 by Lee Tobin McClain

All rights reserved. No part of this book may be used or reproduced in any manner whatsoever without written permission.

Without limiting the author's and publisher's exclusive rights, any unauthorized use of this publication to train generative artificial intelligence (AI) technologies is expressly prohibited.

This is a work of fiction. Names, characters, places and incidents are either the product of the author's imagination or are used fictitiously. Any resemblance to actual persons, living or dead, businesses, companies, events or locales is entirely coincidental.

For questions and comments about the quality of this book, please contact us at CustomerService@Harlequin.com.

TM and ® are trademarks of Harlequin Enterprises ULC.

 Harlequin Enterprises ULC
22 Adelaide St. West, 41st Floor
Toronto, Ontario M5H 4E3, Canada
www.Harlequin.com

Printed in U.S.A.

CONTENTS

Also by Debbie Macomber

MIRA

Visit the Author Profile page
at Harlequin.com for more titles.

THE SHERIFF TAKES A WIFE

Debbie Macomber

One

"What do you *mean* you're in labor?" Christy Manning asked her sister.

"I didn't say that...exactly," Taylor Palmer said, her palms flattened against her protruding abdomen. She lowered her eyelashes, taking a long, slow breath.

"You can't be in labor! I just got here. My suitcases are still in the trunk of my car." Christy bolted to her feet and shoved the dark curls away from her face with both hands. She'd been driving for nearly three days to be with her sister for the birth of this baby, but she hadn't counted on the blessed event happening quite so soon.

"What do you want me to do?" she asked, regaining her poise. In her opinion, there was plenty of reason for alarm. The Lazy P, Russ and Taylor's cattle ranch, was miles outside Cougar Point, the closest town. And there wasn't a neighbor in sight.

Taylor's husband, Russ, was driving his sister, Mandy, over to a friend's house and doing a couple of errands before heading back to the ranch. At most he'd be gone only an hour, or so he'd claimed.

But a lot could happen in an hour.

"I'm not convinced this is the real thing," Taylor said in an apparent effort to reassure Christy, but her hands caressed her stomach as she spoke. "I've never been in labor before, so I'm not exactly sure what to expect."

Trying to gather her scattering wits, Christy circled the kitchen table. First and foremost, she needed to keep calm. Mentally she reviewed the recent classes she'd taken through the local library. She knew CPR and enough karate to defend herself. Great. She could knock someone out and then revive him. A lot of good either of those skills was going to do her in this situation.

She swallowed a feeling of impending panic. She wasn't even supposed to be in Montana. Her mother was the one who'd planned to make the trip, only Elizabeth Manning had taken a fall and broken her leg. She was having trouble getting around and would be little or no help to Taylor. Since Christy had a couple of weeks of vacation due, she'd volunteered to come and stay with her sister. It wasn't any sacrifice on her part; Christy and Taylor had always been close.

Unfortunately no one had bothered to tell her she was going to be stuck alone on a cattle ranch with her nine months' pregnant sister, who was "feeling funny."

It all seemed unreal. Christy had arrived late the night before. Too late to do more than greet everyone, haul her overnight bag into the guest bedroom and fall exhausted into bed.

"Stop looking like you expect to deliver this baby on your own," Taylor said, smiling up at her sister.

"But, Miss Scarlett, I don't know nothin' about birthin' no babies," Christy wailed in a Southern drawl.

She might be teasing, but what she said was the honest-to-goodness truth.

None of this was supposed to be happening—at least not like this. Taylor should be living in Seattle with the rest of her family. Instead, Christy's older sister had gone to Montana a year earlier and to everyone's surprise married a cattle rancher three months later.

At the time, Christy couldn't imagine what had possessed her cultured, cosmopolitan sister to marry someone like Russ Palmer. Especially in Reno, without a single family member present.

Their father hadn't been pleased at being cheated out of the chance to walk his daughter down the aisle, but once he'd met Russ, the rancher had won him over. Russ had reassured everyone in the family without even trying. Taylor and her husband had flown to Seattle at the end of May to celebrate her parents' wedding anniversary. It was then that he'd met Christy and her three brothers.

Taylor winced and her eyes drifted shut again. Her display of pain effectively cut off Christy's thoughts. She held her breath until she saw the tension slowly ease from her sister's body. "What happened?"

"I felt a funny pain, that's all. Don't worry. It wasn't anything."

"A funny pain? And you don't want me to worry?" Christy echoed. She couldn't keep the panic out of her voice. "Then why do I have this urge to boil water?"

Taylor, forever calm and serene in a crisis, grinned. "Don't worry. I've been having these pains off and on for the past week, but…"

"But what?" Christy asked.

"But these feel…different. I don't know how to explain it." She rose haltingly to her feet. "I think it might be a good idea if I got dressed."

"Right," Christy said, as if the idea was a stroke of genius. "Me, too." With her arm around what remained of Taylor's waist, Christy led her sister down the hallway that went to the master bedroom. "Do you need any help?"

"Don't be ridiculous!" Almost before the words had left her lips, Taylor let out a cry and pressed one shoulder to the wall while clutching her stomach.

Christy was instantly alarmed. "What is it?"

"Oh…my." Wide-eyed, Taylor turned toward Christy. "Hurry and get some towels. My water just broke."

"Your water broke," Christy repeated in a stupor. She threw her hands toward the ceiling. "Her water just broke." Rushing into the bathroom, she returned with enough towels to soak up a flood.

Taylor was still leaning against the wall, breathing deeply, her eyes closed. Christy dropped the towels onto the floor, far more concerned about Taylor than she was about a little water. "Are you all right?"

Her sister answered with a nod that said otherwise.

"I'm calling the doctor," Christy told her. "Don't you dare move. Understand?" The panic was stronger than ever, but Christy managed to swallow it. Taylor needed her; there wasn't time to be concerned with her own fears.

Taylor's doctor was in Miles City, sixty miles away, and the hospital was there, too. As far as she could tell, they were an hour or more from help. Christy spoke to Dr. Donovan briefly, and when she explained what had happened, the doctor suggested Taylor come to the hospital immediately.

"I'm not going without Russ," Taylor insisted when Christy relayed her conversation. "Russ will be back any minute."

Christy started to balk. It wasn't her fault that Taylor's husband had such a bad sense of timing.

"You don't know Russ the way I do," Taylor said, even before Christy had a chance to reason with her. "If he came home and found us gone—"

"I'll leave him a note. He'll understand. Then as soon as he's back, he can join us."

"No."

Christy had heard that tone of voice often enough to realize these was no way she could budge that stubborn streak of Taylor's. "We can't just sit here and wait," Christy moaned.

"Of course we can. Now relax!"

"Me, relax? You're the one having the baby."

"I'm fine. Baby Palmer and mother are both calm and prepared."

Baby Palmer. Her only sister was about to become a mother. This wasn't new information, but until this moment Taylor's pregnancy had seemed abstract. Yet here they were alone together, and suddenly this baby was very real. This tiny life depended on Christy, and the thought was terrifying. Yet nothing she said would convince Taylor to leave for the hospital without Russ.

The next thirty minutes felt like thirty years. Christy changed into jeans and a sweatshirt, forced down another cup of coffee and looked out the kitchen window every three seconds.

Outwardly Taylor still seemed calm, but Christy could tell from the pain that flashed on her sister's face that the intensity of the contractions was increasing.

"Maybe you should call the feed store. If Russ isn't there, then contact Cody."

"Great idea!" Christy leaped at the possibility of bringing someone else into the picture. The sooner the better. "Just a minute," she said. "Who's Cody?"

"Cody Franklin…he's the newly elected sheriff and a good friend. I don't know what his schedule is, so try the office first. If he's not at work, his home number's written in the front of the phone book."

Calling anyone, including the National Guard, sounded like an excellent plan to Christy. She found the impossibly thin phone book in the drawer. Good grief, she'd ordered from menus thicker than this.

Christy phoned the feed store first. The lady who answered said Russ had left a half hour earlier, and she hadn't a clue where he'd gone. Christy accepted this with a shrug. At the rate things were developing, she was about to take an advanced course in childbirth.

Christy found the sheriff's home number right where Taylor said it would be. She punched it out and waited impatiently for someone, anyone, to answer.

"Hello," a groggy voice muttered on the fourth ring.

"Hi, oh, thank God you answered." Christy was so relieved, she wanted to weep. She gulped in one giant breath and rushed to explain. "You don't know me. I'm Christy Manning, Taylor Palmer's sister, and Russ left an hour ago and promised he'd be back but he isn't and Taylor's water broke and she's in labor. She keeps insisting she won't leave for the hospital until Russ comes home, but he isn't here, and I don't know anything about delivering babies."

A short silence followed. "Taylor's in labor?"

"That's what I just finished saying. The second and

equally important factor is that Russ, the father of this about-to-be-born-baby, isn't here. He said he'd only be gone an hour, but he's late, and Taylor really should be leaving for the hospital."

"Where did he say he was going?"

"The feed store. But he left there thirty minutes ago and…and *disappeared*." That might be an exaggeration, but the situation called for a minor stretching of the truth, although she realized she'd made it sound as if he'd been abducted by aliens.

"I'll find him and be there as soon as I can."

The relief that washed over Christy felt like a cool evening rain after the hottest day of summer. Taylor needed her, and the last thing Christy wanted to do was reveal how much this situation frightened her. She'd made this trip to help Taylor with the baby. As in diaper, hold, burp. Not *deliver*.

She coaxed Taylor into the living room and had her lie down on the sofa. The ease with which Christy was able to convince her revealed a great deal about Taylor's condition. Although she struggled to disguise it, her dauntless older sister was scared. The pains were obviously far stronger than Taylor was willing to admit.

A whole lifetime seemed to pass before Christy heard a car barreling down the driveway. Taylor sighed audibly and relaxed against the pillows Christy had placed behind her back. "That's Russ now."

Christy hurried to the back door. She didn't recognize the car as Russ's, but that was the least of her worries. The four-wheel-drive Cherokee hadn't even come to a stop before her brother-in-law leaped out of the front seat.

He raced up the steps. "Where's Taylor?" he demanded.

Numb with relief, Christy sagged against the doorjamb and pointed toward the living room. She was about to follow her brother-in-law when a second man climbed out of the driver's seat.

Christy couldn't pull her eyes away from this tall, long-limbed stranger. It was all she could do not to throw her arms around him in thanks. "You must be Cody."

He touched the rim of his Stetson. "At your service. You must be Taylor's sister," he said, sauntering toward her.

"Christy Manning," she said in an authoritative voice, as if she had the situation completely under control and frequently delivered babies while vacationing. She stepped forward to offer the sheriff of Custer County her hand. In truth she was so grateful he'd found Russ that she was close to tears.

A few seconds later, Russ came out, carrying Taylor. "You ready?" he asked his friend.

"Russ, put me down," Taylor insisted. "I'm too heavy."

"We'll argue later, but at the moment you're about to give birth to my son," Russ reminded her with a worried frown.

"Our baby could very well be a girl," Taylor began. "You're still so pigheaded you refuse to—"

"I swear you're the only woman on God's green earth who'd argue with me at a time like this."

"I'd think you'd be used to it by now," Taylor mumbled, but her voice faded as a fresh contraction overtook her. She closed her eyes, pressed her hands to her belly and breathed deeply.

Russ's distraught gaze connected with Christy's.

"I'll get her suitcase," Christy said as she rushed into the master bedroom. When she reappeared, Cody took the single bag from her hands and put it inside the car. Taylor and Russ were already situated in the back seat, and the passenger door was open for Christy. Without another word, she climbed inside and snapped the seat belt in place.

The ride to the hospital took a full hour. Christy didn't need to look at the speedometer to know Cody was traveling well above the speed limit. If anything, she had to stop herself from pleading with him to go even faster.

Taylor did an admirable job of disguising the extent of her discomfort, but it was apparent to all that the sooner she was under medical supervision the better. Russ was calm and collected.

It turned out that the carburetor in Russ's truck had started acting up, and he'd pulled over to the side of the road. Cody had found him bent over the engine, trying to fix it so he could make it back to the ranch.

Christy held herself tense until they reached the outskirts of Miles City. Only then did she feel herself start to relax.

Within ten minutes of their arrival at the hospital, Taylor was in the labor room with Russ at her side. Cody and Christy were relegated to the waiting room, where they leafed through six-month-old issues of *Time* magazine.

Soon bored with those, Christy found her gaze wandering to Cody. Fine lines fanned out from the corners of his dark eyes, and sharply cut grooves bracketed his mouth. He was tanned, his skin weathered by the sun and wind. He had the kind of rich bronze coloring that others strived to achieve under a sunlamp. His hair was thick and as dark as his eyes and cut military short. He wasn't handsome or stunning or anything else she could easily put a name to, but he was beyond a doubt the most uncompromisingly masculine man she'd ever seen. Immediately she experienced a faint stirring of guilt.

James. Dear, sweet James. Always so patient and understanding. She shouldn't even be *looking* at another man, not when she had James.

Cody glanced up from his magazine, and their eyes met. Christy managed to fake a smile. He returned it with a smile of his own and went back to reading. Christy made a pretense of doing the same thing. Despite her best efforts, her gaze wandered back to the sheriff again and again. It was somewhat embarrassing to realize that she wasn't studying him as a representative of law and order but as a man. Cody Franklin was incredibly male. Incredibly...incredible. Everything about him spoke of strength and purpose: his walk, the square set of his jaw, even the way he sat with his ankle resting over his knee. Disturbed by her unintended focus on the sheriff, she flipped through the pages of a two-year-old issue of *People*. Something was definitely wrong with her. No doubt it had to do with Taylor and the baby. Babies were said to stir up lots of feelings and buried emotions. What astonished her was that she should find this man so attractive.

Enough!

More determined than ever, Christy reached for another magazine and gazed unseeing at its pages.

"I take it you just arrived in Cougar Point?" Cody surprised her by asking.

"Last night," Christy said, setting aside the dog-eared

issue of *People*. "Actually, it was early this morning when I went to bed. Russ left the house about the time I came down for coffee, and the next thing I knew, Taylor was telling me she was having these 'funny' pains, only I wasn't laughing, and neither was she."

"How long after that did you call me?"

"Too long," Christy said vehemently. "Taylor claimed the pains were nothing to worry about. I knew I shouldn't have listened to her. Good grief, what does she know?"

Cody smiled, and her eyes were immediately drawn to his full sensual mouth. Frustrated with herself, she quickly looked away.

"Don't be so hard on yourself. You handled the situation exactly the way you should have." He turned back to the periodical. Christy picked up another one herself, but when she glanced up, she saw Cody studying her. "I don't mean to stare," he apologized, "but I can't get over how much you and Taylor resemble each other."

That was almost worth a laugh. She'd hardly been able to keep her eyes off Cody Franklin from the moment they got to the hospital, and *he* was apologizing for staring at *her!* As for the part about the two sisters looking alike, Christy took that as a compliment. Taylor was stunning. In fact, Christy couldn't remember a time when her sister had been more beautiful than she was right now. Taylor was the beauty, not Christy. She didn't mean to sell herself short; she knew she was reasonably attractive. Perhaps the biggest difference was that Taylor had spunk. Her older sister had always displayed such tenacity, such mettle. When it came to dealing with their headstrong father, Taylor had more courage than the rest of them put together.

Anyone looking at the two sisters would know they

were related; Christy was willing to grant the sheriff that much. Their deep blue eyes were a distinct family trait, also shared by their three older brothers, as was the slightly upturned nose.

The two sisters styled their hair differently. Taylor kept her thick chestnut hair long, whereas Christy preferred hers short in a breezy wash-and-wear style.

Christy was about to make some comment along the lines of what a peaceful community Cougar Point seemed to be when they saw Russ.

Cody and Christy stood as Russ approached, his eyes slightly dazed.

"Taylor's ready to go into the delivery room."

"So soon?" Christy's heart was in her throat. "We just got here." She paused long enough to check her watch—and restrain her panic. "We've only been here twenty minutes. How could she possibly be ready for the delivery room?"

"I don't know.... The nurse told me the baby's coming *now*."

"It wasn't supposed to be this soon."

Russ wiped a hand down his face. "You're telling me? If Cody hadn't found me when he did..." He left the rest unsaid, but the implication was obvious.

Christy slumped back into the chair, her knees about to buckle. From everything she'd read and heard, babies were supposed to take their time, especially the first one. What about those twenty-hour labors her friends had described in minute detail? What about all the talk of first labors dragging on and on? Apparently Taylor hadn't been listening.

Russ returned to the double doors, then looked back into the waiting room. He swallowed hard, and Christy realized that if she'd been shaken by the news, it had affected Russ far more profoundly.

"Are you all right?" Cody asked her.

"Of course," she lied. "I'm not the one who's having a baby minutes after I arrive at the hospital." A fact for which Christy was eternally grateful. She wasn't nearly as courageous as Taylor; in fact, when it came right down to it, she considered herself a watered-down version of her older sister. All her life Christy had admired Taylor, wanting to be more like her. Instead, she was complacent and congenial, never causing her parents a moment's concern. Their father once claimed he owed every gray hair on his head to Taylor and every laugh line to Christy. His two daughters were the joy of his life, he often said.

"You look like you're going to faint," Cody said, watching her closely.

"Don't be ridiculous," she snapped, then instantly regretted her sharp tongue. She darted Cody an apologetic smile.

"Come on," Cody suggested, "let's walk. It'll help pass the time."

"Pass what time?" she muttered. "We've been here for about twenty minutes, and already Taylor's being wheeled into the delivery room."

"Come on, you could do with some activity—get your circulation going."

Christy merely nodded. Emotions were coming at her from every direction. Her first concern was for Taylor and the baby. The thought of this precious life, created in love, stirred a realm of deep feelings inside Christy. Her stomach started churning, her palms were sweating, and her heart seemed to be doing a jig. She couldn't have uttered a word had her life depended on it.

They walked the entire length of the hallway and stopped in front of the nursery. Christy carefully studied the row of newborns swaddled in pink and blue blankets and unexpectedly found tears clouding her eyes. Normally she wasn't sentimental or weepy. She didn't dare look over at Cody. He'd assume… She hadn't a clue what he'd assume, but it wouldn't be good.

"Christy?"

"The babies are really beautiful, aren't they?" she whispered, her gaze on the five infants.

"Yes, they are," he answered softly. He stood behind her and rested his hands on the curve of her shoulders. His touch was light, but it offered her a steadiness and comfort that had been lacking all morning. He didn't say anything when she brushed the telltale moisture from her cheeks, and Christy was grateful.

She didn't know what had come over her in the past few hours. She turned to face Cody, placed her hands on his forearms and stared up at him, her eyes bright with unshed tears.

Nothing seemed real anymore. It was as if she'd been walking around in a dream. A living fantasy was beginning to unfold right before her. Perhaps she'd spent too many hours on the road. Otherwise she wouldn't be looking into the darkest brown eyes she'd ever seen and thinking the things she was thinking.

Cody was staring back at her with the same wonder and surprise. He seemed about to say something important when the doors at the other end of the hall opened and Russ stepped out, wearing a green surgical gown and a large smile. Seeing him, both Christy and Cody rushed forward.

"It's a boy," Russ announced, his eyes shimmering with tears. He let out a wild shout of joy, grabbed a shocked Christy around the waist and boisterously whirled her around.

"Congratulations," Cody said, coming forward. The two men exchanged hearty handshakes, then hugged, slapping each other on the back.

Russ didn't speak for a moment and seemed to be composing himself. "He weighed in at eight pounds, three ounces, and he's the ugliest little critter you ever saw. Taylor kept saying how beautiful he is, and all I could see was this furious pink face bawling as loud as anything. His legs were pumping like an oil rig. That boy is madder than a wet wasp."

Christy felt tears in her eyes as she pressed her fingers to her lips. "How's Taylor?"

"She's fine...more than fine. That woman's incredible. I don't know what I ever did to deserve her, but I intend to thank God every day for the rest of my life." He half turned toward the doors he'd come through. "I've got to get back. They're taking Eric into the nursery now, and the delivery room nurse said I could watch him being washed and dressed. If I have anything to say about it, I'll do the washing and dressing myself."

"You're naming him Eric?" Christy asked as she moved one step forward.

Russ nodded. "Eric Russell, after your father and me. Taylor insists."

"That sounds like a perfectly wonderful name to me," Christy whispered, surprised at the emotion that clogged her throat. Her father would be so proud, the buttons would pop right off his shirt.

"If you two walk over to the nursery, you might be able to see him, too," Russ added excitedly. "Taylor will be out of the delivery room anytime. I know she'll want to talk to you both, so stick around for a little bit, okay?"

Christy and Cody had already started in that direction when Russ stopped them. "Hey, one last thing. Taylor and I talked it over, and we want the two of you to be Eric's godparents."

Christy exchanged a meaningful glance with Cody before they simultaneously nodded.

"We'd be honored," Cody answered for them.

"Truly honored," Christy repeated, her throat tightening even more.

In her excitement Christy whirled around to face Cody—except that she hadn't realized he was quite so close. She flattened her hands against his chest as she smiled up at him, her joy overflowing now that her nephew was safely born.

Cody returned the smile. His dark eyes were alive with emotion.

Slowly, moving as if he were hypnotized, Cody slipped his arms around her waist and raised her from the ground. Her hands clutched his shirt collar as his eyes delved into hers.

"I believe congratulations are in order, don't you?"

"Yes," she said, hugging him, afraid he was going to kiss her, equally afraid he wouldn't.

How would she ever explain kissing another man to James? How would she rationalize allowing Cody to hold her like this when she'd promised to spend her life loving someone else?

Two

"Oh, Taylor, he's so beautiful," Christy whispered. "Russ held him up for me to see and…" She paused, unable to continue. The minute she'd seen Eric, her heart had swollen with such a profound sense of love that it had been impossible to suppress her tears.

"You're crying," Taylor said softly.

Christy rubbed her cheeks. She reached for her sister, and they hugged with an intensity she'd never felt before. This wealth of emotion, of happiness, took Christy by storm.

"I love you, Taylor. I really do. And I love Eric, too. He's beautiful, perfect. I feel absolutely ecstatic." She straightened and gave a breathy laugh. "I want to throw open the windows and tell the world my sister just had a beautiful baby boy."

"Did you get a chance to talk to Mom and Dad?"

Christy nodded. The moment her mother heard the news she'd started weeping and then her father had taken the phone. His own voice hadn't sounded all that steady, either. Russ had done most of the talking with Christy crowded close beside him. When it was her turn, she seemed to jabber on like a magpie, but couldn't stop herself.

Following the conversation, Russ and Cody had gone to the hospital gift shop to buy a box of cigars. Christy had spent these few moments alone with her sister.

"I'm sorry I frightened you," Taylor said apologetically, "but I didn't want to leave for the hospital without Russ."

"I understood. I wasn't worried." On the contrary, Christy had been nearly frantic, but it didn't matter now that everything had turned out so well.

Her sister sighed. "I'm glad you were able to meet Cody."

At the mention of the other man's name, Christy abruptly looked away, feeling uneasy. She hadn't had the chance to tell Taylor and Russ about her engagement to James Wilkens. Unfortunately the diamond ring James had given her was still at the jeweler's being sized. If she'd been wearing the ring, it would've been a logical introduction to her announcement. She'd meant to surprise her sister and brother-in-law with the big news as soon as she'd arrived, but it had been so late and everyone was exhausted. Then, before Christy knew it, it was morning and Taylor had gone into labor.

Now the timing was all wrong. Tomorrow, she promised herself, she'd tell Taylor. Everything would be less hectic then. But even as she formed that decision, Christy hesitated, not fully understanding why.

Her head spun and her thoughts skidded to a halt. Who did she think she was fooling?

She *did* know why.

Cody Franklin had hugged her when Russ had come

to tell them about Eric. Now, an hour later, the way she'd felt in his arms still caused her pulse to accelerate. He'd pulled her close, and the feeling of being held by this man was completely and utterly natural, as instinctive as breathing or sleeping. It was as if they'd known each other all their lives. As if their relationship was one of long standing.

Without his saying a thing, Christy knew he'd experienced the same lavish range of sensations. They'd stared openly at each other, neither speaking. If Russ hadn't been there, Christy couldn't help wondering what would've happened. What they would've said to each other. If anything.

But Russ had been there, and after an awkward moment, Cody had released her. He'd dropped his arms with a reluctance that sent blood pounding through her veins until she grew dizzy simply remembering.

James was her fiancé! Yet she had to struggle to bring his image to mind. Her parents had been thrilled with the news of their engagement, but Christy had known they would be. Her father had told her often enough that James, an attorney, would make her an excellent husband. They'd been dating on and off for nearly two years, almost from the first week Christy had been hired as a paralegal at James's law firm. Their relationship, however, hadn't turned serious until three months ago. Until then, their dates had been casual get-togethers with mutual friends. Then they'd started working together on an important case. It had been a real coup for James to be assigned to defend Gary Mulligan against the Internal Revenue Service, and if everything went well, it could mean a partnership for him.

"Christy?"

She turned to her sister. "Sorry. Were you saying something?"

"Just that I'm glad you met Cody today."

"He…seems very nice," Christy answered, and sighed with relief when the nurse walked into the room, distracting her sister's attention from the subject of the sheriff. The woman brought in a huge bouquet of red roses in a tall crystal vase.

"Oh, my," Taylor breathed, reaching for the card. She tore open the small envelope and read the message. Immediate tears filled her eyes. "They're from Russ."

"How sweet."

Taylor smiled softly as a faraway look came into her eyes. Christy speculated that her sister was recalling the first time she'd met Russ and all that had happened since. Russ might not have been the man her family would've chosen for Taylor, but one fact had been clear from the instant they flew to Seattle to attend their parents' anniversary party. Russ Palmer loved Taylor. Beyond question. Beyond doubt. Whatever reservations Christy and her brothers held regarding this marriage had been quickly dissolved.

Footsteps from behind Christy told her Russ and Cody had returned.

"Russ…" Taylor held out her arms to her husband. "The roses are so beautiful. Thank you."

Christy's brother-in-law walked across the room, and his eyes closed as he took his wife into his arms. He whispered something in her ear; Taylor smiled and nodded. The scene was an intimate one, and Christy felt like an intruder. She backed away, not looking at Cody until it was impossible to avoid him.

"Hello, again," he said. His voice was low and his

smile contained a warmth and depth that multiplied a hundredfold all the sensations she'd experienced earlier, the very feelings she was trying to put out of her mind. Once again Christy was struck by the possessiveness she felt looking at him, studying him. For the past hour she'd been trying to understand why she should feel anything toward him. Nothing had come to her. No insights. Nothing.

They were barely more than strangers, and yet she felt completely comfortable with him. At the same time, he rattled her composure unlike anyone she'd ever met. It seemed absurdly ironic to be so flustered by a man and still feel so sheltered.

Cody glanced toward Russ and Taylor. "Would you like to go down to the nursery to view our godson?"

She nodded, gladly accepting an excuse to leave husband and wife alone.

Together she and Cody walked down the familiar corridor until they stood in front of the large nursery window. But it wasn't the newborns that captured their attention. They made comments about little Eric and the other babies, but what interested them most was each other. After a while they gave up the pretense of looking at the newborns.

"Russ phoned the ranch and is having a couple of his hands drive a car over for him," Cody said after a while. "He's planning to spend the day with Taylor."

Once more Christy nodded. It seemed all she was capable of doing. Being this close to Cody felt like being trapped in a magnetic force field. It didn't matter how much she resisted, she was drawn to him.

With a determined effort, she diverted her attention to Eric again. The infant was sleeping, swaddled in a pale blue receiving blanket. A long-sleeved T-shirt covered his tiny arms and fists. He was so small, so adorable.

Cody's eyes followed hers, and when he spoke, his voice was filled with astonishment. "He's really something, isn't he?"

"Yes." Her voice was a whisper. "And to think we could've ended up delivering him."

"We?" Cody joked. "In all my years of law enforcement I've been spared that. Thank God."

Standing behind her, Cody's large hands held her shoulders, as if he'd been holding and touching her for a lifetime. It felt right and good to have this man so close. A small shudder skimmed down her spine at the innocent contact.

Cody must have noticed it, because he turned her around to face him, his eyes narrowing slightly. "You're trembling."

She couldn't deny it. This man she hardly knew confused her, bewildered her. The worst part was that she couldn't understand why. She'd met and dated any number of attractive, compelling men before. Yet none of them had ever overwhelmed her the way Cody did.

"Are you cold?"

"No," she answered quickly, flustered by his questions.

"What's wrong?"

How could she possibly explain something she couldn't grasp herself? "Nothing."

His eyes found hers, and she could've sworn they went several shades darker. "Does this happen often?"

"No." She shook her head. "Does it to you?" Christy swallowed, astonished she'd had the courage to ask him such a personal question.

"No," he answered after a moment. "Never."

She pulled her gaze away, baffled by his openness. His honesty. It was exactly what she'd longed to hear. And what she'd feared.

"I… I need to get back to the ranch," she said, seeking an excuse to do something, anything to end this heightened awareness between them. "Taylor asked me to make some phone calls for her."

Cody lowered his eyes to her lips, his look, unhurried and sensual, as intimate as a kiss. Christy's stomach became a churning mass of doubts, mingled with an abundance of misgivings. She wanted to blame this feeling on the chaotic events of the day.

Slowly, almost unaware of what she was doing, Christy raised her own eyes to meet Cody's. He didn't look too comfortable. In fact, he seemed as perplexed and hesitant as she.

"I need to get back myself," he murmured.

Not until that moment did Christy realize the only way she had of returning to Cougar Point was with Cody. A sinking feeling assailed her. She couldn't possibly avoid an hour or more with him in the intimate confines of his vehicle.

Cody Franklin had no idea what was happening between him and his best friend's sister-in-law. To be honest, he hadn't paid Christy Manning much attention until they were in the hospital waiting room. She'd been terribly agitated, flipping through one magazine after another. Cody doubted she'd read a single word.

Then Russ had appeared and said that Taylor was ready for the delivery room, and Cody had watched as Christy started to completely unravel.

He'd suggested they take a short walk in an effort to help her relax. He didn't know how much comfort he'd be to her, since he was a stranger, but the least he could do was try. He knew from his years as a lawman that some physical activity might help take her mind off her sister.

It was when they'd stopped to look at the babies in the nursery that Cody had felt the faint stirring of something more. Faint stirring, hell, it was like a fist to his gut!

From that moment on, some emotion had started to awaken deep within him. He experienced a lost sensation, as if he were charting unknown land, and each turn led him farther away from all that was familiar. He was suddenly at a loss for words; he'd planned to involve her in conversation, occupy her with inane chitchat about Seattle and her job to keep her from thinking about Taylor, but he hadn't asked a single question.

Every time Cody started to speak, he got lost in her eyes. He'd never seen a woman with eyes quite this blue. They reminded him of the coldest days of winter, when everything around him seemed to anticipate the promise of spring. When she smiled, those same blue eyes brightened even more, and it was like watching sunshine emerge after rain.

She'd look at him, and Cody swore he could see all the way to her soul. She was guileless and genuine and so lovely, it was all he could do not to stare at her, something he'd already apologized for once that day.

Twice he'd placed his hands on her shoulders. It wasn't his habit to comfort women with physical gestures, and he didn't understand his own actions. When he'd first held her, she'd obviously been shaken by Russ's news about Taylor, and he'd reached out in an effort to steady her.

The moment his hands had closed over her shoulders, his heart had begun racing like a runaway train. That hadn't happened since he was thirteen and had kissed a girl for the very first time.

Twenty-two years had passed, and the impact now was nearly as strong. Every minute with her he learned something new about himself, and every emotion he discovered only bewildered him more.

"I'm sorry if it's an inconvenience for you to take me out to the ranch," Christy said, sliding into the front seat of his four-wheel drive.

"It isn't a problem." The only difficulty it created was of his own making. He was caught in some mysterious web of yearning. Perhaps, in some strange way, this all had to do with Russ and Taylor. He couldn't help envying the happiness his friends had found. Taylor was the best thing that had ever happened to Russ Palmer, and now Russ was a father.

Cody paused, half expecting to feel a twinge of jealousy or resentment. When he was introduced to Taylor a year ago, he'd wanted to date her himself, but she'd already met Russ and it was clear that she was falling in love with him. Cody had stood on the sidelines and watched their romance unfold, amused at the way they'd both fought it so hard.

No, jealousy hadn't prompted these feelings; he was convinced of that. His only reaction was happiness for his friends—a pure sense of shared joy.

The drive, which had seemed like four hundred miles earlier in the day with Taylor and Russ in the backseat, went quickly on the return trip. Christy said little, but neither seemed uneasy with the silence. Occasionally Cody would look over at her, and their eyes would meet. Each time, some magic would pass involuntarily between them, some entrancement. After a while it became a challenge to discover what fascinated him about Taylor's sister, and he found his gaze repeatedly drawn to her as he attempted to analyze his attraction.

She was pretty, but no prettier than any number of women he'd dated. Not as beautiful as Becca. He paused, surprised that he didn't immediately feel a jolt of pain as he thought about her. It had been three years since Becca had turned his life upside down. He tried not to think of her at all, tried to ignore her memory as though he'd never known her at all. For the most part he succeeded... For the most part.

"Would you like to stop and get something to eat?" Cody asked as they neared Cougar Point. He wasn't hungry so much as reluctant to leave her.

He should've been exhausted. He'd had only a couple of hours sleep in the past forty-eight. Instead he felt alive. Reborn.

All he knew was that he'd met a woman, a warm, caring, generous woman, and he felt as if his life was starting over again.

"I'm starved," Christy said enthusiastically. "I was so concerned about Taylor this morning that I forgot to eat breakfast."

"I haven't had anything, either."

"I got you out of bed when I phoned, didn't I?"

Cody nodded. Hell, he'd give his right hand to have her wake him every morning. "I worked the graveyard shift last night."

"You must be exhausted."

On the contrary, Cody had never felt more energetic. "Not at all," he said, mustering a smile to reassure her.

"There are a couple of decent restaurants in town, but if you're interested in breakfast, the best place to eat is the bowling alley."

"Great."

Cody had expected her to laugh or to question his choice. She was, after all, a city girl, and he doubted that anyone in Seattle had ever taken her out to eat at a bowling alley. But she accepted his choice enthusiastically.

Since it was midafternoon by this time, the parking lot was nearly deserted. Christy didn't wait for him to come around and open the door for her, a fact that didn't surprise him. Taylor hadn't waited for him to open her door the one time he'd gone out with her, either.

Cody chose a booth toward the back of the restaurant and slid into the red vinyl seat. Christy sat across from him and reached for the menu, which was tucked between the sugar bowl and the salt and pepper shakers.

"Howdy, Cody," Mary Andrews said as she came over to the table, carrying two water glasses. She glanced curiously at Christy.

"This is Taylor's sister, Christy Manning. Christy, Mary Andrews."

"I don't suppose Taylor had her baby, did she?" Mary asked.

Christy's eyes softened as she nodded. "This morning. Eric Russell Palmer weighed in at eight pounds, three ounces."

Mary grinned from ear to ear. "That's terrific. You don't mind if I let folks know, do you?"

Christy shook her head. "Please do."

Still grinning, Mary pulled a small pad from her apron pocket. "What can I get for you two?"

"I'll have the breakfast special," Christy said, closing her menu. "With coffee."

"So will I," Cody said, sliding his own menu back into place.

Mary wrote down their order, then walked back to the kitchen.

For a long time Cody said nothing. Partly because he didn't know what to say and partly because he didn't feel the need to fill the silence with small talk. He was comfortable with Christy. He hadn't felt that way with any woman, ever. He looked over at her and wondered if she was experiencing this same sense of serenity, and instinctively knew she was. "What are you thinking?" he asked as Mary filled two cups with coffee.

Christy added cream to hers, took a sip and smiled. "If we're Eric's godparents, does that mean the two of us are related?"

A grin lit his face. "I suppose it does. I'm just not sure how."

"Me, neither."

One thing he did know: the idea of being linked to Christy pleased him immeasurably. "Tell me about yourself." He wanted to know everything there was to know about her from the time she was in preschool to the present.

"I'm the youngest of five."

"Spoiled?"

"Terribly."

He deliberately drew his gaze away from her mouth, which had fascinated him for several minutes. Beyond question, he knew he was going to kiss her. He didn't know when. Soon, if possible. Nor did he know where. Only that it was quickly becoming an obsession.

"What about you?" Christy asked, pulling a napkin from the holder and spreading it across her lap, taking time to smooth it out. She seemed to be avoiding eye contact with him. That didn't surprise Cody. He'd been blatantly staring at her every chance he got. Her mouth enthralled him as nothing ever had. Soft. Pink. Moist. Just right for kissing.

"What about you?" she repeated, and the question seemed to echo.

"I was born in Miles City," he said, focusing on his coffee. "In the same hospital as Eric, as a matter of fact."

"Was your father a rancher?"

"No. He was a lawman, just as his father was before him. The Franklins have a long tradition of upholding law and order in Custer County."

"Did you always want to work for the sheriff's department?"

"Always. For as long as I can remember I dreamed of wearing a badge."

"They must be proud of you," she said in a way that made his heart quicken. What she was said was true. But his father and grandfather would never know he'd been elected sheriff; his two younger sisters were the only family he had left.

Cody didn't want to talk about himself, not when there was so much to learn about her. "What did *you* want to be when you were a kid?"

"Not a paralegal," she said, then looked away, as if the words had slipped out before she could stop them. "I didn't even know what they were until high school. Sad to say, my dreams were far more traditional. I wanted to be a mommy."

"And now?"

"And now," she repeated in a whisper, frowning.

She was saved from having to answer by Mary, who brought two platters to their table. Each was heaped high with steaming hash browns, scrambled eggs, sausage and toast.

Their conversation ceased as they both picked up their forks. Neither spoke for several minutes.

"I didn't realize how hungry I was," Christy said, reaching for the small container of jam. She peeled back the cover and scooped out the preserves with her knife.

"Where's Mandy?" Cody asked, remembering Russ's teenage sister, who lived with Russ and Taylor, for the first time that day.

"She's with a friend. Russ phoned from the hospital and told her about Eric. She had lots of questions and was sorry she missed all the excitement."

Cody pushed his empty plate aside. Mary stopped by the table to refill their coffee mugs and take away Cody's plate.

"You might as well take mine, too," Christy said, leaning back in the booth. She placed her hands over her flat stomach and sighed. "I can't believe I ate all that."

"Can I get you anything else?" Mary asked.

"Nothing, thanks," Cody answered for them.

Mary set the bill on the table and walked away with a quick backward wave.

They left the restaurant a few minutes later. Cody opened the door for Christy, insisting on the courtesy because he enjoyed doing something, however small, for her.

She seemed preoccupied and anxious on the ride to the Lazy P. He started to ask her how long she planned to stay, but even before he'd finished the question, he knew she wasn't listening.

"I'm sorry. What did you say?" she asked, glancing at him.

"It wasn't important." He pulled off the main road and headed down the long, dusty driveway. This time of year the road was filled with ruts deep enough to send them both bouncing around the interior of his Cherokee if he wasn't careful to watch where he was driving. In several spots he slowed down to ten or so miles an hour. Then he was forced to ask himself if it was his car he was concerned about—or the fact that the sooner he arrived at the ranch, the sooner he'd have to leave Christy.

Once he reached the ranch yard, he turned off the engine and climbed out of the cab. Christy had opened the car door, offering him just the excuse he needed to touch her. His hands slid around her slim waist and he lifted her down.

She hadn't been expecting his help and, caught off guard, she fell forward. She made a small sound as her hands came into contact with his chest.

Neither moved. Cody couldn't believe how good it felt to have her in his arms again.

"I'm sorry," she whispered.

"I'm not." Cody had never been one to beat around the bush, as the saying went. "Not in the least," he added.

Her hands were against his chest, and he wondered if she could feel how fast his heart was beating, wondered if she had even an inkling of what he was feeling.

"Thanks for breakfast and the ride home," she murmured, but made no effort to move away from him.

Heat radiated from where her hands were touching him, warming him in ways he couldn't understand but didn't question. She tensed her fingers as if to pull away, but if that was her intention, she didn't follow through.

Cody raised his hand to the side of her neck. His fingers stroked the kitten-soft skin there, and he watched, fascinated, as she slowly closed her eyes.

Once more his gaze sought her mouth. Her lush, vulnerable mouth. Never had it looked more inviting than it did at that moment.

It seemed only natural to kiss her. Hell, he'd been thinking about doing exactly that for hours, but now that the opportunity presented itself, he hesitated. It was as if an inborn defense mechanism flashed a warning through his system. Kiss Christy Manning and you'll never be the same again, it seemed to be saying.

But the words of caution counted for nothing. Cody couldn't have stopped himself if he'd wanted to. Whatever came after, whatever life held for him, whatever the cost, he was going to kiss this woman.

Unhurriedly, deliberately, he pressed his lips over hers. She murmured something, Cody didn't know what, and he felt the movement against his mouth.

Her lips were everything Cody had dreamed they would be. Warm. Moist. Devastating. With a whimper she responded immediately. It was as if he'd never kissed a woman before this moment.

Her arms made their way around his neck as she leaned into him. Her softness melded into his hardness, and white-hot sensation seemed to explode inside him. Cody kissed her again and again, his hands in her hair, cradling the back of her head. He kissed her until his breathing became labored. Until he heard her moan, and then realized it was his own sigh of longing that echoed in his ears. Still he didn't release her. He held her against him, never wanting to let her go.

Only when Christy stiffened did Cody slacken his hold. Slowly he opened his eyes to discover her looking up at him, her beautiful eyes bright with tears. He frowned because he didn't understand. Then, in a heartbeat, he did. The kissing had affected her as profoundly as it had him.

"I know what you're thinking," he whispered, lifting her chin with his finger, dropping his mouth to hers, unable to resist.

"You don't," she said. "You couldn't possibly know."

"But I do," he countered. "You're thinking this is the craziest thing that's ever happened to you. I know because that's exactly what I'm thinking. We just met this morning, and yet I feel I've known you all my life."

Her eyes widened as if his words had hit their mark.

"All of this is because of Taylor and Russ," she told him. "Their happiness, their excitement must be rubbing off on us. Don't you see how foolish this is?"

"No." He didn't mean to be blunt or obtuse. He was nearly thirty-five years old and long past the age of playing games. Christy was younger, but she knew, the same way he did. She might choose to deny it, but he wouldn't.

"Are you saying you didn't want me to kiss you?" he asked, trusting her to be honest, because he didn't believe she could be anything else.

It took her a minute to answer him, and when she did her voice was raspy. "That's the problem.... I've never wanted anything more."

Three

Christy woke early the next morning after a restless night's sleep. She'd tossed and turned so frequently that the sheets had been pulled loose from the bed and the bedspread had slipped onto the floor. Staring up at the ceiling, Christy slowly expelled her breath while mulling over the events of the day before.

So much had happened.

Taylor's son had been born, and Christy had been introduced to the newly elected sheriff of Custer County.

However, Christy had more than *met* Cody Franklin. He'd taken her to breakfast late in the afternoon, and when he dropped her off at the ranch, he'd kissed her—and she'd let him. More than *let* him; she'd encouraged him. What she'd told him was true. She'd never wanted anyone's kiss more.

Admitting as much certainly wasn't one of her more intelligent moves, but then it hadn't been her mind doing the talking. It had been her heart.

Once again she tried to focus her thoughts on James. He'd been so sweet the evening he'd given her the engagement ring. They'd gone out for dinner, sitting at the table with candlelight flickering and soft music playing in the background. Christy had noticed that he'd barely touched his meal. He seemed nervous, then started talking nonstop. Normally James was a calm, quiet man, not easily agitated. He'd been rambling for about fifteen minutes, and Christy couldn't figure out where the discussion was leading. She'd told him so. Then James had gotten flustered.

Before Christy could react, James pulled a ring box from the inside of his suit pocket. He'd been so endearing, so wonderfully sweet as he held out the diamond, letting the ring speak for him.

By then Christy had become so flustered herself that all she could do was stare at the lovely solitary diamond glittering up at her. James had withdrawn it from its velvet bed, and without a word she'd given him her hand.

The entire thing hadn't taken more than a few seconds. She'd promised to become his wife, promised to pledge her life to him without a word of love spoken between them. James cared for her, Christy felt assured of it. He wouldn't have offered her the ring if he didn't. By the same token, she loved him. Otherwise she wouldn't have accepted his proposal.

Afterward, James had been ecstatic as he'd hugged and kissed her. The ring was too large and had nearly slipped off her finger as she'd shown it to her parents that same night. Both Eric and Elizabeth Manning had been thrilled with the news of Christy's engagement to the up-and-coming attorney.

It wasn't until two days later, just before she left for Montana, that the first of the doubts had come. She loved

James, she reminded herself, repeating it again and again on the endless drive across three states.

James was a good man. He'd been a friend long before they'd become romantically involved, and judging by everything she'd read, friends made the best husbands.

Perhaps the most convincing argument for this marriage was how comfortable Christy felt with him. Her parents thought the world of James; in fact, they seemed more excited than she was about the prospect of his joining the family. Her father talked of little else, promising Christy the wedding of the year.

But if she'd been experiencing a few niggling doubts before she left Seattle, they'd multiplied a hundredfold since she'd arrived in Montana and met Cody Franklin.

Cody.

For more reasons than she dared explore, she struggled to push every thought of the sheriff from her mind.

With a determination born of pride and a sense of fairness and truth that had been ingrained in her from birth, Christy decided to tell Russ, tell someone, anyone, about her engagement. She climbed out of bed and got dressed, then went in seach of her brother-in-law.

Russ, however, had already left the house. A note was propped against the sugar bowl, explaining he'd be with his men that morning, and she shouldn't look for him before noon. He also wrote that he wouldn't be able to visit Taylor and the baby until that evening. He signed his name, adding that Christy should make herself at home.

Defeat settled over Christy. She couldn't keep quiet about herself and James much longer and still hold her head high.

It took only an hour to straighten up the house. She

cooked herself some eggs, then realized she wasn't hungry. Russ, on the other hand, had apparently fixed himself a breakfast large enough to feed five men. He'd made a minimal effort to clean the kitchen; clearly, he'd been in a rush.

With time to spare, Christy wandered outside, wanting to investigate what she could of the grounds. Since Russ was visiting Taylor that evening, she'd drive to the hospital in the afternoon.

One hand leading a chestnut horse paused and stared at her when she appeared.

"Good morning," Christy said cheerfully.

"Howdy." The lanky cowboy straightened and touched the rim of his hat. He looped the reins around a fencepost, then walked toward her. A fistful of cigars with pale blue bands was sticking out of his shirt pocket, evidence of Russ's eagerness to spread the news of his son's birth.

"You must be part of Mrs. Palmer's family."

"Christy Manning," she said, holding out her hand. "I'm Taylor's sister."

The middle-aged man took pains to remove his thick leather glove and clasped her soft palm in his callused one. "Pleased to make your acquaintance. Russ is out this morning, but I s'pect he'll be back soon. Most folks call me Billy Joe."

"Good to meet you, Billy Joe," Christy said, looking toward the barn. Several horses stuck their sleek heads over the stall doors, glancing at her with open curiosity.

"If you'll excuse me," Billy Joe said, backing away from her. His horse was saddled and waiting, prancing in place. "This gelding's anxious to be on his way."

"Of course. I'm sorry. I didn't mean to hold you up."

"No problem." He mounted the gelding in a single smooth motion. Pulling back on the reins, Billy Joe nodded at her once more, then galloped out of the yard.

Left to her own devices, Christy wandered toward the barn, stopping in front of the first stall. The name Shadow was burned into a wood plaque above the door.

"Howdy, Shadow," Christy said. "You look like a friendly horse." Friendly enough, at any rate, for her to venture petting his nose. She stroked it a few times while the gelding took pride in revealing his teeth and nickered his approval.

Seeing a large barrel of grain near the middle of the barn, Christy stepped over to it, intending to reach for a handful of oats. She didn't know much about horses, but figured a handful of oats would win approval.

"I thought I might find you in here," a deep male voice said from the barn door.

Christy's heart shot to her throat. Cody. She turned to see him silhouetted against the morning sunlight. Tall, lean and dark. He wore jeans and a western shirt with a string tie and was so strikingly handsome that for a moment all she could do was stare.

"Hello," she said, returning to her task, her hands trembling. It wasn't fair that he should have this effect on her. But then, she was learning that little in life was fair.

Her hand loaded with grain, she walked back to Shadow's stall.

"Be sure to feed that to him with your palm flat, otherwise he might inadvertently bite you," Cody warned, moving toward her.

Christy was grateful for the advice and did as he suggested. Shadow ate the oats quickly, and when he'd finished, Christy wiped her hand on her jeans. Her heart was hammering so hard, she was certain Cody could hear it.

"Did you sleep well?"

"No," she answered honestly. Her back was to him, but that didn't help. She felt warm and dizzy just knowing he was there.

"I couldn't, either." His voice was soft and raspy. Sensual. "I only had a couple of hours of sleep the night before, so I should've nodded off the minute my head touched the pillow. But I didn't. I couldn't."

Christy found a strange comfort in knowing his sleep had been as unsettled as her own. "I...tossed and turned most of the night, then finally drifted off toward morning."

"Me, too."

When he'd left her the night before, she'd stood inside the house and watched him drive away, feeling restless and uneasy. That disquiet hadn't dissipated until the moment he'd stepped into the barn. Cody spoke, and instantly the emptiness had started to leave her, as if a sense of order had been restored to her life.

Except that it wasn't right. Everything was very, very wrong.

"We need to talk."

"Yes," she whispered. She'd meant to tell Russ about James, knowing her brother-in-law would mention the fact to Cody. But this was better. She could tell Cody herself. Explain before either of them got hurt. Before things went too far.

Honesty really was the best policy. She'd grown up believing that. Practicing it.

Christy was searching for just the right words, irritated with herself for not having thought this out beforehand. There should be an easy way to say it. The truth shouldn't be this difficult.

Then Cody was behind her, so close she could feel the heat radiating from his body. His hands settled over her shoulders, his touch light and warm and reassuring. Slowly he turned her around so she faced him.

Their eyes locked, and Christy's throat went tight. His were beautiful, as dark and rich as the finest coffee. They were the eyes of a man who'd only recently learned to dream. Wistful eyes. Pensive eyes.

"Every time I'd try to sleep, all I could think about was you." His tone said that he'd struggled long and hard against allowing her to dominate his thoughts.

"It was the same with me." She shouldn't have told him that. Shouldn't admit his effect on her in one breath and then tell him about James in the next. "But I—"

"I couldn't stop thinking about how good you felt in my arms."

She knew exactly what he was saying because she'd experienced the same thing herself. He felt good to her, too, the kind of good that made everything feel right even when it was wrong. The kind of good that never diminished, never ceased.

"You felt it, didn't you?" He seemed to need confirmation from her.

She gave it reluctantly, breathlessly, lowering her eyes. "Yes."

They lapsed into silence then, as though neither of them knew what else to say. There didn't seem to be any need for words. Christy understood what Cody was thinking and feeling as clearly as if he'd spoken.

I need to kiss you again and discover if last night was real. He asked her with his eyes.

No, her heart cried. She couldn't allow it. If Cody kissed her again, she'd be forced to confront issues she dared not face. Cody Franklin was a stranger. James was her fiancé. Her friend.

I've frightened you.

No, came the cry from the farthest corner of her heart. *Yes,* she countered immediately. Cody stirred emotions she didn't know she was capable of feeling. Emotions she'd never experienced with any man. Each time they were together, her awareness of him became more intense. This shouldn't be happening to her. Not now. Not *ever.* She was engaged to another man.

Frowning, Cody took one step toward her. Christy's heart surged.

Don't, please, don't, she pleaded silently. *I can't refuse you. I can't refuse myself.*

But Cody had apparently given up listening to the cries of her heart. When she looked at him, he was both watchful and silent.

Before another second could pass, he reached for her, and whatever resistance she'd been able to muster burst like the white filaments of a dandelion in the wind. His mouth found hers, smooth and firm against her softness. She moaned in protest, but her small cry soon became a sigh of welcome, of need, of pleasure.

A tenderness blossomed within her, the sensations so exquisite they shocked her even more than they had a day earlier. It shouldn't be this good, this wonderful, she told herself over and over, wanting to weep with frustration. Yet it was better than anything she'd ever experienced.

Cody continued to kiss her with a passion and an excitement that left Christy clinging to him.

"I can't believe this," he murmured, and her mind

echoed his words. She was struggling with reality, and felt lost and weak.

Cody bent his head and dropped a succession of kisses down her neck and along her jaw until she moaned. He responded with a small, throaty sound and quickly joined their mouths again, kissing hers softly.

Christy went weak with need. She was melting from the heat. Burning up with fever. Consumed with a sweet warmth that threatened to devour her. "No," she whimpered. "We can't do…this."

Cody raised his hands and held them against the sides of her face.

He was going too fast for her. Her own body was going too fast for her. She felt as though she were sitting on a runaway horse, galloping out of control, being propelled farther and farther away from reason.

"I feel as if I've been waiting for you all my life," Cody whispered, wrapping his arms completely around her. His hand reached up to smooth the hair from her temple. "I can only imagine what you must think of me coming here like this."

Her eyes remained closed, and her dark world continued to spin without restraint. Even when she opened her eyes, everything was blurred and out of focus, her thoughts hopelessly addled.

"I didn't mean to shock you," he said.

"You didn't. I shocked myself."

Cody worked his thumbs sensuously across the high curve of her cheekbones. He frowned as he felt her tears. "I hurt you?"

"No…" she murmured, looking away. Now she understood the restless feeling she'd experienced all night.

She'd been haunted by his kiss, haunted by the emotions and the need he'd created within her.

All of this had to stop. Now. This instant. She pressed her forehead against his solid chest, needing his strength in order to find the courage to say what she had to say.

His hand lifted her hair, his touch gentle as though fingering strands of silk.

"I fall apart when you kiss me," she confessed.

His throaty laugh was filled with amusement and tenderness. "*You* fall apart?" He captured her hand and pressed it over his heart. "See what you do to me?"

She didn't need to touch him to realize how his pulse was churning beneath her palm. Unable to watch the disillusionment in his eyes when she told him about James, she closed her own.

"I've never felt anything for anyone as strongly as I have for you," she said softly. Then she didn't say anything more for a long moment, carefully formulating her words.

Cody obviously sensed that she felt troubled because he tucked his finger under her chin and raised her head. His gaze caressed her. "Christy?"

"Please listen," she whispered, her voice trembling. "There's something you should know, something I meant to tell you from the first, only—"

"Cody, what are you doing here?" Russ's voice echoed through the barn like thunder. "Everything's all right with Taylor, isn't it?" Christy's brother-in-law stopped abruptly when he saw Cody's arms around her waist. He removed his Stetson and wiped his forehead with the back of his hand. "I wasn't interrupting anything, was I?"

* * *

"Your timing couldn't be worse," Cody barked, glaring at his friend.

Russ didn't appear the least bit concerned. He tossed a load of baling wire into his pickup and promptly reached for another. If anything, he looked amused.

"This isn't funny."

Russ paused. "Now that's where I disagree. You just met Christy. Until yesterday you hadn't so much as set eyes on her. I don't mind telling you, Franklin, I've never known you to work so fast."

"Shut your fool mouth before you say something I'll make you regret," Cody grumbled. His threat wasn't worth a dime and Russ knew it, but he felt he had to respond.

"She is a pretty little thing, isn't she?" Another wheel of wire landed on top of the first with a loud, discordant clang. He turned to stare at Cody when he didn't answer right away. "Isn't she?" he repeated.

"Yes," Cody admitted grudgingly.

"For a moment there, it looked like the two of you had been kissing." Once more Russ paused, a grin turning up the edges of his mouth.

"I *was* kissing her," Cody said, challenging Russ to make something of the fact if he wanted to. He was as uncomfortable as he could ever remember being with his friend. Russ was curious to learn what was going on between him and Christy, but unfortunately Cody could think of no way of explaining his feelings for Christy, especially with the mood Russ was in. His friend seemed to find the situation downright comical.

"I guessed as much." Russ wiped the sweat from his brow, but Cody had a sneaking suspicion that he did so to cover a smile. Not that Russ had any trouble poking fun at him and letting him know it.

After Russ arrived, and the three of them had exchanged pleasantries, Christy excused herself and left, saying that she was driving to Miles City to visit Taylor and Eric. Cody would have offered to go with her, but he was working swing shift and it wasn't likely that he'd be back before he was scheduled to go on duty.

"You're not going to get closemouthed with me now, are you?" Russ was asking. "I can't say I've ever seen you take to a woman the way you have to Taylor's sister. What's different about Christy?"

"What was different about Taylor?"

Russ chuckled. "Touché. But if you remember correctly, all Taylor and I could do at first was argue. Never met a woman who could irritate me as much as she did."

"You didn't stay angry at her for long."

Russ shook his head. "No, can't say I did. She'd make me so furious I couldn't think straight. Before I could stop myself, I'd say or do some fool thing I'd end up regretting. That certainly doesn't seem to be the case with you and Christy, though. You two can't seem to keep your hands off each other."

Cody decided it was best to ignore that comment. "You and Taylor worked things out, and that's what matters."

Some of the humor disappeared from Russ's dark eyes. "We did, didn't we?" A faraway expression came over him. "Did you get a good look at him, Cody?"

Before Cody could respond Russ continued. "The nurse handed me Eric, and I swear something happened to my heart. It was the craziest thing, holding that baby in my arms and loving him so much my throat got all clogged up. I couldn't have said a word if my life depended on it. Before I knew what was happening, tears were rolling down my face. *Me.* I can't remember the last time I cried. I've never felt anything as incredible as holding my son.

"You know, I loved Taylor before the baby was born, but it pales in comparison to what I felt for her as she struggled to give birth to Eric. I've always thought of women as the weaker sex, but I was wrong." He shook himself as if waking from a deep sleep, his eyes as somber as Cody had ever seen.

"You have reason to be proud."

"I bought every box of cigars the gift shop owned."

"I know. I was with you."

"Hell, I don't even smoke."

Cody laughed. "I know that, too." He hesitated, uncertain how to proceed. "About Christy... You don't have any objection to my seeing her, do you?"

"So you plan to take her to Sitting Bull Lookout?" The ridge above the town had been their favorite necking place as teenagers.

"Probably," Cody answered, trying to hold back a grin.

Russ tucked his hands in his hip pockets. "Then you really are serious?"

"I've never been more serious in my life," Cody admitted without a pause.

Taylor was sound asleep when Christy got to the hospital. Her sister's long hair spread out over the white pillows like spilled coffee. Her eyes were closed, her breathing deep and even.

Tiptoeing into the room so as not to disturb her,

Christy pulled out the lone chair and sat. Although she'd
been on the road for more than an hour, she remained as
upset and nervous as when she'd left the house.

She felt like weeping. She felt like rejoicing. No
woman should experience such conflicting emotions.

The obedient, do-what's-right-at-all-costs part of her
kept reminding her of James. Loyal, hardworking James,
who loved her.

All her life Christy had done what was right. She'd
never been rebellious. She'd been a model child. A model
sister. Respectful. Considerate. Thoughtful.

She felt none of those things now.

The look Cody had given her just before Russ stepped
into the barn would be forever burned in her mind. It was
the kind of look a woman dreams of receiving from a
man sometime in her life. A lover's look. One so intimate
and personal that it could never be explained to another.

If this intense feeling between her and Cody was
wrong, then why did Christy feel so good inside? Why
did she long to throw up her arms and shout for joy?
If this was being rebellious or disrespectful, then all
Christy could say was that she was entering puberty
later than the normal teenager. About ten years later.

Taylor stirred and opened her eyes. "Christy," she
said, yawning. "When did you arrive?"

"About five minutes ago."

"You should have woken me."

"And interrupted your nap?" she teased. "How are
you feeling?"

"Wonderful." A soft smile touched her eyes. "Eric
spent most of the morning with me. Oh, Christy, he's
so adorable. We became acquainted with each other. I

counted his fingers and toes, and he taught me about breast-feeding."

"You look happy."

"I am… I really am."

Christy settled farther down in the chair. Trying not to be obvious, she stared at the floor, studying the pattern in the white tile. "Cody took me out to eat when we left here yesterday."

"In Miles City?"

"No. We went to the bowling alley in Cougar Point."

"I'm glad." There was a pause. "He's a good man."

Christy knew that instinctively. "I thought so, too. I like him, Taylor. I really do."

"Why do you look so guilty?"

How could she look or feel anything else? But Taylor wouldn't understand. Her sister had no way of knowing about the lovely engagement ring being sized at the Seattle jewelers.

They chatted for a few minutes before Taylor settled back against the pillows and sighed.

"What was that all about?"

"What?"

"That sigh," Christy said.

"Oh… I was just thinking about you and Cody. I'm really pleased you like him so much. Frankly, I've been concerned about you seeing so much of James."

Christy was surprised she didn't give everything away right then and there. "Oh?" she managed.

"He's nice, don't get me wrong, but he's so boring. To be honest, I've never understood what you saw in him."

"But he's kind."

"So is Big Bird!" Taylor argued. "I think James is a

nice guy, but he isn't the right one for you, and I can't understand why you continue to date him."

"How can you say that?" Christy demanded, forcing the argument. James had been a child prodigy, a recognized genius by age ten. He graduated from high school in his early teens, and from law school at twenty. At twenty-five he was close to becoming the youngest partner in Atwater and Beckham's long, distinguished history. "James is a a really nice man."

"True," Taylor agreed readily enough. "But he isn't the right one for you," she said again.

"You're wrong." A simple way to end this argument would be for Christy to announce her engagement, yet she hesitated, interested in hearing her sister's opinion.

"James is everything you say, but you're not in love with him and never have been," Taylor announced with a challenging smile.

"You sound so confident of that."

"I am. You couldn't possibly be in love with James if you're this interested in Cody Franklin."

Any objection Christy might have posed died a quick and quiet death.

"I think," Taylor said, holding out her hands to her sister, "you came to Montana at exactly the right time."

Four

"Can I hold Eric?" Mandy Palmer asked minutes after Taylor was home from the hospital. "I barely got a chance to look at him before," she added, casting an accusing glance in the direction of her older brother.

"Of course," Taylor said, leading the teenager into the living room. Russ followed, leaving Christy standing alone in the kitchen with Cody.

She busied herself at the stove, praying the sheriff would go with the others.

He didn't.

"You've been avoiding me," he said softly, leaning against the kitchen counter and crossing his arms over his chest. It was all Christy could do not to stare at him. If she did, he'd be able to read the longing in her eyes, and he'd realize she'd been miserable and unhappy and at odds with herself.

She'd needed these two days to think. To come to grips with herself. To decide.

The answers hadn't come easily. She'd wrestled with the most momentous decision of her life. The resolution had come, but not without a price. She felt exhausted, frightened and on the verge of tears.

She couldn't deny Cody's words. She *had* been avoiding him. She'd astonished herself at how clever she'd been about it. Clever enough so no one would have guessed.

Except Cody.

"Why didn't you answer my calls?" he asked.

"I came to spend time with Taylor, to help her. I've been busy...."

No one had bothered to tell her that Cody had been invited to Taylor and Eric's welcome-home dinner. She wasn't prepared for this.

From the way everyone had disappeared the minute Taylor arrived, Christy shouldn't be surprised to find herself alone with Cody. It seemed as if it had all been prearranged.

"Christy, talk to me," he pleaded, his frustration evident. "Tell me what's wrong."

"Nothing. It's just that I've been so terribly busy." So terribly confused. So terribly guilty. Cowardly, too, since she'd been juggling with her conscience, her scruples and her sense of fairness.

If anything, this time away from Cody had enlightened her. The first day she'd been trapped in the restless, lost sensation she'd experienced the night before, after he'd left.

The second day, however, she'd found peace. It was a strained peace and would be so until she went home to Seattle and talked to James. Nevertheless, she'd reached a decision.

For a good part of the afternoon, Mandy and Christy had worked together to get the house ready for Taylor's return with Eric. No one had said Cody would be returning with them.

No one had given her a word of warning. She didn't know what to say to him just now, and the truth seemed unwieldy. Awkward.

"I don't blame you if you're frightened," Cody continued, his voice low. "I'm frightened myself. The first time we kissed I felt like I'd been hit by a freight train. The second time it was even more powerful.... Deep down I'd hoped it was somehow tied up in the emotion surrounding Russ, Taylor and the baby, but it isn't."

"I don't think it is, either."

"If you're looking for an explanation of what's going on between us, I can't give you one. All I know is what I feel."

Sometimes, Christy believed, a lifetime of doing the right thing could be subverted by pure sensation. This had certainly proved true with her and Cody.

"Talk to me."

Slowly she turned, witnessing for herself the tenderness, and the confusion, in his eyes. Without uttering a word, she walked over to him and slipped her arms around his waist. He placed his own around her, anchoring her to his chest as he expelled a harsh breath.

"Can you tell me what's troubling you?"

She nodded, almost giddy with relief and release. Raising her head, she smiled up at him, longing to reassure him. Part of her yearned to put this behind them and blurt it all out. She wanted to tell him about James and the engagement and how meeting him had turned her world inside out. But there wasn't enough time to untangle this mess before dinner. They needed privacy to discuss it in detail, time to reach an understanding.

She glanced regretfully toward the living room.

"Do you want to steal away?" Cody asked. "Go somewhere else?"

That was exactly what she did want, but they couldn't leave. Tonight was an evening to celebrate. Taylor and Eric were home for the first time, and leaving would be selfish and thoughtless.

"Forget I asked that," Cody murmured. "I'll be patient."

"So will I. We'll make some excuse after dinner," she suggested, then on impulse lightly brushed her lips over his.

Cody, however, wanted more. Much more.

Placing his hands on each side of her neck, he pulled her tighter to him and wove his fingers through her short hair as he brought his mouth to hers.

"I swear," Russ exclaimed loudly, walking into the kitchen, "I can't leave these two alone for a moment." The words were followed by the sound of his laughter.

Languidly Cody eased his mouth from Christy's and slowly opened his eyes. "How about getting lost for the next few minutes?" Cody said.

"Fine with me," Russ agreed, "but I don't think that fried chicken's going to want to wait much longer."

"Oh, my," Christy said, abruptly breaking away. She'd completely forgotten about the dinner she and Mandy had so carefully planned. She grabbed a pot holder and moved the grease-spitting skillet from the burner. Heaving a sigh of relief, she brushed her bangs off her forehead.

"Need any help?" Mandy asked, sauntering into the kitchen. Russ's teenage sister lived with him and Taylor, and from everything Christy had heard, Mandy was the one responsible for bringing Russ and Taylor to-gether. Because of a summer job and other commit-ments, Mandy had been away from the house during most of Christy's visit and Christy was only beginning to get to know her. And like her.

"No. I've got everything under control here."

Russ contradicted her under his breath, but Christy chose to ignore her brother-in-law's comment. She was relieved when the two men vacated the kitchen.

With Mandy's assistance, dinner was ready fifteen minutes later. Mandy called everyone, and they gathered around the dining room table. Russ escorted his wife, his eyes tender as he seated her.

Taylor, wearing a loose pale blue dress that comple-mented her eye color, looked wonderful. Every woman should look so good three days after giving birth, Christy mused.

"Oh, Christy... Mandy," Taylor said, studying the table. "This is fantastic. You must've spent the whole day cooking—and in this heat!"

"It wasn't a problem," Christy said automatically.

"Yes, it was," Mandy countered smoothly. "It took all afternoon, but we had so much fun it was worth it. Your sister's great!"

"I think so, too, but you shouldn't have gone to so much trouble." Taylor gestured at the three different kinds of salads, the platter of fried chicken and two separate desserts.

"But we did," Mandy said, reaching for the potato salad, "so you might as well enjoy it."

Christy shared a secret smile with her older sister. She admired Mandy for her openness and her honesty. Had she answered, she would've quickly allowed Taylor and the others to believe she'd managed to whip up a three-course meal in a matter of minutes without the slightest trouble.

Eric stirred just as they were finishing dinner, and Taylor immediately started to rise. Russ put his hand on her arm, stopping her.

"Let me?" He made it a question.

"He probably needs his diaper changed," Taylor warned.

"So? I can do it. Just how difficult can changing a diaper be?"

Christy and Taylor exchanged a meaningful glance. When she pulled her gaze away from her sister, Christy's eyes sought out Cody. The sheriff gave her a look of exaggerated shock.

"Did I hear correctly?" he teased. "Did Russ Palmer volunteer to change a diaper?"

"Apparently so," Taylor said, pretending to be as awed as Cody.

"All right, you guys, cut it out," Russ warned, shouting from the master bedroom.

"I don't know if I can let a moment like this pass without witnessing it myself. Does anyone have a camera?"

"You're not taking any damn picture," Russ roared, his voice booming through the house. His words were quickly followed by the squalling cry of an infant. A fraction of a second later Russ shouted for Taylor.

Christy tossed her napkin aside and left the table with her sister, wondering if she could help. Mandy was the only one content to let the others deal with the baby while she finished her meal.

The three of them crowded around the bassinet where Russ struggled with the diaper and pins. He was grumbling, and his face was creased with a deep frown as if he were performing major surgery.

"I marry the most modern woman in the world. She won't let me open a car door for her, insists on paying for her own dinner when we go out on a date, but will she use disposable diapers? Oh, no, she's got to torment me with cloth ones."

"They're better for the environment," Taylor said, gently pushing her husband aside. She dealt efficiently with the diaper-changing, completely unfazed by the task.

"That's all there is to it?" Cody asked, making fun of his friend's inability to handle such an uncomplicated situation.

"If you think it's so easy, you try it."

"I will, but probably not for several years." Cody looked at Christy, and the mental image of Cody holding a baby in his arms, their baby, filled her mind. She looked away, not wanting anyone to witness the emotion she was feeling.

Russ watched as Taylor lifted the dirty diaper from the bassinet. "What are you going to do with that… thing?" He wrinkled his nose as he asked the question.

"I'm putting it in the diaper pail in the bathroom."

"You're not keeping those smelly diapers in there, are you?" he said as he followed Taylor down the hallway. Christy could hear him listing his objections.

Once more Christy and Cody were left alone, this time with Eric. The infant lay on his back, squinting his blue eyes as he gazed up at them. His mouth made small sucking motions.

Unable to resist, Christy reached into the bassinet and lifted Eric out. He gurgled contentedly in her arms as she sat on the end of the bed. Cody stood next to her, studying the newborn. He lovingly smoothed his large hand along the side of the baby's head. Eric's tiny hand closed around Cody's index finger.

"Look," Cody said excitedly, as if Eric had broken an Olympic record. "I think he recognizes us."

"And well he should! We're his godparents," Christy reminded him. She turned to smile at Cody and once more found herself lost in his eyes.

In that brief moment Christy saw a reflection of everything she was feeling. Until now, whenever they looked at each other, their eyes brimmed with questions and doubts.

But this time was different. Christy saw in Cody an understanding. They'd each lost the need for answers or explanations.

"How long will you be in Cougar Point?" Cody asked.

"My vacation is two weeks."

Both seemed to calculate the number of days remaining before she'd need to go home.

Cody's expression told her he wanted to spend every available moment he could with her. It was what Christy wanted, too, more than she'd wanted anything in her life.

"I'm working day shift tomorrow," he told her softly, his look tender. "What about dinner?"

"I'd like that." Which was definitely an understatement.

The air between them seemed to spark with sensuality. Cody leaned toward her, and Christy knew beyond a doubt that he intended to kiss her. He hesitated a fraction of an inch from her mouth before regretfully backing away.

"I'd bet my last dollar if I kissed you, Russ would interrupt us."

"He probably would. He seems to have an incredible sense of timing, doesn't he?"

As soon as she spoke, her brother-in-law stuck his head in the doorway. "What's taking you two so long? Mandy's got the coffee poured."

"See what I mean?" Cody whispered.

Christy nodded and stood, placing Eric over her shoulder and rubbing his back. He was so tiny, so perfect, and her heart swelled anew with love for him.

Taylor and Russ were sitting in the living room when Cody and Christy appeared. Their looks were openly curious—as if they were waiting for the couple to make an announcement.

Christy didn't think it would do much good to try to disguise what was going on between her and Cody. Her sister knew her far too well, and clearly Russ was equally familiar with Cody.

Christy handed the baby over to Taylor, dropping a kiss on his forehead as she did. By tacit agreement, she and Cody sat at opposite sides of the room. Being close to each other only intensified the attraction, and no doubt the curiosity.

"So," Russ said, glancing from Cody to Christy, sporting a wide grin.

"Russ," Taylor warned in a low whisper.

"What?"

"Do you have to be so obvious?"

Russ blinked, apparently at a loss to understand his wife's censure. "I didn't say anything, but if I did venture to mention the obvious, I'd say something along the lines of how happy I am that my best friend and your sister have apparently hit it off so well."

"To tell you the truth, I couldn't be more pleased myself," Taylor added, smiling.

Cody crossed his legs and picked up his coffee. "I'm glad to hear Christy and I have made you two so happy."

Russ chuckled at that, amusement glistening in his eyes. "Do you remember that time in the sixth grade?" Russ asked.

"I'm not likely to forget it."

"What are you two mumbling about now?" Taylor demanded.

"We were eleven."

"You were eleven," Cody corrected. "I was ten."

"Right," Russ agreed. "We'd been good friends for several years and had started to notice some of our other buddies turning traitor."

"Turning traitor?" Christy repeated.

"Liking girls."

Since Christy was the youngest of the five Manning children, she couldn't recall her brothers sharing similar feelings. "What did you two do?" she asked.

"The only thing we could," Russ explained, grinning again. "We were losing our best friends left and right, so Cody and I made a pact and became blood brothers. We made a solemn vow never to associate with any of the guys who'd turned traitor and liked girls."

"Especially pretty ones with dark hair and bright blue eyes," Cody remarked, looking at Christy, who possessed both. His mouth quivered, and she realized he was only a breath away from laughing outright.

"And which of you broke this sacred vow first?"

"Cody did," Russ said.

"Russ," Cody responded, the two speaking almost simultaneously.

"Boys, please," Taylor said in what Christy was sure was her best schoolteacher voice.

"Cody gave Mary Lu Hawkins a valentine that year," Russ reminded him.

"My mother forced me to do it," Cody insisted. "I never liked Mary Lu Hawkins, and you know it."

"That's not what I heard."

Listening to Cody and Russ was like being present at an exchange between her own brothers. A strong sense of family was an integral part of who she was. She loved their frequent get-togethers and had missed Taylor dreadfully over the past year.

"Is it always like this between these two?" Christy asked her sister.

"Sometimes worse," Taylor answered.

"Russ was the ultimate traitor," Cody said, setting his coffee mug aside. "He married a dark-haired, blue-eyed woman, and worse, I wasn't even invited to the wedding."

"No one was," Mandy inserted as she came in from the kitchen, drying her hands on her apron skirt. "Not even me. Russ's very own sister."

"I swear you're never going to forgive me for that, are you?" Russ grumbled. "Just wait till you fall in love, little sister, then you might be more understanding."

Mandy straightened her spine and threw back her shoulders. Her eyes narrowed as she glared across the room at her brother. She reminded Christy so much of her older sister confronting their father that she nearly laughed out loud.

"It may come as a shock to you, big brother, but I've

been in love several times." Mandy evidently considered herself a woman of the world.

Russ didn't hide his opinions on *that* issue. He rolled his eyes.

"Russ," Taylor said softly.

"Now what did I do?" he asked. At the rate he was going, his foot would remain permanently in his mouth. "All right, all right, I—*we* made a mistake by not including you in the wedding ceremony. There. Are you satisfied?"

"No. I want you to admit that I'm old enough to be in love."

"Mandy!"

"Admit it." It was clear that brother and sister were often at odds, yet Christy sensed the deep and abiding love they shared.

"Don't look at me, Russ Palmer," Taylor said bluntly. "You got yourself into this."

"I suppose that at fifteen a mature teenage girl may have experienced her first taste of love."

"May have?" Mandy repeated. "That's not good enough."

"Hey, the girl wants blood," Cody murmured.

"She's likely to get it, too," Taylor said, apparently for Christy's benefit.

"All right, I'll admit it. There! *Now* are you satisfied?"

Mandy smiled graciously and nodded. "Thank you, brother dearest."

"You're welcome, sister sweetest." He turned his attention away from Mandy. "Listen," Russ said, looking at Cody and Christy and then back at his friend. "If you two ever get married, whether it's to each other or anyone else, take my advice and don't elope."

"If Mandy was upset about not being at the wedding, that was nothing compared to how strongly Mom and Dad felt about it," Taylor said. "Dad seemed to feel I'd cheated him out of an important part of fatherhood by not letting him escort me down the aisle."

From somewhere deep inside, Christy forced a smile. This talk about weddings was making her decidedly uncomfortable. What her sister said was true enough; her parents had been bitterly disappointed not to hold a large wedding for their oldest daughter. It was one of the reasons they were so pleased when Christy announced that she and James would be getting married. Almost immediately they'd started talking about the church ceremony, with a reception and dance to follow.

"I think it's time for us to go, don't you?" Cody said to Christy, unfolding his long legs and standing. He walked across the room in three strides. "See you later, Taylor, Eric. Oh, and you, too." He nodded at Russ with a grin. "Thanks for dinner, everyone."

"Where are you two headed?" Russ wanted to know, making no effort to disguise his interest.

"Out." Cody turned to Christy, and his smile was like the warm fingers of sunlight in winter. They'd known each other such a short while, and it seemed inconceivable that she could feel like this. But she did. The feelings she and Cody shared were too complex to put into words.

"When will you be back?" Russ asked his sister-in-law, as if he wasn't completely convinced his best friend was safe in her company.

"Who appointed you my guardian angel?" Cody asked sarcastically, his eyebrows raised.

"I'm only looking out for your best interests," Russ explained, continuing the game. "Good grief, man, she's pretty with dark hair and blue eyes. We learned way back in the sixth grade that those are the ones to watch out for. You've got to be careful. Look what happened to me!"

"What did happen to you?" Taylor asked, her brow wrinkling with the question.

"You should know. Before I realized it, I was saddled with a wife. I don't mind telling you, Franklin, I'm worried about you."

"If I'm responsible for the security of an entire county, you can trust me to take care of myself."

"Saddled?" Taylor asked, her voice ominously low. "You found yourself *saddled* with a wife?"

Russ instantly looked guilty. "Maybe saddled wasn't the best word."

"Then I suggest you search for another."

"Ah…" Russ rubbed his hand across his neck.

"He's talking off the top of his head," Cody said, defending his friend. He turned toward Russ. "If I were you, I'd plead for leniency and remind her how crazy in love you are."

"How about I was *favored* with a wife?" Russ muttered. He seemed quite pleased with his choice of word.

Taylor glanced at Christy, a smile playing at the corners of her mouth, then shook her head. "You'll have to do better than that."

"Taylor, come on, I'm having a serious discussion with my friend here. All I'm trying to do is impart a few words of wisdom before Cody makes the same… before he ends up…"

"Ends up what?" Taylor prompted.

It took Russ a moment to answer. "Blessed?" he offered, confident he'd smoothed things over.

"Blessed is an acceptable word."

"I think we should get out of here while the getting's good, don't you?" Cody asked, reaching for Christy's hand, entwining their fingers.

"I couldn't agree with you more." The solid ground beneath her feet seemed to shift as she realized that once they were alone she'd need to explain about James. Dragging in a steadying breath, she looked at Taylor. "I won't be gone long."

"If I get worried, I'll call the sheriff," Taylor teased.

The phone rang, and Mandy shot out of the living room.

Russ escorted Christy and Cody to the back door.

Mandy appeared, stretching the long telephone cord into the kitchen. She seemed confused as she held out the receiver to Russ. "I think it must be a wrong number. Maybe you should talk to him."

"All right."

Cody chuckled. "I never thought I'd be grateful for a phone call. I had the impression Russ was going to make us listen to more of his pearls of wisdom."

They were all the way down the steps when the back door swung open with enough force to send it crashing shut.

"Christy." Russ stood on the top of the steps, hands on his hips, his eyes squinting against the setting sun.

"Yes?" She turned to face her brother-in-law. The humor in his eyes had been replaced with a fierce anger that transformed his handsome features.

Cody took a step forward. "What is it?"

"The phone," Russ said. "It's for Christy. Someone named James Wilkens."

She gasped softly before she could stop herself.

"He claims he's her fiancé."

Five

"Cody, please," Christy began, her heart in her eyes. "I can explain."

"You mean it's true?" Russ shouted.

"It's not as bad as it sounds—if you'd take the time to listen." Both of her hands gripped Cody's forearm as she boldly held on to him, not wanting to let him go for fear she'd never see him again.

"Are you engaged or not?" Cody asked. His dark eyes burned into hers, searing her conscience far more deeply than any words he could've spoken.

"I was going to tell you about James...."

Cody's face tensed as though she'd delivered a crippling blow to his abdomen. He lowered his gaze to her hands, which clenched his arm tightly.

"I see." The two words were cold, his voice remote.

She moistened her lips, unsure she could trust her voice. "Please let me explain."

"What's there to say? It's simple, isn't it? Either you're engaged or you're not." He pulled himself free and turned his back to her.

"Cody." She tried once more, hating the way her voice wobbled as she pleaded for patience and understanding.

One stern look told her he wasn't willing to grant her either. Her heart seized painfully as she slowly dropped her hands and stepped away from him.

Without another word, Cody climbed inside his Cherokee, slammed the door and drove away as if the very demons of hell were in hot pursuit.

Christy went completely still. She couldn't move. Couldn't breathe.

How long she stood there, Christy had no idea. Nor could she put order to her thoughts. Just a few minutes ago she'd been sitting across the room from Cody, laughing with him, sharing secret smiles, her whole being permeated with gladness and joy. How natural it had seemed to be together. As natural as the sun setting. As natural as rain.

"Are you going to talk to your fiancé or not?" Russ demanded, his voice sharp with censure.

Christy stared at him for a moment before she realized James was still on the phone. Nevertheless, she stood where she was and watched the plume of dust that trailed behind Cody's vehicle. After a while it faded away, taking with it the promise of something wonderful.

Russ waited for her at the top of the porch steps. Christy lowered her eyes as she moved past him. He didn't need to say anything for her to feel his reprimand.

The telephone receiver was resting on a small table in the hallway. Christy dragged in a deep, calming breath and reached for it. "Hello, James." She prayed her voice revealed none of her turmoil.

"Christy. How are you?" He sounded anxious, concerned.

"Fine, just fine. Taylor had the baby, but I suppose you've heard about that already. I doubt Mom and Dad could keep quiet about Eric. He really is precious." She knew she was chattering but couldn't seem to make herself stop. "Montana is a beautiful state. I haven't seen much of Cougar Point yet, except the bowling alley. I had breakfast there the other morning, only it was really the middle of the afternoon—the day Eric was born, actually."

"You ate breakfast at a bowling alley?"

"There's a restaurant there and the food's good—excellent, in fact."

"That's nice."

"How are you?" Christy felt obliged to ask.

"Fine. I miss you." He dropped his voice slightly as if he'd admitted something he shouldn't. "The office seems empty with you away."

James wasn't a man who was comfortable with expressing his emotions. Showing affection was difficult for him. The fact that he'd called and said he missed her was practically equivalent to another man standing on a rooftop and shouting at the top of his voice that he was madly in love.

"I… I've been busy."

"I was hoping you'd call me."

His disappointment echoed in each word.

"I'm sorry, James, really I am. It's just that everything happened so fast. I didn't even have a chance to unpack my bags before Taylor went into labor. She came home from the hospital today, and we…we were just having dinner." That was a slight exaggeration, but she needed an excuse to get off the phone before she did something stupid like weep uncontrollably or tell him about Cody.

"You're having dinner? Why didn't you say something sooner? No wonder it took you so long to get to the phone."

Christy leaned against the wall, closed her eyes and swallowed. She felt guilty about by her minor deception, contaminated by the way she was deceiving him in an effort to cut short this painful conversation.

James deserved so much more than this. The guilt was killing her, and it demanded all the self-control she possessed to keep from blurting everything out.

"I'll let you go, but before I do I want you to know I got the diamond back from the jeweler. It'll be ready when you return from your sister's."

"Oh, g-great," she stammered, trying to inject some enthusiasm into her voice.

"Goodbye, Christy. Give my regards to Taylor and her husband and congratulate them both for me."

"I will. Bye, James. Don't work too hard."

"No, I won't."

She replaced the receiver, her fingers curled tensely around it as she waited for the recriminations to rain down on her. She felt an overwhelming sense of wrongdoing, a surge of remorse.

Raised voices came at her from inside the living room.

"The least you can do is listen to her," Christy heard Taylor shout.

"What possible explanation could she have? Either she's engaged or she isn't."

"Listen to me, Russ Palmer. I won't have you yelling at my sister. Whatever's happening between her and Cody is her business. It doesn't have anything to do with us."

"Like hell I'm going to stay out of it. We're talking about Cody here—my best friend. I thought he was your friend, too."

"He is."

"Then you can't expect to sit idly by and watch him get hurt."

"Please," Christy said, stepping into the room. She couldn't bear to have them arguing over her. "Please... don't fight."

The room went silent, a silence so intense it seemed to throb like a giant heart. Taylor's gaze, clouded with doubt and uncertainty, locked with Christy's. Russ's eyes were filled with reproach.

Russ and Taylor continued to stare at her. Russ was angry and made no effort to disguise his feelings. Taylor, usually so strong and confident, couldn't hide her confusion.

Christy suspected her sister was as troubled as her husband. Only Taylor wouldn't allow herself to voice her misgivings because of family loyalty.

"Sit down," Taylor suggested. She motioned toward the recliner where Christy had sat earlier. "You're so pale. Are you sure you're all right?"

"Why didn't you tell us you were engaged?" Russ asked, barely giving her time to compose herself. "And if you and James are getting married, why aren't you wearing a ring?"

"Russ, please," Taylor said, "let her answer one question before hitting her with another." Directing her attention to Christy, Taylor widened her eyes. "We're waiting."

Folding her hands in her lap, Christy squeezed her

fingers so tightly they hurt. "James asked me to marry him two days before I left Seattle."

"He didn't give you an engagement ring?"

"Of course…it's being sized now."

"I see," Taylor said, frowning. "And you didn't mention it to anyone? Do Mom and Dad know? I'm your sister, for heaven's sake! The least you could've done was mention it to me."

"Taylor," Russ said gruffly, then reminded her of her own words. "She can only answer one question at a time."

"I didn't have a chance to tell you when I first arrived. Remember? Then first thing the next morning you went into labor and… I met Cody."

"You had no business leading him on," Russ snapped.

"I didn't mean to," she cried, and raked her fingers though her short hair, praying Taylor and Russ wouldn't condemn her. "It just…happened. We were both so excited about the baby and afterward we went out to eat. Then Cody drove me home and…and I knew he was going to kiss me. I realize it was a mistake not to say anything to him, but I was afraid…" Afraid that if she *had* said something he wouldn't have touched her, and she'd wanted his kiss so much.

Unable to meet her sister's eyes, she glanced at the coffee table as the tears spilled down her cheeks.

"Who's this James character, anyway?" Russ asked Taylor. "Did we meet him?"

She nodded. "He's the attorney Christy introduced to us last summer."

"Not the…" He hesitated.

"Why didn't you tell me?" Taylor apparently considered it a personal affront that Christy had kept the news to herself. "We had plenty of time to talk while I was in the hospital and you were there every day."

"I tried," Christy said in her own defense. "But every time I mentioned James, you changed the subject. And when I finally managed to drag him back into the conversation, you started telling me how dry and boring you think he is and what a mismatched couple we are. What was I supposed to do? Tell you I'd agreed to marry the man you'd just finished criticizing?"

"Oh, dear," Taylor whispered. "Now that you mention it, I do remember you trying to bring James into the conversation."

"Fine. You two got that settled, but what about Cody?" Russ stalked to the other side of the room and stared out the front window. "I can't, I *won't* let this happen to him a second time. Not when it's in my power to prevent it." Gradually he turned around, his shoulders squared and his jaw tightly clenched.

"A second time?" Christy echoed.

When Russ didn't respond right away, she looked at her sister, who was busy with Eric. Either that or she was avoiding eye contact. "Taylor?"

"It happened several years ago," Russ began grudgingly. "A woman by the name of Rebecca Morgan moved into town. She was from somewhere in the south and had the sweetest manners you can imagine. She was the type of woman a man could fall in love with. Becca was perfect. Beautiful. Demure. Charming and…" Russ shook his head. "Who would've guessed?"

"Guessed what?" Christy asked.

"Becca made it obvious from the moment she moved into town that she was attracted to Cody. Every time he turned around there she was, batting her eyes at him, doing those things you women do to let a man know you're interested."

"I could make a comment here, but I won't," Taylor muttered.

"Soon Becca and Cody were seeing a lot of each other. You have to understand, Cody isn't easily taken in, especially by a pretty woman. Until recently." He frowned at Christy as he said it. "But Becca did more than interest him. For the first time in his life, Cody was in love. It showed in everything he said and did.

"Cody's always been popular with the folks around here, and his happiness seemed to rub off on everyone. Most folks liked Becca, too. They couldn't help it. There was plenty of talk about the two of them getting married." Russ walked over to the ottoman and sat down. "A month or so after she moved into town, a series of baffling robberies started happening."

"You don't mean to say Becca..."

"Not her personally. She was part of a team. They worked a scam in small cities all across the western states. Apparently the heat was on in several of the larger cities, and she and her partner decided to try their hand in smaller towns. They were successful, too. Becca would move someplace and get involved with a deputy from the local sheriff's office. One way or another she'd get information about shipments of money to the town banks. Then she'd pass that information to her partner. It was all cleverly done. Whenever a shipment of cash was due to arrive, Becca would make sure she was no-where nearby. Two banks were robbed, and a couple of stores lost valuable equipment all within the second month she was in town. But no one suspected her. How could they? She was just as sweet as honey."

"How long did it take Cody to realize it was Becca?"

"Not long, a few weeks, but he felt like the biggest fool who ever lived and you'll never convince him differently. He took responsibility for everything, blamed himself for not picking up on the scam sooner."

"But he loved her. Trusted her."

Russ's dark gaze collided with Christy's. "I know. He arrested her and her partner and testified against them."

"Surely no one blamed Cody!"

"No, everyone in town was as taken in by her as he was. But Cody felt as responsible as if he'd personally handed over the money. It's his job to protect and to serve and he felt he'd let the entire county down, although he worked his fool head off until every penny was returned. Even that wasn't enough. Cody felt he had to resign from the department."

"No." Christy's response was immediate. True, she'd only known Cody a short while, but in that time she'd learned how important law enforcement was to him.

"Thankfully some of us were able to talk some sense into him. He made the mistake of falling in love with the wrong woman—but then again, it was all due to his efforts that Becca and her friend were caught. If it hadn't been for Cody, no one knows how long their little scam would've worked or how many other communities would've been bilked. Unfortunately Cody didn't see it that way."

"He's only human." Christy felt a burning need to defend him.

"Becca used him. But worse than that, she made him feel like an idiot. It's taken three years for him to live it down, at least in his own mind. The way most folks figure it, Cody did Montana a good deed by putting Becca Morgan and her partner behind bars."

"That's why he wouldn't run for sheriff until last year?" Taylor asked, shifting the baby in her arms.

"It's been his life's dream to be elected sheriff of Custer County, but it took all this time for him to agree to run. I suppose he felt he had to prove his worth all over again. The crazy part is that he could've won hands down *any* year, including the year he was involved with Becca."

"I didn't know," Taylor said softly.

"It's not something that's talked about a lot," Russ explained. "The subject is such a painful one, it's best forgotten."

"Then Becca's still in prison?" Christy managed to ask. Learning how Cody had been deceived was painful for her, too. The knowledge that justice had been done somehow made it easier to accept.

"From what I understand, she's tried to contact Cody a few times, claiming she really was in love with him, and still is. To hear her tell it, she was a helpless pawn in all this. She says she was a victim of blackmail. But Cody won't have anything to do with her."

"I can certainly understand that," Taylor said.

"You aren't comparing me to Becca, are you?" Christy asked bluntly, feeling even more wretched.

"You're no thief," Russ said abruptly. "I'm not worried about you bilking the good citizens of Cougar Point, if that's what you think. No…" He rubbed the back of his neck. "After Becca something changed in Cody. He rarely dated. He closed himself off, became more pensive, introspective. It was as if he'd lost trust in women."

Taylor nodded. "I can't say I really blame him."

"I don't, either," Christy added, realizing as she did so that she was condemning herself.

Russ frowned. "That's why I was so pleased about what happened after he met you. When he looked at you, it was like seeing the old Cody all over again, the man who smiled and joked and didn't take everything so seriously. I don't know what went on between you." He hesitated and glanced at his wife. "Taylor's right when she says it isn't any of my business, but I won't stand by and let you take advantage of him."

"I wouldn't... I couldn't."

"Then why didn't you tell him you were engaged?"

Christy felt as if she'd been backed into a corner. "I planned to. I never intended to keep it a secret, but I needed time to think. You may not believe this, but I'd hoped to talk to Cody about James tonight. I was going to tell him everything."

"Are you planning on marrying James?" Taylor asked, her eyes seeking Christy's.

The question came as a shock. "No. I couldn't—not after meeting Cody."

"Then why didn't you break the engagement when you had the chance?" Russ asked. "You were just talking to him. It would've been a simple matter to tell him then."

"I can't do it over the phone," Christy said, jerking her head upward. "James is a good man. He deserves better than that. He hasn't done anything wrong. I hate to hurt him...." She paused when hot tears threatened to spill down her face. Biting her lower lip, she drew in a shuddering breath.

"Christy's right." Taylor's words cut through the emotion of the moment. "This is a delicate situation. You can't expect her to call James and break off the engagement. That would be heartless. This is best done in person. James may be a bit dull, but he's a decent human being."

"Is...is there any chance Cody will talk to me?" Christy wanted to drive into town and explain that she had no intention of going through with the marriage.

"I doubt he'll have anything to do with you," Russ answered, confirming her worst fears.

"Wait until tomorrow," Taylor advised. "Give him an opportunity to think everything through."

"He asked me out to dinner…. But I'm not sure if he'll show up."

"He won't," Russ said. "I know him better than anyone, and I can tell you, as far as he's concerned, whatever was between you is over."

Christy's shoulders sagged with defeat. "I was afraid of that."

"Don't make it sound so hopeless," Taylor muttered.

"She's engaged, for crying out loud. What do you expect Cody to do?" Russ said. "Ignore it? He isn't going to do that."

"But I have every intention of breaking off the engagement."

"I doubt that'll make any difference to him. I'll be surprised if he even listens to you."

"That's not true," Taylor said confidently. "Cody's a reasonable man, and it's obvious that he's attracted to you."

"He isn't anymore." Russ shook his head for emphasis.

Taylor shot daggers at her husband. "Russ Palmer, kindly allow me to finish."

"Feel free, but you've got to understand. After Becca, Cody doesn't have a lot of trust in the opposite sex."

"My sister isn't another Becca," Taylor insisted.

"You and I know that."

A short silence followed before Christy said, "Cody's smart enough to know it, too." She wanted to believe that. Needed to believe it. But whether that was the case or not was something she'd soon discover.

Cody slammed his fist against the steering column. He was parked on the ridge that overlooked Cougar Point and had been sitting there for the past hour, collecting his thoughts.

Frustration and anger mounted with each passing minute. Drawing in a deep breath, he rubbed his face with both hands, certain he'd almost made a world-class fool of himself for the second time.

When was he going to learn? Women weren't to be trusted. Especially pretty blue-eyed ones who looked as pure as freshly fallen snow. On the outside they were all sweetness, but inside… His thoughts skidded to an abrupt halt despite his best efforts to think badly of Christy.

He couldn't compare Becca with Taylor's sister. The two women had little, if anything, in common. Becca was a con artist. Christy wouldn't know how to deceive anyone.

But she had.

She'd deceived him.

Once more he rubbed his hand down his face. Had she really? Hadn't she said there was something she needed to tell him? He'd stood in Russ's kitchen, looked into her beautiful eyes and had seen for himself the turmoil inside her. He'd been unable to grasp what was troubling her.

But right now all Cody could think about was himself. For the first time in years he'd been able to feel again. For the first time in years he'd been whole.

The only thing he felt now was an ache that cut far deeper than anything he'd known before. His feelings for Christy had been a cruel joke.

"You don't honestly expect Cody's going to come, do you?" Taylor asked as Christy sprayed her carefully styled hair. She'd spent the past half hour fussing with her makeup and hair, hoping that if she looked her best, it would lend her confidence.

"No. But I want to be ready in case he does."

"You've been restless all day," her sister said.

"I know. I can't help it. Oh, Taylor, I can't bear to let things end this way between Cody and me. Everything felt so…so right with us."

"It's hard, isn't it?"

She nodded, fighting the need to rush to him and make him understand. "His eyes were so cold. I didn't know anyone could look so…" She couldn't think of a word strong enough to describe her fears.

For much of the night she'd wrestled with the sheets and blankets, trying to find a comfortable position. Once she did and closed her eyes, the disdainful look on Cody's face would pop into her mind. Her eyes would fly open, and the need to explain to him would dominate her thoughts again.

She'd spent most of the night composing what she was going to say. All day she'd been mentally rehearsing it so when the time came she'd be ready.

But she didn't feel ready now. She felt uneasy and scared, as if nothing she could say or do would make a difference.

"If he doesn't come, what do you plan to do?"

"Go to him," Christy said firmly. "He made a date, and he's going to keep it whether he wants to or not."

A quick smile flashed from Taylor's eyes, and her lips quivered with the effort to suppress it. "I see."

"I mean it. If Cody isn't man enough to give me a chance to explain, then he deserves what he's going to get."

"And what's that?"

"I haven't decided yet, but I'll think of something."

"Yes, I'm sure you will," Taylor said on her way out of the bathroom.

Once she was finished, Christy joined her sister, who was busy with dinner preparations. "Let me help," she insisted, feeling guilty that Taylor was stuck with the cooking. The very reason Christy was in Montana was to help with the household chores while Taylor recuperated.

"Don't be silly. I'm perfectly fine. Besides, you might mess up your makeup." Leaning against the counter, Taylor surveyed Christy's attire. "Personally I'm betting Cody's not going to be able to take his eyes off you."

"Oh, Taylor, do you really think so?" Looking her best was important to Christy. If Cody was going to slam the door in her face, which was a distinct possibility, then she wanted him to know what he was missing.

"There's something different about you," Taylor went on to say, her expression somber. She crossed her arms and cocked her head to one side.

"You mean the eyeliner. I'm using a different shade."

"No, this doesn't have anything to do with eyeliner.

You're not the same Christy I left when I moved away from Seattle."

"I'm older," Christy said, "and hopefully more mature."

Taylor paused to consider that. "I suppose that's part of it, but there's more."

"Oh?"

"You were always the 'good daughter.'"

"You make it sound like you were the bad one, and that isn't the least bit true."

"But we both know I love an argument," Taylor said, "and Dad was always willing to comply. We were so often at odds."

"But you and Dad loved and respected each other. It wasn't like some families."

"I know. It's just that we're so different. About the worst thing I can remember you doing was running around the house with a pair of scissors in your hand."

"I did go swimming in the community pool without a bathing cap that one time, remember?"

"Ah, yes, I'd forgotten about that. You renegade!"

They laughed. Taylor was right; Christy had never caused a problem, never been in trouble. The good daughter. Too good, in some ways.

"You realize Mom and Dad are going to be disappointed when they find out you aren't going to marry James."

"Probably more disappointed than James," Christy joked.

Taylor frowned slightly. "Are you sure you're doing the right thing?"

The question was unexpected. "Of course. Very soon

after I met Cody, I knew I should never have agreed to marry James. I…"

"Then why did you?"

"Well…because we're friends and we'd been working together a lot, and it just seemed…like a good idea."

"Your decision had nothing to do with Mom and Dad?"

"I…ah…"

"I don't mean to pressure you or sound like a know-it-all, but if you check your motives, I think you might discover that you accepted James's proposal for all the wrong reasons. It suited Mom and Dad for you to marry him, and you went along with it because you were trying to please them. Am I right?"

"I…" Christy lowered her eyes as a tingling extended from her stomach to her arms and down her fingers. She loved her parents so much and wanted to make them proud of her. Her marrying James would certainly have done that. Christy had been so concerned about doing what her parents thought was right that she'd never considered if it was best for her.

"Christy?"

"You make me sound so weak, so insecure."

"You're not. You're loving and gentle and good. James is a fine young man, but he's not the one for you."

Without question her parents would be upset with her, but in time they'd realize she was doing what was best for both her and James.

Christy left the Lazy P soon afterward, not waiting to see if Cody was going to come for her or not. From the way he'd left the evening before, she suspected he had no intention of keeping their dinner date.

She found his place without a problem and parked her

car. She took several minutes to compose herself before making her way to the front door.

An eternity passed before he answered her knock. "Christy?"

"I believe we have a dinner date," she said boldly, damning her voice for shaking. She didn't want him to guess how terribly nervous this confrontation made her.

"A dinner date? You and me? Forget it, sweetheart. If you want to go out, call your fiancé."

Six

"I'm not going to marry James," Christy explained in a voice that demanded Cody listen to her and at the same time begged for his understanding. Cody wasn't in the mood to do either. From the moment he'd left Christy the night before, he'd fought to push every thought of her from his mind.

With very little success.

"Who you marry or don't marry is none of my business," he said, his words sharp and abrupt.

Christy flinched at his disdain, and it was all Cody could do to keep from reaching for her and asking her forgiveness.

"Please, if you'd give me a chance to explain...."

She was so beautiful, with her cobalt-blue eyes and sweet, innocent face. Until he'd met Christy and Taylor, Cody had never seen eyes that precise shade of blue.

He groaned inwardly, struggling against the need to take her in his arms and bask in her softness. Equally strong was the instinctive urge to protect his heart and his orderly life from the havoc she was sure to bring.

Cody was the sheriff-elect, but there was little that could terrify him the way this woman did. It was essential to keep his eyes off her. Everything about her was sensual and provocative. It was difficult enough to fight her, but the battle grew even fiercer as he struggled with his own desires. This was much harder than he'd ever imagined it would be.

"At least talk to me."

Her voice was soft and compelling. The mere sound could drive him straight through the bounds of what was fast becoming his limited self-control.

"I think you should leave."

There, he'd said it. He didn't mean it, but he'd said it, and that little bit of resistance lent him a sense of control, which had been sadly lacking to this point. Christy wasn't aware of that, but he was.

"I'm not leaving until you've listened to me."

"Then you're going to have to do your talking from the street." It astonished him how forcefully he came across. He blocked the doorway as he leaned indolently against the jamb, trying his best to suggest that he hadn't a care in the world.

She hesitated, then surprised him by nodding. "Fine. If that's what it takes, I'll shout at you from the middle of the street, loud enough for the entire block to hear."

"You're wasting your time." He'd played these games with another woman once, and he wasn't about to fall into that trap a second time.

Feeling suddenly confident, he straightened, leaned forward and braced his hands against her shoulders, keeping her at arm's length. It was a risk to touch her, but one he was prepared to take. Perhaps he felt the need to convince himself that he could be close to her and not want to kiss her....

His plan backfired the instant she looked directly up at him. To complicate matters, she flattened her hands on his chest. His heart reacted immediately, and he was sure she could feel the effect she had on him. Maybe touching her wasn't such a smart move, after all.

"I meant what I said." He narrowed his eyes, hoping she'd take the hint and leave. In the same breath he prayed she wouldn't.

"You have every right to be angry," Christy continued, her eyes pleading with him. "I don't blame you. I intended to tell you about James and me. Remember when we were in the kitchen before dinner? I told you there was something I had to talk to you about."

She didn't give him a chance to answer. Not that it mattered; he did remember, all too well.

"It was never my intention to mislead you. I would've explained everything except James phoned before I had the chance."

Cody felt himself weakening. This wasn't supposed to be happening. He should be a tower of strength. A bastion of fortitude. With little more than a shrug of his shoulders he ought to send her packing. One woman had mercilessly used him before. Only an idiot would allow it to happen again.

"I realized the first time you kissed me that I could never marry James," she persisted. "Maybe even before then. I know it should've been a simple decision, but it wasn't. I had to think everything through. The answer was so obvious, so clear—but it frightened me."

She was frightened! Cody was shaking in his boots!

He dropped his hands; touching her had been a tactical error.

"So you've broken it off?" he asked, hating the way his hopes rose at the possibility that she was free.

Christy dropped her eyes. "Not exactly. But I promise you I will the minute I get back to Seattle."

Cody's blood turned to ice. So she intended to string him along. At least she was honest about it, but frankly that didn't count for much.

"I know it sounds bad," she said softly. "You might think it'd be better if I told James now. I thought so myself, but then I realized it wouldn't be right. James doesn't deserve to be treated so heartlessly. He's a good man—it would be wrong to call him and just tell him I'd met someone else. It's cruel to do it over the phone."

Cody snorted a soft laugh. She was a candidate for the loony bin if she expected him to buy into that. Either she was engaged to James or she wasn't. Either the wedding was on or it was off. As simple as that.

"All right," she said, and he could see her fighting to hold on to her composure. "If you can't accept that, I'll phone James and talk to him right now."

"Fine." He led her into the house and didn't stop until he reached the kitchen phone. Feeling slightly cocky, he lifted the receiver and handed it to her, fully expecting her not to go through with the call. She was putting on a brave front, but he was sure she had no intention of following through.

She stared at the receiver for a moment before taking it out of his hand. When she did, Cody saw how deathly pale she'd gone.

She offered him a quick, reassuring smile. "You're right," she said weakly. "I shouldn't be thinking about

James's feelings at a time like this. You have feelings, too. It's probably best to get this over with now. James will understand. I know he will." As if her fingers weighed a thousand pounds, she lifted her hand and slowly punched out a series of numbers, then closed her eyes as she waited. "He's probably still at the office."

After what seemed like an inordinate amount of time, and a short conversation with the receptionist, Christy replaced the receiver. "James already left. He must be home by now. I'll try there—only..." She looked up at him, her eyes wide and full of tension. She was willing to do this because Cody demanded it of her, but it was so hard. To know she was humiliating *James,* causing him pain...

"Only what?" he prompted.

"Could you kiss me? I seem to need it right now."

His mouth found hers even before she'd finished speaking. He'd planned to brush his lips gently across hers. This wasn't the time for anything more.

To be on the safe side, he kissed her again—just so he'd know for a fact that he could walk away from her in the blink of an eye.

That was Cody's second tactical error of the evening.

She tasted like heaven, sweet and warm. His mouth continued to move over hers until her lips parted. She sighed deeply and sagged against him. Then she buried her face in the curve of his neck. Her breathing was as hard and uneven as his own. His hands were splayed across her back, and he held on to her with what little strength he'd managed to reserve.

"Give me a moment and I'll phone James at his house," she whispered, her voice raspy.

Cody framed her face in his hands. "No," he whispered. "No?"

"I'm not happy with the situation, but you're right. Breaking the engagement by phone would be insensitive. I can wait until you get back to Seattle and talk to him face-to-face."

She lowered her eyes in gratitude, her thick lashes sweeping her cheek. "Thank you."

He nodded.

"Oh, Cody, please believe me, I'm going to end it. I'm being as completely honest as I can."

"I know."

"You do?"

He nodded. He wrapped his arms around her and rested his chin on her head. "I don't know where that leaves us," he said. "Or even where we go from here."

"I don't, either," Christy whispered, but he felt her sigh of contentment as she relaxed against him.

"You're as jumpy as a grasshopper," Russ teased three days later. "I swear you keep looking out that window as though you expect the Mounted Police to come riding over the hill."

"Not the Mounted Police, just one handsome sheriff."

"Ah, so you're seeing Cody again."

"I've seen him every night this week." Christy could feel herself blush as she said it, which was exactly the reaction her brother-in-law was looking for.

"Quit teasing my sister," Taylor said. She was sitting at the kitchen table, Eric nestled in her arms, nursing greedily.

Every time Christy watched her sister with the baby, she felt astonished at how easily Taylor had taken to motherhood. She acted as though she'd been around infants all her life. She seemed so comfortable, so *confi-*

dent with her son, whether she was breast feeding him or diapering or rocking him to sleep.

"Where's Cody taking you this afternoon?" Taylor asked, glancing up at her.

"He wouldn't say. It's supposed to be a surprise, but I have a sneaking suspicion we're headed into the wild blue yonder." At her sister's raised eyebrows, she explained. "I think he's planning to take me for a plane ride. He told me earlier that he has his private license and twice now he's mentioned flying."

"I thought you were afraid of planes," Taylor commented. When it was first decided that Christy would come to Montana, she'd immediately rejected the idea of flying into Miles City. Driving to Montana appealed to her far more. Neither Taylor nor their mother had pressed the issue.

"I'm not excited about flying," Christy admitted.

"But you don't mind going up in a plane with Cody?"

"No." She trusted him beyond question. Enough to place her life in his hands.

"If I were you, I'd make sure his little surprise doesn't involve horses," Russ warned, and his eyes connected with his wife's as though they were sharing some well-kept secret.

"Cody doesn't ride that often."

Russ poured himself a cup of coffee and joined Taylor at the kitchen table. He smiled at his son while speaking to Christy. "You certainly seem to know a great deal about the sheriff's habits."

"I..." Christy could feel warmth invade her cheeks. She hated the way she blushed whenever the subject of Cody was introduced.

She and Cody had spent every available moment together. With her vacation vanishing like melting snow, each day was more precious than the one before. It was as if they were cramming several months of a relationship into two short weeks.

Cody wasn't pleased that she remained technically engaged to James, but he'd graciously accepted the situation. It wasn't easy for him, but he never questioned her about the other man, or brought James into their conversation.

For his part, Cody had never said anything to Christy about Becca and the way he'd been duped by the other woman. Knowing what she did made her more sensitive to his needs, made her love him all the more.

Christy did love Cody. This wasn't infatuation or hormones or anything else. For some reason, unknown to them both, they were meant to be together. She knew it. He knew it. Yet Christy never spoke of her feelings, and neither did Cody.

She understood his hesitancy. He couldn't talk freely about their relationship while James was still part of her life.

Once she was back in Seattle and had broken the engagement to James, then and only then would she tell Cody she loved him. And he in turn would be free to tell her what she already knew.

Christy would've liked to hear it sooner, but if Cody could display this much patience, she could do no less.

"I don't know when we'll be back," Christy said. "Is there anything I can do for you before I leave?" she asked, looking at Taylor.

Her sister grinned. "Just have a good time."

"I will." She was already having the time of her life.

"I was in town earlier today," Russ said. He paused to be sure he had their full attention.

"So? You go into town at least twice a week," Taylor reminded him.

"Noah Williams, who works at the insurance agency, stopped me." Once more he hesitated as if this news was significant.

"Old Man Williams stops anybody who'll listen to him," Taylor interjected. "That man is the biggest gossip in three counties, and you know it."

Russ rubbed the side of his jaw. "Yeah, I suppose I do."

"Would you say what's on your mind and be done with it?" Taylor grumbled.

Russ chuckled. "All right. Noah claimed he'd heard that the sheriff's about to take a wife. A pretty one, too. He said word has it she's a relative of mine."

"Oh?" Christy asked, willingly playing into his hands. "And did this relative of yours have a name?"

Christy remembered Cody introducing her to the town's sole insurance agent. He'd also told her that Noah Williams was well acquainted with most folks' business, whether they were his clients or not.

"Said he didn't recall the name, but he thought it was something like Cathy or Christine. Or Christabel."

"Funny. Very funny," Christy muttered, looking out the window, hoping to see Cody's truck.

"I'm telling you right now," Russ said, chuckling again, "the secret's out. The sheriff's gonna take himself a wife."

The next afternoon, Christy was lying on her back in a meadow not far from the ranch house, chewing on a long blade of grass. Cody had taken her flying the previous day, just as she'd guessed, and the experience had been exhilarating, not frightening at all. He lay beside her now, staring at the darkening sky. A series of clouds was rolling in, obliterating the sun, but they'd both decided to ignore the threat of rain.

"Looks like there's a storm coming," Cody said.

"Let it. I don't mind, do you?"

"That depends." He rolled onto his stomach and leaned on his elbows as he gazed lovingly down at her. He didn't seem any more eager to leave the site of their picnic than Christy.

The afternoon had been ideal. Cody had arrived at the house early in the day, and Christy had met him with a basket full of goodies. Russ complained that she was taking enough food to feed a small army...of ants.

"Depends on what?" she asked, smiling up at him.

"On who I'm with." As if he couldn't stop himself, he leaned over her and pressed his mouth to hers. Then his lips moved along the side of her face and into her hair. He paused and went still as he breathed in the scent of the cologne she'd dabbed behind her ears.

Other than the few kisses they'd exchanged over the past days, Cody hadn't touched her. It wasn't that he didn't desire her, didn't need her. But he held himself back—held himself in check.

Christy understood and in many ways approved.

The physical attraction between them was more powerful than either had ever experienced. It wasn't something to be trifled with.

He kissed her again lightly, softly, gently.

Christy slid her hands up his chest and put her arms around his neck. He kissed her again, his breath hot and quick. "We should stop now," he warned but made no effort to move away from her.

"Yes, I know," she concurred.

He brushed his thumb back and forth over her moist lips as if gathering the needed resolve to pull away from her. She gazed up into his dark, troubled eyes and saw his hesitation. His hands were trembling as he started to roll away from her.

"No." Her cry was instinctive. Urgent.

"Christy…"

"Shh." She sank her fingers into his hair at the sides of his lean, rugged face, raised her head from the soft patch of grass and touched her mouth to his.

His hands tangled with her short curls as he moved the upper half of his body over hers, anchoring her to the ground. Their frenzied kissing seemed to go on and on.

"Enough," he said breathlessly. "We have to stop."

Christy wanted him so desperately; the hunger to love him all but consumed her, and she moved fitfully beneath him.

"Christy," he said, "we're headed for trouble if we don't stop…*now.*"

"I thought sheriffs were trained to deal with any kind of trouble." Her tongue outlined his mouth even as she spoke.

Cody moaned.

Christy sighed.

There didn't seem to be anything strong enough in this world or the next to pull them apart. Christy felt as if she'd been created for this man, for this moment. The love between them was as inevitable as the setting sun. As natural as the ocean waves caressing the shore or the wind stirring the trees. Her blood seemed to vibrate in sympathy, a vibration that grew more insistent—until she realized something was amiss. It wasn't her blood that was pounding in her veins, but rain that was pounding the earth. The clouds burst over them, drenching Christy within seconds.

Cody brought his hands to her face, framing it as he slowly raised his head. His eyes sought hers.

"Cody, it's pouring!"

He responded by kissing her again. "You taste too sweet to move."

"You're getting soaked."

"So are you." He grinned. "And I don't mind if you don't."

"I don't."

"Good." Once more his mouth connected with hers.

A moment later, Christy leaned against him. "We... almost made love."

"I promised myself we wouldn't," he whispered. "And this is a promise I mean to keep." His hands closed around her upper arms. "Understand?"

Christy nodded.

"I mean it, Christy."

"Yes, sir." She teased him with a salute.

Deftly he reversed their positions, smoothly rolling over and taking her with him so she was poised above him. She straddled his hips and arched her head back as the rain pummeled her face. Brushing away her hair, she smiled at the dark, angry sky.

"I suppose I should be grateful," Cody murmured.

"For the rain? Why?"

"You know why."

"Yes," she whispered, "but in some ways I wish..." She let the rest fade, because they were aware of what would have happened if Mother Nature hadn't intervened when she did.

Seven

"You're *sure* you want to babysit?" Taylor asked, as though she expected Christy to change her mind.

"You're going," Christy said, ushering her older sister to the kitchen where Russ was waiting impatiently. It was the first time Taylor had left Eric, and she was having second thoughts.

"This night is for you and Russ."

"I know but—"

"I have the phone number to the restaurant, the home nurse, the doctor and the hospital. If anything the least bit out of the ordinary occurs, I'll phone someone, so quit worrying."

"Eric's never had a bottle," Taylor protested.

"It's still Mama's milk. He's a smart baby. He'll adjust." After Taylor had spent a long—and hilarious—afternoon learning how to operate the breast pump, each ounce was more precious than gold.

"Christy, I'm not convinced this is such a good idea, after all."

"Don't be ridiculous. Eric will probably sleep the entire time you're away."

"Are you going to let me take you to dinner or not?" Russ's voice boomed from the kitchen. "I'd like to remind you the reservation is for six." After a hard day on the ranch, Russ got too hungry to wait much beyond that for the evening meal.

Cody was the one who'd come up with the idea of the two of them babysitting Eric while Russ and Taylor took an evening for themselves. It was Christy's last night in Cougar Point. First thing in the morning she'd start the long drive across three states. Although she'd been gone less than two weeks, it felt as if an entire lifetime had passed.

"Cody's here," Russ called out. "Just how long does it take you women to put on a little war paint, anyway?" His voice lowered, and Christy could hear him conversing with the sheriff. Her brother-in-law was saying that Taylor and Christy were the two most beautiful women in the county as it was. He contended that they didn't need makeup, and he was having a heck of a time understanding why they bothered with it.

"Hold your horses," Taylor cried, poking her head out the bathroom door and calling down the hallway into the kitchen. "I'll only be a minute."

"Famous last words if I ever heard 'em," Russ grumbled.

As it turned out, her brother-in-law was right. Taylor spent an extra five minutes fussing with her hair and adding a dash of perfume to her wrists. When she'd finished, she checked Eric, gave Christy and Cody a long list of instructions, then reluctantly left the house with her husband.

Cody brought his arm around Christy as they stood on the back porch, watching Russ hold open the car door for Taylor. Christy smiled when Russ stole a lengthy kiss.

"Well," Cody said after Russ had pulled out of the yard, "they're off."

"I don't think they'll win any races."

"No," he chuckled, "I doubt they will." He turned her into his arms and kissed her softly.

"Oh, honestly," Mandy said, scooting past them and down the porch steps. "You two are as bad as Russ and Taylor. If it was me doing these PDAs, you can bet I'd be in big trouble. It seems to me that people over twenty-one get away with a whole lot more than they should."

"PDAs?" Christy asked. "What's that?"

"Public Displays of Affection," Cody whispered close to her ear. As if the temptation were too strong to resist, he caught her lobe between his teeth.

"Cody," she cried, "behave yourself."

"Hey, where are you going?" Cody demanded when Mandy started toward the barn. "I thought you were planning to stick around and chaperone the two of us."

"I'm going to the movies."

"In the barn?"

"Don't be cute with me, Cody Franklin. Just because you've been elected sheriff doesn't mean you can control *my* life."

"You're not the one I want to get cute with."

"Obviously. I figured you two would appreciate a little privacy. Billy Joe's driving me over to Melissa's, and I'm going to the movies with her. She got her license last week."

"I heard rumors along those lines," Cody said with a grin.

"Just don't go sending Bud or any of the other deputies out to tail us." Mandy wagged an accusing finger in Cody's direction. "I know you'd do it, too. Melissa's still a little nervous, and the last thing she needs is a sheriff's car following her into town."

"You think I'd radio for someone to follow her?" Cody sounded aghast that Mandy would even hint at something so dastardly.

"You'd do it if you thought you could." But she was smiling as she spoke.

Billy Joe, Russ's ranch foreman, stepped out from the barn, freshly shaved. His hair was wet and combed down against the sides of his head. "You ready?"

"Yup," Mandy said, walking toward his battered red pickup.

Taylor had explained that the foreman was interested in Melissa's widowed mother and had been seeing her for the past few months. Apparently Mandy and Melissa were working together to stage an evening alone for the two adults.

Eric wailed loudly, and after bidding Mandy farewell, Christy hurried inside the house and into the master bedroom. Eric was lying in the bassinet waiting for someone to answer his summons.

"What's the matter, big boy?" she asked, reaching for him. His damp bottom answered that question. "So you wet your diaper, did you?" she chided playfully, giving him her finger, which he gripped fiercely.

"I'll change him," Cody said from behind her.

Christy arched her brows in feigned shock. "This I've got to see."

"I'll have you know I've changed more than one diaper in my lifetime."

"That may be true, but it seems to me you took great delight in teasing Russ when he offered to change Eric."

"I've had more practice than Russ, that's all." Cody took a fresh diaper from the pile of folded ones on the dresser. "Both of my sisters have children, and being the generous uncle I am, I've helped out now and then. It's not nearly as difficult as Russ seems to think."

"All right, since you're so sure of yourself, go ahead and I'll see to our dinner." Carefully she handed Cody the baby, then walked to the kitchen.

Taylor had set a frozen pepperoni pizza on the kitchen counter. The only place in Cougar Point that served pizza was the bowling alley; Taylor could go without a lot of luxuries, but she needed her pizza. Every time she was in Miles City, she bought three or four pepperoni pizzas from a nationwide chain, brought them home and promptly froze them.

"I hope you're in the mood for pizza," Christy called, setting the gauge on the oven to the right temperature.

"You mean Taylor's willing to share one of hers? Without us having to ask?"

"I didn't even have to bribe her."

"I may volunteer to babysit more often," Cody said as he entered the kitchen, holding Eric against his shoulder. His large hand was pressed against the infant's tiny back.

Christy paused when she saw them, and her heart beat so fast, it actually hurt. Cody looked so natural with a baby in his arms. As natural as any father. Turning away in an effort to disguise her emotions, she clasped the counter with both hands and waited for the aching tenderness to pass.

She was engaged to an attorney in Seattle, a good friend she'd known for several years, and not once had she pictured him as a father. The fact that they'd likely have children someday had barely crossed her mind.

Yet here she was with Cody and her nephew, and the sight of this big, rugged man holding this precious child was enough to bring tears to her eyes.

"Christy, could you give me…" He hesitated when she didn't immediately respond. "Christy?"

She swallowed the lump in her throat, smeared the tears across her cheek and turned, smiling as brightly as she could. She doubted she'd be able to fool Cody, but she intended to try.

"What's wrong?" His question was filled with concern.

"Nothing…"

"If that's the case, then why are you crying?"

She didn't know how she could explain it, not without sounding as though she required long-term therapy. She was crazy in love with one man, and engaged to another. In a few hours she'd be leaving Cody behind. There were no guarantees, no pledges, no promises between them.

Nothing.

There couldn't be anything while she was engaged to James.

James. Two weeks away from him and she had trouble remembering what he looked like. Inconsequential details occurred to her—that he drank his tea with milk and hadn't worn a pair of jeans since he was thirteen years old. He was endearing, hardworking and brilliant.

And he loved her. At least he thought he did, the same way she'd once assumed she loved him.

The phone rang, startling Eric, who let out a loud wail. Cody whispered reassurances while patting the baby's back.

"I'll get that," Christy said, grateful for the intrusion.

"It's probably Taylor calling to check up on us." She hurried into the hallway, wanting to catch the phone before it rang again and frightened Eric a second time.

"Hello," she sang out cheerfully. "This is Palmer's Pizza Parlor. May I take your order?" Taylor would get a kick out of that.

Silence followed.

"It appears I've dialed the wrong number," a male voice said stiffly.

"James? Oh, dear… I thought it was Taylor. This is Christy."

Cody heard Christy's laughter end two seconds after she answered the phone. He knew almost immediately that the man on the other end of the line was her fiancé.

Cody was instantly overwhelmed by confusion and an equally large dose of good old-fashioned jealousy. He was so resentful of Christy's engagement that a long painful moment passed before he could clear his head. He'd never been the jealous type, and now he was all but blinded by it.

He shouldn't have been surprised that James—he had trouble thinking about the other man without tightening his jaw—would call Christy. If Cody was the one engaged to her and she was a thousand miles away, he'd phone her, too. Frequently.

That realization, however, was no comfort. Before many more hours passed, Christy would be leaving Cougar Point. In another two days she'd be back with James. Her weeks with him in Montana would be little more than a fading memory.

Cody wasn't willing to kid himself any longer. There was no use trying to hide from it, or deny it or ignore it.

He was in love with Christy Manning. He'd pledged a thousand times that he'd never allow this foolish emotion to take hold of his life again. So much for all the promises he'd made himself. So much for protecting his heart.

Dammit all, he was in love!

But Cody was realistic enough to put their relationship in the proper perspective. Or at least try. Christy was engaged to a hotshot Seattle attorney. He, on the other hand, was a backwoods sheriff. Christy might be infatuated with him now, but once she returned to the big city that could easily change. Believing these few days together meant more to her could be dangerous.

She was going to break the engagement. Or so she claimed. But now something was troubling her. Cody had sensed it when she was fussing with the pizza. When he'd first arrived, she'd been her usual warm, happy self. She'd joked with him as though she hadn't a care in the world.

Cody frowned. Since the afternoon of their picnic when they'd gotten caught in the downpour, Cody had noticed subtle changes in her. She seemed more spontaneous, more open with him.

He was willing to admit there'd been numerous intricate transformations in their relationship over the past ten days. They'd spent hours together, getting to know each other, growing to love each other.

And for most of that time, Cody had to struggle to keep his hands off her.

He found himself studying her at every opportunity, and whenever he did he liked what he saw. She captivated him. When they were alone together, he'd learned how dangerous it was to kiss her—and how difficult it was to stop. She'd press her soft body against his, and it was a test by fire of his limited control.

In the distance Cody heard the anxiety in her voice as her phone conversation with the other man continued. Not wanting to listen in, Cody opened the screen door and walked outside, carrying the baby. He sat on the top step and let his gaze wander across the acres of prime pastureland.

"See all those pesky cattle, Eric?" he whispered to the baby held securely against his shoulder. "It'll all belong to you someday. Take some advice, though, boy…" He was about to tell Russ's son not to get involved with women because all they did was cause a man grief.

But he stopped himself. Christy hadn't caused him grief or trouble. If anything, she'd brought him the truest joy he'd ever felt. He hadn't realized how lonely he was. Nor had he known how isolated his life had become until she'd walked into it, bold as could be.

Okay, he mused, sighing deeply. He was in love. It wasn't supposed to happen, but it had. Damned if he knew what to do next. For a man in his thirties he'd had precious little experience with it. The one other time he'd committed his heart to a woman, it had cost him dearly. He hadn't been willing to place himself at risk again. Not until he met Christy.

Fifteen minutes passed before Christy finally joined him. He heard her moving behind him in the kitchen and felt the swish of the screen door as it opened.

"That was James," she said as she sat down on the step beside him.

"I heard." He didn't mean to be, but he sounded flippant, uncaring.

"He…he's called two other times."

"That's none of my business," he informed her curtly.

"I know, but I want to be honest with you. Are you angry?"

"No."

"You sound angry."

"I'm not." And pigs fly, he told himself.

For a long moment Christy didn't say anything. She sat there looking like an angel, smelling like something out of a rose garden. How was a man supposed to resist her when she gazed at him with those large blue eyes of hers?

"I...almost told him about you. It was on the tip of my tongue to try to explain. But James seemed so pre-occupied. He was visiting my parents, and I spoke to them, too, and..." She shrugged. "It was impossible."

"Why's that?" He made a determined effort to take the starch out of his voice.

She hesitated before answering. "My mom and dad like James a lot."

"I'm sure he's perfect son-in-law material."

Christy ignored that comment, which was probably best. He knew he wasn't dealing with this situation well. In fact, he was making a real jackass of himself.

"Now...now that I've had these two weeks with you, I think I accepted his proposal more to please my parents than because I was in love with James."

"I see." Several questions popped into his mind. Christy was a kind person, affectionate and empathetic, someone who tried to please others. Her parents, James, *him*.

"They like Russ, too," she hurried to add.

Cody didn't know what that proved, and frankly he wasn't in the frame of mind to ask.

"Or at least they do now. At first—" She stopped abruptly, as if she'd already said too much.

Cody didn't doubt that the week to come, when she confronted James and her family, would be one of the most difficult of her life. If she went through with it, if she decided to break off the engagement, after all.

"I...can't bear for us to spend our last night together arguing," she whispered.

Cody forced himself to relax. He couldn't bear it, either. He lifted his free arm and placed it around her shoulders, drawing her closer to him and Eric. She turned and smiled shyly up at him. With unhurried ease he lowered his head until their mouths met. The kiss was long and slow and when he raised his head, Cody felt dizzy with yearning.

"Oh, Cody," she moaned, her fingers clutching his shirt collar, her eyes closed. "I hate to leave you."

He hated it, too, feared it more than he'd feared anything. He dreaded the moment she'd drive away from him.

Fear and dread. Fighting those emotions wasn't how he wanted to spend their last hours together.

"Are you sure you haven't forgotten anything?" Taylor asked for the tenth time. They stood beside Christy's car, Taylor in her housecoat, Christy in her traveling clothes—a comfortable pair of faded jeans and a long-sleeved T-shirt.

"I'm positive I've got everything." She'd checked the house twice, and even if she'd inadvertently left something behind, she'd be back. Soon, she hoped. As soon as she could clear up the situation with James. As soon as she was free.

Taylor hugged her, and Russ stepped forward, holding Eric. He placed his free arm around Christy and squeezed tight.

"Drive carefully," Taylor said, "and phone the minute you arrive in Seattle. You know I'll worry until I hear from you." Tears brimmed from her sister's eyes as she reached for Christy one last time. "I really hate to see you go."

"I'll phone," Christy promised. As for the part about hating to leave, that went without saying.

"Where's Cody?" Russ asked, frowning.

"He's got the day shift," Christy explained. Although she'd spent until the wee hours of the morning saying goodbye to the sheriff, she half expected Cody to come barreling down the driveway before she headed out.

"Be a good little baby," she whispered to Eric, kissing his brow. "Remember your Aunt Christy." With no more reason to delay, she opened her car door and climbed inside.

As she was driving toward the road, Christy looked in the rearview mirror and caught sight of Taylor slipping her arm around her husband's waist. She rested her head on his broad chest and leaned against him, as though she needed his strength, his support.

The scene was a touching one, and Christy found herself blinking back tears.

She was still sniffling as she headed for the highway that would connect her with the interstate. It would be a straight shot to Seattle after that.

Christy planned to make the best time she could. The sooner she got home, the sooner she could set her life in order.

Reaching across the seat, she located the thermos of coffee Taylor had insisted she take with her. Holding it between her legs, she struggled to unscrew the cap. It was difficult to do with one hand. She'd just about given up when a flashing blue and red light was reflected in her rearview mirror.

Cody.

Christy eased to the side of the road, turned off the engine and threw open the door. It was impossible to hold her emotions at bay a moment longer.

Her gaze was blurred with tears, but it didn't matter. Cody had come to her.

By the time she'd climbed out of her car, he was out of his. Not waiting for an invitation, she rushed toward him, sobbing, so grateful he'd come.

He caught her, encircling her waist with his arms and lifting her from the ground. His lips found hers, their mouths connecting with such force that it threw her head back. Christy didn't mind; she was as needy as Cody. As hungry. As lost.

He continued to kiss her, saying with his body what he couldn't with words. That he loved her, needed her and was desperately afraid of losing her.

Christy understood and responded to each doubt.

"There's a side road about two miles back. Do you know where I mean?"

She nodded, remembered having driven past it minutes earlier.

"Meet me there?"

"Yes."

By the time she climbed back into her car, Christy was trembling from the inside out. Her stomach felt tight, and her heart was pounding. Cody made a U-turn and led the way. Christy followed willingly.

He pulled onto the dirt road, stirring up layers of fine

dust, partially obliterating his vehicle. He drove past a wide curve, then he parked at the side. Christy watched as he reached for his radio. She got out of her car and waited for him.

"I told dispatch I wouldn't be available for the next fifteen minutes," he explained, his dark eyes holding hers. "I know it's not long enough to say what I want to say, but it's all the time I dare take."

Christy nodded.

He brushed his fingertips over her damp cheek. "You've been crying."

"I...couldn't get the thermos open."

"That's why?" he asked softly.

"No, of course it's not. I don't want to go. Oh, Cody, it's so much harder to leave you than I thought it would be." She tried unsuccessfully to swallow a sob.

"Don't cry," Cody pleaded. He held her against his chest and lowered his head. When he kissed her, it was with desperation and urgency, his mouth slanting over hers. She clung to him, giving as much as she took.

He kissed her neck, nuzzled it. Christy let her head fall back, allowing him to do whatever he wished. She was his for this moment, this hour, this day.

His warm mouth skimmed the length of her throat, planting moist kisses along her shoulder blade...then lower, much lower.

Slowly, as if he was calling upon all the self-control he possessed, Cody raised his head. "Letting you go is the hardest thing I've ever done," he whispered. He smoothed the hair away from her face and kissed her again.

A well-modulated voice came over the radio of the patrol car, reminding them both who and what Cody was.

A man who'd pledged to serve and protect. As much as he would've liked to stay with her, the time had come for them to return to their separate lives.

"I'll follow you to the county line," he told her. He held open her car door, looking very much like the dignified sheriff he was. There was little evidence of the loving interlude that had passed between them.

A nod was all Christy could manage. She slid into the driver's seat. Her hand closed around the key. Cody held on to her door, his eyes trained directly ahead.

"I guess this is goodbye," she said hoarsely. "At least for now."

He nodded. "For now. You'll drive carefully?"

"Of course."

Again he nodded, closed her door and then stepped back. He seemed about to say something else, but then changed his mind.

Christy waited for him to enter his patrol car before starting her engine. She sent him a smile and glanced in her rearview mirror as she entered the main road.

True to his word, Cody followed her for several miles. In the distance she read the sign that stated she was leaving Custer County. An immediate knot formed in her throat, making it difficult to swallow.

Her rearview mirror showed Cody's red and blue lights flashing. She pulled over and stopped. Cody eased the patrol car in behind her.

He was out of his vehicle before she had a chance to free her seat belt. Lowering her window, she looked at him expectantly.

"One last thing before you go." His voice was deep and gravelly. "I love you, Christy. Come back to me."

Eight

"James," Christy said quietly, "you know I consider you one of my dearest friends. I've always heard good friends make the best husbands...no," she mumbled, her hands tightening around the steering wheel. "That doesn't sound right. Think, Christy, think!"

She'd just crossed the Idaho-Washington border and was within six hours of Seattle and home. Every mile, every minute, led her closer to the confrontation with James and her parents.

For the past two days Christy had carefully rehearsed what she planned to say, outlining her speech, inordinately conscious of each word.

James would be devastated, her parents shocked.

When it came right down to it, Christy was more worried about confronting her parents than she was James, especially her father, whom she adored. Eric Manning always seemed to think he knew what was best for her; for the most part, Christy had agreed with him. And he'd decided James would be the perfect husband for his youngest daughter.

The hours sped past, far too quickly to suit Christy. As she approached the outskirts of Seattle she found that she was traveling well below the speed limit, which produced several heated stares from her fellow travelers.

Once she'd arrived at her apartment building and had unloaded her car, Christy paced her living room restlessly. She'd assumed that once she was surrounded by everything that was familiar, some of the uneasiness would leave her.

It didn't. In fact, she was more agitated now than ever.

Gathering her courage, she decided to call her family and deal with them first. She planned to ask if it was convenient for her to come over, hoping it would be. The she could quickly put an end to this madness.

Once she was alone with her parents, she'd tell them she intended to break her engagement. Her argument was prepared, her decision unshakable.

Her first choice would've been to do it over the phone, but that would be the cowardly way out. Her only option was to confront them together. Once that was finished she'd go and see James.

As she reached for her phone, her stomach tensed. She wasn't sure what to expect from her parents or James and tried not to dwell on how they'd react to her news. She closed her eyes and prayed someone would answer before she lost her courage and hung up the phone.

"Hello."

"Jason?" He was her second-oldest brother and the handsomest of the lot, or so he liked to claim. At thirty-two he was a "catch," only he enjoyed playing the field far too much to settle down with any one woman.

"Christy? When did you get back?"

"Just a few minutes ago." How odd she sounded.

Christy prayed Jason wouldn't notice. "What are you doing there? Are Mom and Dad around?"

"I'm here 'cause I took the day off. Mom and Dad are out but they'll be back any minute." He paused. "You don't know yet, do you?"

"Know what?" Jason loved playing games, dangling bits of information in front of her like bait, making her hungry for more.

"Never mind."

"Jason, I've been on the road for two days, and to be frank, I'm not up to any of your trick questions." Under normal circumstances Christy would have been amused and played along, but not now.

"Hey, sweetie, no trick questions with this one. All I can say is you have a real surprise waiting for you. Mom's slaved every day since you've been gone, so if I were you, I'd make my presence known soon."

"Thank you so much," Christy muttered sarcastically. "Talking to you is like looking through a telescope with the lens cap on."

"Always happy to oblige," Jason responded with a light chuckle. "Just drop by the house soon.... In fact, the sooner the better."

Christy intended on doing exactly that. "I'll be over in fifteen minutes. By the way, how's Mom?" Breaking her leg had kept Elizabeth Manning at home for several weeks, and Christy knew how terribly disappointed her mother had been about missing this important time with her eldest daughter and newborn grandson.

"Mom's doing great. Especially now..." He didn't finish the enigmatic statement, and Christy refused to fall into his hands by asking what he meant. "If you don't mind, I'll stick around for a while, too. I'd like to get a look at your face once you find out what's been going on around here. Mom's in seventh heaven. At the rate things are going, you're likely to end up in one of those celebrity magazines."

"Cute, Jason, very cute." Christy had no idea what he was talking about, but that was typical of her older brother. Over the last few years, his comments had taken on a biting edge. Christy didn't know what his problem was, but she wished he'd straighten out whatever was wrong.

In an attempt to delay the unavoidable, Christy played back the messages on her answering machine while she leafed through two weeks' worth of mail. Anyone who mattered wouldn't have phoned because they'd know she was out of town, but she couldn't help being curious.

There were several beeps, indicating that whoever had called had hung up before leaving a message. Probably salesmen.

Deciding it was a waste of time, Christy started for her front door when Taylor's voice, hesitant and unsure, came over the tinny speaker. "Christy, call me as soon as you get home. Something's come up that we need to discuss."

There was an uncharacteristic note in her sister's voice, an uncertainty that suggested something was terribly amiss.

Puzzled, Christy returned to the phone and placed a long-distance call to Cougar Point. Mandy answered, sounding as cheerful as ever.

"Taylor's not here," Russ's sister explained. "She drove into Miles City for Eric's first appointment with the pediatrician. Do you want me to have her call you once she gets back? I don't think it'll be too much longer. I know she was anxious to talk to you."

"No. I'm headed to my parents' house now. I'll phone again later." Hopefully by that time everything would be settled. She could contact Taylor and Russ and then talk to Cody. The mere thought of him made her go weak. Seemingly by accident they'd found each other and unexpectedly discovered what it meant to fall in love. Neither of them had been looking for this, neither of them fully understood why it had happened, but it was right. Right for Cody. Right for Christy.

After two long days on the road, she was physically exhausted and mentally depleted. She'd considered delaying this confrontation until she was well-rested and relaxed, but she knew she couldn't do that. The engagement to James hung over her head and she wouldn't find peace until all the obstacles were cleared out of the road that would lead her back to her sheriff.

Her parents' luxury vehicle was in the driveway when Christy drove up. Jason's car was in the street, and Christy parked her own behind his. Even before she'd turned off the engine, her father had opened the front door and was walking toward her, arms outstretched.

Eric Manning embraced his daughter, hugging her tight. From the time she was little Christy had always felt a special closeness to her parents. Most of her friends had rebelled in one way or another against their families, but never Christy. She'd never felt the need.

"When did you get back?" her father asked.

"Not even half an hour ago." She slipped her arm around his thickening waist and they walked toward the sprawling brick house. The lawn was a soft, lush green. Many a happy hour had been spent racing across this very same grass. Echoes of her childhood laughter seemed to mock her now.

Elizabeth Manning stood in the entryway, her left leg encased from her foot to just below her knee in a hot pink cast. She broke into a broad smile as Christy approached the front door.

"Sweetheart, it's so good to have you home."

"It's good to be home, and before you ask, yes, I brought tons of pictures of Eric."

"Oh, that's wonderful, I can't tell you how excited we are that Russ and Taylor named him after your father."

Christy stepped into the house. It was a large home built into a hill overlooking the freeway that cut a wide path through the heart of Seattle. The basement opened onto an enormous, landscaped yard with a profusion of flower beds and space for a vegetable garden, whose bounty spilled over to friends and neighbors every summer.

"How's the leg?"

"Better," Elizabeth said, dismissing her daughter's concern with a quick shake of her head. She was walking with a cane now, leaning heavily upon it. Christy knew her mother well enough to realize Elizabeth Manning would never want to burden her children with the fact that she was in pain. But her mother did look much healthier, Christy mused. The sparkle was back in her eyes, and a flush of excitement glowed from her cheeks. Christy couldn't remember how long it'd been since she'd seen her mother so happy. No doubt the birth of their third grandson was responsible.

"You're looking terrific," Christy said, kissing her mother's cheek.

"Actually, sweetie, we have you to thank for that,"

her father murmured, sharing an enigmatic smile with his wife.

"Me?" Apparently they were playing the same game as Jason.

"Eric, let's not discuss this in the entryway."

Her father chuckled, and Christy noted that his eyes seemed brighter, too. He certainly was in one of his better moods. Christy would like to think it was all due to her arrival and the fact that she'd brought pictures of their grandson. But somehow she doubted it, especially after having spoken to Jason.

Her second-oldest brother was sitting in the family room in front of the television when Christy walked in. He was wearing a Seattle Mariners baseball cap, which he had on much of the time.

"Welcome home, little sister," he greeted her. He stood and hugged her, then stepped back, wiggling his eyebrows.

"All right, you guys," Christy said, claiming the easy chair next to Jason. "What's going on around here?"

Her father's mouth started to quiver, as though he was having difficulty holding back his excitement. He shared another look with his wife of thirty-five years.

"If you'll recall, your mother's spirits were low after she fell and broke her leg. Missing out on this special time with Taylor and Russ depressed her."

"I didn't even realize how melancholy I'd become until Eric mentioned it," Elizabeth said. "Sometimes I swear he knows me better than I know myself."

Christy felt herself nod.

"Your father's the one who came up with the idea for an engagement party."

"An...engagement party," Christy echoed, coming halfway out of her chair, appalled and dismayed.

Her mother pressed her fingers to her lips, almost giddy with delight. "We knew you'd be pleased."

"I... I..." Christy was at a complete loss for words. Somehow she managed a smile and slumped back into the cushions of the overstuffed chair.

"You can't imagine what fun we've had," Elizabeth continued, her voice animated. "I'm afraid your father got carried away. He insisted we order the best of everything. We've rented the Eagles Hall, got the invitations mailed—engraved ones. Oh, sweetie, I can hardly wait for you to see them. We spent hour after hour with the caterers. I can't even *begin* to tell you what a fabulous time I—we—had planning every detail of this party. I can't help feeling proud of everything we accomplished in such a short time."

"It was just what your mother needed," Christy's father inserted smoothly, looking equally delighted. "Elizabeth's been like a kid again from the moment we decided to go through with this."

"I see." Christy went completely numb. It seemed impossible that no one was aware of it.

"I suppose we're a pair of old fools, but when Taylor married Russ in Reno, your father and I felt cheated out of a large family wedding. We've been looking forward to throwing one for years."

"When?" It was torture getting the word past the tightness that all but blocked her throat.

"That's the crazy part," Jason told her. "Mom and Dad put this entire thing together in two weeks."

Christy still didn't understand; not much of the conversation made sense. Her look must have conveyed her confusion.

"The party's tomorrow night," Elizabeth said, her face radiating her excitement.

"Tomorrow night?"

"I know it sounds crazy, and we took a chance booking it so close to the end of your vacation, but there were only a few dates available at the Eagles Hall, and it was either tomorrow night or three months from now."

"In fact, the only reason we were able to get the hall is because of a last-minute cancellation," Eric said. "I had no idea we'd need to book this sort of thing so far in advance."

"James?" No one seemed to notice she was having trouble speaking, which Christy supposed was a blessing of sorts.

"He knows, of course, but we decided to keep it a secret for you. A welcome-home surprise."

Christy nodded, hating the way she continued to sit in her parents' home, saying nothing when it felt as if the foundations of her world were crumbling at her feet. Her mother and father and Jason were all looking at her, waiting for some response, but for the life of her, Christy couldn't give them one.

Her eyes met with her brother's.

He winked broadly. "Mom and Dad are sparing no expense. If the wedding's half as elaborate as the engagement party, then your big day's going to be spectacular."

Eric Manning chuckled. "It isn't every father who has a daughter as special as Christy."

Christy forced a smile although she longed to stand up and beg them to put an end to this craziness. She didn't love James. She loved Cody. She couldn't possibly go through with an engagement to a man she didn't intend to marry.

She glanced from her mother to her father, both of them staring at her with bright, eager smiles, as though waiting for her to burst into a song of praise for their efforts.

"I… I…" The words froze on her lips.

"Honey, look," Elizabeth murmured devotedly to her husband. "Christy's speechless. Oh, sweetie, you don't need to say anything. Your father and I understand. If anyone should be giving thanks, it's me. I was so miserable after my fall. Planning this party was the best thing in the world for me. I've loved every minute of it. Keeping it a surprise has been so much fun."

There had to be a plausible excuse she could use to avoid this farce of an engagement party. "I don't have a dress." The words escaped her lips almost as quickly as they formed in her mind.

"Not to worry," Elizabeth said, her eyes glowing even brighter. "I thought of everything, if I do say so myself. I went shopping the other day and picked out a dress for you. If you don't like it, or it doesn't fit, we can exchange it first thing in the morning."

First thing in the morning. The words echoed in her ears. "I… I'm supposed to go back to work." That sounded reasonable to her. After two weeks away from the law firm, Christy was expected back. They needed her. They were short-staffed without her. She couldn't demand additional time off to exchange a party dress.

"No need to worry about that, either," Eric said. "James has that covered. He talked it over with the office manager, and she's given you two extra days off with pay."

"Tomorrow, of course, will be filled with all the last-minute details for the party," Elizabeth rattled on, rubbing her palms together.

"You didn't tell Taylor?" Her older sister would've said something to her; Christy was sure of it.

"Well, not right away. I mailed her a long letter and an invitation so it would arrive the day you were scheduled to leave Montana. I'm guessing she has it by now. I couldn't take the chance of mailing it any sooner for fear you'd find it, and I didn't want to say anything when we phoned in case she inadvertently let the cat out of the bag. I wanted to keep this a surprise."

"I see," Christy murmured.

"Your father and I don't expect Taylor to fly home for the party, not so soon after having the baby. She and Russ will come out for the wedding. Which is something else we need to discuss. Talk to James, sweetie—the sooner we have a date, the better. There's so much to do, and I so want this wedding to be carefully planned. I can't tell you how much I've learned in the past two weeks. Right after the party tomorrow night, we're going to sit down and discuss the wedding."

Christy nodded, simply because she lacked the courage to explain there would never be a wedding, at least not one in which James was the bridegroom.

"You are surprised, aren't you?" Jason demanded, looking exceptionally cocky, as though he was the person responsible for pulling this whole affair together.

Surprise was too mild a word for what Christy was experiencing. Even shock and dismay were too mild.

Horror and panic more aptly described her feelings.

James! She needed to talk to James. He'd help her. He'd understand, and then together they'd clear up this mess. Together they could confront her parents and make *them* understand.

She stood before she realized what she was doing. Everyone in the room seemed to be staring holes straight through her. Glancing around, she offered them each a weak smile.

Always dutiful. Always obedient. Never causing a concern or a problem. Christy was about to destroy her good-girl image.

But first she had to talk to James.

Two messages were waiting for Christy on her answering machine when she returned late that afternoon. The first was from Cody and the second from Taylor.

Christy didn't answer either.

Instead she sat in her living room, staring into space, weighed down by guilt, pressured beyond anything she'd ever experienced and entangled in circumstances beyond her control.

How long she stayed there Christy didn't know. Here she was safe. Here she was protected. Here she could hide.

That small sense of security, however, quickly disintegrated. Knowing there was nothing else she could do to stop the progression of events, she stood and walked into the kitchen. She paused in front of the phone, then abruptly picked it up before she had a change of heart.

Cody wasn't home, and she left an all-too-brief message. Her next call was to Taylor.

"Christy, what's going on?" Taylor burst out the instant she recognized her younger sister. "I got this crazy letter from Mom about a surprise engagement party for you. What's happening?"

"You mean about the party?" Christy asked. Her voice lacked any level of emotion. She had none left.

"Of course I mean the party," Taylor cried. "Do you mean to say you're going through with it?"

"I don't have any choice."

"Christy, you can't be serious! What about Cody? I thought you were in love with him. I may be out of line here, but I could've sworn you…" She inhaled deeply. "I'd better stop before I say something I shouldn't. Just answer me one question. Do you or do you not love Cody Franklin?"

Christy wiped the tears from her face and nodded wildly. "You know I do."

"Then it seems to me you're allowing Mom and Dad to dictate your life."

"You don't understand," Christy whimpered.

"What's there to understand?"

"Mom broke her leg—" She couldn't go on, wondering if she should even try to describe this hopeless mess. Even if she did it was doubtful Taylor would understand.

"I know about Mom's accident," Taylor returned impatiently.

"She was terribly depressed afterward. I saw it, we all did, but apparently it didn't go away like everyone expected it would. Then Dad came up with the brilliant idea of planning this engagement party."

"Oh, dear."

"Mom put everything she had into it, and now—"

"Christy, I know it's difficult, but you've got to remember Mom and Dad planned this party without consulting you."

That was true enough, but it didn't change the facts. "I can't humiliate them. I thought if I talked to James, told him about Cody, everything would work out, but then I discovered I couldn't do that, either. I wanted us to face Mom and Dad and make some kind of decision together about the party, but that's impossible now. Everything's so crazy.... I can't believe this is happening."

"Do you mean to say James doesn't know about Cody yet?"

Christy closed her eyes.

"Christy?"

"I...couldn't tell him." She stiffened, waiting for the backlash of anger that was sure to follow.

After a short silence, Taylor said, "You *couldn't* tell James about Cody?"

The trouble she had forming the words was painfully obvious. "You heard me."

There was another silence. "I see."

"How could you possibly *see?*" Christy demanded, keeping her voice level, when she wanted to scream at the accusation she heard in her sister's voice. "I went to him, fully intending to tell him everything."

"Then why didn't you?"

"For two months James has been preparing for the most important trial of his career."

"You mean to say you're worried about James's *career?* At a time like this?"

Christy ignored her sister's outburst. "A businessman from Kirkland... You must know Alfred Mulligan. He's the one who does all those crazy television ads. Anyway, he's been charged with cheating on his taxes. The whole case is extremely complicated, and you know as well as I do how messy this kind of thing can get when the federal government is involved." She waited for Taylor to agree with her.

"What's that got to do with anything?"

Christy hated the angry impatience she heard in her sister's voice. It was all too clear that Taylor was upset with her. Christy felt Taylor's disapproval as strongly as a slap. All her life she'd experienced love and approval, especially from her family, and it hurt more than she could bear to feel such overwhelming censure from her only sister.

"You don't understand," Christy tried again. "James has been working day and night for weeks to get ready for this trial. It was scheduled for the first of next month, but he learned this afternoon they've called the case early. He's making the opening statement tomorrow morning."

"I'm afraid I don't understand the relevance of all this."

"I don't expect you to. James has worked himself into a frenzy. I've never seen him like this. So much hangs in the balance for him."

"That's fine, but I still don't—"

"He has a chance to win this case, but it's going to be difficult," Christy went on, cutting off her sister's protest. "James knows that. Everyone does, but if by some miracle he can pull this off, it could mean a partnership for him."

"Oh, Christy," Taylor said with a groan.

"If I broke off the engagement now, it could ruin everything for him."

"That's James's problem, not yours."

"Maybe it is his problem. I don't know anymore. I do know that I can't do this to him. Not on the eve of the most important trial of his career. Not when James has finally been given the chance to prove himself. If anything went wrong, I'd always blame myself."

The silence hummed as Taylor considered her words. "What about Cody?" she asked finally. "Have you given any thought to *his* feelings?"

"Yes." Christy had thought of little else. Never in her life had she asked more of a person than she was asking of Cody. Another woman had destroyed his trust, and there was nothing to assure Christy that he'd want anything to do with her after this.

As painful as it was, as difficult, she found she couldn't humiliate her parents and risk destroying James's chances with this case.

Even if it meant she lost Cody.

Nine

Something was wrong. Cody felt it instinctively, all the way to the marrow of his bones. Christy had left two separate messages on his answering machine, and every time he'd played them back, he'd felt an achy, restless sensation. It wasn't what she'd said, but how she'd said it. She sounded lighthearted and cheerful, but beneath the facade, Cody heard unmistakable confusion.

He'd tried to phone her back, but to no avail. Unable to sleep, he rose in the early morning hours and drove around the back roads outside town, trying to make sense of what was happening. Or not happening.

He couldn't find the answers, not when he didn't understand the questions.

His greatest fears were about to be realized. Once again he'd fallen in love, involved his life with a woman who couldn't be trusted.

Christy isn't Becca, his heart shouted, but Cody had virtually given up listening.

The sun had barely crested the hill as Cody sat in his Cherokee, looking at the valley below, pondering what he should do. If anything. Dammit all, he should never have let this go so far. Becca had taught him everything he needed to know about women and love.

Dawn burst over the hillside, with golden rays of sunlight splashed against the rugged landscape, and small patches of light on the horizon.

Cody released a jagged sigh, then started his car. As much as he'd like to turn his back on the entire situation and pretend the past two weeks with Christy hadn't happened, he knew the effort would be futile.

He glanced at his watch, knowing Russ and Taylor would be up and about. He needed to talk.

The light from the kitchen window glowed as Cody approached the ranch house. He pulled in to the yard, turned off the engine and waited until the door opened and Russ appeared on the back porch.

Climbing out of the car, Cody joined his friend.

"I thought that was you," Russ said, opening the door in mute invitation.

Cody removed his hat and set it on the peg while Russ walked over to the coffeepot and automatically poured him a mug.

"Taylor's feeding Eric," Russ said. "She'll be out in a few minutes."

Cody nodded and straddled a high-backed wooden chair.

Russ sat across from him. "Personally I don't think this thing with Christy is as bad as it sounds. Although, to be honest, if I was in your shoes, I don't know what I'd do."

Cody hadn't a clue what his friend was talking about but decided not to say anything, hoping Russ would explain without him having to ask.

"How're you holding up?"

"Fine." Cody was about to drop the charade and ask his friend what was going on when Taylor came in, wearing a long pink housecoat. Her hair was mussed and fell to the middle of her back. She offered Cody an apologetic smile, and once more he was left to interpret the meaning. His gut was tightening, and he didn't know how much longer he could go on pretending.

"Good morning, Cody," Taylor greeted him, helping herself to a cup of coffee. It seemed to Cody that her smile conveyed more concern than welcome.

It was all Cody could do not to leap to his feet and demand someone tell him what was happening.

"I suppose you're here to talk about Christy?" she asked gently. If Russ hadn't said a word, Cody would've guessed something was wrong just from the way Taylor was looking at him—as if she wanted to put her arms around him and weep.

"Christy's been on my mind," he answered brusquely.

"You realize she doesn't have any choice, don't you?" Taylor added. Her eyes, so like Christy's, appealed to him to be open-minded. "Russ and I've gone round and round about this and—"

"Any choice about what?" Cody demanded. His friends exchanged a surprised look.

"You mean Christy didn't get hold of you?"

"No."

"Then you don't know about the engagement party?"

"All I got was two messages in which she sounds like Mary Sunshine. I *knew* she wasn't telling me something. I sensed that right away."

It took a moment for the news to hit him. Engagement party? That meant she was still involved with… If he hadn't already been sitting down, Cody would have needed a chair fast. He'd heard of men who'd had their feet kicked out from under them, but he'd never understood the expression until then.

"Oh, dear." Taylor reached for her coffee and it was clear that she was upset. Her hands trembled, and her eyes avoided meeting his.

Cody transferred his attention to Russ, who looked as uncomfortable as his wife. "What's going on?" Cody asked in a deceptively calm voice.

Once more, husband and wife exchanged glances as if silently deciding between themselves who would do the talking. Apparently Russ presented his wife with the unpleasant task, because she swallowed, then turned to Cody. "My sister's caught in a series of difficult circumstances."

"What the hell does that mean?"

"Apparently my mother took the two weeks while Christy was here in Montana to plan an elaborate engagement party. It seems her spirts needed a boost, and my father thought involving her in planning a party would help. Unfortunately he was right. Mom threw herself into the project and arranged the event of the year, starring Christy and James."

"Are you telling me she's going through with it?"

"She doesn't have much of a choice. The celebration's scheduled for this evening."

This second bit of information hit Cody with the same impact as the first. "You've got to be kidding!"

"I wish we were," Russ said, his expression annoyed. "My in-laws mean well, but Christy's trapped in this fiasco simply because there isn't time to cancel it now."

"What about James?" Cody asked, stiffening as he

mentioned the other man's name. Every time he thought about the Seattle attorney, he struggled with anger and jealousy. James Wilkens had far more claim to Christy than he did. They both loved her, but it was James who'd given her an engagement ring. It was James her parents wanted her to marry.

"James is another problem," Taylor whispered.

Cody didn't understand. "You mean he's refusing to release her from the engagement?"

"He doesn't know Christy intends to break it off," Russ said without preamble.

Cody would've accepted just about anything more readily than he did this news. Christy had played him for a fool, used him the same way Becca had, for her own selfish purposes—whatever they might be.

"She's going to tell James everything," Taylor said heatedly in her sister's defense.

Cody didn't bother to comment, still reeling from this last news.

"When I talked to her, she'd just returned from seeing James. She'd gone to him with the best of intentions, wanting to tell him about you and break off the engagement before it went any further. She was hoping the two of them could discuss the engagement party and decide what could be done."

"She didn't say a word about me to James, did she?" At Taylor's wilted look, Cody decided that was all he needed to know. He stood, emptied the contents of his mug into the sink and set it on the counter so hard that it almost shattered.

"She couldn't tell him," Taylor cried. "If you love Christy the way you claim, you'll listen long enough to find out why."

Cody did love Christy, but he didn't know how much more battering his heart and his pride could take. He stood frozen, waiting for Taylor to continue.

"If she told James about you, she might put his entire career in jeopardy." For the next ten minutes Russ and Taylor took turns explaining the situation as best they could.

"Christy doesn't have any choice but to follow through with this farce of a party, don't you see?"

Taylor did an admirable job of presenting her sister's case; Cody would give her that.

She kept her pleading eyes focused on him. "If it'd been up to her, she would've ended the engagement five minutes after she got home."

Cody didn't respond, although it was apparent his friends were waiting for him to say something.

"You've got to appreciate the situation Christy's in," Taylor went on. "What would *you* have done had the circumstances been reversed?"

Cody closed his eyes, pondering the dilemma. What would he do?

He just didn't know.

"Oh, sweetheart!" Christy's mother exclaimed, stepping back to examine the effect of the full-length layered blue dress. "You look like an angel. Eric, come and see."

Eric Manning, wearing a white tuxedo with a pale blue cummerbund the same shade as Christy's dress, stepped gingerly into the living room. He eyed his youngest daughter and nodded approvingly. "You make an old man proud," he said with a warm smile.

"You've never looked lovelier," her mother added.

Christy managed a smile. She had no idea how she

was going to make it through this party. She might be able to fool her parents, but surely someone would notice. Rich would. Of her three brothers, she'd always been closest to Rich. He'd take one look at her and immediately guess that something was wrong.

Not that it would make any difference. She'd stand before family and friends and pretend to be madly in love with James, pretend to be an eager bride-to-be. But the only thing Christy was eager for at the moment was to put this evening behind her.

"I'd like to propose a toast to the happy couple, my sister Christy and the love of her life, James Wilkens." Rich Manning raised his champagne glass to the couple.

Christy grinned at her brother and fought the urge to empty her champagne glass over his head. Of all the guests, she'd expected him to realize how miserable she was. Instead, he'd unwittingly made things even worse.

Smiling faces nodded appreciatively at her brother's words before the party-goers sipped the vintage champagne. The round of toasts had been going on for several minutes. Christy wasn't sure how much more of this she could endure.

Her father had proposed the first toast, followed by her uncles and all three of her brothers. Each seemed to add something to the list of blessings they wished for her and James.

Christy swallowed another sip of champagne as her fiancé stood at her side, tall and debonair. She could barely look at him without being overwhelmed with guilt. They'd spent two hours in each other's company, and neither had spoken more than a handful of sentences.

In retrospect Christy wondered how she could possibly have agreed to spend the rest of her life with James. He was wonderful, but it was increasingly obvious that they were painfully mismatched.

Hoping she wasn't being conspicuous, Christy scanned the gathering, wondering if it was possible for anyone to read her thoughts. Not that it would do any good.

"Would you like something to eat?" James asked, glancing toward the linen-draped tables where trays of hors d'oeuvres lay waiting.

Christy shook her head, positive she wouldn't be able to keep down a single bite. "Nothing for me, thanks. What about you?"

"I'm fine," James answered.

The music started, and a handful of couples were making their way to the gleaming wooden floor. "I've always been terrible at this sort of thing," James confessed, reaching for Christy's hand. "But I suppose it's expected of us."

Christy nodded, wanting nothing more than to escape. A path was cleared as James led her to the dance floor and slipped his arm around her waist, careful to maintain a respectable distance between them. The music was slow and melodious, a love ballad, whose words seemed to ridicule her more than anything that had preceded the dancing.

James smiled into Christy's eyes as they moved across the floor. Soon other couples joined them.

Her fiancé seemed to relax a little more now that they weren't the only two on the floor. For that matter so did Christy. "I'm sorry I haven't been myself this evening," James murmured regretfully.

Christy was ashamed to admit she hadn't noticed.

Her whole attention had been focused on simply getting through this ordeal.

"The Mulligan case is going to take up a lot of my time over the next few weeks, and I can only hope you'll be patient with me."

Christy was horrified to realize she'd forgotten all about the trial and how important it was to him. "Oh, James, I'm so sorry. I didn't even ask how everything went this morning."

"Not as well as I'd hoped," he mumbled under his breath.

"I'm sorry," she said again. "But I understand you're going to be busy. In fact, it might actually work out for the best. You see, I met—" She wasn't allowed to finish.

"I knew you'd be understanding," he said, cutting her off. He smiled gently and drew her toward him. "You always have been."

"You, too," she whispered sarcastically, but James didn't respond.

Closing her eyes, she tried to pretend it was Cody's arms around her. That was the only way she'd be able to continue this farce. Keeping his image in her mind gave her a sense of purpose, a means of enduring this disastrous night.

After a respectable number of dances, James escorted her off the floor. Until then Christy hadn't noticed how tired and defeated he looked. Several family members insisted on dances with her, and Christy found herself on the floor with a number of uncles, her brothers and longtime family friends.

James was doing his duty, as well, keeping the women from both families occupied. She did see that he managed to do so without dancing with any of them, and that made her smile, however briefly.

It wasn't until the end of the evening, when Christy decided she just might survive, that her aunt Lois, her mother's youngest sister, asked the impossible question. "When's the date for the wedding?"

The whole room went silent. The music ceased, and everyone turned to stare at Christy and James. They were sitting together in a long row of folding chairs against the wall. It was the first time they'd sat down that evening.

Christy felt like a cornered animal. The cracker in her mouth seemed to go down her throat whole.

"You don't have an engagement party without letting those you love know when you're planning the wedding," Aunt Lois said.

James glanced at Christy. "We haven't had a chance to discuss a date, have we, darling?"

"No," Christy muttered. It wouldn't look good to announce that she was counting the days until she could break the engagement. If she was going to discuss a wedding date with anyone, it would be with Cody. But he hadn't asked her, and after he learned about this evening, Christy doubted he'd ever want to see her again.

"Springtime is always lovely for a wedding." Aunt Lois stood directly in front of her, waving her arms, demanding the attention of Christy and everyone else. "George and I were married in May, and the flowers were gorgeous." Pressing her gloved hands together, she released a slow sigh of remembered happiness.

"But May's almost a year away," Elizabeth Manning objected loudly, walking across the dance floor to join this all-important discussion. "Why wait so long? I was thinking more along the lines of November."

"November?" Christy echoed.

"The leaves are always so pretty then. You know how I love orange, brown and yellow," she said, looking at her daughter.

Already Christy could see her mother's mind working, plotting and planning. She'd enjoyed making the arrangements for the engagement party so much that she couldn't wait to start on all the pomp and ceremony of a formal wedding.

"With your dark coloring, Christy, an autumn theme would be perfect."

"Personally I favor a December wedding," Eric Manning shouted. He'd obviously had more than his share of champagne.

"December?" Elizabeth shrieked, shaking her head. "Never."

"All right," Eric countered. "Let's ask Christy and James which date they prefer. This is, after all, their wedding."

"Ah." Christy couldn't think. Her mind froze along with her hands, which were raised halfway to her mouth, her fingers clutching a delicate artichoke canapé. In a panic she looked at James, her eyes wide in speechless appeal. If ever she needed rescuing, it was now.

"What do you say, sweetheart?" her mother asked.

By some miracle Christy managed to lower the cracker to her plate. "I... I haven't given the matter much thought."

"When George and I decided to marry, we couldn't do it fast enough," Aunt Lois informed the group.

"November," James said decisively. "Your aunt's right. There's no need to put off the wedding."

"We don't have to choose a date *now,* do we?" Christy asked. "Not when you're so busy with the Mulligan case."

His hand patted hers gently. "This trial will be over soon enough, and I've been selfish not to consider your feelings. Naturally you and your mother will want to start making all the necessary arrangements."

"November would be perfect." Elizabeth Manning opened her purse and withdrew a small appointment calendar. "Let's pick the date right now. How does the twelfth sound?"

Once more Christy found herself speechless. "Ah…"

"The twelfth sounds grand," James said triumphantly, and lightly touched his lips to Christy's cheek. "Isn't that right, darling?"

The whole world came to an abrupt halt, awaiting Christy's reply. The walls seemed to be falling in around her, until she could hardly breathe.

"Christy?" her mother probed, eyeing her curiously. "November 12 would be a beautiful day for a wedding, don't you agree?"

Cody slowly patrolled the deserted streets of Cougar Point, but his mind wasn't on the job. The crime wave of the century could be happening before his very eyes, and Cody doubted he would've noticed.

How could he? The only reason he'd agreed to take this shift was in an effort to forget that Christy was with James tonight.

While Cody dutifully served his constituents, Christy was sipping champagne with her attorney fiancé. No doubt his diamond was firmly placed on her ring finger and she was having the time of her life.

It hurt.

The pain was as real as anything he'd ever endured. Except that it hurt more. There wasn't a thing he could do to alter the chain of events that had led Christy into this predicament. Apparently there wasn't much she could do, either.

He tried to remind himself that the woman he loved would go to great lengths not to hurt others, even if it meant hurting herself. But Christy wasn't the only one suffering.

Cody felt like a casualty of circumstance. And there was nothing he could do....

It was late when he rolled into the station—after eleven. He got out of the patrol car and saw Russ's pickup truck parked out front. Frowning, he made his way inside.

Russ Palmer unfolded his long legs and stood. "About time you got here."

"Problems?"

Russ nodded. "A few. I thought it might be a good idea if we talked."

The anxiety that had been following him around all night grew more intense. "I'll meet you in ten minutes."

Since the bowling alley was the only restaurant in town that stayed open this late, Cody didn't need to mention where they'd meet.

Russ was already in the booth, holding a white ceramic mug, when Cody walked inside. Cody slid in across from him, wondering how his friend had come to pick the same booth he'd sat in with Christy. He'd been in love with her then and hadn't even known it.

"What's so all-fired important to bring you out this time of night?" Cody asked.

"Taylor."

That didn't explain a lot.

The cook brought out a second mug for Cody and returned to the kitchen. Russ stared after the other man.

"You don't mean Taylor, you mean Christy, right?"

Russ nodded glumly.

"What did she do now? Run off with Gypsies? Marry the garbageman?"

"Worse."

"I suppose this has to do with the engagement party."

Once more Russ nodded. "Apparently no one guessed her real feelings. It seems everyone was too concerned about how much liquor made it into the punch bowl to ask Christy how *she* felt about the whole thing."

"I should be grateful for that?"

"No," Russ answered. "She went through the evening like a real trooper. She loves her family, and she did this for their sake, but she didn't like it."

"She's not the only one."

"I can well imagine," Russ said with a sympathetic sigh. "I know how I'd feel in the circumstances."

"I'm not sure what to do anymore." Cody rubbed his face wearily. "Tell me what happened. I can deal with that better than not knowing."

Russ seemed uncertain where to begin.

"Just spit it out," Cody said, trying to persuade himself he should forget he'd ever met Christy Manning.

"She's sick. Started throwing up at the party. Taylor talked to her and said Christy's in pretty rough shape."

For all his effort to portray disinterest, Cody's heart raced at the news. "What's wrong?"

"It's not what you think."

"If she's feeling as bad as you say, then why didn't she contact me?"

"She's been trying to reach you for two days."

"I've been busy. What was I supposed to do? Phone her and suggest she enjoy her engagement party? I have some pride left, and frankly I'm holding on to it."

"She needs to talk to you. Call her."

Cody shrugged.

"If you've been avoiding her, don't. She doesn't deserve this. Not now."

"I've tried phoning," Cody confessed, as if admitting to a shortcoming in his character. "She's never there."

"You didn't leave a message?"

"No," he answered reluctantly. What was there to say in a message that would help their situation? As far as he could see, nothing.

"She's at her apartment now. Take my advice and put each other out of this misery. Talk to her."

Ten minutes later Cody unlocked his front door, turned on the light and walked into his living room. He scowled at the phone—but he didn't know who he was trying to kid. He practically lunged at it, he was so hungry for the sound of Christy's voice.

He dialed the Seattle number Russ had given him, and Christy answered even before the first ring had finished.

"Cody?" Her voice caught on his name before he had a chance to speak.

"Hello, Christy," he said in a voice that, to his own ears, sounded stiff and cold.

"Thank you for calling me."

Before he could respond, she asked, "Did Taylor tell you?"

"Tell me what?"

"What happened at the party."

"No." There was more? "Russ came into town and asked me to call you. He alluded to something but never said exactly what. Go ahead and tell me."

A slight hesitation followed. "I…it isn't easy."

"Dammit, Christy, what's going on now?" The possibilities that came to mind did little to put him at ease.

"I want to be honest with you," she said, her voice shaking. "I…" She paused, and Cody could hear her drag a deep breath through her lungs. "Something happened at the party tonight…something I never intended."

Cody wanted to come across as nonchalant, but he couldn't. He expelled his breath, trying to think of what she might have done that would make him stop loving her.

Nothing. She could do nothing. Even if she were to inform him that she'd given in to the pressure and married James that very night, it wouldn't be enough. He'd still love her. He'd always love her.

"November 12," she whispered.

"I beg your pardon?" She'd gone from guessing games to riddles.

"The wedding's set for November 12."

Ten

Christy rolled over and glanced at the illuminated dial of her clock radio. It was 10:00 a.m.

This was supposed to be her first day back at the office, but she'd had to phone in sick. A flu bug was what she'd told Marcia, the office manager, who was sympathetic enough to suggest Christy stay home. But it wasn't the flu that was making her ill.

It was something else entirely. Christy was heartsick, afraid she'd lost Cody forever. She felt trapped, doing what was right for everyone but herself.

Now she was wide awake, and the day stretched out before her. She could occupy herself with mindless game shows on television, but that would only use up an hour or two. Reading would help pass the time—if she could concentrate. She might even give some thought to phoning Cody.

No.

That was out of the question. Cody didn't want to talk to her, not anymore. She'd said everything she could to make him understand her predicament two nights earlier.

The conversation had gone reasonably well until she'd told him she'd been forced to set a date for the wedding.

An unexpected sob tore through her throat, and fresh tears flooded her eyes. She'd done a lot of weeping over the past days. Damp, crumpled tissues lay scattered across her bedspread where she'd carelessly discarded them.

She loved Cody, and nothing she'd been able to say had convinced him of that. Cody, being a sheriff, saw life in terms of black and white. Either she'd agreed to the wedding date or she hadn't. Unfortunately Christy had sanctioned November 12, more or less, when pressured by James and her entire family. As soon as she confessed as much, her telephone conversation with Cody had ended abruptly.

She'd pleaded with him for understanding, tried to assure him she'd never willingly marry James, but it hadn't helped. They'd hung up with Cody promising to contact her after he'd had time to think.

Nearly thirty-four hours had passed. Surely he'd had adequate opportunity to come to some kind of decision.

The doorbell chimed, and sniffling, Christy reached for another tissue. She blew her nose before tossing aside her covers and climbing out of bed. She intended to send her visitor, whoever it was, away. She was in no mood for company.

With her luck, it was probably her mother wanting to discuss color schemes for the bridesmaids' dresses. If her car hadn't been parked directly in front of her door, she wouldn't even bother answering.

"Who is it?" she asked, squinting through the peephole and seeing no one.

"Cody Franklin."

"Cody...oh, Cody." Christy threw open the door. For one wild second she did nothing but stare into his wonderful face, convinced he'd been conjured up by her imagination. Before another second could pass, she launched herself into his arms.

Cody dropped his suitcase, clasping her around the waist with both arms. He hauled her to him with joyful abandon. Their mouths met in a kiss so fierce, it threatened to steal her breath. He held her as if he was starving for the taste of her, and meant to make up for every minute of every day they'd been apart.

Christy's arms encircled his neck, her mouth finding his. She kissed him over and over in an agony of need.

With a shudder Cody tore his mouth from hers and spread a wildfire of kisses over her face. His arms were around her waist, and her feet dangled several inches off the ground as his chest heaved with deep breaths.

Weeping for joy, Christy pressed her head against his shoulder, feeling completely at ease for the first time since she'd left Montana. She was in Cody's arms. Nothing could hurt her again.

"It might be a good idea if we went inside," he whispered.

Christy nodded. Slowly he released her, and she slid down.

"How'd you get here?" she asked, searching the parking lot for signs of his Cherokee.

"I flew," he explained as his hand stroked the tumbling curls away from her face. "I couldn't leave things between us the way they were. At least not without talking this out face-to-face. I took three days' vacation, hoping we could put an end to this craziness."

Christy was hoping for the same thing. She took his

wrist and pulled him inside her small apartment. She closed the door, then turned to face him, her hands behind her.

From the moment she'd come home, she'd stood alone against what seemed like overwhelming forces. Her mother needed her. James needed her. Everyone wanted a part of her until she felt as if she were being torn in two.

"How...how'd you know I was home?" she asked once her mind had cleared enough to process her thoughts.

"I phoned the law firm from the airport. They told me you were out with the flu."

Christy couldn't believe what she was hearing. Cody had phoned her at the office!

"You disapprove?" His eyes narrowed.

"No." But her heart was thumping loudly. It wasn't likely anyone had given his inquiry a second thought. Even if they had, she wouldn't be around to answer their questions.

"But the fact that I talked to someone who knew you *and* James upset you, didn't it?" He started to pace her living room. Four long strides covered the entire length of it. He buried one hand in his back pocket while the other massaged the muscles of his neck. "You're so afraid your precious James is going to find out about me."

"That's not true," she denied vehemently. Too late, Christy realized she probably was the most pathetic sight he'd ever seen.

Her eyes were red and swollen, and she wasn't even dressed. The five-year-old pajamas she was wearing were as sexy as dishcloths. Not that any of this seemed to bother Cody, who was apparently far more interested in arguing with her than ravishing her.

In her emotionally fragile condition Christy was much too weak to withstand a heated verbal exchange. She'd already heard from Taylor, who knew without a doubt what would be best. Russ, too. But they weren't listening to *her*. It was easy for them to dish out advice when they were a thousand miles from the situation.

She was the one on the front line, the one who'd have to face their parents. She seemed to be the only one who appreciated the long years of hard work that had led James to this point in his career. She couldn't, *wouldn't,* ruin his chances now.

If Cody Franklin expected her to buy their happiness at another's expense, then he didn't really know her at all.

He turned to face her. Boldly she met his eyes, staring down the hot accusation she saw in them.

Suddenly Christy felt his anger start to dissolve, replaced with doubt and pain. Defeated, he expelled a harsh breath. His shoulders sagged. "Forget I ever mentioned James. I didn't come here to fight about him."

"Why did you come?"

He didn't seem to have an answer, or if he did, he wasn't willing to supply it just yet. He looked away from her and plowed his fingers through his hair. "To talk some sense into you and end this confusion before we both go insane."

How Christy wished it was that simple.

"This isn't as complicated as you're making it," he said. "Either you're serious about loving me or you aren't. It should be a matter of setting the record straight, but—"

"I do love you."

"Then why are you wearing another man's ring?" he demanded. He stalked toward her and pulled her hand from behind her back. He frowned as he found her ring finger bare.

"I've only worn James's diamond once. The night of the engagement party," she said, surprised by how strained her voice sounded. "I took it off the minute I walked in the door and haven't put it on since."

Cody's large, callused hand curled over her fingers as he shut his eyes. The muscles in his jaw clenched. Then, moving slowly, as though hypnotized, he lowered his mouth to hers.

Her lips trembled under his and Christy closed her eyes as hard as she could, wanting to shut out the realities that kept them apart. She longed to block out everything, except the man who was holding her so gently.

"We need to talk," he whispered.

"Isn't 'I love you' enough?" she asked. Although he struggled to hold her at bay, Christy spread nibbling kisses at the curve of his neck. She wanted him so much....

Cody released a ragged sigh and propelled himself away from her. He moved so fast and so unexpectedly that Christy nearly stumbled. Bewildered, she caught herself just in time.

By then Cody had put the full distance of the living room between them. "In case it's slipped your mind, I'd like to remind you that you're an engaged woman."

It seemed she was allowed to forget that when she was in Cody's arms. She blinked back her pain. Throwing this farce of an engagement at her now was cruel and unfair.

"If you flew all those miles to remind me of that, then you made a wasted trip." Humiliation tainted her cheeks and it was all she could do not to cover her face with both hands and turn away from him.

For several minutes neither of them spoke. She sensed that they both needed time to compose themselves. Cody continued pacing, while Christy stood rooted, leaning against the door, requiring its solidity to hold her upright. It was a shock to discover how badly she was trembling.

"I need to ask you to do something," Cody said crisply, as if whatever he was about to say didn't involve him.

"All right."

"Break the engagement to James." His dark eyes cut into her with sharp, unquestioning demand.

"Of course. You know I will as soon as I can—"

"I want you to do it now. Today."

Full of anguish and regret, Christy shut her eyes. This had tormented her from the moment she got home and talked to James. Surely Cody realized she didn't want to stay engaged to another man.

"Christy?"

"I…can't break it off. Not yet. You know that. James has been working for three months getting ready for this trial. He was as prepared as any attorney could be, and yet one thing after another has gone wrong for him. I can't add to his troubles by—"

"We have no business seeing each other," Cody interrupted. "We didn't when you were in Montana, and we have even less of an excuse now that you're home."

"But I love you."

Her words fell into an uncomfortable silence. Cody

didn't answer for so long that she began to worry. His expression told her nothing.

"Love doesn't make everything right," he said, his eyes darkening with bitterness. "I wish it did, but the way we feel about each other doesn't alter one damn thing. You're promised to another man, and that's all there is to it."

"But… Cody—"

"Not only do you have his ring, you've set a wedding date."

"I explained all that," she whispered, feeling utterly defenseless.

"There's something you don't seem to understand," Cody said, frowning heavily. "I'm a man of honor, a man of my word…"

She nodded. "I couldn't love you as much as I do without knowing the kind of man you are."

"Then you must realize that I can't continue this. You must know how it makes me feel."

She stared at him, barely able to believe she'd been so stupid and selfish. Cody wasn't being possessive or jealous. It wasn't his pride that was injured or his ego. It was his sense of fairness. A matter of honesty.

He slowly shook his head. "For both our sakes, I wish I could be different. I'd like nothing better than to steal away with you for a few days, hold you, kiss you. More than anything else in this world I want to make love to you, but I can't allow that to happen."

Christy wanted all those things, too.

"The fact that you were committed to James bothered me when you were staying with Russ and Taylor. The fact that you didn't want to break the engagement over the phone wasn't unreasonable and I understood it."

Christy now wished she'd put an end to everything two weeks ago. If she had, her life would be so much simpler.

"It wasn't easy to keep my hands off you then, and it's a lot more difficult now." His voice was tight, and he didn't slacken his stride as he continued to pace. "I can't do this any longer. Either you break it off with James, right now, today, or it's over. I'll fly back to Montana and this will be the last time I see you."

Christy felt as if the entire ceiling had come crashing down on her head.

"The last time?" she repeated, struggling to keep her voice from rising.

"Christy, look at it from my point of view."

"I am. All I'm asking for...all I need is for you to be a little more patient. The trial will be over soon."

"I've been more than patient already."

"But it'll only be for a while. I swear to you," she said urgently, "I'll break it off with James at the first opportunity. But I can't do it now."

Once again her words fell into a void and she was left to wonder at his thoughts. "Cody...please," she whispered when she couldn't tolerate the silence anymore.

He pivoted sharply. "I know you. You're warm and loving, and you won't do anything that might hurt another person. You refuse to disappoint anyone—except yourself."

If he understood her so well, then surely he'd be patient just a little longer. She was about to say that when he added, "You've allowed your parents to manipulate you all your life."

"That's not true," she burst out, wanting to defend herself, angry that he'd even suggest it.

"They handpicked a husband for you, and you went along with it."

Her shoulders slumped, but her indignation had yet to cool.

"You didn't love James then and you don't love him now. Or so you claim."

"I love *you*," she cried. "How many times do I have to say it?"

"Yet when James offered you an engagement ring, you accepted his proposal."

"I... I..." Her outrage went limp for lack of an argument. Everything he said was true, but it had happened before she'd met Cody.

"You're so eager to take care of everyone else you're willing to sacrifice your own happiness."

"All I need is a few more days, just until this trial..." She didn't finish, since nothing she said was going to change his mind.

"Frankly I have a strong suspicion that you're going to wake up one fine morning married to dear old James and not realize how it happened."

"That's ridiculous." She folded her arms to ward off an unexpected chill. "I swear to you that will never happen."

"You swore to me you were going to break the engagement when you arrived back in Seattle, too. Remember?"

His eyes challenged her to deny it. She couldn't. He met her stare, but it was Christy who looked away first, Christy whose gaze flickered under the force of the truth.

"But how could I have known about the engagement party?" she asked weakly. Then, gaining conviction, she said, "You're not being fair. To even suggest I'd go ahead with the wedding is—" she searched for the right word "—ludicrous."

"Is it really?"

"Of course it is! You make me sound like some weak-willed... I can't imagine why you'd want anything to do with me if that's how you feel."

"I love you, Christy, and it's going to hurt like crazy to walk away from you. My request isn't unreasonable, although I know you don't agree with that."

She leaned against the door frame. "You can't ask me to make that kind of decision! Not right this minute. I need time...." In the back of her mind she was desperately praying the Mulligan case would be thrown out of court that afternoon and this whole regrettable affair could be laid to rest.

She might win the lottery, too, but she couldn't count on it.

"Is the decision that difficult?" Cody asked, frowning. "That on its own says something, whether you admit it or not."

Christy shut her eyes and took a deep breath. The man she loved, her entire future, was about to walk out the door, and she knew of no way to stop him short of destroying another person's happiness.

Straightening, she glared at Cody across the room. "I don't know what's right anymore," she said defiantly. "How can I? All everyone does is make demands of me. First it's Mom and then James and now...you."

Then she started to cry. She couldn't help it. Her shoulders shook and her chest heaved as the sobs convulsed her and tears cascaded down her cheeks.

She heard Cody mutter a swear word. "Christy, please, I can't stand to see you cry," he whispered hoarsely.

He could break her heart, but he couldn't stand to see her cry. Christy found the thought almost laughable.

Cody moved across the room and took her in his arms. His hands stroked the hair away from her brow. With him she felt secure. With him she felt warm and protected. She hid her face in his shoulder as the emotion worked through her. He held her until she was able to draw in a deep, shaky breath. Christy could feel her control slipping back into place.

Still Cody held her, his hands caressing her back. For the longest time he said nothing. He continued to hold her close, and after several minutes Christy became aware of how intimate their position was.

She sighed longingly and tested her discovery by tenderly kissing his neck. A moment passed in which she waited for him to protest or ease himself away.

Experiencing a small sense of triumph when he didn't, she leisurely investigated the warm, tantalizing skin, making slow, moist circles over the hollow of his throat.

"Kiss me," she whispered. "Oh, please, Cody, just kiss me. I'll be all right if you do that."

He didn't immediately comply; in fact, he seemed inclined to ignore her, as if nothing would be proved, nothing would be solved by kissing.

He froze when she placed her hands on each side of his strong face, sliding her lips up his jawline and over his chin until their mouths were joined.

Cody pulled his mouth from hers. His whole body seemed to be shaking as he inhaled. He walked over to her sofa and sat on the edge, his elbows on his knees.

"What are we going to do?" He shook his head in despair. "I'm not strong enough to walk away from you," he said starkly. "I thought I could."

"I won't let you go." She sat next to him, resting her forehead on his shoulder, and sighed. "I love you so much.... I'd give anything to marry you today."

Cody went stock-still. "What did you just say?"

Eleven

"I won't let you go, Cody. I can't," Christy repeated.

"Not that," he said, bolting to his feet. He started pacing again, and when she didn't immediately speak, he added, "It was after that."

She frowned. "I love you?"

"Not that, either. The part about marrying me today."

"I would." She didn't feel any hesitation in saying as much. Almost from the first day she'd met the sheriff of Custer County, she'd known she was going to love him all the days of her life.

"Will you marry me, Christy?" His expression was so open and sincere that she felt tears stinging her eyes.

"Oh, yes," she whispered. She'd probably be the only woman in the world engaged to two men at the same time, but that couldn't be helped.

"I mean now."

"Now?"

"I'd like us to be married this afternoon."

Her heart responded with a quick, wistful beat, but

Christy didn't see how a wedding, that day, would be possible.

"Maybe it's different in Montana, but Washington state has a three-day waiting period after we apply for the license."

A satisfied smile lifted the corners of his mouth. "Idaho doesn't."

"That may be, but Idaho's over 350 miles from here. If you're only going to be in Seattle three days, we'll end up spending two of them on the road."

"That's easily fixed. I'll rent a plane." He smiled a breathtaking smile that was so appealing, she thought she'd die a slow death if he didn't make love to her soon. "Am I going too fast for you?"

"No," she rushed to assure him, although her mind was abuzz. "It's just that I'm having trouble understanding. What about James?" She hated mentioning fiancé number one, but she had to be sure they were doing the right thing for the right reasons.

"What about him?"

"Will I…do I have to tell him about the wedding? I mean, it won't make much difference if he learns I've married you a couple of days from now or even next week. I'm only suggesting I delay telling him because of the trial."

Some of the happy excitement left Cody's eyes. "I'll leave that up to you. As far as James is concerned, I don't know what's right or wrong anymore. All I know is that I love you more than I thought it was possible to love any woman. It scares me to think I could lose you."

"There isn't the slightest chance of that."

His smile was sad. "I meant what I said earlier about being afraid you'd end up married to James. I've had nightmares about it, wondering if I'd get a call in the middle of the night. I actually dreamed that you phoned to explain how everything got out of your control and you'd married James before you could come up with a way to stop the ceremony."

"I would never allow such a thing."

He gave her a distrusting look, and although it injured her pride to admit it, Christy could understand Cody's concern.

"I feel a whole lot better making *sure* that couldn't happen." The warmth in his eyes removed the sting his words might have inflicted. "I learned a long time ago to cover all my bases. Marrying like this might not be the best thing, but we're making a commitment to each other, and heaven help me for being so weak, but I need that."

Heaven help *him!* Christy felt herself go soft. "Oh, Cody, I love you so much."

"Good," he said, his voice slightly husky, "because you're about to become my wife."

He smiled, completely disarming her. If Christy had a single argument, which she didn't, one of those devastating smiles would have settled it.

"How soon can you be ready?"

"An hour?"

"I'll check the phone book and make the arrangements while you dress." He took her hands and helped her to her feet, pausing long enough to plant a kiss on her unsuspecting lips.

In a daze Christy walked into her bedroom and searched through her closet for something special enough for her wedding. Smiling to herself, she walked to the door and leaned idly against it. "The whole thing's off. I don't have anything decent to wear," she said, teasing him.

Cody sat at her kitchen table, leafing through the impossibly thick yellow pages. He glanced up and chuckled. "Don't worry about it. Whatever you put on is going to come off so fast it'll make your head spin."

Christy chose a soft pink suit she'd purchased the year before at Easter. Carrying it into the bathroom, she closed the door. Quite by accident she caught her reflection in the mirror above the sink and gasped at the pitiful sight she made.

Leaning over the sink, she studied the woman who stared back at her. Her short dark hair was a mess, as if it hadn't been combed in weeks. Her eyes were another thing. Christy had always considered her distinctive blue eyes to be her best feature. Now they were red-rimmed and bloodshot as if she'd been on a two-day drunken spree. Her lips were red and swollen, although she attributed that to Cody's kisses. That man could kiss like nobody's business. She went weak all over again, remembering the feel and taste of his mouth on hers.

Bracing her hands against the sink, she was forced to admit that she was probably among the most pathetic creatures on earth. Yet Cody had looked at her as if she was gorgeous.

The man definitely loved her. That worked out well, since she definitely loved him.

Cody couldn't keep still. He couldn't seem to make himself stop pacing Christy's living room. Four steps, turn, four more steps, turn again.

He glanced at his watch. She was already five minutes past the hour she'd told him she'd need. What could be taking her so long? She'd locked herself in the bathroom, and he hadn't heard a peep since. His mind was beginning to play cruel tricks on him. Perhaps she'd changed her mind about going through with the wedding and, not wanting to hurt his feelings, she'd climbed out the bathroom window.

That thought revealed the shocking state of his mental condition more than anything he'd said or done in the past two hours. He'd flown into Seattle with one purpose. Either he'd settle this craziness between him and Christy or he'd end their relationship.

He hadn't counted on her enthusiasm. She'd been giddy with happiness when he'd arrived. Okay, he was the giddy one. He'd had no idea she was going to throw herself into his arms the moment she opened the door. Not that he'd minded... A slow smile relaxed his mouth. Everything had progressed naturally from there.

Cody had always considered himself a strong man. Not muscular or brawny, although he could hold his own and often had. His real strength, he felt, was his stubborn determination. He liked to think he had a will of iron.

Christy had proved him wrong in world-record time.

During the early-morning flight, he'd given himself a pep talk, outlining everything he intended to say. He'd planned to meet with her, explain his position and ask her as calmly and unemotionally as possible to make her decision.

It was either James or him.

If she chose the attorney, Cody was prepared to accept her choice serenely and walk out of her life.

Other than the rocky beginning of that conversation, everything had gone as he'd hoped. Never mind that Christy had managed to break down his resolve within five seconds. The instant she was in his arms, he could feel himself start to weaken.

No woman, not even Becca, had ever had as much control over him.

Now he and Christy would be flying into Coeur d'Alene, Idaho, and getting married. Smiling, Cody settled against the back of the sofa. He recalled when Russ and Taylor had come back to Cougar Point after serving as chaperones for the drill team, traveling with a busload of high school girls to Reno. They'd left town barely speaking to each other and arrived home a few days later married.

Cody could still remember how surprised everyone was. Most folks agreed Taylor was the best thing ever to happen to the opinionated Russ Palmer, but there'd been skeptics, too.

Understandably. Taylor was a city girl. Russ was a rancher. Taylor had only been in town three months.

But when folks in Cougar Point learned that Cody had married Christy after knowing her less than *one* month, there'd be even more raised eyebrows.

That didn't disturb Cody in the least. He loved Christy beyond a doubt, and next month when he stood before the citizens of Custer County to be sworn in as sheriff, she'd be at his side. It would be the proudest moment of his life, and he wanted her with him.

The bathroom door opened, and Christy stepped out. Cody turned around to inform her that she was twelve minutes late. His teasing comment wilted before ever making it to his lips.

She was stunningly beautiful, dressed in a pink linen suit. Her hair was perfect, her makeup flawlessly applied. Christy Manning was so beautiful, Cody couldn't help staring at her. It took more effort than he could believe just to close his mouth. He was too tongue-tied to utter a single word.

"Do I look all right?" she asked, gazing at him expectantly.

For the life of him, all Cody could do was nod.

Christy smiled and held out her hand. "Then let's get this show on the road."

The ceremony itself took place later that evening in a wedding chapel overlooking the crystal blue waters of Lake Coeur d'Alene. Between the time they obtained the license, purchased a pair of gold bands and made the arrangements for the wedding itself, Cody half expected Christy to express some doubts.

She didn't. When she repeated her vows, Christy's strong, clear voice had sounded so confident and poised, he couldn't help marveling—and feeling both humbled and honored by her love.

The flight back to Seattle brought them into the airport shortly before midnight. In the space of one day Cody had traveled from Montana to Washington state, then had flown a two-seater Cessna from Seattle to Coeur d'Alene and back again. He should've been exhausted, but he wasn't. In fact, he felt more alive than he could ever remember being in his life. All he had to do was glance at Christy, who delighted in flashing him a sexy, slightly naughty smile, to feel the blood shoot through his veins.

They returned the Cessna to the hangar and headed toward his rental car. He held the door for her and pressed a light kiss on her lips when she climbed inside. She leaned against him, and it took all his restraint not to deepen the kiss right then and there.

He needed a moment to let his mind clear. "Where to, Mrs. Franklin?" he asked, sliding behind the wheel of the car.

She responded with a blank look.

"Choose any hotel you'd like." He wanted the best Seattle had to offer for Christy. A honeymoon suite. Champagne. Silk sheets. Room service.

"But I didn't pack anything," she protested.

Cody was about to comment that she wouldn't need any clothes, but he didn't get the chance.

"I have this white silk baby doll gown. Would you mind if we went back to my apartment so I could put a few things together?"

"Your wish is my command, Mrs. Franklin."

Resting her head against his shoulder, Christy sighed audibly and murmured, "I like that in a man."

At the apartment complex, he went inside with Christy. His own suitcase was still there.

Christy hurried into the bedroom, then reappeared a moment later. She walked shyly up to him, then placed her hands on his chest. Cody gazed down at her as she slipped her arms around his neck and kissed him soundly.

Cody's response was immediate. He cradled the back of her head as he returned her kiss—and then some. Soon she was weak and pliant in his arms.

"What was that for?" he asked when he found his breath.

"Because I'm so happy to be your wife."

Cody locked his hands at the small of her back and glanced longingly toward her bedroom.

Christy reached up, kissed his cheek and deftly removed the Stetson from his head. Cody frowned when she tossed it Frisbee fashion across the room. It landed on a chintz-covered cushion as neatly as if he'd set it there himself.

Next her fingers were busy working loose the knot of his tie. "Christy?" Her name tumbled from his lips. "What are you doing?"

"Undressing my husband. I've decided I don't want to go to a hotel room, not when we're both here. Not when I can't wait another minute for us to act like a married couple."

"You're sure?" He didn't know why he was questioning her; he wanted her so much that he was trembling.

"Very sure." After discarding his tie, she began to unfasten his shirt buttons.

Cody's hands roved her back, his fingers seeking and not finding a zipper.

She peeled open his shirt and lightly ran her long nails down his bare chest. Shudders swirled down his spine as she nuzzled his neck, nibbling and sucking and licking her way to the throbbing hollow of his throat.

"Christy," he pleaded, his hands on her bottom. "Where's the zipper to your skirt?"

Smiling, she broke away long enough to remove the suit jacket and kick off her heels, which went flying in opposite directions. She twisted around and unfastened the button at her side, then slid the zipper open so the skirt could fall past her hips and pool at her feet. Stepping out of it, she reached behind her for the row of buttons that ran down the back of her silk blouse.

"I can do that," he said eagerly. His fingers fumbled awkwardly with the tiny buttons, but he managed. Her blouse and her lacy bra followed the path of his shirt, landing on the carpet somewhere between the sofa and television.

Unable to wait a second longer, Cody kissed her, his tongue surging into her mouth. The minute she leaned into him, Cody felt his body heat rise to the boiling point.

Slipping her arms around his neck, Christy let her head fall back, grazing his bare chest with her breasts.

He groaned, fighting the rising flames of his passion. She was slowly, surely, driving him out of his mind.

"Christy," he begged, not knowing exactly what he was pleading for. Not for her to stop, that much he knew. *More,* he decided. He needed more of her.

Tucking his arms behind her knees, he lifted her up and carried her into the bedroom. The only light was the soft illumination from the single lamp in the living room.

Gently he placed her on the bed, and they hastily finished undressing each other. Cody looked down on her, nestled in the thick folds of a lavender comforter. She was so beautiful that for a moment he was lost to everything but the woman before him. He longed to tell her what he felt, and knew it would be impossible to put into words.

Lightly he ran his hands over her breasts and smiled....

Afterward he lay on his back with Christy beside him, her head on his shoulder, her arm draped over his chest. Cody sighed as she cuddled her body intimately against his.

Her eyes remained closed, her smile dreamy. "I guess I'm not a good girl anymore."

"Oh, yes, you are. Very good, indeed..."

* * *

"What are you doing now?" Cody murmured.

He was half asleep, Christy saw as she caught his earlobe between her teeth. "I'm making a citizen's arrest."

"Oh, yeah? What's the charge?"

"I'll trump something up later."

"Christy, hey, what are you wearing?"

"My new silk nightgown."

"I like you better with nothing on."

Ignoring his complaints, she straddled his hips and leaned forward to kiss his chin.

"Mmm, you smell good…flowers, I think."

"Remember, you're the one who emptied an entire bottle of bubble bath into my tub."

"You didn't object."

"How could I? You were doing your husbandly duty and pampering me…only…" She paused and drew in a soft breath as he closed his hands over her breasts. "I didn't realize it could be done in a tub."

"It?" he teased.

"Cody, I was supposed to be the one arresting you, remember?"

"Say it." He raised the silk gown high on her leg and began to caress her thighs with both hands.

"It embarrasses me to say it… Cody," she whimpered as his finger executed the sweetest of punishments.

"You *are* going to say it."

She couldn't utter a single word. She hadn't known her body was capable of giving her any more pleasure than it already had.

"I love it when you blush," he murmured.

Christy rested her head on his chest, listening to the

steady, even beat of his heart. "Are we ever going to sleep?" she asked.

"Nope. The way I figure it we've got about forty-eight hours before my plane leaves, and at the rate we're going we can make love—"

"I'm too tired."

Christy felt him smile against her hair. "I am, too." he said. "We'll make up for lost time in the morning."

"In the morning," she echoed as her eyes slowly drifted closed.

A horrible racket woke Christy several hours later. She bolted upright and glanced at her clock radio. Just after 4:00 a.m.

Cody was already out of bed and reaching for his pants.

"Christy?"

The slurred voice belonged to none other than her brother Rich. She'd given him an extra key to her apartment. He stopped in often, but had always phoned first.

"It's my brother. He has a key. Stay here. I'll get rid of him."

"Your brother?"

"Shh." She grabbed her robe, then kissed Cody before hurrying into the living room.

Rich stood by the door, looking like an errant schoolboy. "Hi," he said, raising his right hand.

"I don't suppose you know what time it is?"

"Late," he offered.

"How about early."

"How early?"

"Too early," she told him, praying he wouldn't notice the two sets of clothes spread from one end of the living room to the other. She marched across the room and gripped his elbow, turning him toward the door.

He gave her a hurt look. "You're sending me back into the cold?"

"Yes."

"I didn't drive here. I couldn't," he said. "I know you probably can't tell, but I've had a teeny bit too much to drink."

"I noticed."

"I was hoping you'd make me some coffee, listen to my woes and let me sleep on your couch."

"I have to be at work in a few hours." A slight exaggeration. Besides, when she didn't show up at the office, everyone would assume she was still home with the flu.

"Pamela cheated on me," Rich blurted. "I need some advice and I need it from a woman. Just hear me out, okay?"

Not knowing what else she could do, Christy moved into her kitchen and started making a pot of coffee. Rich pulled out a stool at her kitchen counter and plopped himself down. "Apparently she's been seeing him all along."

"Who?"

"Pamela."

"No, who's she been seeing?" This conversation was frustrating Christy.

"Hell if I know his name. Some jerk."

"It isn't like you were crazy about her."

"Maybe not, but I always thought she was crazy about me. What is it with women these days? Isn't anyone faithful anymore?" he said plaintively.

"Ah..."

Rich squinted into the darkened living room. "Hey,

what's going on here?" Standing, he walked over to the chintz-covered chair and picked up Cody's Stetson. He glanced back at his sister.

"I can explain," she said in a weak voice.

Frowning, he returned to the kitchen and carefully placed the Stetson on her head. Several sizes too large, it rested well below her hairline in the middle of her forehead.

"Is there something you wanted to tell me?" he asked.

Twelve

"Who the hell are you?" Rich demanded.

Christy shoved the Stetson farther back on her head to find Cody walking out of the bedroom.

"It sounded like you might need a little help explaining things," her husband said casually.

Rich pointed at his sister and his mouth fell open. His eyes had narrowed, and disdain and disbelief marked his handsome features.

"It's not as bad as it looks," Christy said, ignoring his censure. Acting as nonchalant as she could, she poured him a cup of coffee.

Swiveling his gaze between Cody and Christy, Rich shook his head. "It looks pretty darn bad, little sister." He stared at the trail of clothing on the living-room carpet. His mouth twisted with disgust as he started toward the front door. "In fact, I don't think I've got the stomach to listen to you."

"You'll listen to her," Cody warned grimly, striding toward Rich. The two men stood no more than two feet apart, glaring at each other ferociously.

"And who's going to make me? You?" Rich's sarcasm was sharp. "If that's what you think, I've got news for you, cowboy."

"Rich, shut up," Christy said. "The least you can do is hear what I have to say."

"I don't listen to—"

"Don't say it," Cody interrupted, his words so cold they almost froze in midair. "Because if you do, you'll live to regret it."

Rich mocked him with a smile. "Listen, Mr. Marlboro Man, I've taken about enough from—"

"Stop it, both of you!" Christy marched out from her kitchen. She stood between her husband and her brother, a hand on each man's chest, and glanced up at Rich. "I'd like to introduce you to my husband, Cody Franklin. Cody, this stupid oaf is my third-youngest brother, Rich."

"Your husband!"

"My husband," she echoed softly. She dropped her hands and slipped her arm around Cody's waist, leaning against him, needing his solid strength.

"I'll have you know," Cody muttered, "you interrupted my wedding night."

"Your husband," Rich repeated a second time, stalking across the room. He retrieved Christy's bra from the floor and twirled it around on one finger. "I don't suppose James knows about this?"

Christy snatched her underwear out of her brother's hand. "As a matter of fact, he doesn't."

"This is getting even more interesting." Sitting on the sofa, he picked up Cody's shirt and made a soft tsking sound with his tongue. "What about Mom and Dad?"

"They don't know, either," Cody said forcefully.

"Aha," Rich snickered, "the plot thickens."

"I'm so pleased you find this amusing." Christy moved hastily about the room, picking up pieces of discarded clothing, more embarrassed than she could ever remember being.

Cody poured himself a cup of coffee and joined Rich, sitting on the opposite end of the sofa. "I'm a good friend of Russ Palmer's," he said by way of explanation.

Rich nodded. "So my dear, sweet sister met you when she was in Montana visiting Taylor?"

"Cody's the one who drove her to the hospital," Christy added. She sat on the side of the sofa and curved her arm around Cody's broad shoulders.

"Then this was what you'd call a whirlwind courtship." Rich studied the two of them. "Exactly how long have you known each other?"

"Long enough," Cody answered, making it plain he didn't much care for this line of questioning.

"We didn't mean to fall in love so fast," Christy continued, wanting to untangle any doubts Rich had about her relationship with Cody. "It just happened."

"You might have mentioned it to James."

"I probably should've phoned and told him while I was still in Montana, but it seemed wrong to break the engagement over the phone, and then when I got home—"

"The surprise engagement party," Rich said, groaning loudly. "I can see that you were trapped. Mom put her heart and soul into that party. You couldn't back out without humiliating her. Not at the last minute like that."

"I wanted to tell James right away, but that didn't work out, either." The hopelessness of the entire situation nearly overwhelmed her. "The Mulligan trial was called early, and he's immersed himself in the most complicated case of his career. He's got to be emotionally and physically at his peak for that."

"Yeah, that's right," Rich commented. "I'd forgotten about that."

"The timing couldn't be worse. I can't tell James about Cody and me until he's through with the trial. And yet…"

Rich released a long, sympathetic sigh. "You do seem to have your problems, little sister."

Cody leaned against the back of the sofa. "You can imagine how I felt when I learned she'd been roped into that engagement party. To complicate matters, she set a date for the wedding."

Rich did a pitiful job of disguising a smile. "November 12, wasn't it?"

"That's not funny, Rich, so cut the comedy, will you?" Christy playfully punched his upper arm.

"You have to admit, it's kind of amusing."

Christy found very little of this amusing. She was deliriously pleased to be Cody's wife, but he was flying out of Seattle in another day, and she'd have to return to her job and live a complete lie with James and her parents. She wouldn't be able to keep up this charade for long.

"Perhaps this predicament is comical to someone else," Cody said grudgingly, "but trust me, it isn't if you're one of the parties involved."

Rich was quick to agree. "So the two of you decided to take matters into your own hands and get married."

Christy nodded. Her eyes met Cody's, and they exchanged a loving look. His fingers linked with hers. "It must sound crazy."

"Hey, it works for me," Rich said, "but I wouldn't be

in your shoes for all the tea in China when you tell Mom and Dad what you did."

"Why not?" Cody asked with a dark frown.

"They were cheated out of one wedding when Taylor married Russ without a single family member present. I can only speculate what they'll say when they hear Christy did the same thing."

"They'll skin me alive," she muttered. In all the excitement, in all her enthusiasm, Christy had forgotten how much her mother was looking forward to planning her wedding—which would be far more elaborate than the engagement party. As they left the Eagles Hall that dreadful night, Elizabeth Manning had been filled with ideas and opinions and excitement.

"Your parents won't do any such thing," Cody insisted.

"Cody, you don't know them." Christy felt a return of the nausea that had overtaken her at the party. Elizabeth Manning might never forgive her, and she'd always done what her mother thought best. Until now.

"They won't say a word," he said softly, "because I won't let them."

"But you don't understand—"

"If your parents are looking for someone to blame, they can deal with me. I was the one who insisted you marry me now. You just went along with it."

"Because I'm crazy in love with you and because I want to be your wife more than I've ever wanted anything."

"Hey," Rich said, raising both hands, "if both of you want to stand in front of the firing squad, I'm not going to stop you."

A chill descended on the room. "I take it there was a reason for this unexpected visit," Cody said pointedly.

"I was having woman problems," Rich mumbled.

"I thought there was something bothering you the night of the party." Although Rich hadn't enlightened her with the details, Christy should've known something was amiss. Otherwise he would have noticed how upset she was that evening.

"I may be having a few problems," Rich continued. "But they're nothing compared to what you two are facing. Married to one man while engaged to another—that, little sister, takes the cake."

"How kind of you to point it out." Yawning, she covered her mouth with her hand. "I'll make you a bed on the sofa and you can spend the rest of the night there."

"And interrupt your honeymoon?"

"It's already been interrupted," Cody reminded him. "If there's any justice in this world, I'll be able to return the favor someday."

"No chance of that. I'm swearing off women. The whole lot of them," Rich said with an emphatic shake of his head.

"Oh?" Christy had heard that song before.

"It's true. They're fickle, money-hungry, material-istic—"

"Thank you very much," Christy said, standing.

"With a few exceptions." He eyed his sister and smiled in apology.

"Now where was it you said you wanted to go for dinner?" Cody asked, reaching for his suit jacket.

"What's the matter with eating here?" Christy asked, not wanting to leave the apartment. Everything had been idyllic, and she was almost light-headed with happiness. To walk outside these protected walls might well invite trouble, and she'd had enough of that to last her a lifetime.

"I thought you wanted to dine out?"

"Not really." At the time he'd made the suggestion, Christy hadn't been able to think of an excuse. Now her mind overflowed with them, only she doubted Cody would consider any of them sensible.

She checked her freezer and extracted a package of pork chops. "I could wrestle us up some grub in no time." She turned around and grinned. "Am I beginning to sound like a Montana woman?"

"No. You're beginning to sound like a cattle thief." He moved behind her, slid his arms around her waist and nuzzled the curve of her neck.

"I'm a good cook."

"I know."

"How could you? Every time I go to make something for us, you interrupt me with...you know."

"Are you still having trouble saying the words?"

"No..." She giggled softly. "You've cured me of that." Twisting around, she leaned against the refrigerator door with her hands primly linked in front of her. "I can talk about making love about as often as you want to do it."

"Then let's get out of here before you give me any ideas."

"I like giving you ideas."

Cody glanced at his watch. "It's well past dinnertime and I'm hungry."

She moistened her lips. "You want me to say some of the other words you taught me?"

"Christy...no."

"Come here." She beckoned him with her index finger. "I'll whisper a couple of humdingers in your ear."

Cody ignored her. "I'm not going to let you sidetrack me."

"Oh, but I enjoy sidetracking you."

"That's the problem," Cody said. "I like it, too." He cleared his throat and changing tactics, grabbed his hat. "As your husband, I command that we leave for dinner now."

"You command?" She couldn't help laughing.

"That's right," he said, his mouth quivering with a suppressed smile. "I've got to teach you that I'm wearing the pants in this family."

"If that's the case, then why are they so often unzipped?"

Cody actually blushed, and Christy smiled.

"Because I'm a needy husband," he said gruffly. "Are you complaining?"

"Oh, no." She sent him a saucy grin. "Because I happen to be a needy wife. In fact, I seem to be experiencing a need right now. Is it hot in here to you?"

"Christy?" Cody's voice contained a low note of warning.

"It seems very hot…much too hot for all these clothes." She jerked the light sweater over her head and let it fall to the floor. Next she lowered the straps of her bra. "There," she said with a deep sigh, offering Cody what she hoped was a tantalizing display of her assets. "That feels better."

Cody stood his ground for a couple of minutes. Then he removed his hat and sent it flying across the room.

Silently Christy rejoiced.

"What about those jeans? Aren't they making you hot, too?" Cody asked.

"Maybe they are. Only I can't seem to open the snap." He didn't seem to notice that she hadn't tried.

"I see." He stepped over to her and made short work of her bra, then cupped Christy's breasts, his hands firm and insistent.

Sighing, Christy closed her eyes, giving herself over to a host of delightful sensations. Cody used one hand to stroke her breast, his other hand busy at the opening of her jeans. The zipper purred, and Christy was filled with another small sense of triumph.

She shivered helplessly as Cody slid her jeans down her hips. Her bikini underwear followed and that was the last thing she noticed for some time. Other than Cody, of course...

Christy's gaze fell reluctantly on Cody's luggage, which lay open on her bed. The lump in her throat seemed to grow larger every minute, until she could hardly swallow. She'd decided earlier that she wasn't going to be emotional when he left. They'd talked everything out earlier, planned for their future as best they could.

"You called the office?" Cody asked, putting a clean shirt in the suitcase.

"Yes... I told them I still had the flu." Lying didn't come easy to Christy. She felt as though she'd dug herself into a deep pit.

"What did they say?"

"Marcia, she's the office manager, said it's a slow week and not to worry about it, but she did make a point of asking me if I'd be in on Friday, which seemed a little odd."

"What about James?"

"He was at the courthouse." Her eyes widened at the unexpectedness of the question.

"When's the last time you heard from him?"

"Ah…" She had to stop and think. "The day after the engagement party. We talked briefly, and he explained that he wouldn't be able to keep in touch while the trial's going on." Under normal circumstances she would've seen him at the office, even if it was only for a few minutes, every morning. The fact that he hadn't made an effort to contact her said a good deal about their relationship.

"I see." Cody was obviously surprised.

"He's very intense and single-minded."

"Do you think he'll get an acquittal?"

"I don't know," she said.

"Whatever happens, this can't go on much longer. You realize that, don't you?"

"It won't be more than a few days." In discussing the situation they'd agreed on a time limit. Even if the trial dragged on for more than a week, Christy had promised to return James's ring and tell her parents that she and Cody were married.

"I still think we should tell your parents now."

"Not yet," she pleaded. The way Christy figured it, she'd start dropping hints so the fact that she'd married Cody wouldn't come as such a shock. After Cody flew back to Montana, she intended to drop by the family home and casually point out that James hadn't called her once since the party. She was hoping her parents would conclude that perhaps he wouldn't be the best husband for her, after all.

"Christy, I'm worried." Cody stood in front of her,

his face concerned. "I don't like leaving you, especially under these circumstances."

"You know I love you."

His mouth curved into a sensual smile. "Beyond a doubt."

"Good." She put her arms around his waist and hugged him close. His heart beat strongly and evenly, offering her reassurance. In time they'd look back on these bleak days and laugh, she told herself. Someday, but not now.

"I'll phone you twice a day," he promised in a husky whisper. "Morning and night."

"I'll need that."

"So will I."

A sigh of regret rumbled through his chest as he dropped his arms. "It's time to go."

Neither of them seemed inclined to talk on the ride to the airport. Once Cody had checked in at the airline counter, he hugged Christy and kissed her lightly. It was as if he dared not kiss her the way they both enjoyed for fear he wouldn't be able to walk away. She understood all too well.

"Take care of yourself," she whispered.

"You, too."

She nodded, barely conscious of the way she clung to him. "Of course. We'll talk tonight. And before we know it, we'll be together."

"Together for good," he added. "I've got to go."

She closed her eyes tightly to keep from crying.

Cody kissed her again, only this time his mouth was fierce and wild. He released her by degrees, his reluctance tearing at her heart. With everything in her, Christy longed to board the plane with him. How much easier it would be to leave with Cody and then call James and her parents. But Christy knew she couldn't abandon her responsibilities. Cody understood that, too; she was sure of it. Christy Manning Franklin had always done the right thing, even if it was sometimes for the wrong reasons.

The next morning Christy returned to work for the first time since she'd left for vacation. What a difference a few weeks could make. She wasn't the same woman anymore.

"Christy." James's voice rose as he hurried over to her desk. "You're back. I hope you're feeling better."

For all his brilliance, James had very little experience of life. That was even more obvious to Christy now, and it made her feel oddly protective of him. She smiled as he reached for her hand, squeezing her fingers. Kissing her, even in an empty office, would have been unthinkable. He'd never been openly affectionate, but he was tender and good, and Christy couldn't ignore her guilty conscience.

"I'm much better, thanks. How's the Mulligan case going?"

He frowned and briefly looked away before responding. "Not too well."

"How much longer do you think it's going to be?"

"I'm hoping to wrap everything up by the end of next week."

"That long?" She couldn't keep the disappointment out of her voice.

James frowned again. "I didn't realize how negatively this case was affecting you."

"It's just that…" She couldn't very well announce that

she was looking for the right moment to tell him she was married to someone else.

"I know, darling." He said the last word softly, as though fearing someone might overhear him. "This is a difficult time for us both, but it'll soon be over, and we can get on with our lives."

Now that Christy had a chance to study him, she saw that he seemed exhausted. Deep lines were etched around his eyes and mouth. Clearly James wasn't sleeping well.

"The case is going worse than you expected, isn't it?"

James sighed. "It's difficult to hide something like this from the one you love. Yes, it's going much worse."

"Is there anything I can do?" Christy found herself asking.

"Nothing," he said, giving her a rare smile. "But your concern is greatly appreciated." He looked at his watch. "It's time I left for the courthouse. I won't be back for the rest of the day."

Christy nodded.

"I suppose we should meet for dinner. After all, it's been a long time since we've gone out. But—"

"Don't worry," Christy interrupted. "I understand." If she was having trouble dealing with a short conversation as James was walking out the door, an entire evening in each other's company would've been unbearable.

"Have a good day," he said gently.

"You, too."

He nodded, but his expression was somber. It was all too apparent that he didn't think he'd be having anything resembling a satisfactory day.

At lunchtime Christy looked up to find Marcia standing at her desk. The office manager had been with the firm for over fifteen years and was one of the finest women Christy knew.

Christy smiled. "Do you need something, Marcia?" After a three-week absence, her desk was piled high with folders.

"Can you come into one of the conference rooms for a minute?"

"Sure."

Leading the way, Marcia paused in front of the wide oak doors and grinned sheepishly. "It's good to have you back from vacation, Christy. It made all of us appreciate how much your bright smile adds to our day." With that she opened the door.

Christy was greeted with a chorus of "Surprise" from her fellow workers. A large cake sat in the center of the table, surrounded by several gaily wrapped packages. She must have looked stunned, because Marcia placed one hand on her shoulder and explained. "It's a wedding shower for you and James."

Thirteen

A week had passed since Cody had come back to Cougar Point. By far the longest week of his life. He wanted Christy with him, hungered for her smile and the way her eyes darkened when she looked up at him in that suggestive way.

He loved Christy, and marrying her had helped him cope with the ridiculous set of circumstances in which they found themselves trapped.

He wasn't pleased that she was still engaged to James, but there seemed little he could do about it. If it had been up to him, he'd have settled it before flying out of Seattle, but Christy had been adamant that she was doing the right thing in waiting. Cody wasn't convinced, but the decision had been hers, and he didn't feel he could go against Christy's wishes.

So they were husband and wife. Cody *felt* married. It was as if he'd lived his entire life waiting for this woman. In the too-brief days they'd been together, Cody knew he'd changed. His life's purpose had been focused on his career, and in many ways it still was. Christy, however, added a new dimension to his personality.

She'd taught him to dream.

Unlike Russ, who'd always planned on marriage, Cody had given up hope of ever finding the right woman. It hadn't been a conscious decision; in fact, he wasn't fully aware of it until he met Christy.

He was getting downright philosophical, he mused. Christy gave his life a deeper meaning, and their marriage made everything else more...important, somehow.

Someone brighter than he was would have guessed what was happening the first time they'd kissed. He still recalled feeling lost and bewildered. When he learned she was engaged to marry James, Cody had been even more shaken than he dared to admit.

James. The other man's name brought a grim frown. Reluctantly Christy had shown him a picture of the attorney. He looked clean-cut, professional, intelligent. But he guessed that James Wilkens lacked passion. It was difficult to imagine James allowing a little thing like falling in love to overcome his inhibitions.

Throwing off his anxiety about Christy's engagement, he stood, moved into his kitchen and poured a cup of coffee. He was supposed to be packing, getting ready for his move to Miles City, but because of everything that had happened between Christy and him, he'd delayed until the last minute.

Almost everything in the living room was inside cardboard boxes, and Cody headed absently toward the bedroom, intent on getting as much accomplished that evening as he could.

He recognized his mistake immediately.

Christy had never slept on his bed, never even been in

this room, but the fires she sparked to life within Cody were more evident there than anywhere else.

Feeling helpless, missing her so much, Cody sat on the end of the bed. He'd married himself one little hellcat. A smile tempted his mouth. She was a seductress in bed, and an angel out of it.

His need for her was insatiable. Half the time they were so impatient for each other that they hadn't bothered to use any birth control. They'd discussed that; if she were to get pregnant, Cody wouldn't mind. In many ways it would please him tremendously, although he admitted the timing would be all wrong for her. Christy had enough pressures on her already.

A week. They'd been apart for seven days, and it felt like an eternity. Dammit all, he wanted her with him.

Now. Not two days from now.

Not next week. *Now.*

His patience was wearing paper-thin. He picked up the phone and called the number he knew by heart. Christy answered on the second ring.

Her voice softened when she heard his. "Soon," she promised in a seductive whisper that nearly drove him crazy.

"How soon?" he demanded.

"A couple more days."

"Forgive me for saying this, but didn't you claim it would be 'a couple of days' a couple of days ago?" His voice was sharp despite his best efforts.

"Yes, but there are complications."

"Aren't there always?"

"Cody, please, don't be angry with me…"

"I called because I love you."

"I love you, too," she said, sounding a little bewildered. Cody realized he'd probably pushed too hard and backed off, spending the next few minutes telling his wife he loved her.

When he replaced the receiver, he was more frustrated than ever.

Cody was enjoying breakfast in the bowling alley early the following morning when Russ showed up. It wasn't unusual for Russ to eat in town, but rarer since he'd married Taylor.

The rancher slid into the booth across from Cody. "I thought I'd find you here."

"You looking for me?" he asked.

"You could say that." Russ turned over the ceramic mug and waited until the waitress came by and filled it for him. He reached for the menu. "You look like hell."

"Nice of you to say so," Cody muttered.

"I didn't come here to pick a fight."

Their friendship was too good for this kind of bickering. "I haven't been sleeping well," Cody admitted reluctantly, sipping his own coffee. Truth be known, he hadn't had a decent night's sleep since he'd flown home from Seattle.

"How's Christy holding up?"

"A lot better than I am." She always managed to sound cheerful, as if it was perfectly normal for a couple to be married three days and then separated for weeks.

"You sure about that?"

Russ's question caught Cody off guard. He narrowed his eyes, wondering if Russ knew something he didn't. Russ's attention seemed to be on the menu.

"I'm not sure of anything," Cody answered thoughtfully. "What makes you ask?"

Typically Russ shrugged. "Nothing in particular." He set aside the menu, declined to order breakfast when Mary delivered Cody's and sat there looking superior. "Go ahead and eat," he said, motioning toward the plate of sliced ham, eggs, hash browns and toast.

"I wasn't planning on letting my meal get cold," Cody informed him frostily. His nerves were shot, and the last thing he needed was his best friend dropping obscure hints.

Cupping the mug with both hands, Russ leaned back in the booth. "Who else knows you and Christy are married?" he asked after a moment.

"Everyone except James and her parents." Christy's three older brothers were all aware of the fact that they'd eloped. Cody had spoken to the two oldest brothers, Paul and Jason, before he'd left Seattle. Rich had been the first to discover their secret, of course, and he'd quickly let the others in on it.

"Should I thank you for the fact that Mrs. Simmons stopped me in the street yesterday with a jar of her watermelon pickles?" Cody asked, eyeing Russ. "She says she heard the sheriff had taken himself a wife and wanted to give me a small gift."

"Ah... I might've mentioned something to Mrs. Simmons," Russ said, hiding a smile. Mrs. Simmons handed out homemade preserves at every opportunity. Each family in town ended up with at least one jar every year.

Russ took another drink of his coffee. "I guess you and everyone else in town figured out Taylor got pregnant on our honeymoon."

Cody was having trouble following this conversation. "What's that got to do with anything?"

"Nothing," he said with an enigmatic smile.

"Listen, Russ, if you know something I don't, spit it out, would you? I'm in no mood for games. Is something going on with Christy that I don't know?"

"Did she tell you about the wedding shower?"

Cody scowled. "No. When was this?"

"Last week. The girls in the office held it for her, threw it as a surprise."

"That was nice."

"It wasn't for you and Christy," Russ barked. "What's with you, man? The shower was for Christy and James."

Cody rubbed his face. She hadn't said a word, not a single word about any wedding shower. And now that he knew, Cody thought that, maybe, just maybe, Christy did sound a little less cheerful than usual. He was fast losing his perspective.

"I bet she hasn't told you something else, either."

Cody resented having his brother-in-law tell him things Christy hadn't even mentioned. "You mean there's more?" he asked darkly. "Did her mother take her shopping and spring for a five-thousand-dollar wedding dress?"

"Nothing quite so drastic," Russ said with a hint of a smile. "I overheard Taylor on the phone last night. She was talking to Christy."

"What did Christy say?"

"I don't know. I only heard half the conversation."

Cody had talked to Christy, too. He'd hung up with a restless feeling he couldn't identify, but he'd attributed it to the fact that she was still in Seattle when he wanted her in Montana.

"And?"

"And when I asked Taylor, she seemed reluctant to say much. But I heard her discuss symptoms."

"Symptoms?"

"I tried to tell you earlier," Russ informed him with a look that questioned Cody's intelligence, "but you got so damn defensive, I shut up." Russ shook his head. "Taylor got pregnant in Reno. Think about it, Cody. Taylor and Christy are two of *five* children. Doesn't it seem obvious to you that the Manning women are a fertile lot?"

"Christy's not pregnant," Cody said with a confidence he wasn't feeling. He felt his head start to spin.

"You're sure of that?"

"She'd say something if she even suspected. I'd bet on it."

"Of course. She tells you everything."

"I'd like to think she'd confide in me," Cody said, growing more uncertain.

"If she didn't tell you about the wedding shower, you can damn well wager she wouldn't mention that she's hanging her head over a toilet every morning."

Cody felt as if he'd been kicked in the stomach. Christy was pregnant and too concerned about protecting her parents and James to risk telling him.

Hell, she *couldn't* tell him. He hadn't made it easy for her, had he? Missing her the way he did, Cody was irritable and impatient while Christy carried the brunt of the load.

Hastily he slid out of the booth and put on his hat. He'd been looking for an excuse to put an end to this nonsense, and now he had one.

"Where you going?" Russ demanded, reaching across the table for Cody's untouched breakfast plate. He leaned forward and retrieved the salt and pepper shakers.

"Seattle."

Chuckling, Russ nodded. "That's what I thought."

"Enjoy your breakfast," Cody muttered sarcastically.

"Thanks," he responded between bites, "I will."

Christy had been feeling blue all day. Cody wasn't home when she'd tried to call, and that depressed her even more. Nothing made sense. Nothing. She felt weepy and excited. Confused and elated. Engaged to one man. Married to another. She might be pregnant. It might be the beginning of an ulcer. She didn't know which.

She couldn't sleep, although she desperately needed to.

Her appetite was nil. After going through the bother of fixing herself spaghetti and a salad for dinner, her meal sat uneaten on her kitchen table.

Feeling wretched, she sank down in front of the television and turned on the movie channel, silently chastising herself for not writing thank-you notes to her friends from the office. Sending notes of appreciation for gifts she intended to return seemed a ridiculous thing to do.

A 1940s war movie with an incredibly young John Wayne and Maureen O'Hara was on, and she was soon caught up in the fast-paced action. How minor her troubles seemed compared to those on the screen.

Damp tissues crowded her end table. She was sniffling ingloriously when her doorbell chimed.

Whoever was on the other side was certainly impatient. The doorbell rang a second time before she was halfway across the carpet. "Hold your horses," she said peevishly. She wasn't interested in company.

Christy quickly changed her mind.

"Cody," she whispered when she saw her husband.

"Oh, Cody." Without another word she broke into tears and flew into his arms.

Seconds later, his mouth was on hers in that urgent, hungry way that was so familiar between them. Cody directed her into the living room, then closed the door with his foot, all the while kissing her.

Christy's hands roamed his face when he released her. She giggled and locked her arms around his neck, holding on to him for everything she was worth.

"Oh… Christy, I missed you," he breathed. His hands caressed her face. Then he was kissing her again and again as if he'd never get enough of the taste of her.

"I've been so miserable without you," Christy admitted, feeling weepy and jubilant at the same time.

"Me, too, love." He looked at her for a long moment, frowning, then smiling, then frowning again.

"What is it?" Christy asked, reacting to his confusion but not understanding it. She sensed a wonder in him, too, as if he couldn't quite believe they were married.

Christy believed it. Their love was the only thing that had gotten her through the trauma of the past week.

"Are you pregnant?" he asked without preamble, running his splayed fingers through her hair. His hold on her tightened, but Christy doubted he was aware of it.

Involuntarily her eyes widened at his question. "I… I don't know yet."

"You've been ill?"

"Yes… How'd you know that?" Usually she'd been sick in the mornings, but often in the afternoons, too. If she was looking for a pattern, there wasn't one. She was confused and anxious, and not knowing where to turn, she'd called her sister. "Taylor?" Christy had never dreamed that her older sister would say anything to Cody. She'd counted on Taylor to be discreet.

"No," Cody admitted, scowling. "I had breakfast with Russ this morning. Rather Russ ate *my* breakfast while he cheerfully pointed out that Taylor got pregnant while they were still in Reno and—"

Christy interrupted him. "You came because of that?"

"No." Cody dropped his hands and stepped away. "Well, not completely. I did come in part because I was afraid…no, afraid's the wrong word. I was concerned for you. I came for another reason, too."

He was so sincere, so forthright. "Yes?"

His eyes darkened. "You didn't tell me about the wedding shower."

Christy's gaze fell. "I couldn't."

"I realize that now, and I realize a whole lot more. This has to be the end of it, Christy." His eyes burned into hers. "As your husband—the man that loves you—I can't let you continue this charade any longer."

Spontaneous tears filled her eyes as she nodded. "I don't think I can pull it off another day. I…thought I was doing what was best for everyone involved, but I see now that I was only prolonging the agony—mostly my own. You were right, so right. There'll never be a good time to tell Mom and Dad. I did us both a terrible disservice by refusing to acknowledge that."

Cody's lips brushed her forehead. "Don't be so hard on yourself."

"There's no one else to blame. It's just that it's really difficult for me to disappoint my parents. I love them both so much, and they're so fond of James."

"But they don't have the right to pick your husband for you."

"I know." She exhaled softly. "I would've liked to have spared James this, but he has to know. I... I did him a disservice by not telling him the afternoon I came home. James isn't as emotionally fragile as I've made him out to be."

Cody's eyes flared briefly before he spoke. "How soon can we get you in to see a doctor?"

"A doctor?" she asked. "Why?" Sure, she'd been overprotective of James and reluctant about telling her parents the truth, but that didn't mean she needed medical help.

"If you're pregnant—"

"Oh, that," she said, relieved. "Taylor recommended I buy one of those home pregnancy test kits, which I did this afternoon. Only I decided I could deal with *not* knowing better than I could handle knowing. Does that sound crazy?"

Cody chuckled. "No. But do you mind satisfying my curiosity? I, for one, am anxious to find out if I'm going to become a father."

"You definitely are," she said, loving the way Cody's face brightened at her words. "The only question is whether or not it's going to be nine months from now."

Cody's arms were around her, his eyes filled with a tenderness that made her knees grow weak. "The test takes about twenty minutes," she said, sliding her hands up the front of his shirt.

"Twenty minutes," Cody repeated.

She moistened her lips, thrilled when her husband's narrowed gaze followed the seductive movement of her tongue.

"Are you suggesting what I think you're suggesting?" he whispered.

Christy nodded.

"But if you're pregnant, will it hurt the baby?" His voice was hoarse, and a dark flame seemed to leap to life in his eyes.

"Not according to Taylor."

"You're sure?"

"Positive. Besides, it'll do this baby's mother a whole lot of good."

Christy lay contentedly in his arms, her long, sleek body nestled intimately with his. If they spent the next ten years exactly like this, Cody wouldn't have a single complaint. He loved this woman. He loved everything about her.

"Are you disappointed?" she asked softly, rolling over so she could look at him when he answered.

He kissed her, his mouth clinging to hers, his hands caressing her. "You've got to be kidding."

They'd been on fire for each other from the moment he'd arrived. Their hands had trembled as they'd hurriedly undressed each other, their mouths eager, filled with promises and pleas.

Raising herself on one elbow, Christy smiled dreamily down on him and lovingly traced her fingers over the hard angles of his face as though memorizing every feature. To Cody's way of thinking, that was unnecessary. He never planned to leave her again.

"I wasn't talking about the lovemaking," she said. "I was referring to the pregnancy test."

His arm curved around her trim waist. "No. When the time's right, we'll start our family and not because we were in too much of a hurry to—"

"May I remind you how much of a hurry we were in a few minutes ago?"

"No, you may not." He clasped her around the waist and they both dissolved into laughter.

A woman he could love *and* laugh with—how did he get so lucky?

"It might be a good idea if I went over to my parents' house alone," Christy said. She looked up at him beseechingly. "Please, Cody?"

"I won't hear of it, Christy," he answered in a voice that brooked no dissent. "We're in this together."

"But…"

"You phoned James?"

"You know I did. He'll arrive at my parents' within the hour." James had sounded surprised to hear from her, and even more perplexed when she explained she needed to speak with him urgently. He'd offered to come to her apartment, but when she'd suggested they meet at her family home in an hour, he'd agreed.

"How did Rich find out we're telling your parents?" Cody asked, frowning.

Her scoundrel of a brother had been visiting their parents when Christy called and in fact had answered the phone. There must have been something in her voice that conveyed her intent, because Rich had made it clear he planned to stay around for the fireworks display. That comment reminded Christy that the coming scene was bound to evoke plenty of emotion. Christy wished Cody would wait for the worst to pass before he presented himself as their latest son-in-law.

"Don't even think of arguing with me," he said. "We're doing this together."

"All right," she murmured, holding in a sigh. "The way I figure it, we'll have forty-five minutes to explain everything to my parents before James arrives."

"Good." Cody nodded.

"Are you ready?" she asked, and her voice trembled despite every effort to maintain an optimistic facade. Her heart felt frozen with fear. Although she'd wanted to handle this on her own, she was grateful Cody had chosen to go with her.

They spoke infrequently on the drive to her parents' home. When they did, it was to murmur words of encouragement, or reinforce how much they loved each other.

As they pulled in to the driveway, another car came in after them. "Oh, no," Christy breathed.

"What's wrong?"

"It's James." Christy climbed out of the car, not waiting for Cody. She turned to face her fiancé. "You're early," she said, struggling to keep the annoyance out of her voice.

"I called your parents, and they suggested I come now." James's gaze narrowed as Cody came to stand behind her and rested his hand on her shoulder.

It was clear that James took offense at the familiar way Cody touched her. His eyes went cold as he demanded, "Who is this?"

Fourteen

Christy felt Cody's hand tighten involuntarily. The two men glared at each other like hostile dogs who'd inadvertently strayed into each other's territory. She supposed it wasn't a complimentary analogy, but it seemed fitting.

"James, this is Cody Franklin," she said, hating the unexpected way her voice squeaked.

"So the gang's all here," Rich shouted, coming out the front door, ready to greet the two men. "I suppose you're wondering why I've called this meeting." He laughed, obviously in a playful mood.

Christy glared at him, wondering what he was doing.

"Do you mind waiting a few minutes?" Rich asked. "Jason and Paul are on their way."

"As a matter of fact, I do mind," Christy snapped. She gripped Rich hard by the elbow and forced him back into the house. "Please introduce Cody to Mom and Dad," she said.

Rich's mouth fell open. "Me? No way, little sister. I happen to value my neck."

"I'll take care of everything," Cody said, slapping

Rich on the back. "You have nothing to fear but fear itself."

"James," Christy said reproachfully, turning to face the attorney, "it would have helped matters if you'd come when I suggested, but since you're here now, we'll settle this in the kitchen."

She walked into the house and passed her mother, who was watching her curiously.

"We'll talk in the kitchen," Christy reminded James when he hesitated in front of Elizabeth Manning and shrugged.

"Christy?" her father called. "What's going on here?"

"I'll explain everything in a few minutes, but first I have to clear something up with James."

"Actually, I'll be more than happy to explain," Cody said, stepping forward. He offered Eric Manning his hand, and they exchanged a brief handshake as Cody introduced himself.

"Exactly what's going on?" James wanted to know as they entered the kitchen.

Christy stopped at the huge round oak table. She pulled out a chair and sat down, then gestured for James to do the same.

He complied, but with some hesitation. "You never answered my question. Who is that man?"

"Cody Franklin."

"That doesn't explain much."

"No, it doesn't," she agreed readily. With a sigh, she wondered where she should even begin. "He's from Montana."

"Ah, that accounts for the cowboy hat."

"We met when I went to spend time with Taylor. Cody's the new sheriff of Custer County."

James nodded, urging her to go on. She'd explained the easy part; everything else was hard.

Unable to stay seated, Christy surged to her feet and frowned as she organized her thoughts. "Sometimes, not often I think, but sometimes when two strangers meet something happens...something special." She paused and looked at James, hoping, praying she'd see a glimmer of understanding. She didn't.

"You're talking about fairy tales," he said, and laughed as though she'd made a poor joke. "Are you going to break into song next?"

Christy ignored the question. "A special magic, a chemistry that flows between the two of them," she went on. "There was magic when Taylor met Russ. At first they both resisted it and—"

"Yes, yes," James interrupted, "but what have your sister and her husband got to do with anything?"

"Cody and I experienced that same...chemistry," she announced, astonished this genius attorney could be so obtuse. "Neither of us was expecting to fall in love."

"You didn't," James said flatly, dismissing her claim.

"But I did."

"You can't be in love with Franklin. It isn't possible when you're in love with me."

"James, please, let me explain—"

He interrupted with an upraised hand. "Christy, darling, what you experienced for this man is a simple case of homesickness. It's perfectly understandable, and forgivable. We were only engaged a day or two, and after working so hard for all those weeks, it only makes sense that you'd look to another man for companionship."

"James," she said, taking both of his hands in her

own, "that's not the case. I wish it was that simple, but it isn't."

"Nonsense." James hadn't been touted as a brilliant attorney without reason. With infuriating ease, he twisted everything she said around to suit his own purposes.

"I love Cody." She said it forcefully enough, she prayed, for James to accept it as truth.

"As I already said, that isn't possible." He stood, placing his hands on her shoulders, his look indulgent. "You love me, remember? Otherwise you wouldn't have agreed to become my wife."

"I agreed to your proposal because I *like* you. And because it pleased my mother and father," she cried.

"Christy." He said her name softly, as if she were a petulant child. "I'm sure you're mistaken."

"I'm not." Her hands on his forearms, she stared directly into his eyes. "I love Cody Franklin so much I married him."

It hurt Christy to watch the transformation come over his face. She hated the pain she saw. The disbelief. The humiliation.

"It's true," she said before he could question her.

Anger flickered in his eyes. He jerked his arms free from her and dropped them to his sides.

"When?"

"Does it matter?"

"No, I guess not." His eyes drifted briefly shut. That said more than any words he could have spoken.

She took a moment to open the clasp of her purse and take out the diamond ring he'd given her. When she handed it back to him, James stared at the velvet box as if he'd never seen it before. "Keep it."

"No, I can't."

He removed it from her hand and turned away long enough to shove it into his coat pocket. When he looked at her again, he was able to mask the pain, but she knew him well enough to realize how deeply she'd hurt him. Causing him such intense suffering was the most difficult thing she'd ever had to do. James didn't deserve to be treated this way.

"I intended to tell you the minute I got home from Montana," she said in her own defense, the words coming so fast they nearly blended together.

"The engagement party," he supplied for her. "You tried to tell me then, didn't you?" He didn't wait for her to answer. "I sensed something was wrong and trapped you into setting a wedding date." He scowled. "On a subconscious level I ignored the obvious, immersed myself in my work, hoping whatever had happened with you would pass. I know I made it difficult to talk to me. But am I that unreasonable that you couldn't have told me the truth?"

"That wasn't it." Christy felt it was important to correct that impression. "I just didn't feel I could. You were so heavily involved in the Mulligan case and I didn't want to—"

"I'm still involved."

"I know. But the worst of it's over, and I couldn't go on pretending. I'm sorry, James, sorrier than you'll ever realize."

He snickered, but didn't openly contradict her.

"I'm terribly fond of you and I'd give anything to—"

"Fond." He spit out the word as if it were an obscenity. His vehemence was a shock. James wasn't a passionate man. Rarely had Christy seen him reveal any emotion, in or out of a courtroom.

Once more she tried to explain. "I don't expect you to understand how difficult this was for me. That would be asking too much of you." She knew she sounded shaken, but she couldn't help that. "If there was any possible way I could've done this without hurting you, I would have."

He didn't respond.

"You're a wonderful man, James, and someday a woman will come into your life—the right woman. And you'll know what I mean."

"You were the right woman. Or so I believed."

"I'm sorry. So very sorry."

He shook his head as if he didn't quite believe her. His hand was buried in his pocket, and Christy guessed he'd made a tight fist around the diamond.

"I only wish you the best," she whispered.

He breathed deeply, then nodded, although Christy had the impression he didn't agree with her. She was about to say something more when a thunderous shout came from the direction of the living room.

"Your father?" James asked.

Christy nodded. "Cody must have told him."

James's gaze continued to hold hers. "You'll be all right?"

"Of course."

He seemed to accept that. "Can I kiss you, one last time?"

In response she opened her arms to him, her eyes brimming with unshed tears. James reached for her, his touch gentle. He held her close for just a moment, then pressed his mouth to hers.

He broke away, and his finger touched her cheek, his eyes clouded. "Be happy, Christy."

"I will."

With that he turned and walked out of the kitchen. Christy stood by the window and watched him move down the walkway, then climb inside his car. For what seemed an eternity, James sat in the driver's seat with his hands gripping the steering wheel as he stared straight ahead.

Christy couldn't delay the confrontation with her family any longer. Squaring her shoulders, she walked into the living room to find her brothers, Paul, Jason and Rich, perched on bar stools as though viewing a stage performance.

"Christy," her mother sobbed, dabbing a tissue under her nose, "tell us it isn't true."

She moved next to Cody and sat on the arm of the chintz-covered chair. She slipped her hand into his. "Cody and I were married last week."

"Married!" Her father stormed to his feet as if she'd desecrated the Constitution of the United States.

Confused, Christy's eyes went to Cody's.

"I hadn't gotten around to telling them that part yet," he told her.

"Married," her mother repeated. "It can't be true. Christy would never do anything so… We have a wedding to plan. You couldn't possibly have gone off and gotten married without telling your own mother and father. It isn't like you to do something so underhanded."

"I thought they knew," she whispered, bewildered. "I heard Dad shout, and I thought… I assumed."

"All I said," Cody explained, "was that you wanted

a little privacy with James so you could return his engagement ring."

"Oh." She swallowed and closed her eyes for a moment. "Well, Mom and Dad," she said brightly, looking at them once more, "I see you've met your new son-in-law."

"Welcome to the family," Paul said, holding up a soft drink can in tribute. "From what Rich said, you're a friend of Russ's."

Cody nodded.

"But you couldn't possibly be married," her mother whimpered, turning to Eric as though he could explain everything.

"Trust me, Mom, we're married."

"They're married," Rich said, saluting them with his own can of soda. "I should know. I was at their wedding night."

"Hear, hear," Jason cried, wearing the ever-present baseball cap. "Wait a minute. At their *wedding* night?"

"I don't find any of this humorous or in good taste," Eric roared. "Your sister's turned down the best man in three states for some…some small-town lawman. Bad enough that Taylor had to marry a country boy, but Christy, too? Never!"

"Dad," Christy reminded him softly, "the deed is done."

"But, Christy," Elizabeth wailed, "I bought the material for the bridesmaids' dresses and we've put down a deposit on the hall for the reception, and—"

"I didn't mean to cheat you out of a wedding, Mom. I really didn't."

"What will we say to our friends?" Her mother appeared to be in a state of shock. She'd gone deathly pale, and her shoulders jerked as she tried to gain control of her emotions.

"If you're worried about what to tell your friends," Paul said, sounding knowledgeable, "I'd suggest the truth."

"Stay out of this," Eric shouted, dismissing his eldest son with a shake of his head. "We're in one hell of a mess here."

"How's that?" Cody asked.

"Christy's married to you is how," Eric informed him none too gently. "My daughter doesn't belong in the country. She was born and raised in the city. We've already got Taylor living out in the sticks. I won't allow Christy to be out there slopping hogs or whatever you do in that backwoods community."

"Dad!" Christy was outraged. "It's *my* decision. And Cougar Point isn't any backwoods community. Besides, we won't be living there."

"You're moving to Washington state?" Elizabeth asked Cody, her eyes wide and hopeful.

"Sorry, no."

Her mother drooped against the back of the sofa and reached for a fresh tissue. She wadded it up and pressed it over her eyes as if to block out this horrible scene.

"Cody's the sheriff," Christy said, wanting to impress both of her parents with the fact that he was a responsible citizen. "We'll be living in Miles City once he's installed."

"A sheriff should please them," Jason said under his breath, speaking to his two brothers.

"I think they prefer an attorney over a sheriff," Rich concluded when neither parent responded to Christy's announcement.

"I recognize that this is all rather abrupt," Cody said in a reasonable voice. "I don't blame you for being shocked. I can't even blame you for being concerned. You wouldn't have raised a daughter as wonderful as Christy if you weren't the kind of people who'd care about her happiness."

"That's good," Paul whispered to Jason. "He's going to win them over with flattery."

"Will you three shut up," Eric yelled, infuriated with his sons and not bothering to disguise it.

"Dad, please try to understand," Christy tried again. "I fell in love with Cody."

"Falling in love is one thing, but marrying him on the sly is another."

"While she was engaged to James, I might add." Rich apparently didn't know when to keep his mouth closed. Both Eric and Cody sent daggers his way. Guarding his face with his hands, Rich pretended to ward off their attack.

"I can only say I love you both," Christy said. "I'd never intentionally do anything to hurt you. In fact, most of my life I've done everything I can to please you, right down to becoming engaged to James."

"I can't believe I'm hearing this," Eric said to his wife. "We raised her the best we knew how, and now this."

"Darling, we thought you loved James," her mother pleaded.

"I thought I did, too, until I met Cody." Her hand clasped Cody's, and she smiled down at him. "I know I made mistakes, lots of them."

"*We* made mistakes," Cody corrected, his gaze holding hers.

"No one's making a list," her father mumbled, "but if I were—"

"Nothing on this earth will ever convince me I made a mistake marrying Cody." Her father obviously wasn't willing to accept what they'd done. As Christy suspected, her family would need time to come to terms with her marriage and the fact that she'd be leaving the Seattle area.

"I gave my week's notice when I returned from vacation," Christy said. It had been one of the low points of her life, telling Marcia she was quitting her job in order to prepare for her wedding. The lie had all but choked her.

"You're leaving your job?"

"She couldn't very well continue working with James," Eric muttered to his wife. "And from the sounds of it, she intends to live in Montana."

"Poor James," Elizabeth said with a regretful sigh. "He would've made such a good husband."

"I'll make Christy a good husband, too," Cody promised. "I love your daughter."

An awkward silence followed Cody's words. "My daughter doesn't belong in Montana, and she deserves a decent wedding with her family around her. Christy's not the type of girl a man takes to a justice of the peace."

"We were married by a minister." Christy knew even before she spoke that there was little she could say to appease her father. He wasn't accustomed to having his authority challenged. Not even by a sheriff.

"It might be best if we gave your parents a chance to get used to the idea," Cody suggested.

Christy agreed, but leaving her family home was one of the most difficult tasks of her life.

Paul, Jason and Rich followed them outside.

"They'll come around," Paul said to Cody as they exchanged handshakes. Paul was tall and silver-blond, the only one in the family who'd inherited that coloring.

"Just give 'em a year or three," Rich said with less than diplomatic cheer. "Grandkids will be sure to win 'em over. There *will* be children, won't there?" He was eyeing Christy as if a good stare would tell him if she was in the family way.

"Don't worry about a thing," Jason said, throwing his arm over Cody's broad shoulders. "Mom and Dad will accept your marriage before you know it."

"They've got two days," Cody said darkly.

"Two days?" Christy echoed, a little stunned, although she shouldn't have been. Cody's life was in Miles City, and he'd recently taken three days of his vacation to spend with her. He couldn't afford to take off any more, not during this important period of transition.

"Is that too soon for you?" he asked, his eyes revealing his concern. "I figured that would give us enough time to get your things packed and shipped."

She nodded, slipping her arms around his waist. Her life was linked to Cody's now, and there was no turning back.

They hadn't gone through airport security yet, but Christy delayed, glancing around the terminal building, certain if she stayed there long enough her parents would rush in and throw their arms around her, telling her how much they loved her and how they wished her and Cody well.

Only they hadn't come.

"Honey," Cody said patiently. "They aren't coming. We have to go."

"I know, but I'd hoped. I...thought they'd at least want to say goodbye."

Christy hadn't heard from them in the two hectic days they'd spent packing up her apartment. She'd tried not to let it affect her, but she'd always been close to her parents, and being shunned this way hurt more than anything they could have said.

"Give them time," Cody said—he'd been saying that a lot—and it seemed as if her pain belonged to him, too.

Christy offered him a brave smile and nodded.

They joined the security line, then hurried to their departure area, arriving just as their flight was called. Christy realized there was nothing left to do but board the plane that would take her away from everything that was familiar and bring her to a whole new life.

"You're not sorry, are you?" Cody asked once they were seated and about to take off.

"No." Beyond a doubt Christy knew she was meant to be with Cody. She would've preferred to have her parents' blessing. But if she had to do without it, then she'd learn to accept that.

Cody was her love. And now he was her life.

Since Paul, Jason and Rich all worked days and hadn't been able to come to the airport to say their goodbyes, the three of them had taken Christy and Cody to dinner the night before.

Everyone had made an effort to have a good time, and they all had.

Only something vital had been missing. No one said anything. No one had to.

Eric and Elizabeth Manning weren't there. And what

was missing was their love. Their blessing. Their approval.

Christy didn't know when she'd see her parents again.

"Oh, Cody," Christy whispered, stepping back to study her husband in his full dress uniform. "You look… wonderful."

They'd been in Miles City, Montana, a week. In that time they'd moved into their first home, unpacked their belongings and gone about making a place for themselves in the community.

"When will Russ and Taylor get here?"

"Oh," she said, still a little awed by how handsome Cody looked. "I forgot to tell you Taylor phoned. They're going to meet us at the courthouse for the installation."

"Good." He straightened the sleeves of his crisp uniform jacket. "Well, I'm ready."

"I'm not," Christy told him. "In case you haven't noticed, I'm not dressed yet."

Cody wiggled his eyebrows suggestively. "All the better to seduce you, my dear."

Christy giggled. "I do believe you've seduced me in every room of this house, Sheriff Franklin. More than once."

"There's time—"

"There most certainly is not." She scurried past him. She wasn't quick enough, and with little effort, Cody caught her in his arms.

"Cody," she warned him. "We…can't. You don't want to be late for your own installation. And I don't want to arrive at the ceremony looking like a disheveled mess."

Cody hesitated. "Well…"

She entwined her arms around his neck and kissed him soundly.

"Shameless hussy," he said with a grin as he unwound her arms. "Get dressed before I change my mind."

"Yes, sir." Mockingly she saluted him.

A half hour later they entered the courthouse. Judge Carter would be doing the honors, and the room was filled to capacity. Christy was escorted to the front row of reserved seats. Many of the citizens of Cougar Point were in the audience.

The ceremony was about to begin when Taylor, carrying Eric, and Russ slipped into the chairs to her right. That left two empty seats on her left. Christy was so busy greeting her sister that she didn't notice the vacant chairs had been filled. She turned to smile and introduce herself to her seatmates, and to her astonishment saw her parents.

"Mom. Dad." Without warning, tears flooded her eyes. She looked at Cody, who was standing at the podium with Judge Carter. When she nodded toward her family, Cody's face brightened.

"Are you willing to forgive your father for being a stubborn old cuss?" Eric asked in a low voice.

Christy nodded, shaken by the intensity of her relief. She hugged him and then her mother, who was as teary-eyed as Christy.

When the ceremony was over, Cody joined them. Christy's husband and father faced each other. Eric Manning offered his hand first, and the two exchanged a hearty shake.

Judge Carter came forward to introduce himself a few minutes after that, and soon they were all talking at once.

A small reception followed, and Cody held Christy's hand as he led the way.

"Thank you," she whispered.

He shook his head. "Honey, as much as I'd like to take credit for bringing your parents out here, I can't."

"Not that," she said, smiling up at him from the very depths of her soul. "Thank you for loving me."

"That," he said softly, "was the easiest thing I've ever done."

"Eric Manning," Christy could hear her father say over the din of raised voices. "I'm the sheriff's father-in-law. We're proud of the boy. Glad to have him in the family."

"Not as glad as he is to be part of it," Cody murmured, smiling at his wife.

* * * * *

Visit the Author Profile page
at Harlequin.com for more titles.

THE SOLDIER'S REDEMPTION

Lee Tobin McClain

To the staff and volunteers
at Animal Friends of Westmoreland. Thank you
for letting me work alongside you to learn how a
dog rescue operates…and thank you for being a
voice for those who cannot speak for themselves.

And the people, when they knew it, followed him:
and he received them, and spake unto them
of the kingdom of God, and healed them
that had need of healing.
—*Luke* 9:11

One

Finn Gallagher leaned his cane against the desk and swiveled his chair around to face the open window. He loved solitude, but with overseeing Redemption Ranch's kennels, dealing with suppliers and workers and the public, he didn't get enough of it. These early-morning moments when he could sip coffee and look out across the flat plain toward the Sangre de Cristo Mountains were precious and few.

He was reaching over to turn on the window fan—June in Colorado could be hot—when he heard a knock behind him. "Pardon me," said a quiet female voice. "I've come about the job."

So much for solitude.

He swiveled around and got the impression of a small brown sparrow. Plain, with no identifying markers. Brown tied-back hair, gray flannel shirt, jeans, no-brand sneakers.

Well, she was plain until you noticed those high cheekbones and striking blue eyes.

"How'd you find us?" he asked.

"Ad in the paper." She said it Southern style: "Aaa-yud." Not from around here. "Kennel assistant, general cleaning."

"Come on in. Sit down," he said and gestured to a chair, not because he wanted her there but because he felt rude sitting while she was standing. And his days of getting to his feet the moment a lady walked into the room were over. "I'm Finn Gallagher. I run the day-to-day operations here at the ranch."

"Kayla White." She sat down like a sparrow, too, perching. Ready for flight.

"Actually," he said, "for this position, we were look-ing for a man."

She lifted an eyebrow. "That's discriminatory. I can do the work. I'm stronger than I look."

He studied her a little closer and noticed that she wore long sleeves, buttoned down. In this heat? Weird. She looked healthy, not like a druggie hiding track marks, but lately more and more people seemed to be turning in that desperate direction.

"It's pretty remote here." He'd rather she removed herself from consideration for the job so he wouldn't have to openly turn her down. She was right about the discrimination thing. With all their financial troubles, the last thing Redemption Ranch needed was a lawsuit. "A good ten miles to the nearest town, over bad roads."

She nodded patiently. And didn't ask to be withdrawn from consideration.

"The position requires you to live in. Not much chance to meet people and socialize." He glanced at her bare left hand.

"I'm not big on socializing. More of a bookworm, actually."

That almost made him like her. He spent most of his evenings at home with a dog and a good book, himself. "Small cabin," he warned.

"I'll fit." She gestured at her petite self as the hint of a smile crossed her face and was just as quickly gone. "I'm relocating," she clarified, "so living in would be easier than finding a job and a place to stay, both."

So she wasn't going to give up. Which was fine, really; there was no reason the new hire had to be male. He just had a vision of a woman needing a lot of attention and guidance, gossiping up a blue streak, causing trouble with the veterans.

Both his mother and his boss would have scolded him for that type of prejudice.

Anyway, Kayla seemed independent and not much of a talker. The more Finn looked at her, though, the more he thought she might cause a little interest, at least, among the guys.

And if she were using… "There's a drug test," he said abruptly and watched her reaction.

"Not a problem." Her response was instant and unambiguous.

Okay, then. Maybe she was a possibility.

They talked through the duties of the job—feeding and walking the dogs, some housekeeping in the offices, but mostly cleaning kennels. She had experience cleaning, references. She liked dogs. She'd done cooking, too, which wasn't a need they had now, but they might in the future.

Now he wasn't sure if he wanted to talk her into the job or talk her out of it. Something about her, some hint of self-sufficiency, made him like her, at least as much as he liked any woman. And they did need to hire someone soon. But he got the feeling there was a lot she wasn't saying.

Would it be okay to have a woman around? He tested the notion on himself. He didn't date, didn't deserve to after what he'd done. That meant he spent almost no time around women his age. A nice, quiet woman might be a welcome change.

Or she might be a big complication he didn't need.

"What's the living situation?" she asked. "You said a cabin. Where's it located?"

He gestured west. "There's a row of seven cabins. Small, like I said. And a little run-down. Seeing as you're female, we'd put you on the end of the row—that's what we did with the one female vet who stayed here—but eventually they'll fill up, mostly with men. Veterans with issues."

She blanched, visibly.

He waited. From the bird feeder outside his window, a chickadee scolded. The smell of mountain sage drifted in.

"What kind of issues?" Her voice came out a little husky.

"PTSD related, mostly. Some physical disabilities, too. Anything that would cause a vet to give up hope, is how the owner of the ranch puts it. We give residents a place to get their heads together, do some physical labor and help some four-legged critters who need it. The idea is to help them get back on their feet."

She looked away, out the window, chewing on her lower lip.

He took pity. "We don't allow any firearms. No drugs or alcohol. And we have a couple of mental health specialists and a doctor on call. Planning on a chaplain, too."

Once we start bringing in enough money to hire one, he almost added, but didn't. "If somebody's problems seem too much for us to handle, we refer them elsewhere."

"I see." She looked thoughtful.

They should've put what kind of nonprofit it was in the ad, to screen out people who were scared of veterans. But the truth was, they'd limited the ad to the fewest words possible, economizing.

"I can show you around," he said. "If you like what you see, we can talk more."

He was pretty sure that conversation wouldn't happen, judging by the way her attitude had changed once their focus on veterans had come up.

He hoisted himself to his feet, grabbed his cane and started toward the door.

She'd stood up to follow, but when she saw him full-length, she took a step back.

It shouldn't surprise him. Even with the inch or so he'd lost from the spinal surgery, he was still six-four. And he'd been lifting to work off some steam. Pretty much The Incredible Hulk.

It had used to work in his favor with women, at least some of them, way back when that had mattered.

"You're military?" she asked as he gestured for her to walk out ahead of him.

"Yep." He waited for the fake *thank you for your service*.

She didn't say it. "What branch?" she asked.

He was closing the door behind them. When he turned to answer, he saw that she'd moved ahead and was kneeling down in front of a little boy who sat on the floor of the outer office, his back against the wall, holding a small gaming device.

Finn sucked in a breath, restrained a surprised exclamation, tried to compose himself.

Kid looked to be about five. Freckle faced and towheaded.

Just like Derek.

His emotions churning, he watched her tap the boy's chin to get his attention. Odd that such a small boy had been so quiet during the, what, half hour that they'd been talking. Derek could never have done it.

"My son, Leo," she said, glancing up at Finn. And then, to the boy: "We're going to walk around with Mr. Gallagher. We might have a place to stay for a bit, a tiny little house."

The boy's eyes lit up and he opened his mouth to speak. Then he looked over at Finn and snapped it shut. He scooted farther behind his mother.

Could the kid be afraid of his limp or his cane? Could Kayla? But if she couldn't deal with that, or her kid couldn't, then they needed to take themselves far away from Redemption Ranch. His problems were minor compared to some of the veterans who would soon be staying here.

And beyond that, what kind of risks would a young kid face in a place like this? The vets he wasn't really worried about, but a little kid could be trouble around dogs—if he was too afraid of them, or not afraid enough.

No kids were going to be hurt on Finn's watch. Never again.

"This way," he said, his voice brusque. He'd show them around, because he had said he would. Unlike a lot of people, he didn't retract his promises.

He touched her back to guide her out. As he felt the

ridge of her spine through the shirt, she looked up at him, eyes wide and startled.

He withdrew his hand immediately, his face heating. He hadn't meant his touch to be flirtatious, but apparently it had come off some weird way.

He could already tell this wasn't going to work.

Kayla pulled Leo close beside her as she walked ahead of the square-shouldered soldier into the open air. Her mind raced at strategic pace.

She'd gotten a good feeling about the job when she'd seen it, reading the *Esperanza Springs Mountaineer* in the café where they'd had an early breakfast. Live in— check. They needed a place to live. A good thousand miles away from Arkansas, remote and off the beaten path—check. That was the big priority. Work she could handle—check. She liked dogs, and she liked working hands-on.

A wholesome, healthy, happy environment that would help Leo heal… Of that, she wasn't yet sure.

As for her own healing from her terrible marriage, she wasn't expecting that, and it didn't matter. She wasn't the type to elicit love from anyone, her son the exception. She knew that for sure, now.

The man striding beside her—and how did a guy stride with a cane, anyway?—looked a little too much like her bodybuilding, short-haired, military-postured ex. Finn had spooked her son to the point where, now, Leo pressed close into her side, making it hard to walk.

But it wasn't like she was going to become best friends with this Finn Gallagher, if she did get this job and decide to take it. It wasn't like she'd reveal anything to him, to anyone, that could somehow lead to Mitch finding them.

The mountains rose in a semicircle around the flat basin where the ranch was situated, white streaks of snow decorating the peaks even at the end of June. There was a weathered-looking barn up ahead of them, and off to the right, a pond with a dock and a rowboat.

This place drew her in. It was beautiful, and about as far from Little Rock as they could reasonably go, given the car she was driving. If she were just basing things on geography, she'd snap this job up in a minute.

But the military angle worried her.

"Would we live there?" Leo pointed. His voice was quiet, almost a whisper, but in it she detected a trace of excitement.

They were approaching a small log cabin with a couple of rustic chairs on a narrow porch. As Finn had mentioned, it was the end of a row of similar structures. Sunlight glinted off its green tin roof. One of the shutters hung crooked, but other than that, the place looked sturdy enough.

"This is the cabin you'd live in if this works out," Finn said, glancing down at Leo and then at her. "The vet who lived here before just moved out, so it should be pretty clean. Come on in."

Inside, the cabin's main room had a kitchen area—sink and refrigerator and stove—along the far wall. A door to one side looked like it led to a bathroom or closet. A simple, rough-hewn dining table, a couch and a couple of chairs filled up the rest of the small room. With some throw rugs and homemade curtains, it would be downright cozy.

"Sleeping loft is upstairs," Finn said, indicating a sturdy, oversize ladder.

Leo's head whipped around to look at Kayla. He loved to climb as much as any little boy.

"Safe up there?" she asked Finn. "Anything that could hurt a kid?" She could already see that the sleeping area had a three-foot railing at the edge, which would prevent a fall.

"It's childproof." His voice was gruff.

"No guns, knives, nothing?" If Finn were like Mitch, he'd be fascinated by weapons. And he wouldn't consider them a danger to a kid.

"Of course not!" Finn looked so shocked and indignant that she believed him.

"Go ahead—climb up and take a look," she said to her son. Leo had been cooped up in the car during the past four days. She wanted to seize any possible opportunity for him to have fun.

She stood at the bottom of the ladder and watched him climb, quick and agile. She heard his happy exclamation, and then his footsteps tapped overhead as he ran from one side of the loft to the other.

Love for him gripped her hard. She'd find a way to make him a better life, whether here or somewhere else.

"I'm not sure this is the right environment for a child," Finn said in a low voice. He was standing close enough that she could smell his aftershave, some old-fashioned scent her favorite stepfather had used. "We need someone who'll work hard, and if you're distracted by a kid, you can't."

"There's a camp program at the church in Esperanza Springs. Thought we'd check that out." Actually, she already had, online; they had daily activities, were open to five-year-olds and offered price breaks to low-income families.

Which they definitely were.

Finn didn't say anything, and silent men made her nervous. "Leo," she called, "come on down."

Her son scrambled down the ladder and pressed into her leg, looking warily at Finn.

Curiosity flared in the big man's eyes, but he didn't ask questions. Instead, he walked over to the door and held it open. "I'll show you the kennels." His face softened as he looked down at Leo. "We have eighteen dogs right now."

Leo didn't speak, but he glanced up at Kayla and gave a little jump. She knew what it meant. Eighteen dogs would be a cornucopia of joy to him.

They headed along the road in front of the cabins. "Is he comfortable with dogs?" Finn asked.

"He hasn't been around them much, but he's liked the ones he's met." Loved, more like. A pet was one of the things she'd begged Mitch for, regularly. She'd wanted the companionship for Leo, because she'd determined soon after his birth that they'd never have another child. Fatherhood didn't sit well with Mitch.

But Mitch hadn't wanted a dog, and she'd known better than to go against him on that. She wouldn't be the only one who'd suffer; the dog would, too, and Leo.

"We're low on residents right now," Finn said. He waved a hand toward a rustic, hotel-like structure half-hidden by the curve of a hill. "Couple of guys live in the old lodge. Help us do repairs, when they have time. But they both work days and aren't around a whole lot."

"You going to fill the place up?"

"Slowly, as we get the physical structures back up to

code. These two cabins are unoccupied." He gestured to the two that were next to the one he'd just shown them. The corner of one was caving in, and its porch looked unstable. She'd definitely have to set some limits on where Leo could play, in the event that this worked out. "This next one, guy named Parker lives there, but he's away. His mom's real sick. I'm not sure when he'll be back."

Across the morning air, the sound of banjo and guitar music wafted, surprising her. She looked down at Leo, whose head was cocked to one side.

They found the source of the music on the porch of the last cabin, and as they came close, the men playing the instruments stopped. "Who you got there?" came a raspy voice.

Finn half turned to her. "Come meet Willie and Long John. Willie lives in the cabin next door, but he spends most of his time with Long John. If you work here, you'll see a lot of them."

As they approached the steps, the two men got to their feet. They both looked to be in their later sixties. The tall, skinny, balding one who'd struggled getting up had to be Long John, which meant the short, heavyset one, with a full white beard, his salt-and-pepper hair pulled back in a ponytail, must be Willie. Both wore black Vietnam veteran baseball caps.

Finn introduced them and explained why Kayla was here.

"Hope you'll take the job," Long John said. "We could use some help with the dogs."

"And it'd improve the view around here," Willie said, a smile quirking the corner of his mouth beneath the beard.

Finn cleared his throat and glared at the older man.

Willie just grinned and eased down onto the cabin's steps. At eye level with Leo, he held out a hand. "I'm pleased to meet you, young man," he said.

"Shake hands," Kayla urged, and Leo held out his right hand.

"Pleased to meet you, sir," he said, his voice almost a whisper, and Kayla felt a surge of pride at his manners.

After a grave handshake, Willie looked up at her. "Wouldn't mind having a little guy around here. Always did like to take my grandkids fishing." He waved an arm in the direction of the pond she'd seen. "We keep it stocked."

Kayla's heart melted, just at the edges. Grandfather figures for Leo? A chance for him to learn to fish?

There was a low *woof* from inside the screen door and a responding one from the porch. A large black dog she hadn't seen before lumbered to its feet.

"About time you noticed there's some new folks here," Long John said, reaching from his chair to run a hand over the black dog's bony spine. "Rockette, here, don't pay a whole lot of attention to the world these days. Not unless her friend Duke wakes her up."

Willie opened the screen door. A gray-muzzled pit bull sauntered out.

"Duke. Sit." Willie made a hand gesture, and Duke obediently dropped to his haunches, his tongue lolling out. Willie slipped a treat from the pocket of his baggy jeans and fed it to the dog.

Leo took two steps closer to the old black dog, reached out and touched its side with the tips of his fingers.

"One of our agreements, for anyone who lives in the cabins, is that they take in a dog," Finn explained.

"Gives them a little extra attention. Especially the ones not likely to be adopted."

Leo tugged Kayla's hand. "Would *we* have a dog?"

"Maybe." She put seriousness into her voice so he wouldn't get his hopes up. "It all depends if Mr. Gallagher decides to offer me the job, and if I take it. Those are grown-up decisions."

"Sure could use the help," Long John said, lowering himself back into his chair with a stifled groan. "Me and Willie been doing our best, but…" He waved a hand at a walker folded against the porch railing. "With my Parkinson's, it's not that easy."

"Hardly anyone else has applied," Willie added. "Don't get many out-of-towners around these parts. And the people who live in Esperanza Springs heard we're gonna have more guys up here. They get skittish." He winked at Kayla. "We vets are gentle as lambs, though, once you get to know us."

"Right." She had direct experience to the contrary.

At first, before her marriage had gone so far downhill, she hadn't translated Mitch's problems into a mistrust of all military personnel. Later, it had been impossible to avoid doing just that.

When Mitch had pushed his way into her place well after their divorce was final—talking crazy and roughing her up—she'd gone to the police.

She hadn't wanted to file a complaint, which had been stupid. She'd just wanted to know her options, whether a protection order would do any good.

What she hadn't known was that the police officer she'd spoken with was army, too. Hadn't known he drank with Mitch at the Legion.

The cop had let Mitch know that she'd reported him,

and she still bore the bruises from when he'd come back over to her place, enraged, looking for blood.

Shaking off her thoughts, she watched Long John talk with Finn while Willie plucked at his guitar and then held it out to show Leo. The two veterans did exude a gentle vibe. But then, their wartime experiences were distant, their aggressions most likely tamed through age and experience.

"Let's take a look at the kennels," Finn said and nodded toward the barn. "Later, guys."

Just outside the barn, Finn turned and gestured for Leo to stand in front of him. After a nod from Kayla, Leo did, his eyes lowered, shoulders frozen in a slump.

"I want you to ask before you touch a dog, Leo," he said. "Most of them are real nice, but a couple are nervous enough to lash out. So ask an adult first, and never, ever open a kennel without an adult there to help you. Understand?"

Leo nodded, taking a step closer to Kayla.

"Good." Finn turned toward the barn door and beckoned for them to follow him.

Much barking greeted their entry into the dim barn. Finn flicked on a light, revealing kennels along both sides of the old structure and more halfway up the middle. One end of the barn was walled off into what looked like an office.

Finn walked down the row of dogs, telling her their names, reaching through some of the wire fencing to stroke noses. His fondness for the animals was obvious in his tone and his gentle touch. "All of them are seniors," he explained over his shoulder. "Which is about seven and up for a big dog, eight or nine for a little one."

"Where do they come from?" she asked. The barking

had died down, and most of the dogs stood at the gates of their kennels, tails wagging, eyes begging for attention.

"Owner surrenders, mostly. Couple of strays."

She knelt to look at a red-gold dog, probably an Irish setter mix. "Why would anyone give you up, sweetie?" She reached between the cage wires to touch the dog's white muzzle, seeming to read sadness in its eyes.

"Lots of reasons," Finn said. "People move. Or they don't have money for food and vet bills. Sometimes, they just don't want to deal with a dog that requires some extra care." He knelt beside her. "Lola, here, she can't make it up and down stairs. Her owner lived in a two-story house, so…"

"They couldn't carry her up and down?"

"Apparently not."

"Can I pet her, too, Mom?" Leo asked, forgetting to be quiet.

Kayla looked over at Finn. "Can he?"

"She's harmless. Go ahead."

As Leo stuck fingers into the cage of the tail-wagging Lola, Finn turned toward Kayla. "Most of our dogs *are* really gentle, just like I was telling Leo. The ones that are reactive have a red star on their cages." He pointed to one on the cage of a medium-sized brown dog, some kind of Doberman mix. "Those, you both stay away from. If the job works out, we'll talk about getting you some training for handling difficult dogs."

If the job worked out. Would it work out? Did she want it to?

Finn had moved farther down the row of cages, and he made a small sound of concern and opened one, guiding a black cocker spaniel out and attaching a leash to her collar. He bent over the little dog, rubbing his hands up and down her sides. "It's okay," he murmured as the dog wagged her tail and leaned against him. "You're okay."

"What's wrong?"

"Her cage is a mess. She knocked over her water and spilled her food." He scratched behind her ears. "Never has an accident, though, do you, girl?"

Kayla felt her shoulders loosen just a fraction. If Finn was that kind and gentle with a little dog, maybe he was a safe person to be around.

"Could you hold her leash while I clean up her cage?" he asked, looking over at Kayla. "In fact, if you wouldn't mind, she needs to go outside."

"No problem." She moved to take the leash and knelt down, Leo hurrying to her side.

"Careful," Finn warned. "She's blind and mostly deaf. You have to guide her or she'll run into things."

"How can she walk?" Leo asked, squatting down beside Kayla and petting the dog's back as Finn had done. "Mom, feel her! She's soft!"

Kayla put her hand in the dog's fur, shiny and luxuriant. "She *is* soft."

"She still has a good sense of smell," Finn explained to Leo. "And the sun and grass feel good to her. You'll see." He gestured toward the door at the opposite end of the barn. "There's a nice meadow out there where the dogs can run."

She and Leo walked toward the barn's door, guiding the dog around an ancient tractor and bins of dog food. In the bright meadow outside, Kayla inhaled the sweet, pungent scents of pine and wildflowers.

"Look, Mom, she's on her back!" Leo said. "She likes it out here!"

Kayla nodded, kneeling beside Leo to watch the little black dog's ecstatic rolling and arching. "She sure does. No matter that she has some problems—nobody likes to be in a cage."

A few minutes later, Finn came out, leading another dog. "I see you've figured out her favorite activity," he said. "Thanks for helping."

The dog he was leading, some kind of a beagle-basset mix, nudged the blind dog, and they sniffed each other. Then the hound jumped up and bumped her to the ground.

"He's hurting her!" Leo cried and stepped toward the pair.

"Let them be." Finn's hands came down on Leo's shoulders, gently stopping him.

Leo edged away and stood close to Kayla.

Finn lifted an eyebrow and then smiled reassuringly at Leo. "She's a real friendly dog and likes to play. Wish I could find someone to adopt her, but with her disabilities, it's hard. Willie and Long John can only handle one dog each. I have one of our problem dogs at my place—" He waved off toward a small house next to a bigger one, in the direction of the lodge. "And Penny—she owns the ranch—has another at hers. So for now, this girl stays in the kennel."

If she and Leo stayed here, maybe they could take the black dog in. That would certainly make Leo happy. He'd sunk down to roll on the ground with the dogs, laughing as they licked his face, acting like a puppy himself. He hadn't smiled so much in weeks.

And Kayla, who always weighed her choices carefully, who'd spent a year planning how to divorce Mitch, made a snap decision.

This place was safe. It was remote. Mitch would never

find them. And maybe Leo could have a decent childhood for a while. Not forever, she didn't expect that, but a little bit of a safe haven.

She looked over at Finn. He was smiling, too, watching Leo. It softened his hard-planed, square face, made him almost handsome. But as he watched, his mouth twisted a little, and his sea-blue eyes got distant.

She didn't want him to sink into a bad mood. That was never good. "If I can arrange for the summer camp for Leo," she said, "I'd be very interested in the job."

He looked at her, then at Leo, and then at the distant mountains. "There's paperwork, a reference check, drug tests. All that would have to be taken care of before we could offer you anything permanent."

"Not a problem." Not only did she have good references, but they were sworn to secrecy as to her whereabouts.

"I'll have to talk to our owner, too." His voice held reluctance.

Time to be blunt. "Is there some kind of problem you see in hiring me?"

"I'm withholding judgment," he said. "But we *do* need someone soon, since our last assistant quit. Until everything's finalized, how about a one-week trial?"

"That works." Even if the job didn't come together, she and Leo would get a week off the road.

With dogs.

Meanwhile, Finn's extreme caution made her curious. "You never did mention what branch of the military you served in," she said as he bent over to put leashes back on the two tired-out dogs.

"Eighty-second Airborne."

Kayla sat down abruptly beside Leo, pulling her

knees to herself on the grassy ground. She knew God was good and had a plan, but sometimes it seemed like He was toying with her.

Because this perfect new job meant involvement with a man from the same small, intensely loyal division of the US Army as her abusive ex.

Two

"You sure you're not making a big mistake?" Penny Jordan asked Finn two days later.

It was Saturday afternoon, and they were sitting in Penny's office, watching out the window as Kayla's subcompact sputtered up the dirt road to cabin six, leaving a trail of black exhaust in its wake.

"No." Finn watched as Kayla exited the car and opened the back door. Leo climbed out, and they opened the hatch and stood, surveying its contents. Leo looked up at her, listening seriously, like an adult. "I think it probably *is* a mistake, but I couldn't talk her out of wanting the job. So I went with the one-week trial."

"But she's moving in." Penny, ten years older than Finn but at least twenty times wiser, took a gulp of black coffee from her oversize cup. "That doesn't seem like a trial thing to do."

"They were staying at the campground up toward Harmony." He eased his leg off the chair where he'd been resting it, grimacing. "Afternoon thunderstorms are getting bad. At least they'll have a roof over their heads."

"You're skirting the issue." Penny leaned forward, elbows on the table. "She has a young son."

"I know, and even though she says she's got a plan for childcare, I don't know that it's safe for him—"

"Finn." Penny put a hand on his arm. "You know what I'm talking about."

He wasn't going there. "Guess I'd better get up there and help 'em move in."

"You're going to have to face what happened one of these days," she said, standing up with her trademark speed and grace. "I'll come, too. Gotta meet the woman who broke through your three-foot-thick walls."

"She didn't break through—it's a *trial*," he emphasized. "She knows the deal. And yes, you should meet her, because when she's not working kennels she can do housekeeping for you. Free you up for the real work."

Penny put her hands on her hips and arched forward and sideways, stretching her back. She was slim, with one long braid down her back and fine wrinkles fanning out from the corners of her eyes, the result of years spent outdoors in the Western sun. Not a trace of makeup, but she didn't need it; she was naturally pretty. Big heart, too.

She didn't deserve what had happened to her.

"Speaking of the real work," she said, "we might have two more vets coming in within the next six weeks."

"Oh?"

"Guy's classic PTSD, right out of Iraq. The woman…" Penny shook her head. "She's been through it. Scarred up almost as bad as Daniela was." Penny walked over to the window and looked out, her forehead wrinkling. "I'm going to put her in the cabin next to your new hire. She'll be more comfortable farther away from the guys."

Finn nodded. Daniela Jiminez had only recently left the ranch to marry another short-term resident, Gabriel Shafer. They'd stopped in to visit after their honeymoon, and their obvious joy mostly made Finn happy. He'd never experience that for himself, didn't deserve to, but he was glad to have had a small part in getting Gabe and Daniela together.

They walked down the sunny lane to the cabins. Finn kept up with Penny's quick stride even though he wasn't using his cane; it was a good day.

When they were halfway down, Willie's truck came toward them and glided to a halt. "Hitting the roadhouse for dinner and then a little boot scootin'," Willie said out the window. "You should come along, Finn. Meet somebody."

Penny rolled her eyes. "Men."

"Like Finn's gonna get a lady friend," Long John said from the passenger seat.

"You think you've got better odds?" Finn asked, meaning it as a joke. Everyone knew he didn't go out, didn't date. Those who pushed had gotten their heads bitten off and learned a lesson. Willie and Long John, though, were more persistent than most.

"We've both got better odds because we know how to smile and socialize," Willie said. "Ladies around here love us."

That was probably true. Unlike Finn, they both had the capacity for connection, the ability to form good relationships. He, on the other hand, didn't have the personality that meshed easily with a woman's. Too quiet, too serious. Deirdre had thrown that fact at him every time he caught her cheating.

"Y'all be careful, now," Penny said, giving the two

men a stern look. "You know we don't hold with drinking at the ranch, and that roadhouse is the eye of the storm."

"Rum and coke, hold the rum," Willie promised.

"Scout's honor," Long John said, holding up a hand in mock salute.

The truck pulled away, and a couple of minutes later Finn and Penny reached the cabin driveway where Kayla was unloading her car. She put down her box, picked up a red rubber ball and squatted in front of her son. "You say hello," she told the boy, "and then you can go throw the ball against the house."

The little boy swallowed, and his eyes darted in their direction and away. "Hi," he said and then grabbed the ball and ran to the side of the cabin.

"He's a little shy," Kayla said. She extended a hand to Penny. "I'm Kayla White. Are you Penny?"

"That's right." Penny gave Kayla a frank appraisal. "I'm glad to meet you. Looking forward to having a little help around here. See how you like the work. And how the work likes you. Cleaning up after dogs isn't for everyone."

"I've done worse." Kayla's color rose, like she'd read a challenge under Penny's words. "I appreciate the chance to stay in the cabin, but we're not going to really settle in until the trial week's over. I know the job wasn't intended for a mother and child."

"Sometimes the Good Lord surprises us," Penny said. "Now, what can we do to help you move in?"

"Not a thing." Kayla brushed her hands on the sides of her jeans. "I'm about done. And I can do some work tomorrow, although it'll be limited by Leo. I'm going to have him try that church camp on Monday." She shaded her eyes to watch her son as he threw the ball against the house, caught it and threw it again.

Looking at young Leo, Finn felt the lid on his memories start to come loose. Derek had loved to play ball, too. Finn had spent a lot of time teaching him to throw and catch and use a bat. Things a father was supposed to teach his son.

His throat tightened, and he coughed to clear it. "We'll take care of the work your first day here. You can start on Monday." He was feeling the urge to be away from her and her child.

She looked from Finn to Penny. "Well, but you're giving me a place to stay early. I don't want to be beholden." She pushed back a strand of chocolate hair that had escaped her ponytail and fallen into her eyes.

She was compact, but strong, with looks that grew on you slowly. Good thing she wasn't his type. Back when he was in the market for a woman, he'd gone for bigger, bouncier, louder ladies. The fun kind.

Yeah, and look where that got you.

"I'm with Finn on having you start Monday, but I'll tell you what," Penny said. "We all go down to church on Sundays. Why don't you join us? It'll give your son a chance to get to know some of the other kids while you're still nearby. That should make his first day at camp a little easier."

Finn turned his face so Kayla couldn't see it and glared at Penny. Yeah, he'd hired Kayla—temporarily—but that didn't mean they had to get all chummy in their time off.

Still, it was church. He supposed he ought to be more welcoming. And he knew Penny missed her grown daughter, who for inexplicable reasons had sided with her father when Penny's marriage had broken up. If Penny wanted to mother Kayla a little, he shouldn't get in the way.

Kayla bit her lip. "I'd like to get Leo to church," she said. "We went some back home, but…well. It wasn't as often as I'd have liked. I want to change that, now."

So she'd be coming to church with them every Sunday if she took the job? It wasn't as if there was much of a choice; Esperanza Springs had only two churches, so it was fifty-fifty odds she'd choose theirs.

Unless she wanted to get some breathing room, too.

Or maybe she'd leave after a week. He intended to make sure the work was hard and long, so that she didn't get too comfortable here.

Because something about Kayla White was making *him* feel anything but comfortable.

As the church service ended in a burst of uplifting piano music, Kayla leaned back in the pew. Her whole body felt relaxed for the first time in weeks. Months, really.

The little church had plain padded benches and a rough-hewn altar. Outside the clear glass windows, the splendor of the mountains put to shame any human effort at stained glass artistry.

Leo had sat with her for half the service, reluctantly gone up to the children's sermon and then followed the other kids out of the sanctuary with a desperate look back at Kayla. She'd forced herself not to rescue him and had made it ten minutes before giving in to her worries and going to check on him. She'd found him busily making crafts with the other young children, looking, if not happy, at least focused.

Now beside her Penny stretched, stood and then sat back down. "Hey, I forgot to mention that Finn and I help serve lunch after church to the congregation and some hard-up folks in the community. Would you like to join us? If you don't feel like working, you can just mingle until lunch is served."

The pastor—young, tanned and exuberant—had been visiting with the few people remaining in the pews, and he reached them just as Penny finished speaking. "We find we get more people to come to church when we offer a free meal," he said and held out a hand to Kayla. "Welcome. We're glad to have you here. I'm Carson Blair."

"Kayla White. I enjoyed your sermon."

He was opening his mouth to reply when two little girls, who looked to be a bit older than Leo, ran down the aisle at breakneck speed. They flung themselves at the pastor, one clinging to each leg, identical pouts on their faces.

"Daddy, she hit me!"

"She started it!"

The pastor knelt down. "Skye, you need to go sit right there." He indicated a pew on the left-hand side. "And, Sunny, you sit over here." He pointed to the right.

"But…"

"We wanted to play!" The one he'd called Sunny looked mournfully at her twin.

"Sit quietly for five minutes, and you can play together again."

Kayla smiled as the pastor turned back toward the small circle of adults. "Good tactics," she said. "I have a five-year-old. I can't imagine handling two."

Finn pushed himself out of the pew and ended up

standing next to Kayla, leaning on his cane, facing the pastor. "Had a phone message from you," he said to the pastor. "I'm sorry I didn't return it. Weekend got away from me."

"We all know your aversion to the phone," the pastor said, reaching out to shake Finn's extended hand.

"To conversation in general," Penny said. "Finn's the strong, silent type," she added to Kayla.

"Don't listen to them," Finn advised and then turned back toward the pastor. "What's up?"

"I was hoping to talk to you about your chaplain position. I know you can't pay yet, but I'd be glad to conduct vespers once a week, or do a little counseling, as long as it doesn't take away from my work here."

"I'll keep that in mind."

Finn's answer didn't seem very gracious for someone who'd just been offered volunteer services.

The pastor looked at him steadily. "Do that."

"We certainly will," Penny said. "But speaking of work, that lunch won't get served without us. You coming?" she asked Kayla.

"Absolutely. Lunch smells wonderful. I'm happy to help, if it will get me a plate of whatever's cooking."

"We all partake," the pastor said, shaking her hand again vigorously. "We're glad to have you here. It's rare that we get a fresh face."

"Won't be so rare soon," Penny warned. "We have a couple of new veterans coming in. And I'm working on getting Long John and Willie to church, too."

"You know the church does a van run," the pastor said. "Sounds like you'll need it. And we'll gladly welcome the men and women who served our country."

Finn jerked his head to the side. "Let's go."

In the church kitchen, organized chaos reigned. Finn handed aprons to Kayla and Penny and then donned one himself, choosing it from a special hook labeled with his name.

"Why do you get your own apron?" she asked, because there didn't seem to be anything special about it.

"It's king-size," he said ruefully. "Those little things barely cover a quarter of me. Last Christmas, the volunteers went together to buy me this tent."

"And in return," a white-haired woman said, "we make him carry all the heavy trays and boxes. Isn't that right, Finn?"

"Glad to, as long as you save me a piece of your strawberry-rhubarb pie, Mrs. Barnes."

Kayla was put to work dishing up little bowls of fruit salad while Penny helped Mrs. Barnes get everyone seated and Finn pulled steaming trays of chicken and rice from the ovens. A couple of other ladies carried baskets of rolls to each table and mingled with the guests, probably fifty or sixty people in all.

It wasn't a fancy church. As many of the congregation members wore jeans as dresses and suits, and seating for the meal was open. That meant there was no distinction between those who'd come just for the food and those who'd come for the service first. Nice.

The children burst into the room and took over one corner, stocked with toys and a big rug. Kayla waited a minute and then went to check on Leo. She found him banging action figures with another kid in a zealous pretend fight.

"Hey, buddy," she said quietly, touching his shoulder.

He flinched and turned. She hated that he did that. No matter what, she was going to make sure he gained confidence and stopped feeling like he was at risk all the time. Mitch had never hit him, to her knowledge, but yelling and belittling were almost as bad. And that last time, when he'd broken into their place and beaten Kayla, she'd looked up from the floor to see Leo crouched in the doorway, pale and silent, tears running down his cheeks.

"Leo is quiet, but he seems to fit in," said the woman who'd run the children's program. "He's a very polite little boy. I understand he's going to do the day camp, too?"

Kayla nodded. "Thank you for taking care of him."

"He's welcome to sit at the kids' table and eat. Most of the children do, though a few go sit with their parents."

Kayla turned back to Leo. "What do you think, buddy? Want to sit here with your new friends, or come sit with me and Miss Penny and Mr. Finn?"

Leo considered.

The other boy whacked his action figure. "ATTACK!" he yelled.

Leo made his figure strike back, and the other boy fell on the floor, pretending he'd been struck.

"I'll stay with the kids," Leo said and dived down to the floor to make his action figure engage in some hand-to-hand combat with the one the other boy was holding.

Kayla watched them play for a moment as realization struck her. If she did, indeed, build a better life for Leo, it would mean he'd become more and more independent. He wouldn't be tied to her by fear. He'd have regular friendships, sleepovers at other boys' homes, camping trips.

And where did that leave her, who'd centered her life around protecting her son for the past five years?

It'll leave me right where I should be, she told herself firmly. It would be good, normal, for Leo to gain independence. And if that made her nostalgic for his baby years of total reliance on her, that was normal, too. She could focus on the healthy ways parents and children related, instead of walking on eggshells to avoid offending Mitch.

The lunch went quickly, partly because the serving staff ate in shifts and then hurried back to the kitchen to help with refills and cleanup. Kayla didn't mind. She liked the camaraderie of working with others. And she liked having her stomach—and her son's—full of delicious, healthy food.

She was washing dishes when Mrs. Barnes came up beside her, towel in hand. "I'll dry and put away," she said. "Where are you from, dear?"

"Arkansas," Kayla said vaguely. "Small town." Mrs. Barnes seemed harmless, but Kayla didn't want to get into the habit of revealing too much.

"And what brought you to Esperanza Springs? We don't get a whole lot of newcomers."

Kayla was conscious of Finn nearby, carrying big empty serving dishes back to the sinks to be washed. "I was looking for a change," she said. "I've always loved the mountains, so we thought we'd take our chances in Colorado."

"And what did you do back in Arkansas?"

Kayla didn't see malice in the other woman's eyes, only a little too much curiosity. "I worked for a cleaning company," she said. "Cleaning houses and offices and such." No need to mention that she'd started it, and that it had been doing well. She hoped Janice, who'd taken it over, was managing okay. She'd been avoiding calling her, afraid word would get back to Mitch, but she needed to stop being afraid. She'd call Janice tonight.

The kitchen was getting hotter, and Kayla dried off her hands and unbuttoned her sleeves. As she rolled them up, Mrs. Barnes went still. Behind her, Finn stared, too.

Too late, she looked down and saw her arms, still a traffic wreck of bruises.

"Oh, my, dear, what happened?" Mrs. Barnes put a gentle hand on Kayla's shoulder.

She didn't look at either of them. "I fell."

It wasn't a lie. Each time Mitch had hit her, she'd fallen.

Someone called Mrs. Barnes to the serving counter. She squeezed Kayla's shoulder and then turned away, leaving Finn and Kayla standing at the sink.

He frowned at her, putting his hands on his hips. "If someone hurt you—"

An Eighty-second Airborne tattoo peeked out from under the sleeve of his shirt. The same tattoo Mitch had.

She took a step backward. "I need to go check on Leo," she said abruptly and practically ran out of the kitchen, rolling down her sleeves as she went.

Leo was drawing pictures with the same boy he'd been playing with before, but he jumped up and hugged her when she approached. "Mom! Hector goes to the day camp here, too! He's gonna get me the cubby next to his and bring his Skytrooper tomorrow!" He flopped back down on the floor, propped on his arms, drawing on the same large piece of paper as his new friend.

"That's great, honey." Kayla backed away and looked from Leo to the kitchen and back again. She was well and truly caught.

Her whole goal was to provide a safe, happy home for

Leo. And it looked like maybe she'd found that place. The ranch, the dogs, the church people, all were bringing out her son's relaxed, happy side—a side she'd almost forgotten he had.

But on the other hand, there was Finn—a dangerous man by virtue of his association with Mitch's favorite, dedicated social circle. She knew how the Eighty-second worked.

She grabbed a sponge and started wiping down tables, thinking.

Finn had seen her bruises and gotten suspicious. If she let slip too much information, he might just get in touch with Mitch.

On the other hand, maybe his tattoo was old and so was his allegiance. Maybe he'd gotten involved in broader veterans affairs. Not everyone stayed focused on their own little division of the service.

She had to find out more about Finn and how committed he was to his paratrooper brothers. And she had to do it quickly. Because Leo was already starting to get attached to this place, and truthfully, so was she.

But she couldn't let down her guard. She had to learn more.

As she wiped a table, hypnotically, over and over, she concocted a plan. Once she'd finalized it, she felt better.

By this evening, one way or another, she'd have the answer about whether or not they could stay. For Leo's sake, she hoped the answer was yes.

Three

Late Sunday afternoon, Finn settled into his recliner and put his legs up. He clicked on a baseball game and tried to stop thinking.

It didn't work.

He kept going back to those bruises on Kayla's arms, the defensive secrecy in her eyes. All of it pretty much advertised a victim of abuse.

If that were the case, he was in trouble. His primary responsibility was to the veterans here, and some angry guy coming in to drag Kayla away would up the potential for violence among a group of men who'd seen too much of it.

That was bad.

But worse, he was starting to feel responsible for Kayla and the boy. They were plucky but basically defenseless. They needed protection.

If he sent them away, he'd be putting them at risk.

His phone buzzed, a welcome break from his worries. He clicked to answer. "Gallagher."

"Somethin' curious just happened." It was Long John's voice.

Finn settled back into his chair. "What's that, buddy?" Unlike Willie, Long John had no family, and with his Agent Orange–induced Parkinson's, he couldn't get out a lot. He tended to call Finn with reports of a herd of elk, or an upcoming storm, or a recommendation about caring for one of the dogs.

It was fine, good, even. Finn didn't have much family himself, none here in Colorado, and providing a listening ear to lonely vets gave him a sense of purpose.

Long John cleared his throat. "That Kayla is mighty interested in you."

"What do you mean?" For just a second, he thought Long John meant romantic interest, but then he realized that wasn't likely to be the case. Kayla was young, pretty and preoccupied with her own problems. She wouldn't want to hook up with someone like him. Long John was probably just creating drama out of boredom.

"She came over for a little chat," Long John said. "Talked about the weather a bit and then got right into questions about you."

"What kind of questions?"

"Where'd you serve. How active are you in the local chapter. How many of your military buddies come around. Did you ever do anything with the Eighty-second on the national level. That kind of stuff."

"Weird." Especially since she'd seemed to have an aversion to all things military.

"Not sure what to make of it," Long John said. "She's a real nice gal, but still. All kinds of people trying to take advantage. Thought you should know."

"Thanks." He chatted to the older man for a few more minutes and then ended the call.

Restless now, he strode out onto his porch. The plot thickened around Kayla. If she'd been treated badly by someone, why would she now be seeking information about Finn? Was she still attached to her abuser? Was he making her gather information for some reason?

As he sat down on the porch steps to rub his leg—today was a bad day—he saw Kayla sitting with Penny at the picnic table beside Penny's house. Talking intently.

More information gathering?

Leo played nearby, some engrossing five-year-old game involving rocks and a lot of shouting. Kid needed a playmate. They should invite the pastor's little girls up here.

Except thinking of the widowed pastor hanging around Kayla rubbed him the wrong way.

And why should any of that matter to him? Impatient with himself, he got down on the ground and started pulling up the weeds that were getting out of control around the foundation of his place, like everywhere else on the ranch. Kayla wasn't his concern. She was here on a temporary pass. And even if they did give her the full-time job—which he still questioned—he didn't need to get involved in how she ran her life and raised her kid.

Penny stood and waved to him. "I'll be inside, doing some paperwork, if anybody needs me," she called.

He stood, gave her a thumbs-up and watched her walk inside. That was how they ran the place, spelling each other, letting each other know what they were doing. It'd be quiet on a Sunday, but they liked for at least one of them to be on call, phone on, ready to help as needed.

From the garden area just behind him, he heard a

thump, a wail—"Mommy!"—and then the sound of crying. Leo. Finn spun and went to the boy, who was kneeling on the ground where Finn had been digging. His hand was bleeding and his face wet with tears.

Finn beckoned to Kayla, who'd jumped up from the picnic table, and then knelt awkwardly beside the little boy. "Hey, son, what happened?"

Leo cringed away, his eyebrows drawing together, and cried harder.

"Leo!" Kayla arrived, sank down and drew Leo into her arms. "Oh, no, honey, what happened?"

"It hurts!" Leo clutched his bloody hand to his chest.

"Let me see."

The little boy held up his hand to show her, but the sight of it made him wail louder. "I'm bleeding!"

Kayla leaned in and examined the wound, and Finn did, too. Fortunately, it didn't look too serious. The bleeding was already stopping. "Looks like he might have cut it on the weed digger. Is that what happened, buddy?"

The boy nodded, still gulping and gasping.

"I have bandages and antibiotic cream inside, if you want to bring him in." He knew better than to offer to carry the boy. Only a mother would do at a time like this.

Kayla got to her feet and swung Leo up into her arms. "Come on. Let's fix you up."

There was a buzzing sound, and Finn felt for his phone.

"It's mine," Kayla said. "I'll get it later."

"You can sit in there." Finn indicated the kitchen. "I'll grab the stuff."

Moments later, he was back downstairs with every

size of Band-Aid in his cupboard and three different types of medical ointment.

Kayla had Leo sitting on the edge of the sink and was rinsing his hand.

Leo howled like he was being tortured.

"I know, honey, it hurts, but we have to clean it. There. Now it'll start feeling better." She wrapped a paper towel around the boy's hand and lifted him easily from the sink to a kitchen chair.

She'd been right. She *was* stronger than she looked, because Leo wasn't small.

"Let's see," Finn said, giving the little boy a reassuring smile.

Leo shrank away and held his hand against his chest.

"I won't touch it. I just want to look." To Kayla he added, "I have first-aid training from the service. But it's probably fine. Your call."

"Let Mr. Finn look, honey. Let's count one-two-three and then do the hard thing. Ready?"

Leo looked up, leaned into her and nodded. "Okay."

Together, they counted. "One, two, three." And then Leo squeezed his eyes shut and held out his hand.

Finn studied the small hand, the superficial cut across two fingers. He opened his mouth to reassure Kayla and Leo.

And then memory crashed in.

He'd put a Band-Aid on Derek's hand, not long before the accident. He'd cuddled the boy to his chest as he held the little hand—just like Leo's—in his own larger one. Carefully squeezed the antibiotic on the small scrape, added a superhero Band-Aid and wiped his son's tears.

"It looks fine," he said to Kayla through a suddenly tight throat. "You go ahead and dress it." He shoved the materials at her, limped over to the window and looked out, trying to compose himself.

Normally, he kept a lid on his emotions about his son. Especially his son. Deirdre, yes, he grieved losing her, but she was an adult and she'd made a lot of bad choices that had contributed to her death.

His son had been an innocent victim.

"There. All fixed!" Kayla's voice was perky and upbeat. "You keep that Band-Aid on, now. Don't go showing that cut to your friends. It's a big one."

"It *is* big," Leo said, his voice steadying. "I was brave, wasn't I, Mommy?"

Finn turned back in time to see her hug him. "You were super brave. Good job."

Leo came over to Finn and, from a safe distance, held up his hand. "See? It was a really big cut!"

"It sure was," Finn said and then cleared the roughness out of his throat. "Sorry I don't have any fun Band-Aids. Not many kids come around here."

And there was a good reason for that. Having little boys around would tear him apart.

Change the subject. "You want to watch TV for a few minutes, buddy? I need to talk to your mom."

Leo's head jerked around to look at Kayla. "Can I, Mom?"

She hesitated. "I guess, for a few minutes. If we can find a decent show." She looked at Finn pointedly. "I actually don't allow him to watch much TV."

"Sorry." He headed into the living room and clicked the TV on, found a cartoonish-looking show that he remembered his son liking and looked at Kayla. "This okay?"

She squinted at the TV. "Yeah. Sure."

Her phone buzzed again, but she ignored it.

In the kitchen, she looked at him with two vertical lines between her eyebrows. "What's up?"

"Why'd you grill Long John about me?" he asked her abruptly.

At the sharp question from Finn, Kayla's mind reeled. "What do you mean?" she asked, buying time.

She knew exactly what he meant.

Long John must have gotten on the phone the moment she'd left his cabin. And wasn't that just like a soldier, to report anything and everything to his military buddies.

They're friends, an inner voice reminded her. She'd just met Long John, while Finn had probably known him for months if not years.

Finn let out a sigh. "Long John let me know you were asking all kinds of questions about me. I wondered why."

She studied him for signs of out-of-control anger and saw none. In which case, the best defense was a good offense. "You have a problem with me checking my employer's references the same way you and Penny are checking mine?" she bluffed.

He looked at her for a moment. "No. That's not a problem. It's just that some of your questions seemed pointed. All about my military service."

"That's part of your background," she said.

Finn shook his head. "I'm just not comfortable with having you here if you have any sort of attitude toward the military," he said. "The veterans are the most important thing to us, and believe it or not, they're sensitive. Especially the ones we get here. I don't need a worker who's cringing away from them or, on the other hand, overly curious."

She nodded. "That makes sense." She should have known this wouldn't work. It was too perfect.

The thought of going back on the road filled her with anxiety, though. Her supply of money was dwindling, and so was Leo's patience.

This place was *perfect* for Leo.

She tried to hang on to the pastor's words from this morning. What was the verse? *I know the plans I have for you...*

God has a plan for us.

She straightened her spine. "We'll get our things together tonight and move on tomorrow."

Her phone buzzed for about the twentieth time. Impatient, she pulled it out. She read through the texts from her friend Janice, back in Arkansas, her anxiety growing.

Don't come back under any circumstances.
He tore up your place.
He's raving that he's going to find you.
Get a PFA, fast.

She sank into a kitchen chair, her hand pressed to her mouth, her heart pounding. What was she going to do now?

"Listen, Kayla, I didn't mean you had to leave this minute," Finn said. "You can stay out the week, like we discussed. We can even help you figure out your next step. I just don't think..." He paused.

There was a brisk knock at the screen door, and then Penny walked in. "I called the last reference, and they raved about you," she said to Kayla. "So as far as I'm concerned, you're hired."

Kayla glanced up at Finn in time to see his forehead wrinkle. "Temporarily," he said.

"Long-term, as far as I'm concerned." Penny gave him an even stare.

"We need to talk," he said to Penny.

"All right." She put a bunch of paper in front of Kayla. "Start signing," she said. "Look for the *X*s."

Finn and Penny went out onto the porch, and she heard the low, intense sound of an argument.

From the living room, she heard Leo laughing at the television.

Finn didn't want to hire her. That was clear, and it wasn't only because she'd been nosy. Something else about her bothered him.

Which was fine, because he kind of bothered her, too. She didn't think he was dangerous himself, but he was clearly linked up to the veteran old boys' network. If Mitch started yelling at one of his meetings about how they were missing, the word could get out. Paratroopers were intensely loyal and they helped each other out, and a missing child would definitely be the type of thing that would stir up their interest and sympathy.

She needed to be farther away, but for now, the protection offered by the ranch was probably the safest alternative for Leo. A week, two, even a month here would give her breathing room.

Or maybe Mitch's rage would burn out. Although it hadn't in the year since the divorce he'd fought every inch of the way.

Finn didn't want her here, but she was used to that. She'd grown up in a home where she wasn't wanted.

And Penny had seemed to intuit some of her issues when Kayla had probed about Finn and the ranch during a lull before the church service. She'd said something about men, how women needed to stick together. Penny was on her side.

She could deal with Finn. She didn't need his approval or his smiles.

And she didn't want to depend on anyone. But here, she could work hard, pull her weight.

Finn and Penny came back in. Finn's jaw jutted out. Penny looked calm.

"You can have the job," Finn said.

"However long you want it," Penny added, glancing over at Finn.

Kayla drew in a deep breath, looking at them. "Thank you."

Then, her insides quivering, she picked up the pen and started signing.

Four

Finn headed for the kennels around eight o'clock the next morning, enjoying the sight of the Sangre de Cristos. He could hear the dogs barking and the whinnying of a horse. They only kept two, and Penny cared for them up at the small barn, but she sometimes took one out for a little ride in the morning.

Up ahead, Kayla's cabin door opened, and she and Leo came out.

He frowned. He wasn't thrilled about her working here, but he was resigned to it. He just had to stay uninvolved, that was all.

He watched her urge Leo into the car. Leo resisted, turning away as if to run toward the cabin, but she caught him in a bear hug.

Uh-oh. Wherever they were going—probably down to the church day camp—Leo wasn't on board.

She set Leo down and pointed at the back seat, and with obvious reluctance, the boy climbed in. Through the car's open windows, he heard Leo complain, "I can't get it buckled."

She bent over and leaned in, and he noticed she didn't raise her voice even though Leo continued to whine. She spoke soothingly but didn't give in.

Finn looked away and tried to think about something other than what it would be like to parent a kid Leo's age.

Derek's age.

When she tried to start the car, all that happened was some loud clicking and grinding. A wisp of smoke wafted from the front of the vehicle.

She got out and raised the hood. From inside the car, Leo's voice rose. "If I have to go, I don't want to be late!"

By now, Finn had reached the point where her cabin's little driveway intersected with the road. He looked out over the valley and sniffed the aromatic pines and tried to stay uninvolved. She hadn't seen him. He could walk on by.

He tried to. Stopped. "Need a jump?"

She bit her lip, its fullness at odds with her otherwise plain looks and too-thin figure. She looked from him to Leo. As clear as the brightening blue sky, he could see the battle between her desire for independence and her child's needs.

"I think my starter's bad."

"You need to call for a tow?" He stood beside her and pretended to know what he was looking at. Truth was, despite the fact that he'd sold farm machinery in one of his jobs, car repair wasn't in his skill set.

She shook her head. "I can fix it, if I can get down to town and get the part."

He looked sideways at her. "You sure?"

She blew out a *pfft* of air and nodded. "Sure. Just takes a screwdriver and a couple of bolts. Trouble is, Leo needs to get to camp."

His glance strayed to her mouth again but he looked away quickly, glancing down to the cross around her neck. She wasn't a girl up for grabs, obviously, and even if she were, he couldn't partake. One, because she was sort of his employee—Penny was technically her boss, but he was her direct supervisor. And two, because of what he'd done. He didn't deserve to connect with a woman. He needed to remember his decision in that regard.

No one had ever tested it before, not really.

But there was nothing wrong with giving her and the boy a ride, was there? Any Good Samaritan would do that.

"I planned to head down into town anyway," he said. "I can move up my schedule. Come on. Grab his booster seat and we'll hop in my truck."

She hesitated and looked toward Leo, who appeared very small even in the compact car. "Okay. Thank you. That would be a big help." She leaned in. "Hustle out, buddy. Mr. Finn's going to give us a ride."

"Is our car broken?"

"Yes, but I can fix it," she said, her voice confident.

Leo nodded. "Okay."

Finn carried the booster seat and Kayla held Leo's hand as they walked down the dirt road toward Finn's place and the truck. The piney breeze felt fresh against his face. A mountain bluebird flashed by, chirping its *TOO-too, TOO-too.*

Other than that, it was quiet, because Kayla wasn't a person who had to talk all the time. As a quiet man himself, he appreciated that.

The ride to town got too quiet, though, so he turned on a little country music. When his current favorite song came on, he saw her tapping a hand against her jean-clad thigh. He was tapping the steering wheel, same rhythm, and when their eyes met, she flashed a smile.

They got close to town, and there was a sniffling sound in the back seat. Kayla turned half-around. "What's wrong, buddy?"

"I don't want to go." Leo's voice trembled.

"It's hard to do new things," she said, her voice matter-of-fact.

"My tummy hurts."

"Sometimes that happens when you're scared." She paused, then added, "Anyone would be a little bit afraid, meeting a lot of new people. But we know how to do things anyway, even when we're scared."

"I don't want to." His voice dripped misery.

The tone and the sound brought back Finn's son, hard. He remembered taking Derek to his first T-ball practice, a new team of kids he didn't know. Finn had comforted him in the same way Kayla was comforting Leo.

His breath hitched. He needed to stop making that dumb kind of equation. "You'd better stop crying," he said to Leo. "Buck up. The other boys will laugh at you."

Finn looked in the rearview mirror, saw the boy's narrow shoulders cringe and wanted to knock himself in the head.

Leo drew in a sharp, hiccupy breath.

Kayla was giving Finn the death stare. "Anyone worth being your friend will understand if you're a little scared the first day," she said over her shoulder.

But Leo kept gasping in air, trying to get his tears under control. And that *was* good; the other kids wouldn't like a crybaby, but still. Finn had no right to tell Leo what to do.

No rights in this situation, at all.

And now the tension in the truck was thicker than an autumn fog.

He'd created the problem and he needed to fix it. "Hey," he said, "when do you want the dog to come live with you?"

The snuffly sounds stopped. Kayla glanced back at Leo, then at Finn, her eyes narrowed.

He could tell she was debating whether or not to trust him and go along with this or to stay angry. He'd seen that expression plenty of times before, with his wife. She'd have chosen to hold on to her anger, no question.

"I don't know." Kayla put on a thoughtful voice. "I'd rather wait until this evening when Leo's home from camp. That way, he can help me handle her. That is…" She turned half-around again. "Do you think we're ready to take care of a dog? You'd have to help me."

"Yeah!" Leo's voice was loud and excited. "I know we can do it, Mom."

"Hey, Leo," Finn said, "I don't know the dog's name. She needs a new one. Maybe the other kids at camp could help you pick one out." Actually, the former owners *had* told Finn the dog's name. It was a common curse word. Even now, thinking of their nasty laughs as they'd dumped the eager, skinny, blind-and-deaf dog at the ranch, his mouth twisted.

"Okay!" Leo said as they pulled into the church parking lot. "I'll ask them what we should name her!" He unfastened his seat belt as soon as the truck stopped, clearly eager to get on with his day.

"Wait a minute," Kayla warned Leo as he reached for the door handle. "I need to take you in, and we have to walk on the lines in the parking lot. It's for safety. The teacher told me when I talked to her."

"I'll be here," Finn said as Kayla got nimbly out of the truck and then opened the back for Leo to jump down. They walked toward the building holding hands, Leo walking beside her, moving more slowly as they got closer.

Watching them reminded him of dropping off his son.

He couldn't make a practice of getting involved with Kayla and Leo, he told himself sternly. It hurt too much. And it gave his heart crazy ideas about the possibility of having a family sometime in the future.

That wasn't happening, his head reminded him.

But his heart didn't seem to be listening.

Kayla walked out of the church after dropping Leo off at the camp program, her stomach twisting and tears pressing at her eyes.

If only she didn't have to start him in a new program so soon after arriving in town. But she had to work; there wasn't a choice about that.

He'll be fine. He has to grow up sometime.

But he'd looked so miserable.

The lump in her throat grew and the tears overflowed.

To her mortification, two of the other mothers—or maybe it was a mother and a grandmother—noticed and came over. "What's wrong, honey?" the older, redheaded one asked.

The younger woman came to her other side and startled Kayla by wrapping her in a hug. "Are you okay?"

What kind of a town was this, where complete strangers hugged you when you were sad? Kayla pulled back as

soon as she graciously could and nodded. "I just hate…
leaving him…in a new place."

"Gotcha," the older woman said without judgment
and handed her a little packet of tissues. "I'm Marge.
Just dropped off my Brenna in the same classroom your
boy was in. It's a real good program."

Kayla drew in big gasps of air. "I'm sorry." She blew
her nose. "I feel like an idiot."

"Oh, I know what you're going through," the mother
who'd hugged her said. "I cried every single day of the
first two weeks at kindergarten drop-off." She patted
Kayla's shoulder. "I'm Missy, by the way. What's your
name? I haven't seen you around."

"I'm Kayla. Pleased to meet you." She got the words
out without crying any more, but barely.

"Now, me," Marge said, "I jumped for joy when
Brenna started kindergarten. She's my sixth," she added,
"and I love her to pieces, but it was the first time I had
the house to myself in fifteen years. I don't want to give
up the freedom come summer, so all my kids are in some
kind of program or sport."

Kayla tried to smile but couldn't. Leo had gone willingly enough with the counselor in charge, no doubt
buoyed up by the prospect of telling the other children
he was getting a dog. But as they'd walked away, he'd
shot such a sad, plaintive look over his shoulder. That
was what had done her in.

For a long time, it had been her and Leo against the
world. She had to learn to let him go, let him grow up,
but she didn't have to like it.

In the past year of starting and running her little business, cleaning houses for wealthy people, she'd paid attention to how they cared for their kids. Lots of talking,

lots of book reading. That had been easy for her to rep-
licate with Leo.

A couple of the families she'd really admired had
given their kids independence and decision-making
power, even at a fairly young age. That was harder for
Kayla to do, given how she and Leo had been living,
though she could see the merits of it. "Maybe I should
go back in and check on him," she said, thinking aloud.

"Don't do it," Missy advised. "You'll just make yourself miserable. And if he sees you, he'll get more upset."

"He'll be fine." Marge waved a hand. "They have
your number to call you if there's anything wrong. Enjoy
the time to yourself."

One of the other mothers, a tall, beautifully made-up
blonde, drifted over. "Some of us are going to Flexible
Coffee for a bit," she said to Kayla. "I noticed you're
new. Want to come?"

More small-town friendliness? Kayla appreciated it,
but she didn't quite feel comfortable. She didn't want
to go socialize for an hour or two; she had a car starter
to buy and install.

Before she could beg off, Marge lifted an eyebrow
and pinned the woman with a steady stare. "Glad you're
willing to bury the hatchet, Sylvie—that is, if you're inviting all of us. You haven't spoken to me since Brenna
gave Jocelyn that surprise haircut last year."

Sylvie shuddered. "Right before she had a pageant.
She could have won."

Marge snorted. "Don't pin that on me. Jocelyn wears
a wig to those things, just like every other little beauty
queen."

"I wouldn't expect *you* to understand." Sylvie's once-over, taking in Marge's faded T-shirt and cutoff shorts, wasn't subtle.

Missy rolled her eyes. "Would you two stop fighting? You're going to give Kayla here a bad impression of our town."

The gorgeous Sylvie glanced out into the parking lot and then looked at Kayla speculatively. "That looked like Finn Gallagher's truck. Are you two seeing each other?"

"No!" Heat climbed Kayla's cheeks. All three women looked at her and she realized she'd spoken too loudly. "I work for him, that's all," she said quickly, trying to sound casual. "I'm having car trouble, so he gave me and my son a ride to town."

"Think I'll go say hello." Sylvie sashayed over to Finn's truck.

"One of these days, she's going to land him," Marge said.

"Not sure she's his type," Missy said.

"Long-legged blondes are every guy's type." Marge stretched. "You two going to take her up on her coffee invite?"

"I have to work," Missy said, turning toward the row of cars. "But if you go, call me later with all the gossip, okay?"

"Will do," Marge called after her. Then she turned to Kayla. "How about you. Want to come?"

"I have to work, too." And Kayla wasn't sure she wanted to get in the middle of a lot of gossip. Back in high school, she'd envied the girls who knew everything about everyone and felt comfortable in the spotlight, but no more.

Now she just wanted peace. And peace, for her, definitely meant staying *out* of the spotlight.

"Well, it was nice meeting you. Think I'll go just to see what news Sylvie's gathered," Marge added. "Unless she decides to hook up with Finn right here and now." She nodded toward Finn's truck.

Sylvie had propped her crossed arms on the open window and was leaning in. She ran a hand through her long blond hair, flipping it back.

Kayla felt a surge of the old jealousy. There were women who stood out and got noticed. And then there were women like her. As good-looking as Finn Gallagher was, he'd definitely go for the showier type.

Which didn't matter, of course. Finn could date whomever he chose, and it wasn't her business. She just hoped he could still give her a ride back to the ranch before taking off with Sylvie.

But Sylvie backed away quickly, spun and headed toward the main parking lot where Kayla and Marge still stood.

"Did you get a date?" Marge asked her bluntly.

"Marge! And no. He blew me off again." Sylvie sighed dramatically. "If only I didn't have this attraction to unavailable men. Are we going for coffee or not?"

"I'll meet you over there," Marge said.

"How about you, Kayla?" Sylvie studied her a little too hard. "Come on—join us. I'd like to get to know you."

No way. "Thank you," she said in the fake-nice voice women like Sylvie always inspired in her. "I appreciate the coffee offer, but I really do need to get going. Thank you for helping me with my meltdown," she added to Marge. "I'll see you at pickup, or maybe another day this week. 'Bye, Sylvie."

She hurried off toward Finn's truck, hoping she hadn't been too abrupt.

"What went on just now?" Finn asked as soon as she'd settled inside and fastened her seat belt.

She shrugged. "They asked me for coffee, but I told them I needed to work."

"You know, your shift doesn't start until ten. You could've gone."

"No, thanks."

He looked at her speculatively but didn't ask any questions. "I'd like to take you to breakfast," he said instead.

That jolted her inner alarm system but good. "Why?"

"Because I'm guessing you haven't eaten, and you have a long day of work ahead." He hesitated, then added, "And because I upset Leo, and I want to make it up to you."

"That's not necessary. You fixed it." What did he want with her, inviting her to a meal?

He must have read her wariness, because he spread his hands. "No big deal. I often stop at the Peak View Diner for breakfast. It's cheap, and Long John and Willie will probably be there. They'd love to have a new audience."

Oh. Well, if Long John and Willie would be there…

"Best bacon biscuits in the state." He offered a winning smile that made her breath catch.

Her stomach growled. "Well…"

"Look," he said, "I'm not asking you out, if that's what's worrying you. It's just that Esperanza Springs is a sociable little town. People are curious about you, and it's better for them to meet you than to gossip among themselves."

"Bacon biscuits, huh?" She grinned and lifted her hands, palms up. "I can't turn that down. Just as long as you and Long John and Willie protect me from the gossip hounds."

"Believe me," he said, "nobody can get a word in around those guys' stories, but they really are popular. If people see you're with them—"

"And with you?" she interrupted.

"To a lesser extent, yes. So we'll make an appearance, eat a couple of biscuits and then get back to the peace and solitude I think we both prefer."

She looked at him sideways and gave a slow nod. "Okay," she said and then looked away, afraid of revealing the surge of emotion that had welled up in her at his words.

It wasn't that often that people paid enough attention to Kayla to figure out what she was like inside. And it was even less often that someone shared the same preferences and tastes.

Unfortunately, Kayla was finding Finn's attention and understanding just a little bit too appealing.

That night, Kayla spooned up another sloppy joe for Leo. She sat back in her chair at the little table, pushed her own empty plate away and stretched.

Despite her sore muscles and tiredness, she had a sense of accomplishment.

Working in the kennel had been physical and sometimes hard, but she loved the sweet old dogs already. And she was relieved to know that she could do the work, that it wasn't too hard for her. Finn's directions were clear and easy to understand, and he'd left her to do her job rather than hovering over her.

After work, she'd put the new starter in her car. *Thank you, online videos*. Paying someone to fix something simple like that just wasn't in the budget.

She looked around the bare cabin. That might be her next project, making it look a little homier.

It would be a while before she found a spare hour to dig out her old camera and explore the ranch, take some shots. She was an amateur, but she enjoyed photography. Living in such a beautiful place was making her itch to capture some images.

But for today, she'd gotten the car fixed and dinner on the table and started a job, and that was enough. She'd sleep well tonight.

Leo wiped a napkin across his face and chattered on about his day at camp, his new friends and potential names for the dog. She didn't have the heart to correct him for talking with his mouth full. Fortunately, he seemed to have forgotten that Finn had said he'd bring the dog around tonight, because that didn't seem to be happening.

Or maybe he was just used to men disappointing him, as Mitch had so many times when he'd failed to pick Leo up for visits as planned.

We're free from all that now. She pushed thoughts of her ex away. Instead, she listened to her son chatter and let her shoulders relax, stretching her neck from side to side. She'd better get these dinner dishes washed before she got so sleepy she was tempted to just let it go. This cabin was way too small for that, especially since the kitchen, dining room and living room were just one connected space.

There was a knock on the door, a little scuffling.

Her shoulders tensed again.

"It's Finn, with a special visitor," came the deep voice that was already becoming familiar to her.

"The *dog!*" Leo shouted and jumped up from the table. "May I be 'scused?"

"You may." She smiled and stood up.

Leo ran to the door and flung it open. "Hi, dog!"

"She's here for you if you're ready," Finn said to Kayla, restraining the black cocker spaniel just inside the doorway. "If not, tonight can just be a visit."

Kayla laughed and rubbed Leo's back. "You think you'll be able to get her out of here again? We're as ready as we'll ever be." She knelt down, and Finn dropped the leash, and the dog walked right into her arms.

"She's so sweet!" Kayla rubbed her sides and turned a little, encouraging the dog to go to Leo, who reached out to hug her tight.

"Gentle!" Kayla laughed as the dog gave Leo a brief lick. "Let her go and we'll see what she does."

The dog started to explore, keeping her nose to the floor as she trotted around. She bumped into a kitchen chair, backed up and continued on her quest as if nothing had happened.

When she reached Leo again, she was ready to examine him. She licked his hands and face while he squealed and laughed.

Kayla laughed, too. "Leo must smell like dinner," she said and then looked up at Finn. "Would you like a plate? We have plenty of sloppy joes and corn on the cob." She flushed a little as she named the humble fare. Finn was probably used to better.

Finn looked over at the table, and for a moment something like longing flashed across his face. But it was gone so quickly that she might have imagined it. "It does smell good," he said, "but I already ate with Penny and a couple of the guys. We do meals together occasionally."

Leo rolled away from the friendly dog, and she knelt in a play bow and uttered a couple of short barks.

"She's deaf, but she still barks?" Kayla asked.

"She's not entirely deaf. And she barks when she's excited." He ruffled Leo's hair. "She's excited now. I think she likes you."

Leo looked up at Finn, eyes positively glowing.

Finn slid a backpack off and set it on the floor. "If you're sure you're ready, I'll get out her stuff."

Kayla nodded. "That's fine. I'm just going to get the dinner dishes cleaned up." She hoped Finn would pick up on the fact that she wanted Leo to be as involved as possible.

He seemed to read her mind. "Leo, I need help," Finn said. "If you can just let the dog explore for a few minutes, we'll get out her supplies."

"Supplies?" Leo's eyes widened.

Finn pulled out a food dish and large water bowl. "Now, the thing about dogs and food," he said to Leo, "is that you never want to come between them. This one's gentle, but she's been hungry before and she probably remembers it. Dogs can get a little bit mad if they think you're taking their food."

Kayla couldn't resist: she walked over and knelt to hear the lesson. The dishes could wait.

"Did you choose a new name for her?" Finn asked.

"Shoney," Leo said, looking up at Kayla. "It's the place where my dad and me liked to go for dinner."

Kayla stared blankly at her son. She hadn't realized that was why he liked the name. And wasn't it amazing that a kid could love a dad as mean and inattentive as

Mitch had been? He'd taken Leo out for a meal exactly once since the divorce.

If Finn felt those undercurrents, he ignored them. Instead he continued with the lesson, explaining the leash and the toys and the brush for the dog's hair.

Kayla's shoulders relaxed. Finn was a steady man. He'd arrived when he'd said, bringing the dog, bringing the supplies they needed. He showed Leo how to gently lead Shoney around so that she didn't get hurt running into things. He pulled out a blanket, ragged but clean, and explained that it was the blanket Shoney had been using in the kennel, and would help her feel more comfortable in a new place.

"I used to have a blanket," Leo said, "but we put it away." He hesitated, then added, "I only use it sometimes. In 'mergencies."

Finn nodded. "Makes sense."

Finn wasn't like other men she'd known, her mother's boyfriends or the teasing boys at school, or Mitch. In fact, she'd never met a man like him before.

He glanced over, and she flushed and looked away. She focused on the paneled walls, the curtainless windows, through which she could see the sun turning the tops of the mountains red, making the pasturelands golden. Crisp evening air came through the screen door, a welcome coolness for her warm face.

Leo filled the dog bowl with water and set it in the corner on a towel just as Finn had instructed, pausing often to pat Shoney. Then he returned to the backpack to check out the rest of Shoney's supplies.

"Your son's careful," Finn said approvingly.

"He's had to be." Unbidden, a memory from Leo's younger days pushed into her awareness.

Leo had just turned four, and he'd spilled a glass of juice at the table. Just a few drops had hit Mitch's phone before Kayla had swooped in with a towel, but he'd jumped up, shouted at Leo and raised his fist.

She'd intercepted the blow, but her heart still broke thinking of how Leo had tried to stifle his tears.

"Look, Mom!" His voice now was worlds away from that fearful one, and happiness bloomed inside her.

"What do you have there?" She stood and walked over to him.

"There's a scarf for her!" He held up a pink-checked neckerchief.

"Cool! See how it looks on her."

As Leo crossed the room to where Shoney had flopped down, Kayla looked over at Finn. "You dress your dogs?" she asked teasingly, lifting an eyebrow.

He shrugged and a dimple appeared in his cheek. His gaze stayed fixed on hers. "I like a girl in nice clothes."

"Oh, you do?"

They looked at each other for a moment more, until several realizations dawned on Kayla at once.

She was flirting. She *never* flirted.

She didn't have nice clothes, another fact that put Finn out of her league.

And this situation, living in close proximity to Finn here at the ranch, could get out of control all too easily.

She looked away from him, her cheeks heating.

No surprise that he turned and walked over to Leo, ensuring that their slightly romantic moment was over. "Here's a scoop for dog food," he explained while Kayla finished clearing up the dinner dishes. "She gets one scoop in the morning and one scoop in the evening."

"How can Shoney find her food, if she's blind?" Leo asked.

"Because of her super sense of smell," Finn explained, then put a piece of food on the floor near Shoney. Sure enough, the shaggy black dog found it almost immediately.

Kayla's heart melted, not in a flirty way now, but in a grateful way. As Leo experimented with having Shoney find bits of food, she walked over to Finn and knelt beside him to watch.

"He's being gentle," Finn said. "You've taught him well."

That meant the world to Kayla, for someone to say she'd done a good job. Especially on gentleness, since his male role model had been anything but. "You're really good with him yourself," she said. "Have you spent a lot of time around kids?"

All the joy drained out of Finn's face. He looked away, then rose smoothly to his feet and picked up his now-empty backpack. "You good for now?" he asked, his voice gruff.

"Um, sure. I think so." What had she said wrong?

"Then I'll leave you alone with your new family member. See you, Leo." Finn was out the door almost before Leo could offer a wave.

As she petted the dog and helped Leo get to know her, she mused over the encounter in her mind. It was when she'd mentioned kids that he'd closed off.

There was some kind of story there. And God help her, but she wanted to know it.

Five

The next morning, Kayla tried not to notice Finn's very muscular arms as he pulled the truck into a parking lot in town, just beneath the Esperanza Springs Fourth of July Community Celebration banner.

"Like I said, I'm sorry to make you work on a holiday," Finn said, in the same friendly but utterly impersonal tone he'd taken all morning. "But once we get the dogs settled, you can hang out with Leo and do whatever, until the parade starts." He was acting differently toward her, after the awkward ending to their evening last night. She'd replayed it in her mind, and she didn't think she'd said anything to offend him. Maybe he was just moody. Or maybe she was imagining his distance.

Trying to match his businesslike cordiality, she gave him a quick, impersonal smile as she climbed down from the truck and got Leo out of the back. "No problem. I think it'll be a fun day."

"Will Shoney be okay?" Leo asked. He'd been loath to leave her alone, and truthfully, Kayla had felt the same. Shoney had followed them to the door, and when

Kayla had nudged her back inside so she could close it, the dog had cried mournfully.

Finn nodded down at Leo. "Shoney's been staying in a little cage in the kennel for a few weeks. She'll be thrilled to have your whole cabin to herself for a little while."

Kayla focused on the intensely blue sky and the bright sun that illuminated the broad, flat valley, framed by the Sangre de Cristos. Even on the prettiest summer day in Arkansas, the air didn't have this refreshing crispness to it. "Come on," she said to Leo. "Let's go find Miss Penny. She said you could hang around with her while Mom works."

"Okay," he said agreeably, and Kayla sent up a prayer of thanks for Leo's accepting, nonconfrontational demeanor.

They didn't have far to look, because as soon as they'd turned toward the celebration's central area, Penny approached them. "Hey, Leo, I think they've got some good fry bread for breakfast. Have you ever had Native American food?"

Leo looked up at Kayla, puzzled.

"No, he hasn't," Kayla said to Penny, "and neither have I. But we're both in favor of bread and fried food, so I'm sure he'll love it."

"Come on, kiddo. Let's go!" And the two were off into the small line of food vendors, most still setting up, along the edge of the town park.

Kayla helped Finn lift down the crates. They'd brought five dogs, well-socialized ones who could handle the crowds and noise, healthy ones more likely to be adopted.

"We'll put them in the shade, out of the way, and let

them out one at a time to move around and get some exercise. If you can stay and do that while I park the truck, there won't be that much more to do."

So she let each dog out and strolled around, keeping them leashed but letting them greet people politely. It would be great if all five found homes today.

Suddenly, Axel, the ancient rottweiler Kayla was walking, started barking and pulling at the leash. Kayla got him under control as the other dogs chimed in, barking from their crates. She looked around to see what was causing the ruckus.

Two women walked in their direction, each with two large Alaskan malamutes on leashes. It took a minute, but Kayla recognized the taller woman as Marge from the previous day's camp drop-off.

She stood still as the pair slowly approached, keeping Axel close and smiling a greeting. And then she saw the lettering on Marge's shirt, identical to that of the other woman: Mountain Malamutes.

"We breed 'em," the other woman explained, gathering both of her leashes in one hand and leaning forward to greet Kayla. "I'm Rosa. We're teaming up with you and Finn today to try and get your guys adopted."

"Great, but how?" Kayla was struggling to keep Axel from pulling her off her feet and to speak above the noise of the crated dogs. Meanwhile, the malamutes stood panting, tongues out, alert but quiet. "And how on earth do you get your dogs to behave so well?"

Marge laughed. "Thousands of years of breeding, for starters," she said. "They're work dogs. Plus, we train 'em hard. But Rosa and I, we feel bad about breeding dogs when there are so many rescues who need homes, so we help where we can."

A group of men in Western shirts walked by, most carrying musical instruments, and Kayla recognized Long John's shuffling gait. Willie was beside him, and the two stopped and greeted Kayla as if they'd known her for years instead of days.

"You and young Leo should come hear us play," Willie said, patting her arm.

"That you should," Long John agreed. "We're at eleven and then again at three, right over on the stage they're setting up." He waved a hand toward a flurry of activity at the center of the park.

"I will," Kayla promised, warmed by their friendliness.

As the men walked on, a little girl about Leo's size rushed over and wrapped her arms around Marge's legs. "Mommy!" she cried, sounding upset. She buried her face in Marge's leg.

Marge extracted herself, knelt and studied the little girl's upset face. "What's wrong, baby?"

"Sissy and Jim won't play with me. So I got mad and ran away from them."

Marge's eyes narrowed as she scanned the area. "I'm gonna speak my piece to those two when I find 'em." She looked up at Kayla. "Two of my older kids. They're supposed to be taking care of Brenna."

"Hi, Brenna," Kayla said, smiling at the adorable little redhead. "I think you were in camp with my son, Leo, yesterday."

"Uh-huh." Brenna sucked a finger. "We played on the swings."

"Matter of fact," Marge said, "I think I see him right over there on the playground. Want to run over and see if he wants to play?" Marge turned to Kayla. "Is that okay?"

"I'm sure it is. Let me just text Penny." She did, and the answer came back immediately: Send her over. The more, the merrier.

Brenna took off for the play area, and when she got there, she hugged Leo. And then they started climbing a multilevel wooden structure.

A volley of rapid Spanish rang out nearby, and Hector, the boy who'd played with Leo at church, ran to join Leo and Brenna.

Kayla's breath caught as gratitude swept over her. Some small towns could be clannish, but Esperanza Springs had welcomed her and Leo with open arms.

She was well on her way to falling in love with this place. The natural beauty and the distance from Arkansas were great, but more than that, she already felt like part of a community.

Moments later, Finn returned, in time to direct another truck their way. Then they all helped unload five empty dog crates on wheels, made to look like circus animal carts, but cunningly arranged with harnesses. As Finn and Rosa tested out one of the carts, hooking up a malamute and putting in Charcoal, the largest dog they'd brought from the ranch, Kayla couldn't help clapping her hands. "That's so adorable!"

Marge nodded. "Exactly the reaction we're looking for. And the next step we're hoping for is that people who get swept away with the cuteness will want to adopt the dog."

"And buy a malamute," Rosa called.

"It's a win-win." Finn adjusted the cart, and they all

watched while the malamute trotted in a circle, tail and ears high, pulling the silver-muzzled Lab mix.

"It's working. If it works for Charcoal, it'll work for all the dogs." Finn let Charcoal out of the cart and urged him back into his crate. "Kayla, if you want to take some time off, you're welcome. I'd just need a little assistance at twelve thirty, when the parade's lining up."

"Thanks, boss." She added a sassy smile, forgetting for a moment to be businesslike and keep her distance.

He lifted an eyebrow, the corners of his own mouth turning up.

Kayla forced herself to turn away. She strolled through the grounds, savoring the sights, smells and sounds of a small-town Fourth of July. She'd grown up in Little Rock, and if the city had offered such events back then, her mother hadn't known about them. She and Mitch had taken Leo to a few Fourth of July gatherings, but the kind Mitch favored involved a lot of drinking. They didn't have this wholesome feel.

"Hey." Sylvie, the pretty blonde who'd issued the coffee invite the day before, fell into step beside her. "How's it going? Having fun with our Podunk event?"

"I love it, actually," Kayla said.

"Is your son here?" Sylvie looked sideways at her.

"Yes. He's on the playground." Kayla reached up and ran her fingers along the soft, low branches of a cottonwood tree, enjoying the ambling freedom of walking through the park.

"Hey, listen," Sylvie said. "I know Finn seems like a nice guy, but you should be careful. Especially being a single mom and all."

Kayla straightened. "Why?"

Sylvie looked at her like she was dense. "Well, because no one knows anything about his history, of course!" She opened her mouth as if to say more, but a handsome cowboy waved to her. "Gotta go," she said.

Kayla's walk slowed as she approached the playground. She replayed what Sylvie had said. Was there something she didn't know about Finn? Was he a risk?

That was hard to believe. He seemed safe and trustworthy.

So did Mitch. When they'd first started dating, he'd been so attentive that Kayla had felt like she was living in a fairy tale. Roses, candlelight dinners, unexpected visits just to tell her he was thinking of her. For a girl who'd felt like a mistake all her life, all that romance had been heady stuff. Accepting his proposal had been a no-brainer. He was the only man who'd ever seemed to care.

But even during their engagement, she'd started to feel a little constricted. She'd realized his love was possessive, probably too possessive. She'd told herself it was because he loved her, that at least he wasn't running around on her or burying himself in his work.

Everything had changed when they'd had Leo. Having to share her affections had brought out the crazy in Mitch. And rather than getting used to parenting, growing into it, he'd gotten worse and worse.

She hesitated and then walked over to where Penny was sitting, checking her phone and glancing up at the kids often.

"Thanks so much for watching him," she said. "Can I ask you something?"

"Sure."

"Is there something I should know about Finn? Something that would make me or Leo at risk around him?"

Penny frowned. "Not a thing. Why do you ask?"

"This other mom, Sylvie. She said I should be careful around Finn."

"Nope. He's fine. He…" Penny hesitated. "He's had some heartache in his past. Tragedy, really. But I wouldn't say he's dangerous."

Tragedy. She'd sensed that about him.

She trusted Penny. And the truth was, she trusted Finn.

Mostly.

"Mom!" Leo ran over and hugged her. "This is fun!" He grabbed her hand and pulled her toward the wooden climbing structure. "Watch how high I can go!"

He climbed rapidly to the lookout tower, and Kayla had to force herself to smile and wave rather than climb up herself and make him come down. He was growing up, and this was a safe place. She had to let him spread his wings and fly.

Then he shouted, "Dad!"

Kayla's heart stopped. What on earth? Could Mitch be here?

Leo scrambled down to the ground and she met him there, but before she could grab him, he ran, hard, across the park's grassy area.

She ran after him, arms and legs pumping almost as fast as her heart. She caught up with him at the same moment that he reached a man in military fatigues and a maroon Airborne beret.

Not Mitch. Just the same uniform.

"You're not…" Leo looked up and then backed off of the man. "You're not Daddy." His eyes filled with tears.

"Oh, honey." Kayla's fear turned to sadness for her son. Despite all Mitch's failings as a dad, he was all Leo knew.

"So this little one is an Airborne kid, is he?" The soldier knelt. "Come on—want to try on my hat?" He put it on Leo's head.

"So cute!" Someone snapped a picture. Then another woman, who turned out to be the soldier's wife, took a photo of the soldier and Leo together.

Anxiety bloomed in Kayla's chest. She turned to the soldier's wife, trying to keep the first one in her sights. "What are the photos for?"

"Oh, do you want me to send them to you?" The woman smiled. "You must be his mom. I'm Freida."

Kayla hated to quell the friendliness, but safe was safe. "I don't like photos of my son to be out and about, actually. Would you mind deleting them?"

The woman stared. "I was only trying to be nice. I wasn't going to put them up online or anything."

"Of course. I'm sure you wouldn't. It's just… I'm sorry."

The woman clicked a couple of buttons on her phone. "There. Gone." Her voice was cool, and her meaningful glance toward her husband showed that there was going to be plenty of talk about this at the dinner table tonight.

Kayla shook off her concern, because Leo was crying. She knelt and put her arms around him. "What's wrong, honey?"

"I thought it was Daddy!"

"You miss him, don't you?"

"Yeah. When are we gonna see him?"

That was the question. "Remember how we talked about it. Daddy's not safe for us right now."

"But I miss him."

Her heart broke for a little boy whose father wasn't worthy of the name. But he'd always loom large in

Leo's thoughts, just as her own parents did. "I'm sure he misses you, too," she said. It might be true. As damaged as Mitch was, he still had to have some human feeling for his flesh and blood. Didn't he? "I have an idea. Let's make a scrapbook of pictures of you and the things we're doing. Maybe later, we can send it to him."

Leo nodded, but he was slumped as they walked back across the park.

Fortunately, the presence of the malamutes and the parade cheered him up, and he seemed to forget his sadness as he watched the parade and helped with the dogs. Then they ate their fill of hot dogs and baked beans and potato chips.

Finn approached just as they were scooping up the last of their brownies and ice cream. "Looks good," he said.

"Sit down and join us?" she invited before thinking better of it.

"I'd like to, but I'd better not. Listen, Willie's driving the truck back with the dogs. Long John, too. Dogs don't do so well with fireworks. In fact, a lot of our guys, Willie included, don't like them, either."

"Fireworks?" Leo's eyes widened. "Daddy loved those!"

"Why wouldn't the guys…? Oh," she said as realization dawned.

"Right. The loud noises and flashing lights remind them of…" He hesitated and looked at Leo. "Of some bad things in their pasts."

She smiled to show her appreciation of his tact. He wanted to protect Leo from harsh realities, just like she did. It was breathtakingly different from being with

Mitch. And whatever Sylvie said, Kayla felt that Finn was basically a good guy.

"I want to stay for the fireworks, Mom. I miss Daddy."

She bit her lip. What would be the harm in staying?

"I'm meeting with some of my fellow Airborne Rangers," Finn said. "I'll drive back probably around eleven."

Right. She had to remember, and keep remembering, that Finn was loyal to his own kind. Not to her.

Also, she didn't need for Leo to be getting more memories of Mitch, becoming more unhappy and discontent. "I think we'll go ahead and leave with Willie," she decided.

"No!" Leo jumped up and kicked the picnic table, hard. "Ow!" he cried, obviously feeling the blow through his thin sneakers, the word ending in a wail as he plopped down on the ground to hold his foot. "I wanna stay for fireworks! Daddy would let me!"

She blew out a sigh. This day, that had started out so nicely, was going rapidly downhill. And she didn't know if she was making the right decisions. Didn't know if she was keeping him safer or sending him to the psychiatrist's couch. That was the problem of being a single parent: there was no one to consult with.

She dearly longed to consult with Finn, who was watching sympathetically as she patted Leo's shoulder and studied his foot to make sure he hadn't really hurt himself.

But she had to remember that Finn wasn't someone she should get close to, because his loyalty would inevitably be toward his military brothers, not a civilian woman and child.

Sighing, she turned her back on Leo and walked a few steps away, denying him the attention he was seeking.

Finn nodded once and left the scene, too. He understood that much, at least, and she was grateful.

Leo's crying turned to hiccups and then stopped, and she turned back to him and held out a hand. "Come on. Let's go get in the car with the dogs and Mr. Willie. We'll see how Shoney's doing and take her for a walk." As she'd hoped, the idea of their new dog distracted Leo.

As for Kayla, she wished for all the world that she could stay and simply enjoy the warmth and fun of a small-town holiday.

The next Saturday, Finn came outside and was surprised to see Kayla laughing, standing close to a tall man whose back was turned. Even with her hair in its usual messy braid, she looked beautiful.

In the yard in front of the main house, Leo played with two little girls.

His chest tightened, and he had to force himself not to clench his fists. He started toward the pair, then stopped to take a calming look at the countryside, the flat basin surrounded by white-capped mountains.

Kayla wasn't his, no way. And he had no right to feel jealous that she was spending time with someone else.

He drew in a breath and continued on down. Halfway there, he recognized the pastor.

Which didn't necessarily make him feel any better. Carson Blair was good-looking and well respected, the father of twins just a bit older than Leo. He wasn't such a hulk as Finn, so he and Kayla were better matched physically.

More than that, the pastor wasn't carrying the load of guilt Finn did. On the contrary, he was a good man, a servant of God who had every right to happiness.

All of those logical thoughts didn't stop Finn's feet from moving toward them to see what was going on.

"Hey, Finn," the pastor said, smiling. "We've had an offer of some fishing. Would you like to join us?"

"An offer from whom?" He knew he sounded grouchy. "You need to sign a waiver if your kids are visiting the ranch. Liability issues."

"Didn't even think of that." The pastor gave an easy smile. "Where do I sign?"

Kayla was looking at him, confusion on her face. "Willie invited him, and Leo, too," she said. "He said he's had his grandkids fishing at the pond here. I didn't think you'd mind."

She was wearing her typical kennel uniform, jeans and a T-shirt. As usual, it made her look like a teenager.

It also meant she wasn't dressing up for the pastor. "No problem, just covering our backs," Finn said. "The ranch can't afford a lawsuit."

Kayla gave him a look as if to say that Carson Blair was hardly going to sue them. "I'll go get the waiver. Isn't Penny in the office?"

"Good idea."

That left him standing alone with Carson. "How are the girls?" he asked, just to avoid an awkward silence and the pastor's know-too-much eyes.

"They're doing pretty well. Life's a scramble, though. It sounded nice to come up here and relax for a little while. Get out some of their energy."

Leo chose that moment to glance over. He'd been shouting, but when he saw Finn, he lowered his voice.

Just the effect he wished he didn't have on kids. Although it *was* a useful reminder. Kids might not know exactly *why* he was scary, but they were right to be scared. He wasn't safe to be around.

Kayla came back, forking fingers through her hair with one hand while holding out the waiver with the other. In the past week, her bruises had faded to the point where she let her arms show. Finn could still see them, though. It reminded him that she'd been through a lot and didn't need him adding to her problems.

After the pastor had signed the waiver and run it back inside, they all headed down toward the pond where Willie was waiting, several fishing rods in hand.

"Okay, kids," Willie said, clearly in his element. "I'm going to give you each a fishing pole and show you how to bait it."

"With *worms*?" Carson's daughter—Skye, maybe?— stared into a Styrofoam container, horrified fascination on her face. The other twin and Leo peeked in, too, and a lively discussion broke out, amiably moderated by Willie.

Finn strolled away from the group. Just the smell of the lake, the fresh air, the smile on the old man's face, helped him get some perspective.

He was still raw from losing his wife and child, and probably always would be. What he wasn't used to was developing any kind of feelings for another woman and child. This was the first time his heart had come out of hibernation.

There were bound to be some missteps, some difficulties. He'd made the decision not to get involved again, but it had never been tested before. So this was a new learning experience.

Behind him there was a shout. A splash.

Finn spun and saw Leo struggling and gasping in the

reeds at the lake's edge. Kayla was a few steps farther away, but she ran toward Leo, the pastor right behind her.

Finn got there first, tromped into the mud and reeds, yanking his feet out of the sucking mud with each step. "I'm coming, buddy," he called, keeping his voice calm. "I've got you."

Everyone on the shore was shouting, the two little girls were screaming, but he blocked it all out and focused on Leo. He got his hands around the boy's torso and lifted, and was rewarded with a punch in the face.

He shook it off like you'd shake off a buzzing bee, ignored the boy's flailing and carried him toward shore. Once Leo realized he was safe, he started to cry in earnest and clung to Finn.

The feeling of a little boy in his arms, the relief of saving him, of not losing another kid on his watch, overwhelmed Finn and he hugged Leo right back. Then he put the boy into Kayla's arms.

She sank to the ground, holding and cuddling Leo. "You're okay, you're okay," she said, stroking his hair, using the edge of her sleeve to wipe mud and tears from his face.

He was okay. Praise God.

Kayla looked up at Finn. "Thank you."

He shook his head. "I should have been clear about the safety rules." He'd thought Willie was in charge of the trip and would have told them to stay away from that soggy edge, but apparently not, and he shouldn't rely on someone else. When would he learn that it was his responsibility to keep kids safe?

"That's not a way to end a fishing trip," Willie said. "Let's take a lunch break. The two of you can grab some clean clothes and come back."

"I'll dry right off in the sun," Finn said. "Leo can change if he wants, and then I'd like to see if I could help him catch a fish."

For whatever reason, the boy was afraid of him, and for whatever reason, Finn seemed to want to stop that. So be it. It didn't have to mean anything.

"I'll dry off here, too," Leo said, straightening up and stepping away from Kayla. Trying to be a little man. Finn's throat tightened.

He was hunting around for a bobber in Willie's fishing box when he noticed a small laminated photo. "Who's this?" he asked.

Willie looked at the photo and shook his head. "My granddaughter who died."

Finn stared at the little blonde, obscured by cracked and yellowing laminate. "I didn't know. I'm sorry."

Willie shrugged. "I don't talk about it much, but there's not a day I don't think of her." He sighed. "You get used to it. Not over it, but used to it."

"I haven't."

Willie nodded. "It takes time."

Finn looked at the older man, always upbeat, always quick with a helping hand or a joke to cheer up other people. It was a good reminder: Finn wasn't the only person in the world who'd suffered a loss.

After they'd fished and each of the children had caught at least one, Kayla offered to take the kids to her cabin to get them cleaned up and give them a snack. "And you can meet our new dog," she said to the twins, earning squeals of delight.

Leo and the pastor's twins were getting to be friends. That meant that Kayla and Carson would become friends, too; that was how it went when you were the parents of young children.

It made sense. But he didn't have to like it.

He didn't like the way the departing kids' laughter woke up his memories, either. Derek would have loved to fish and play with dogs. But thanks to Finn's own carelessness, he'd never get to do it.

Finn didn't deserve the kind of happiness that came to good people like the pastor and Kayla.

He roused himself from his reverie and started gathering the remaining gear to take back to his cabin. His leg ached, and he stopped to rub it.

"You're hurting today." Carson Blair knelt and picked up a few loose pieces of fishing gear.

"Yeah." Finn straightened. "Thought you'd be going up to Kayla's with your girls."

"She and Willie said they can handle them for a bit," Carson said. "I'll help you carry stuff up to the main house. It'll give me the chance to talk to you."

He was going to speak to Finn about Kayla. "No need," he said. "I'm fine."

"Are you sure about that?"

The man was annoying. "Yes, I'm sure."

"Well, I'm not," Carson said. "You've got some kind of issue with me, and I'd like to know what it is. I think we could work together, make good things happen, at church and in town and at this ranch, but not if you're mad about something I don't even understand."

The words burst out before Finn could stop them. "You need to leave my employees alone."

Carson raised an eyebrow. "Is that what Kayla is to you? An employee?"

"Yes, and she's got a job to do here. She doesn't need any distractions."

"Funny, she told me she was off today."

"You calling me out?" Finn's fists clenched.

Carson raised a hand like a stop sign. "I'm not calling you out. I'm a pastor. It's sort of against the rules." A slight smile quirked his face. "Besides which, I know my limits. I couldn't take you." He turned and started walking. "Come on. I'll help you carry this stuff up."

Finn hesitated and then fell into step beside the man. The momentary break gave him time to think. He didn't have any right to Kayla, and there was no good reason for him to be throwing his weight around, setting limits.

"Sorry," he said as he fell into step beside the pastor. "Didn't mean to act like a thug."

Carson chuckled. "You're hardly that." He paused. "But…if I might make a suggestion, have you considered talking to someone about your grief issues?"

Finn's ire rose again. "I've got my issues under control."

"Do you?" The pastor's question was mild, but his face showed skepticism. "You seem a little quick to anger. A lot of times, that's about something other than the issue at hand. Although," he added, "I can see why you'd be defensive of Kayla. She's a lovely woman."

Finn glowered.

"And I'm interested in a purely pastoral sense. I don't have time for anything more. But you—" he turned and faced Finn down "—you need to get yourself straight with God before you have anything to offer a good woman like Kayla."

Finn schooled his face for a sermon. And closed his mind against the tiny ray of hope that wanted in. Because getting himself straight with God wasn't going to happen, no matter what a flowers-and-sunshine pastor had to say.

On Monday morning, Kayla took her time strolling toward the kennel for her morning shift.

Magpies chattered and barn swallows skimmed the fields, low and graceful in the still-cool morning air. She lifted her face and sent up a prayer of thanks.

Leo had gone eagerly to camp this morning, none the worse for his tumble into the pond two days before. Just the memory of it sent a shudder through Kayla, but it was rapidly followed by more gratitude, this time for Finn.

He'd been instantly alert and had rescued Leo almost before Kayla had realized the gravity of the situation. Willie and Pastor Carson had rushed in to provide sympathy and comfort.

Having all that support had melted Kayla. She'd been raising Leo virtually alone since his birth. Mitch hadn't been a partner, but a threat to be wary about. And he'd cut her off from most of her old friends.

Kayla was independent; she'd had to be, growing up with her parents.

The sudden, warm feeling she'd gotten, that she and Leo were part of a caring community—that was something she treasured, something she felt a timid wish to build. She'd made a start yesterday at church, introducing herself to more people and signing up for a women's book discussion later in July.

She felt the urge to build something with Finn, too, but she wasn't willing to explore that. Neither, from the looks of things, was he.

He did give her a friendly wave when she walked into

the kennel. "I'm putting the dogs from the first row out into the run. I'll supervise 'em if you clean?"

"Sure." She smiled at him. It was nice he'd phrased it as a question, when in reality he was the boss and could call the shots.

She started removing toys and beds and dishes from the kennels in preparation for hosing them down. The cleaning protocol they'd set up helped prevent disease, and it also made for a nice environment for the animals. For many, it was the best place they'd ever lived.

She opened the door to the last kennel on the end and saw something dark on the floor. Blood.

"Finn!" She left everything where it was and headed to the doorway. "I think that new dog, Winter, is sick." She scanned the field and located the big female, sitting watchful, away from the other dogs.

"What's going on?" Finn had been kneeling beside Axel, but now he stood and came over. "Is she acting different?"

"Take a look at her kennel. I'll watch the dogs."

He went inside and she knelt and called to Winter. She'd been dropped off the previous day by a couple of guys, neighbors of her owner. They'd rescued her from what they said was an abusive situation, but Finn, who'd talked with them, hadn't offered up any more details.

The dog looked over, ears hanging long, cloudy eyes mournful.

"Come here, girl," Kayla encouraged and felt in her pocket for a treat. She checked to make sure no aggressive dogs were nearby and then held it out to Winter.

The dog came closer, walking with a hunched, halting gait, but stopped short and cringed back as Finn emerged from the kennel. He held up his phone. "That was blood.

I called the vet," he said. "Her new-dog appointment was supposed to be today, but he had to cancel. He says he can come out but he has to bring his baby boy."

She nodded, still watching the wary dog. "What do you think is wrong with Winter?"

Finn shook his head slowly, his mouth twisting. "The story is that she had a litter of stillborn pups. The owner got mad and started beating her."

Kayla gasped. "Who *does* that?" Sudden tears blurred her vision. The dog was beautiful, one of God's innocent creatures. That someone would feel he had the right to abuse her…

"The guys who dropped her off say they're going to call him up on animal abuse charges. But they wanted to make sure she was safe first." He studied the dog. "I'll step away. She's probably afraid of men, and for good reason. Maybe you can get her to come over."

It took continued encouragement and the tossing of several treats before the dog got close enough for Kayla to touch her.

"Be careful," Finn said quietly from his position on the other side of the dog run. "She's been treated badly. She may bite."

Kayla clicked her tongue and held out another treat, then carefully reached out to rub the dog's chest. Winter let out a low whine.

"Here, baby. Have a snack." She waved the remaining treat, gently.

The dog grabbed it from her hand and retreated to a safe distance to eat.

"You stay out here with her," Finn said. "I'll get the rest of the kennels clean and then bring the other dogs in. I worry about contagion. No telling what she's picked up."

So Kayla sat in the sun, sweet-talking the old dog. After Finn took the other dogs in, as the day warmed up, Winter approached close enough that Kayla could scratch her ears.

She patted the ground. "Go ahead—relax. Just rest."

But the dog remained alert, jumping up when a chipmunk raced past, then sinking back down on her haunches, head on front paws, eyes wary.

Kayla knew how *that* felt. "It's hard to relax when you're worried for your safety, isn't it?" she crooned. "It's all right. We'll protect you here."

What was true for the dog might be true for Kayla, too. Sometimes, during the past week, she'd felt her habitual high-alert state ebb away. Even now, the hot sun melted tension from her shoulders.

After half an hour, she heard a vehicle approach and a door slam. Soon Finn appeared with a jeans-clad man he introduced as Dr. DeMoise.

"Call me Jack," the tall vet said easily, shifting a wide-eyed baby from one shoulder to the other so he could shake her hand.

"Your son's beautiful," Kayla said. Without her willing it, her arms reached for the baby boy. "Do you think he'll let me hold him?"

"Most likely." The vet smiled his thanks. "He's not real clingy yet."

She lifted the baby from his arms. The child—probably about six months old—stared at her with wide eyes and started to fuss a little. Kayla walked and hummed and clucked to him. Comforting a baby must be like riding a bike: it came back easily. Leo had been colicky, and she'd spent a lot of time soothing him.

Now, holding the vet's baby close and settling him,

longing bloomed inside her. She hadn't let herself think about having another baby, not when she was with Mitch, and not in the difficult year after getting divorced, when she'd been struggling to start a business and fend him off. Now desire for another little one took her breath away.

Forget about it, she ordered herself.

But with Leo growing up so fast…

The baby stiffened and let out a fussy cry, probably sensing her inner conflict. She breathed in and out slowly and walked him around the field.

Once she'd gotten the baby calmed down, she watched as Jack squatted near the dog, who seemed to be in increasing distress. Finn leaned against the fence several feet away, watching.

"I'm wondering if she's got another pup," the vet said finally. "You said her litter was stillborn?"

"And her owner beat her right after she gave birth."

The vet grimaced. "I'm going to need to take her in, but let's see what she's trying to do now, first. Couple of clean towels?"

Finn went inside and the doctor examined the dog and pressed her abdomen gently.

Kayla walked over, swaying gently with the baby. "Is she going to be okay?"

The vet frowned. "I hope so. It's good you called."

"Could she have another live pup?"

"No. Not after almost a day, not likely." He rubbed the dog's ears, gently. "But we'll do our best to take care of Mama, here. She doesn't deserve what happened to her."

"Nobody does." Kayla leaned closer and saw a couple of wounds on the dog's back and leg.

Finn handed the towels to the doctor and then came

over to stand by Kayla. He smiled at Jack's baby, reached out and tickled his leg, and the baby allowed it.

"This one's not afraid of you. Lots of babies are scared of men. At least..." At least, they'd been afraid of Mitch.

"Sammy's been raised by his dad for the last six months," Finn explained as they both watched the vet work with Winter. "He and his wife adopted him, but she passed away, so now he's a single dad."

"Awww." She swayed with the baby to keep him calm.

"Jack is the only vet within thirty miles, so he has a busy practice. When his wife died and he had to care for Sammy full-time... It's been rough."

"Day care?"

"He's got a part-time nanny, but apparently, she's not working out."

The vet rose and walked over to them. "I'll drive my van to the gate so we can get her into the clinic. If one of you wants to come along..."

"I can," Kayla said instantly. "I can take care of Sammy and help with the dog."

"No." Finn frowned. "I'll go."

"But—" She didn't want to let the baby out of her arms.

"I need you to finish up here," he said abruptly.

Jack gave them both a quizzical look. "Whatever you two decide. I'll be right back with the van. Just make sure the dog stays still."

After he'd left, Kayla spoke up. "I just thought, since I've got the baby calmed down—"

"I don't want you going into town with Jack. People will make something of it." His face was set.

Kayla pressed her lips together. It was almost as if Finn felt possessive of her. Which didn't make any sense.

But it *did* feel familiar, and scarily so. Mitch had started out just a little possessive, but that had expanded until he got outraged if she had a conversation with a male cashier or said "thank you" to a guy holding open a door for her.

Finn's attitude was probably about something else. There was no reason a man like Finn should have any feelings at all about her, possessive or otherwise.

But she needed to be careful, and stay alert, and not get too involved. Just in case Finn bore any similarity to Mitch.

Six

That Friday evening, Finn turned his truck into the road
that led to Redemption Ranch with mixed feelings—
mixed enough that he pulled over, telling himself he
needed to check on Winter and her new foster puppy,
crated in the back.

Truth was, he wanted to get his head together before
he got back to the ranch.

The trip to pick up Winter from the vet clinic had
been a welcome opportunity to escape from a work environment that had him in close proximity to Kayla for
much of the day.

He opened the back of the pickup and checked on the
two dogs. Winter lay still, but with her head upright and
alert. The young pup beside her had been a surprise, but
so right that Finn had quickly agreed to take both back
to the ranch.

He took his time adjusting the crates and rubbing
Winter's head through the side bars, aware that he was
just procrastinating on returning to the ranch and Kayla.
He wanted to stay uninvolved, but he couldn't seem to

pull it off. When he'd seen Kayla holding that baby earlier in the week, he'd gotten gushy, romantic, old-movie feelings, until memories crashed in and washed them away in a sea of cold guilt. And then, just to top off his own ridiculousness, he'd gone caveman on her, refusing to allow her to go help Jack. Which was just plain stupid. Jack was single, and eligible, and deserving of happiness, and why *wouldn't* he like Kayla, especially when she'd shown such tenderness toward his son?

But before he'd had the sense to think that through, he'd gotten in Jack's face, insisting that Kayla couldn't go into town with Winter, that he, Finn, had to be the one to go himself.

What was wrong with Finn, that he was acting like a Neanderthal around this woman whose personal life was absolutely none of his business?

Possessive stuff. No matter what his brain said, his emotions wanted to mark her as his.

It was almost like he wanted to be a husband and father again.

Finn pushed the thoughts away by turning up the country music louder. And then was rewarded with songs about hurting love. He released a huff and started the truck again.

He pulled up toward the kennel and tried not to look to the right, at Kayla's place. But there were Penny and Willie, carrying a table from the next cabin down the road and into the yard in front of Kayla's porch. He rolled down a window to see what was going on, and the smell of grilling meat sent his stomach rumbling.

"Come on—join in," Willie called, beckoning with his free arm.

What could he do but pull over and stop the truck?

The cessation of movement started Winter barking, so he had to get her out of the crate. And then the pup cried, so he had to be brought out, too.

And that brought everyone running over to see.

Finn knelt beside Winter and the fragile pup, trying to help them get their bearings. Trying to get his own, as well.

Leo shouted and reached out, and the puppy cringed.

"Careful!" Finn said.

Only when Leo shrank back did Finn realize he'd boomed out the word too loudly.

"You left with one and came back with two?" Penny asked, kneeling to see the dogs and, not coincidentally, putting herself at Leo's height. She put a hand on the kid's shoulder. "That's not her pup, is it?"

"It is now." Finn couldn't help but smile as the puppy yapped up at Winter and she gave him a chastening slurp of her tongue, knocking him into his place. Quickly, he explained how the unlikely pairing had come to pass.

Willie was setting up horseshoes, and Long John sat in a chair, shucking corn. "Looks like a party," Finn said, loud enough for the two older veterans to hear.

"Cooking out. It's Friday." Willlie grinned. "Not that I've worked that hard all week, but habit is habit."

"Do you need a blanket for the dogs to rest on?" It was Kayla's husky voice, and when he turned toward her, he saw that she already had one in hand. Of course, she'd seen the need and filled it, quietly and efficiently. That was who she was.

They settled the dogs off to the side of the picnic table. "Why is there a pup, Mom?" Leo asked, pressing against Kayla's side. "You said she had babies that died."

"I don't know. Ask Mr. Gallagher."

But Leo pressed his lips together and stayed tight by Kayla's side.

Great. Finn had managed to spook the poor kid. "Winter wasn't feeling well after her puppies didn't make it," he said, simplifying and cleaning it up for young ears. "And Dr. Jack had a pup at the clinic who didn't have a mom."

"The Good Lord has a way of working things out," Willie said. "Joy out of sorrow." He gave Finn a meaningful look.

Finn's jaw tightened, because he knew what Willie was thinking. That Finn was supposed to find some kind of redemption out of the loss he'd faced.

It wasn't happening. Not now, not ever.

"This corn's ready to throw on the grill," Long John called.

"Chicken's almost done," Penny said.

"Ooh, I've got to check on my apple cobbler." Kayla hurried inside.

Willie came over to where Finn stood. "You as hungry as I am?"

Finn noticed Leo watching them. On an impulse, he clutched his hands across his abdomen and fake-fell to the ground. "Starving!" he groaned.

Willie laughed and nudged Finn with his boot. "Get up, boy. Them that don't work, don't eat."

Finn jumped to his feet. By now, Leo was smiling, just a little. "I'll do anything," Finn said, "for apple cobbler."

"Then get inside and help her carry out the dishes, and make it snappy." Willie rolled his eyes at Leo. "Think I'll ever be able to make this big lug behave?"

Leo laughed outright. "He's a grown-up! He doesn't have to behave."

"That's where you're wrong," Willie said. "Grown-ups have to behave even better than kids. Right, Finn?"

"I'm going, I'm going." He glanced over at Leo, who was still smiling. "Keep an eye on those dogs for me, will you?"

"Yeah!" Leo hurried in their direction. Finn waited just long enough to see that the boy knelt carefully, not getting too close.

"I'll keep an eye, too," Willie murmured to Finn. "Now, I'm serious. If you want dinner, you'd better help the lady get it on the table."

Finn reached Kayla's small kitchen just in time to see her lift the cobbler out of the oven. Her cheeks were pink and her eyes bright, and he wondered how he'd ever thought her plain.

She met his eyes, and it seemed to him her color heightened. "I... Dinner's almost ready. I hope you'll join us."

"I'd like to." His playful mood from trying to jolly Leo up lingered, and he assumed a hangdog look. "But Willie told me I can't unless I do my share of the work. Give me a job?"

She chuckled, and the sound ran along his nerve endings. "There's never a shortage. You can carry out the plates and silverware. Then come back, and I'll have more for you to do."

"Yes, ma'am." He inhaled. "That smells fantastic."

"I have some talents."

"I can see that."

Their eyes locked for a moment, and Finn was sure he detected some sort of interest, not just casual, in hers.

His own chest almost hurt with wanting to get closer to this woman. And he could barely remember why he'd thought that was a bad idea.

She turned away from him, laughing a little. "Go on. Get to work."

So he carried out the flatware and plates, and then went back for several more loads. Penny called him into action to help at the grill, and then Willie remembered there was a fresh pitcher of lemonade down at his cabin. Long John offered to get it, going so far as to stand up, but Finn waved off the offer and walked down to get it. Limp or no, he was still more able-bodied than Long John.

It felt like a party, but more than that, it felt like family. And Finn, whose relatives all lived back East, hadn't had that sense in years.

Two years, to be specific. Since Deirdre and Derek had died.

But for the first time in a long time, that thought didn't send him into darkness. He set it aside, because he wanted to focus on the here and now, just for a little bit longer.

So they ate their fill of grilled chicken and corn on the cob, Long John's famous coleslaw, and potato salad Penny had picked up from the deli in town. She'd gotten ice cream, too, so when the main meal was over, there was that for the cobbler.

The dogs, Winter and the new pup as well as Shoney, went up and down the long table, begging. Finn couldn't be sure, but he suspected that all the dogs had gotten a few scraps. Himself, he'd concentrated on sneaking food to Shoney, who couldn't see the many crumbs and pieces that dropped to the ground.

Finally, they'd all eaten their fill, and more. Leo asked to be excused and was soon rolling on the ground with the dogs. Penny started clearing dishes. When Finn stood to help, she waved him away. "Take it easy for a bit," she said. "The kitchen's only big enough for one. You, too, Kayla. Sit back and relax."

"No, I'll wash and you can dry," Kayla compromised.

"Seems to me," Willie said, his eyes twinkling, "that a boy of Leo's age might like to play a little Frisbee or catch. But my old bones ache too much to do a game justice." He looked at Finn. "How about you?"

Finn hadn't missed how Leo's eyes lit up. "It'd be good to work off some of this fine food," he said and glanced up at Kayla. "Okay with you?"

"Of course, if he wants to." She turned toward Leo and then shrugged. "Just ask him."

It was tacit permission for Finn to form his own relationship with Leo. And while he knew it wasn't a good idea long-term, some lazy, relaxed, happy part of himself couldn't worry about that just now.

"Think I've got a couple of mitts and a softball down in my storage cupboard," Willie said and started to get up.

"I'll get it if you tell me where." This time, Finn took his cane, wanting to save his leg for the actual game of catch.

And that was how Finn ended up teaching Leo how to throw like a pitcher and how to hold his mitt, while Willie and Long John relaxed in lawn chairs and offered advice.

It felt like an unexpected blessing. Leo, who seemed at times timid as a mouse, was smiling and laughing and, to all appearances, enjoying himself enough that he didn't seem to want to stop.

Out here, tossing a softball back and forth as the sun sank behind the Sangre de Cristos, it was easy for Finn to focus on what was good in his life. This work that benefited other creatures, both human and canine, in a concrete way. This place, with its open spaces and views of the jagged mountain range that seemed to point the way directly to heaven. These people, who'd struggled enough in their lives to understand others rather than judge them.

Back in Virginia, after everything had gone so terribly wrong, he'd sunk too deep into himself, to where he could only see what was bad and wrong inside him. It was the kind of shame and guilt that threatened to make you want to do away with yourself, and although it would have been deserved, and he'd come close, some faint inner light had told him it was wrong. He'd dragged himself to church and talked to the pastor, older than Finn and wiser, about getting a fresh start. He was suffocating in Virginia, and all he'd felt the smallest shred of desire for was the open spaces of the West, where he'd sometimes traveled for work. Next thing, the pastor had been calling his old high school friend, Penny. The job had fallen into place so neatly that Finn, who didn't normally put much stock in God reaching down from the sky and fixing things, felt there'd been some of that going on.

Maybe Kayla and Leo's arrival had been a God thing, too.

Finally, he felt the chill in the darkening air and realized that Leo was yawning, and wondered aloud whether it was time to go inside.

"Not when there's a fire to be built." Willie got up and dragged an old fire-pit bowl from the back of the house. "Hey, Leo, can you give me a hand picking up sticks?"

"And I'll get the logs," Finn said with a mock sigh.

As they taught Leo how to build a fire—with appropriate safety warnings—Finn had a reluctant realization.

He hadn't wanted to get involved with people, especially women and kids. He'd come to Redemption Ranch to focus on making retribution, giving something back to a world from which he'd taken so much away. To lose himself amid the mountains that made even a hulk like him feel small. Not to grow close to a pair of souls who tugged at him, made his heart want to come alive again.

But want to or not, it had happened.

Kayla washed the last dish and handed it to Penny, then let the water out of the sink. "Thanks for helping," she said. "We got done in half the time."

"Yes, we did." Penny hung the pan on the overhead hook.

"No thanks to you," she scolded Shoney, who'd been roaming the kitchen and generally getting underfoot, looking for dropped food and occasionally finding it. Kayla dried her hands, knelt to rub the dog's shaggy head, and then stood and headed for the door. "I'd better go see how Leo's doing."

"He's doing fine." Penny put a hand on Kayla's arm, stopping her. "I can see him out the window. He's with Willie and Finn."

"And he's not acting scared of Finn?"

"Come see." Penny gestured out the window.

Kayla looked and sucked in a breath.

In the background, the setting sun made rosy fire on

the mountains. Swallows skimmed and swooped, catching insects for an evening snack, chirring and squeaking their pleasure. The dogs sprawled on the blanket she'd brought out, the new puppy spooned in close to Winter.

And there was Leo, laughing up at something Willie had said, while Finn looked on fondly.

They weren't related by blood, but they were interacting like three generations. It was what she'd always wanted for Leo.

"Does he have a grandpa?" Penny asked.

Kayla shook her head. "His father's parents have both passed, and my dad…"

Penny was wiping off the counter, but at Kayla's pause she stopped and looked at her.

"My dad's in prison for life." She said it all in a rush, as she did every time she had to discuss her dad with anyone. Then she knelt and pulled Shoney against her, rubbing the shaggy head.

"That's rough." Penny leaned back against the counter, her face sympathetic rather than judgmental. "Did that happen when you were a kid, or later?"

"When I was twelve." She'd remember the day forever, even though she'd tried to push it out of her mind. Coming home from school to police cars every which way in the front yard. The neighbors whispering and gawking. And then her father, coming out of the house, swearing and fighting the two officers who were trying to control him.

It had been another couple of years before she'd gotten her mother to tell her the charge. "He shot a convenience-store clerk," she said now to Penny. "A robbery gone bad. Drugs." She looked at the floor. "The man he killed was the father of three kids. And he disabled a police officer trying to escape."

"Oh, honey." Penny held out her arms, and when Kayla didn't stand to walk into them, she came right over and wrapped her arms around Kayla and Shoney both. "That must have been so hard."

Kayla felt a little pressure behind her eyes, but she had no intention of crying. She cleared her throat and took a step back. "It *was* hard. Kids can be cruel."

"Did you have brothers and sisters?"

"Nope. Just me. I was a mistake."

Penny stared and slowly began shaking her head back and forth. "Oh, no. No, you weren't. God doesn't make mistakes."

Kayla waved a hand. "I know. I know. It's fine. It's just…that's how my parents looked at it, is all."

"You ever talk to anyone about that?" Penny asked.

Kayla's eyebrows came together. "I'm talking to you."

"I mean a therapist."

"No. No way." Her dad's issues, and her mom's problems after the arrest, were part of a big box of heartache she didn't want to open.

"So your parents had issues, let you know they hadn't planned to have you." Penny lifted an eyebrow. "How old were you when you married the abuser?"

Kayla's jaw about dropped. "What? What does that have to do with my folks?"

Penny took the dish towel from Kayla's hands, folded it once and hung it on the stove handle. "I just think it's interesting that you chose a man who didn't value you properly, after being with parents who maybe did the same. Patterns." Penny looked out the window. "We repeat patterns."

The older woman's words hit too close to home. After her father had gone to prison, Kayla had tried to stay close to her mother, as close as the multiple boyfriends and stepfathers would permit. But when her mom had been killed in a drinking-related car accident…yeah. Kayla had connected with Mitch almost immediately, drawn to his self-assurance and dominant personality.

Kayla didn't want to think about what that all might mean, psychologically. Instead, she turned the tables. "Are you speaking from experience?"

"Touché," Penny said. "I sure am. And one day, you and I can sit down and talk about it, maybe. All I know is, I'm not quick to put my trust in any man. But it's important to trust someone. I want you to know you can trust me."

"Why?" Kayla asked bluntly. She didn't understand why Penny was being intrusive, and she *really* didn't understand why she was being kind.

"I've watched how you interact with your son for a couple of weeks now. You're a good mom." Penny smiled at her. "And more relevant to me, you're a good worker. I'd like to keep you around."

A sudden thickness settled in Kayla's throat. "Thanks."

"And when I said what I did about men, I wasn't talking about Finn. He's one of the good ones. So are Long John and Willie, for that matter."

Kayla nodded but didn't speak. Penny might think these men were good, and trustworthy, and probably on some level they were. But on the flip side, they were military men and loyal to their band of brothers.

Men like Mitch.

"We're done in here," she said instead of answering. "Want to go outside by the fire?"

"For a bit, sure." Penny's eyes were hooded, and Kayla was suddenly sorry she hadn't pursued Penny's remarks about men. She got the feeling that the older woman had a story that was plenty interesting, not to mention a few issues of her own.

She led the way, but when she got to where she could see the fire, she stopped. Penny almost ran into her.

Willie was playing guitar, softly, and Long John picked harmony on his banjo. The fire burned low, sending the warm, friendly smell of wood smoke in their direction.

And Leo was sleeping in Finn's arms.

Kayla drew in a deep breath and let it out slowly. There was something about a man who was good with kids. Something about a man big enough to hold a five-year-old boy with no problem, and confident enough in his masculinity to be nurturing.

Penny walked past and perched on a log beside Willie. They spoke for a moment, low, and then Willie launched into another song, a love song Kayla remembered from when she was a kid.

Penny stared into the fire, a remote expression on her face.

Kayla walked over to Finn's side. "Are you okay holding him?" she asked. "He can get heavy."

"It's not a problem." But his face was serious, his eyes a little…sad? Troubled?

So they all sat around for a little while longer, huddling in the warmth of the fire. A circle of humans in the light of the moon, seeking warmth, needing each other.

In the distance, there was a howl.

"What's that?" she asked.

"Coyote," Long John said. "Keep the dogs and the boy near home tonight."

Kayla shivered and scooted her log a little closer to the fire's warmth.

She looked around at the faces, old and young. She'd gotten almost close to these people in the past two weeks, and she never got close. She liked being here, liked being with them.

She especially liked being with Finn, if she were honest with herself. They'd fallen into an easy routine, working together in the kennels, sharing information about the dogs and the weather and the ranch. They laughed at the same jokes on the country-music station, liked the same songs. Both of them usually carried a book around for slow moments, and he'd turned her on to Louis L'Amour.

All the connections were something to enjoy, but also something to be cautious about. She'd liked being around Mitch and his friends at first, too.

Of course, looking back at it, she couldn't miss the warning signs. Why had she chosen Mitch?

There was the obvious fact that no one else had wanted her. And that she'd wanted to have a baby like nobody's business. Still, she should have had more sense.

Unless Penny was right, and it had to do with her parents, her childhood.

Willie played a last riff on his guitar and then looked over at Long John, who'd fallen silent. "That's it for me," he said. "These old bones are ready for bed, early as it is."

"It's not early when you get up for chores." Penny arched her back and stretched.

Both of the older men watched her, identical longing expressions on each weathered face.

Oh. So it was that way. And yet the two were best of friends, and Penny seemed oblivious to the way they'd been looking at her.

As they put their instruments away, Penny stood. "Thanks, everyone. See you tomorrow."

Willie cleared his throat. "Walk you home?"

Penny paused a beat. "No. Thanks, but I'm fine." She turned and headed for the road at a good clip.

"Can't blame a guy for trying," Willie muttered.

Long John gave him a look. "She's the same age as your daughter." He started to heave himself up out of his chair, then sank back with a sigh.

Willie held out a hand, and Long John hesitated, then grasped it and got to his feet. Willie picked up both musical instruments, and the two of them headed back toward their cabins.

That left Kayla alone with Finn, who still held the sleeping Leo in his arms. "I...I'll put out the fire." She felt absurdly uncomfortable.

He nodded. His face was hard to read. Was he enjoying holding Leo or was it a burden for him?

His face suggested something else entirely, but she wasn't sure what.

Finn watched as Kayla hauled a bucket of water to the metal fire pit. She was tiny, but she lifted the heavy bucket easily and poured it on.

That was Kayla—however vulnerable she appeared on the outside, there was solid strength hidden beneath.

She straightened and put her hands to the small of

her back. "I should probably bring another bucket of water, right?"

"Just to be sure. I'm sorry I can't help you."

"You're helping, believe me." She gave her sleeping child a tender glance before taking the bucket back over to the outside spigot.

Finn felt the weight of the five-year-old boy against him as if it were lead. Pressing him down into the lawn chair.

Pressing him into his past.

He'd held his own son just like this. It was such a sweet age, still small enough to fit into a lap and to want to be there.

Leo would soon grow beyond such tenderness.

Derek wouldn't, not ever.

The knowledge of that ached in Finn's chest. Outside of the guilt and the regret, he just plain missed his son.

Would Derek have been shy and quiet, like Leo? Or more blustery and outgoing like his cousins, kids Finn never saw anymore because he couldn't stand his brothers' sympathy?

Kayla sloshed another bucket over the fire pit. "There. No sparks left to cause a fire."

He met her eyes and the thought flashed through him: *there are still some sparks here, just not the fire-pit kind.*

But although it was true, it wouldn't do to highlight the fact. "Do you want me to carry him inside?"

She hesitated, and he could understand why. It was an intimate thing to do. Yet a sleeping five-year-old was substantial, and he could bear the burden more easily than she could. Despite the ache in his leg, he wanted to play the man's role rather than watching a small, slight woman do all the heavy lifting.

Before she could refuse him, he stood, carefully holding Leo's head against his shoulder. The boy stirred a little, then cuddled marginally tighter and relaxed against Finn.

His throat too tight to say anything, he inclined his head, inviting Kayla to lead the way inside.

It was tricky, but he used his free hand and good leg to climb the ladder to the sleeping loft, following behind Kayla. He had to duck his head beneath the slanted roof. When he went to put Leo down, his leg went out from under him and he lurched, making Kayla gasp. But he caught himself and managed to place the boy carefully on his low, narrow cot, made up with faded race-car sheets.

The sight of those sheets hurt his heart a little. Kayla must have packed them up and brought them along, wanting to give her child a taste of home. "Sorry about that," he said, gesturing at his leg. "I wouldn't drop him."

"No, it's fine, thank you! I forgot that climbing might be hard for you."

He shrugged. "My pleasure."

"I guess he's finally used to you," she said as she pulled the sheets and blankets up to cover Leo's narrow shoulders.

"It took some doing, but yeah."

"He…he's seen some scary things. His father…well."

"Same man that gave you the bruises?" he asked mildly.

Her sharp intake of breath wasn't unexpected, but Finn was tired of the distance between them, the concealment, the connections that weren't getting made. Something about this night made him want to throw caution away and nudge her a little, see if the thing he felt was there for her, too.

She ran a hand over Leo's hair, not looking at Finn. "Yes," she said, her voice so low he had to bend closer to hear it. "Same guy."

"If I could get my hands on him, I'd be tempted to do worse to him than he did to you and Leo." Because the words were confrontational, he kept his tone mild.

She glanced up at him, secrets in her eyes. And then she rose, gracefully, to her feet. "It's late."

Yes, it was, and he didn't want to go. He climbed the ladder down ahead of her, so he could catch her if she fell—odd protective urge, since she was probably up and down the ladder a dozen times a day. At the bottom, he waited.

She stepped off the last rung. The slow way she turned, he could tell she knew he was there, close. "Finn…"

He reached out for her, touched her chin. "You're a good mother and a good cook," he said. "Thank you for tonight."

That was all he meant to do; just thank her. But the unexpectedly soft feel of her skin made his hand linger, and then splay to encompass her strong jawline, her soft hair.

She looked up at him through long, thick lashes. There was a light spray of freckles across her nose.

Finn's heart swelled with tenderness, and he lowered his face toward hers.

Seven

Kayla drew in a panicky breath and reached out, feeling the rough stubble of Finn's face. He was going to kiss her and she wanted him to.

But he stopped short and brushed her cheek with his finger. "Your skin is so soft. I didn't shave. I'm afraid I'll hurt you."

She inhaled the piney, outdoorsy scent of him and her heart thudded, heavy and hard. "You won't hurt me," she whispered.

He narrowed his eyes just a tiny bit, studying her, as if to test her sincerity.

And then he pulled her closer and lowered his lips the rest of the way down to hers.

Tenderness and respect? She'd never experienced kissing this way. It made her want to pull him closer, but she didn't dare. And after a moment, he lifted up to look at her. "You're like a tiny little sparrow, ready to fly away."

His whimsical description amused her, cutting through the moment's intensity. "Sometimes I've wished

I could fly," she admitted, her voice still soft, heart still pounding.

"You did fly. You flew here to Redemption Ranch."

Yes, she had. She'd been flying away from something, someone.

From Mitch.

Reluctantly, she stepped back from the warm circle of Finn's arms. She looked at the floor across the room, embarrassed to meet his eyes, because she'd not only enjoyed his kiss, she'd returned it.

"Someday," he said, "I want to hear more about what you flew away from."

She bit her lip. She was starting to trust him, kind of wanted to tell him. Finn's solid protection and support would be such a blessing to her and Leo.

But there, as he crossed his arms and looked at her, was his Eighty-second Airborne tattoo. She still didn't know how attached he was to his unit, how close the bonds of brotherhood went for him.

Just because of who he was, she'd suspect the ties held tight. He was the loyal type, for sure. "The past isn't important," she said, not looking at him.

Something flashed in his eyes, some emotion. "I'm not sure I agree with you. If you don't deal with the past, you can't move forward."

"Moving forward is maybe overrated."

"Like us kissing?"

She huffed out a fake kind of laugh. "Yeah."

He cocked his head to one side, looking at her, his expression a little puzzled. "I don't understand women very well," he said. "And it's late. I should be going."

Something inside her wanted to cling on, to cry out, *No, don't go!* But that was the needy part of her that her mom had despised. The part that had experienced Mitch's attention and glommed right on. "See you tomorrow," she said, forcing her voice to sound casual.

"Actually, not much," he said. "After the meeting tomorrow morning, I'll be away for the weekend."

"Oh." Her heart did a little plummet, and that was bad. She was already too attached, expecting to see him every day.

He must have heard something in her voice. "It's a reunion," he said, indicating his tattoo. "Eighty-second Airborne."

Her heart hit the floor. "Oh."

He laughed a little. "Bunch of old guys telling stories, mostly. But I love 'em. They're my brothers."

Of course they were. He'd do anything for his brothers.

Including, if it came to that, helping one of them find the woman who'd betrayed him and taken away his son. "Finn, about…this," she said, waving a hand, her cheeks heating. "We shouldn't… I mean, I don't—"

His face hardened. "I understand. We got carried away."

"Exactly. I just didn't want you to think…"

"That it meant something?"

It meant everything. "Exactly," she lied.

"Agreed," he said, his bearing going a little more upright and military. "See you."

And he was gone. The little lost girl inside Kayla curled up in a ball and cried at the loss of him.

She was hiding something.

Finn headed toward Penny's place for the dreaded

semiannual meeting with the ranch's finance guy. Bingo, his current dog, loped along beside him.

"You have to act nice if you're coming to the meeting," Finn grumbled to the dog, but Bingo only laughed up at him. "I know. Penny will give you treats to make you behave."

The dog's tail started to wag at the *T* word.

Finn tried to focus on the dog, on the fresh morning air, on anything but the fact that he'd kissed Kayla last night. And she'd responded. She'd liked it.

And then she'd backed right off.

Had she heard the truth about Finn, or remembered it? Was that why she'd pushed him away?

But it wasn't just that. She was secretive, and he wanted to know why. Wanted to know what it was in her past that had her running. If they were going to be involved, he needed to know.

Were they going to be involved?

Probably not. For sure not. He'd made the decision, after losing his wife and son, that he wasn't going to go there again. Up until now, his grief had been so thick and dark that the promise hadn't been hard to keep.

But Kayla and Leo had made their way through his darkness and were battering at the hard shell surrounding his heart. He'd held Leo last night, held him for at least an hour, and the experience had softened something inside him.

Leo needed a father figure. And some part of Finn, apparently, needed a son.

But he didn't deserve a son. He didn't deserve to look forward, with hope, to the kind of happy new life that Derek and Deirdre would never have.

It was just that holding Kayla, kissing her, had been

so very, very sweet. It had brought something inside him back to life.

He reached the main house. A glance at his phone told him he was early, so he settled on the edge of the porch.

If he *did* get involved with Kayla—and he wasn't saying he would, but if it happened—he wanted to know the truth about her. And, he rationalized, she was his employee. He needed to know.

Raakib Khan had served with Finn in the Eighty-second, and they'd had each other's backs. When Raakib came home, he'd started a little detective agency.

Finn called Raakib, shot the breeze for a minute and then gave him everything he knew about Kayla.

"What is your interest, my friend?" Raakib asked.

"She works for me."

"And is that all?"

Finn let out a disgusted snort. After all they'd been through together, Raakib could read him like a book. "That's all you need to know about," he growled and ended the call.

When he looked up, he saw Kayla walking toward him. His face heated. What had she heard?

She gave him a little wave and walked up the stairs toward the conference room. He got to his feet and followed, the dog ambling behind him.

Penny was in the kitchen, putting doughnuts on a tray, so he veered over her way. "You still sure about having Bingo here?"

"I think it's fine. It keeps us all in a good mood and reminds us of our mission."

He leaned closer. "Why is Kayla here?"

Penny shrugged. "I feel like we need all the ideas we can get. We're in trouble, Finn."

"Worse than I know?"

"You'll hear." She handed him the tray of doughnuts. "Carry this in there, will you? I'll be right in."

Their banker was there. A vet out of the Baltic, but you wouldn't have known it from his suit and dress shoes. Well, he was navy, after all.

He seemed to be grilling Kayla.

Finn wanted to protect her, felt that urge, except that she was holding her own. "No, I've never worked for this exact type of organization before," she admitted to Branson Howe. "But I volunteered with a nonprofit for kids, and I've run a business, so Penny thought I might be able to help. With the website or something."

She'd run a business? That was news to him.

Branson was frowning, arms crossed.

"We can use an outsider perspective," Finn said. "It's been just me and Penny since…well, since everything went haywire." He glanced over at Penny, who'd just walked in. Sometimes he worried about how she was dealing, or not dealing, with what had happened.

"It's okay, Finn—you can talk about it." Penny's abrupt tone called her words into question. "Coffee, everyone? We should get started."

"That's what I've been trying to do." Branson glared at Penny.

Undercurrents. You had to love them. Penny and Branson always circled around each other like two dogs getting ready to fight.

"You called the meeting," she said, "so why don't you tell us what's on your mind?"

Finn glanced at Kayla, who lifted an eyebrow back at him, obviously reading the back-and-forth as personal, the way he was. "I'll get you a cup of coffee," she offered. "Penny, do you need a refill?"

She waved a hand, leaning forward to look at Branson. "What's going on?"

"I just got a notice from the IRS." Branson opened his laptop and accepted a cup of coffee. "We missed a payment, and there's going to be a fine attached to it when we make it. We need to get on it and pay so the IRS doesn't flag us as suspicious. If that happens, we'll be in line for a lot of paperwork and audits."

"I thought the taxes, at least, were fine." Penny frowned. "We had an outside firm do them. They said they'd found enough deductions that we didn't have to pay anything."

Branson dropped his head and looked at her. "And you didn't question that?"

"No. I did pay them, of course… Oh." Penny smacked her forehead. "I'm an idiot."

"What?" Finn had to ask.

"I was going to get someone new for this year, but with as busy as I've been, I didn't. The outside firm was the one Harry chose, and I wonder…" She trailed off. "Again. I'm an idiot."

Harry. Penny's ex, and a poor excuse for a man.

"I looked into your tax people." Branson hesitated and looked at Penny. For the first time, a hint of sympathy twisted the corner of his mouth.

"I'm not made of glass. Give it to me straight."

"Apparently, one of the silent owners of your outside firm was Oneida Emerson. That could be why no forms were filed."

"None?" Penny's voice was casual, but her fists made red spots on her arms.

Again, Branson's eyes portrayed a little sympathy. "I'm hoping this is the last bad news I have to give you, from this situation, but I can't promise that," he said.

"Give it to me straight," Penny said. "Do you think we're going to make it? Or do we give up and shut down?"

"The vets and the dogs need us," Finn protested.

As if understanding his safe haven was at stake, Bingo let out a low whine and rested his head on Finn's knee.

"What about the grant we…you…just got?" Kayla asked.

"Can't be used for anything other than what we applied for. Improvements to the physical facility." Even if what they needed most was money for something else.

"What's the fine and back taxes likely to add up to?" Penny asked.

Branson named a number that was twice their operating budget.

Finn groaned and looked over at Penny. She was shaking her head. "If I could get my hands on Harry and his—" She bit off whatever she'd been going to say, but Finn could guess at it.

Even Bingo sighed and flopped to the floor, looking mournful.

"If you could just get some publicity and success stories out there, you might be able to raise enough in donations," Branson said. "You've barely started fundraising. But—"

"That's right," Kayla interrupted. "Everyone wants to support vets, and who can resist the dogs?"

"But we have no money for publicity, is the problem," Penny said. "No time to put together a campaign, either."

"Can't get water from a stone." Branson closed his

folder. "And neither of you has any background at fund-raising."

"You can't give up." Kayla leaned forward and looked in turn at everyone at the table. "Even if you don't have money, there are ways to get the word out."

Finn's heart squeezed as he looked at her earnest expression. It was sweet that she cared, given the short length of time she'd been here.

"I'm listening," Penny said in a dismissive tone that suggested she wasn't.

"Social media, for one. An updated website, for another."

"We have that stuff. It hasn't helped so far."

"Pardon me for saying so," Kayla said, "but it's all out of date. You—we, I'll help—need to keep that fresh and add new content."

"I know you're right," Penny said, "but I'm not posting pictures of the veterans. That's stood in our way."

"Well, okay, not without permission. But aren't there some who will ham it up for the camera? I'm sure Willie would."

Penny snorted out a laugh. "You're right about that."

"Capitalize on the setting. How warmhearted the community is." She sat up straighter, her cheeks flushing a little. "Maybe have an event that brings the whole community up here. And then photograph and video bits of it to use all year."

"It's a good idea," Penny said, "but wouldn't donations just trickle in? If Branson's right, we need money now."

"A fund-raising event isn't likely to bring in enough to weather this crisis, even if you could really get the word out," Branson said. "And what about when the next crisis comes?"

Finn debated briefly whether to speak up. But Kayla had changed the tone of the meeting and it had made him think of an idea that had been nudging at him. "Let me throw something out there," he said. "That old bunkhouse. If we renovated it, we might be able to host people to come up here."

"A working-ranch type of thing?" Penny looked skeptical. "That would take a lot of time, and our staff is small."

"But it's a possibility," Kayla said.

Penny frowned. "Wouldn't we have to have more ranch-type activities? Like riding horses and roping cattle or something?"

Finn snorted. "Not many ranches run according to that model anymore," he said.

"But," Penny said, "that's what people expect at a dude ranch. My sister worked at one for a while, and the Easterners want all the stereotypes."

Branson was shaking his head. "I don't like the liability issues, if you're having people do actual ranch work."

Kayla looked thoughtful. "I think people would enjoy coming out here for the peace." She waved a hand at the window. "Lots of people just want to get away. Relax. Reflect. This is a great place to do all that."

"This is getting to be pretty pie-in-the-sky," Branson said. "We need to pay our bills. You're talking about a renovation, lots of initial investment. You can't afford that."

"We have to start somewhere, Branson," Penny said impatiently. "Kayla and Finn are just suggesting some ideas. Which is more than I hear you doing."

Finn looked at Penny. She wasn't usually confrontational. He couldn't blame her, given that her husband and his girlfriend had absconded with the ranch's funds. But she shouldn't take it out on Branson, who was, after all, a volunteer.

A volunteer who had a thing for Penny, if Finn's instincts were firing right.

Kayla snapped her fingers. "Crowdfunding. The kids' organization I volunteered for did it."

"I don't like it." Branson shook his head. "My niece tried to crowdfund to pay off her college loans, and then got mad when everyone in the extended family didn't donate."

"But this is a real cause," Penny said. "We're not just trying to avoid our responsibilities. Anyone who knows us knows how hard we work."

"*Do* they know, though?" Kayla asked. "Maybe we should do an open house *and* crowdfunding. People in the community could come up and see what we do, see the dogs and whatever vets are willing. We could talk about our mission. If we put that together with an online campaign, we might at least get some breathing room."

Penny tipped her head to one side, considering. Then she nodded. "Worth a try, anyway. It might create some buzz."

Branson threw his hands in the air, looking impatient. "You people are dreamers. Some Podunk carnival isn't going to raise the money you need, not in such a limited time frame."

"How limited?" Finn asked.

"The penalty will go up in two weeks. I don't think—"

"Do you have a better idea?" Penny asked him.

"Good fiscal management, maybe?" He stood up and

grabbed his papers. "If you'll excuse me, I have some other responsibilities to attend to." He nodded at Kayla and Finn and walked out.

Kayla stared after him and then looked at Finn, one eyebrow raised.

"Don't ask me," he said. "Penny and Branson have some issues that go way back."

"Hello, I'm in the room," Penny said. "You don't have to talk about me like I'm not."

"Plus," Finn went on, ignoring her, "I think Branson takes care of his mother and a special-needs daughter. He's stretched pretty thin."

"He is, but that's not an excuse for shooting down every idea we have." Penny grabbed a chocolate-frosted doughnut and bit into it.

"What do you think of it all?" Finn asked her. "Because if you're in, then I think we should go full bore into this fund-raiser. But we shouldn't make the effort if it's all for nothing. You know more about the books than I do."

"I think it's worth a try," Penny said slowly. "But it would be an all-hands-on-deck sort of situation. That means you, Kayla. You brought up some great ideas. Are you willing to help?"

"Of course," Kayla said. "This place does important work. I would hate to see it go under. And the Lord knows I'm used to working against some odds." She did a half smile.

Finn's heart turned over. *Stick to business.* "I can cancel my weekend trip. This is more important."

Penny bit her lip. "I got a call this morning from my daughter."

"That's a surprise, right?"

Penny nodded. "She's been having some contractions. If it's labor—"

"Then you should go," Kayla said instantly. "We can handle things here."

"Yes," Finn agreed. "We can handle it." Penny never asked for anything for herself, always carried more than her share of the load. If she had the chance to mend things with her daughter—and be there when her first grandchild was born—Finn was all in favor.

"You guys are the best," Penny said. "It's probably Braxton Hicks. I should be able to stick around for a few days and help get this project going. And I can do the online fund-raising part from anywhere. It's just that there will be a lot of on-the-ground organization if we're really going to do an open house."

Finn blew out a sigh. Then he looked over at Kayla. "When should we get started?"

Penny and Kayla looked at each other. "No time like the present," Penny said. "Let's make a list."

Kayla grabbed a legal pad and a pen. "For starters, we need to think of what a good open house would be like. Something other people won't think of."

"That's true," Penny said. "We don't want to resort to carnival games and kettle corn. There's got to be something new that we could do to make people really want to come. If we're asking them to drive all the way up here, we ought to have something interesting and different for them."

"Something with the dogs?" Kayla said.

"Yes, but what?" Penny reached for the pad, but her phone buzzed and she glanced at it. Glanced again. Then she stood so abruptly that her chair tilted and would have fallen if Finn hadn't grabbed it.

"She went into labor," Penny said. "It's too early. I have to go."

"How can we help?" Kayla asked.

"I…I don't even know."

"Come on," Kayla said, taking the older woman's arm. "We'll get your things together."

So Kayla helped Penny pack while Finn called the airport, and within two hours he'd driven her there and gotten home again.

All the while, he was thinking.

He and Kayla were now pretty much committed to setting up an open house, and doing it alone. That was a problem, because every time he was near her he wanted to kiss her.

He had to get himself pulled together and realize, remember, what a bad idea that would be. For him, no; but for Kayla and Leo, most definitely. They'd already been through plenty of problems in their lives, and they didn't need him adding more.

For their sake, he had to keep control of his emotions.

The next morning, Kayla knelt in the meadow outside the kennels and watched Finn make his way up the road toward her, his gait unsteady. He was using his cane. It must be a bad day with his leg.

On impulse, she lifted her camera lens and started snapping pictures. With the morning sun glowing on the mountains behind him, the image was riveting. Something she could submit to a magazine or contest, if he gave her permission.

When he got closer she let the camera slip into her lap and surveyed the scene. Across the field, scarlet paintbrush flowers bristled toward the sky, while silvery lupine and blue columbine nodded and tossed in the faint breeze. Sage and pine sent their mingled fragrance down from the mountains. She'd brought Willie and Long John's dogs for the shoot, knowing they could be trusted to remain calm. Now Rockette lay at Kayla's side, big black head lifted to survey the scene. Duke, the grizzled pit bull, sniffed around the rocks, displaying a mild interest in a prairie dog that popped out of its burrow to look around.

Finn disappeared into the barn and came out a moment later, with Winter, the female who'd been abused, at his side. He approached Kayla with a half smile, half grimace. "Showing up as ordered."

"I'm sorry." She moved over to offer him a seat on the end of the bench. "You having a bad day?"

"It happens." He lowered himself onto the bench and propped his cane beside him. "What's our game plan?"

He sounded guarded, and she couldn't blame him. In fact, she was feeling the same way. They'd committed to a couple of weeks of working together on an important project, and that meant they'd have to deal with these undertones between them at some time.

If only they hadn't kissed. That had muddied waters that had only just started to clear as they'd adjusted to working together. Now she couldn't look at him without remembering his tenderness, wishing for it to happen again.

But getting close to Finn meant the risk that he'd discover their connection to the Airborne and that Mitch would find out. She couldn't let that happen, for her own safety but especially for Leo's.

Time to get businesslike. "I'd like to video you first."

His jaw literally dropped. "No way. This isn't about

me. I thought we were going to video Long John and Willie."

"Later. You first. You can talk about your work here, and about your history as a veteran."

"Nope. Not happening."

She blew out a breath, trying to keep her frustration under control. "We agreed yesterday that we'd make a series of short clips of veterans. Who better to start with than the person who pretty much runs this place?"

"*Willing* veterans. Which I'm not." He rubbed his leg and his face twisted again.

"If you're going to ask others to participate," she said, "you should be prepared to do the same. Tell your story. It will help other vets, and this place, and the dogs."

"My life isn't interesting!" He practically spit out the words and then lowered his voice. "It's a mess."

What was his story?

"Anyway," he grumbled, "I'm not exactly photogenic. I hate being on camera."

"You're inspiring," she said firmly. "And you can have the dogs with you. And we can edit it." She picked up the old video camera and panned the area, adjusting the settings. "Ready?"

He glared at her.

She glared right back.

He drew in a breath and let it out in a sigh. "Where do I stand?"

"Just sit right there." He was on a bench against the wood barn siding, Willie's dog, Duke, beside him, and if he wasn't photogenic she didn't know who was. He'd advertise the place better than anything. And he didn't even consider himself handsome, which was part of his appeal.

Now that he'd agreed, Kayla felt flustered. She was used to being behind a camera, but not to talking. "Let me find the questions I brainstormed," she said and went to her bag. *Be calm, be calm*, she told herself. *It's a job. You're just doing your job.*

And saving a ranch.

And making things right for Leo.

And helping dogs and veterans who need it.

She pulled out the sheet of notebook paper on which she'd jotted some questions and skimmed them over. They seemed kind of…shallow, and weak. She wanted to sparkle for Finn.

You're not a sparkling kind of person, said the voices from her past.

But it wasn't all about her.

She heard Finn's booming laugh and looked over. He was watching the two dogs. Rockette was rolling on her back in the grass, and Duke was poking and prodding her with his paw, letting out intermittent barks. Winter sat watching with mild interest.

She swung her camera around and caught footage of the dogs, then of Finn watching them. She walked closer.

"So, Finn, what do the dogs do for you?" she asked.

He looked more relaxed now, as he gestured toward the silly pair. "They're lighthearted, and always accepting, and they never give up. Old Duke here, he can't stop trying to dominate Rockette. And she won't let herself be dominated."

She quirked an eyebrow at him. "She's aware of the women's movement."

"She's her own dog, that's for sure."

"Could you tell us a little bit about the ranch and its mission?"

As he answered that softball question, he relaxed to his theme and was actually good on camera. His passion for the work showed, and he explained their clientele: vets who had lost hope, dogs who had lost their last chance.

She risked going a little more personal. "And what made you decide to work for the ranch? What is it in your background that makes you feel a connection?"

He frowned for a moment and then nodded. "I know what it is to lose hope," he said. "I served with good people. Some didn't come home, and some came home a lot worse off than I am."

When he came to a natural breaking point, she hazarded a more personal question. "Do you mind telling us about your own injury?"

"Do I have to?"

"Yes. Yes, you do." She put a hand on her hip, trying to look stern, and he laughed, and all of a sudden there was that romantic vibe between them again.

She cleared her throat and pulled herself back to a businesslike mind-set. "Seriously, if you don't mind, it will bring something personal to people."

"Okay." He looked off to the side as if collecting his thoughts, and then faced Kayla and the camera again. "I was caught in a building that had been bombed. A beam fell on me and…" He grimaced. "The fracture was too bad to fix just right."

She studied him. "What were you doing in the building?"

He shrugged. "Civilians were caught inside. One of my buddies, too."

"You went in to help get people out, didn't you?" She knew in her heart that it had gone down that way. Finn was a protector to the core. If he could help someone, he would.

"It needed done," he said. "We were able to get all the kids out. This—" he gestured at his leg "—this didn't happen until the last trip."

"Did you get a medal? Or probably more than one." She thought of Mitch's stories of the actions that had led to his medals.

Finn waved a hand. "Not important."

Maybe not, but she would look up his service record when she got the chance, see what medals he'd earned, or ask Penny. Because she was getting the feeling there was a lot more to his service than he'd mentioned before. And to have that in the video would add to its appeal.

Hearing about his heroism only made her more impressed with him. But she needed to remember her concerns. "Could you tell us a little about your division? Aren't the Airborne a tight unit?"

"Best in the army, at least according to us." He flashed a grin. "We're definitely confident, but you have to be if you're going to step out of a plane over enemy territory."

Kayla's stomach tightened. Of course he was proud of his service and his brothers.

Of course, he was loyal to them. Just as Mitch was.

If they knew each other, they'd be loyal to each other. So she simply had to make sure that never happened.

She heard voices in the kennel and quickly ended the interview. She needed to be careful. She was getting so drawn to Finn. Just looking at him now, she felt like it was hard to catch her breath. "Thank you," she said, feeling shy. "That was…well. I really admire what you did, who you are." She felt like a dork, but she couldn't keep it in.

His face hardened. "Don't get too impressed. There's a lot about me that's far less admirable."

Willie and Long John came out through the kennel door, interrupting the awkward moment. "How'd they do as show dogs?" Willie asked, laughing as Duke jumped up on him.

"They were great. They could be pros." She pointed a stern finger at Long John, then at Willie. "Just so you know, I'll be interviewing you next, after the midday shift. And then we'll cut film into a good video we can use to promote our event."

"I'm ready, willing and able," Willie said, puffing out his chest.

"You're a ham." Long John waved a hand. "Now, me, I'd rather stay offscreen. I'm not the handsome dude I used to be."

Kayla smiled at the lanky man. "You're plenty handsome, and I'd guess the women, especially, will love to see you." She touched his arm. "And more important, your example of working through your issues will be inspiring. Both to donors and to vets who wouldn't otherwise think of coming."

"You're a good little lady," Long John said, his voice gruff. "We struck gold when we got you to come work at the ranch."

The praise warmed the hungry child inside Kayla. She put an arm around Long John's waist. "I feel like *I* struck gold, coming here."

"Yeah, sure, we're in the middle of a gold rush, but we also have to work," Willie said, gesturing back toward the kennel. "Those dogs won't exercise themselves."

"Of course!" Kayla hurried to put her camera away,

determined to continue doing well at her regular job in addition to the extra she'd taken on.

"Kayla." Finn spoke quietly. "Why don't you take a break. We can handle the midday shift."

"Oh, no, it's okay. I'm glad to do it."

"Take a break." It wasn't just a suggestion.

He wanted her to leave. He was basically ordering her to leave.

Hot, embarrassing tears prickled the backs of her eyes and she swallowed. "Okay, then," she said. She gathered the rest of her things while the three men went back into the kennel.

She'd thought they had a connection. However reluctantly, Finn had let her in today, at least a little. Revealed something about who he was. She'd had a moment of thinking they were getting closer.

She dawdled on the road back to her cabin, trying to take in the mountains' beauty. Trying not to feel hurt at Finn's rejection.

She was starting to care what he thought, too much. And he was a dangerous man to care about.

But *was* he dangerous?

He didn't seem like the kind of man who would give her up to a fellow soldier. He seemed like he would want to protect her, take care of her.

On the other hand, she hadn't expected betrayal from the police officer she'd gone to when things went south with Mitch. She'd expected an officer of the law to protect her, and look how mistaken she'd been then. She had to remember where these men's loyalties lay.

Faced with an unexpected couple of hours to herself, Kayla walked inside her cabin. Grabbed a glass of iced tea from the fridge—and on impulse, her Bible and devotional book—and went back out onto the porch, Shoney trotting beside her.

She felt confused, like everything was shifting inside her, ready to explode. She didn't have anyone to talk to.

Except God.

She paged through the Bible restlessly, looking out over the fields and mountains. His world. So beautiful and perfect.

She knew He was in charge. You should trust Him. Moreover, there was nothing to do *but* trust Him, since her own power was so limited compared to His.

Her life hadn't been conducive to trusting. Not as a kid, not as an adult.

But God. God wasn't Mitch. God wasn't Finn. God was bigger, incomprehensible and great. He was like the mountains, mysterious, a little scary, and everlasting.

She let her eyes drift over the Psalms until they fell on a line in Psalm 92, one she'd underlined not long ago: *O Lord, how great are thy works! and thy thoughts are very deep.*

She breathed in and out and looked around.

She wasn't going to understand this world. She wasn't going to know what to do, not perfectly.

And no person was going to love away the bad things that had happened to her.

But God could, and would. According to the Book of Revelation, He would wipe away every tear.

She didn't know she was crying until a fat drop splatted on the parchment-thin page. She brushed her knuckles under her eyes and read on.

Read, and prayed, and listened.

Shoney seemed to sense her mood and pressed close against Kayla's legs, and Kayla lifted the dog into her lap. Comfort and affection and unconditional love: God had known she and Leo needed those things, and had provided them through Shoney, whose special needs couldn't take away from her happy, giving spirit.

She nuzzled the dog's soft fur. *Okay, God. I get it. I should be more like Shoney.*

She kept reading and praying all afternoon. It was only when an alarm rang on her phone that she realized she'd have to hustle to go fetch Leo in time.

When she reached her car, she spotted Finn talking to Long John and Willie outside of Willie's cabin. The three men waved, and Willie gestured for her to join them.

She shook her head and mimed pointing at a watch. She got into the car and headed out.

There was a kind of peace in letting it all go, in realizing you weren't in control.

It was something she needed to keep exploring.

When her phone buzzed, she pulled over to take the call, figuring it was Long John asking her to run an errand while she was in town.

She didn't recognize the number. Maybe it was Willie's phone; he didn't use it often, so she'd never put him in her contacts.

"Hello?"

Silence at the other end.

"Hello? Willie?"

More silence. No, not complete silence. Breathing.

Horror snaked through her as she clicked the call off. She fumbled through the settings until she figured out a way to block the number.

She pulled in a breath and let it out slowly.

It was probably nothing. There was no reason to associate a random call with Mitch.

Anyway, once you'd blocked the number there was no way anyone could trace it. Right?

She put the car into Drive and continued on toward town, carefully, both hands on the steering wheel, staying a couple of miles under the speed limit.

She'd better not call attention to herself, lest the law enforcement here be just as corrupt as it had been back in Arkansas.

Eight

Almost two weeks later, Finn listened to the thunderous applause in the community center and smiled over at Kayla, who stood on the other side of the stage. She looked stunning in a white dress that fit her like a glove. Her brown hair fell loose and shiny around her shoulders, and her smile was as joyous as his.

They'd generated so much interest in the ranch, just by talking up the open house with friends and neighbors, that they'd been asked to share their story at the monthly town meeting. The event was tomorrow, and they'd been working like mad, but from the response they were getting, it seemed like it might actually be a success.

As the meeting broke up, people crowded around him, asking questions and offering congratulations. He looked over and saw a similar group surrounding Kayla.

Funny how conscious he was of her at every moment.

"Well, you done it," Long John said, clapping him on the shoulder. "I think you just got the open house a couple dozen more visitors. Folks are excited."

"That thermometer thing you put online is rising up

fast," Willie added, coming up behind Long John and reaching out to shake Finn's hand. In his other hand, he held up his phone, displaying a donation meter already half-full. He squinted over at Long John, then looked back at Finn. "Say, we need to talk to you a minute. In private, like."

"Sure." Finn glanced around, then ushered the two older men toward a quiet corner of the community center. "What's up?"

Long John and Willie glanced at each other. "We've got ourselves an awkward situation," Long John said. "See, we were given a gift card for that new restaurant up Cold Creek Mountain."

"Cold Creek Inn?" Finn whistled. "Nice."

"My daughter wanted to treat us," Willie explained. "Thinks I don't get out enough or some fool thing."

Finn chuckled. "Why don't you ask Dana Dylan to go with you?" He nodded at the white-haired dynamo who'd asked Willie out a number of times.

Willie raised his hands and took a step backward. "No, no way. I don't want to encourage her."

Finn lifted an eyebrow. "Because your heart's somewhere else?"

"His heart ought to go on out with Dana," Long John grumbled.

Finn shouldn't have opened that door. The two men's rivalry over Penny was mostly good-natured, but their friendship was too important to fool with them.

Apparently Willie felt the same way, because he slapped Long John's shoulder. "I'd rather have dinner with my buddy here than any woman. Don't have to clean up my act for him."

"Then you two use the gift card," Finn said. He was still confused about why they'd brought him into it.

"But we don't either of us like that kind of food," Long John said. "Nor a place where you have to get all gussied up to go."

"And it expires tomorrow," Willie said. "If my daughter finds out I didn't use it, she'll be upset."

"So we were thinking…"

"Since you and Kayla are all dressed up," Willie said, "I'd like for you to use it. Tonight." He held out a gilt-edged plastic card with *Cold Creek Inn* embossed in fancy script.

Mixed emotions roiled through Finn's chest. The thought of taking Kayla on a date sounded way too good. Working together as they had been, he was drawn to her more and more. She was a good person—that was the main thing. She tried hard and did the right thing and took care of her son. She said she wasn't a great Christian, that she had a lot to learn, but he'd watched her during church. She had a God-focused heart. The fact that she was gorgeous, at least to him, was just icing on the cake.

But the feelings Finn was having for Kayla were the exact reason he shouldn't be taking her on anything resembling a date. "I think you two should use it," he repeated. "It was meant for you, Willie, not me." And it would be better that way. Better than for him to start something with Kayla that he couldn't finish.

"I'm just not up to it today," Long John said. He gestured down at his body with a disparaging movement of his arm. "My Parkinson's is acting up. I need to get some rest."

"And I'm driving him back," Willie said. "Truth is,

I'm worn-out myself. I'd rather sit at home and watch reruns on the TV then go to some fancy place where I have to figure out what fork to use."

"Give it to somebody else, then," Finn said. He was starting to panic at the idea of doing something so romantic with Kayla. No telling where that would lead, but it was a place he couldn't go. "How about the Coopers. Isn't it their anniversary?"

"Nope," Long John said flatly. "Willie and I, we talked it over. We're giving it to you."

"Hey, Kayla," Willie called across the emptying room. "Come here a minute."

"Willie!" Finn scolded in a whisper.

But it was too late. She was already coming over, her high heels clicking, and again Finn was stunned at how gorgeous she was. "What's up?" she asked.

"Finn wants to ask you something," Long John said. "Come on, Willie. I see that old Pete Ramsey. He's always trying to borrow money. I need to get out of here." And the two men turned and walked away.

Although there were other people in the room—and in fact, Long John and Willie didn't go far before finding a couple of chairs—Finn suddenly felt like he was alone with Kayla.

If they went out to the restaurant, they would truly be alone. The thought created a tsunami of feeling inside him.

He tried desperately to cling to the thought that she might not be trustworthy, that there was some kind of mystery in her past. But he'd just talked to Raakib yesterday, and so far, there was nothing criminal or even dishonest to report.

356 The Soldier's Redemption

"Finn?" Kayla was looking at him quizzically. "What's going on?"

She looked so pretty and sophisticated that he felt like a high school boy asking a girl to a dance. The ease he'd felt working with her was nowhere to be found. He held up the gift card. "Willie wants us to use this."

Behind her, Willie made a sweeping motion with his arm while shaking his head vigorously.

And the older man had a point. What a half-baked way to ask a woman out. "What I mean to say is, would you like to go out to dinner with me? At the Cold Creek Inn?"

Color rose in her face as she looked at him and bit her lip.

Oh, man. He *really* wanted to go out with her.

But did her hesitation mean she wanted to go, or that she didn't? He needed to give her an out. "You must be worried about Leo. You probably can't go."

"Actually," she said, holding up her phone, "I just found out he wants to stay a little bit longer at his friend's house. They're roasting marshmallows." She looked so pretty it made his heart hurt. "And his friend lives up Cold Creek Mountain."

"We do have something to celebrate," Finn said, with a smile and a tone he'd kept in cold storage for years. He stepped fractionally closer without even meaning to. "Today went well, and there's no one I'd like to spend the evening with more than you."

Her mouth opened halfway, and he couldn't take his eyes off her. He felt tongue-tied, until he again noticed wild gesturing behind her. Long John, and now Willie, seemed to be conducting a pantomime coaching session;

Willie was making a rolling motion with his hands, as if to say, *talk to her more, convince her.*

So he started telling her about the restaurant, how fantastic it was reputed to be. "Apparently it looks out over the valley. They have all kinds of fancy game dishes, venison, and wild boar, and pheasant." But was eating wild game really persuasive to a woman? "I think they're known for their chocolate desserts, too," he said, hoping he'd remembered correctly.

"That sounds good." She gave him a tentative smile.

Finn noticed a couple of nearby people glancing their way. "Come over here," he said and guided her a little bit away from the crowd. "If someone heard us talking about the Cold Creek Inn, there goes your reputation."

"Because of going somewhere with you? Really?"

He thought. Not many people knew about what had happened in his past. And if they did know, would they see it as a reason for her to avoid him? He was starting to wonder. "It's a small town," he said, because he couldn't explain.

Although maybe, someday soon, he would. If anyone would look at his past mistakes with compassion, it was Kayla.

She shrugged. "I don't really care what anyone thinks. Do you?"

He didn't care about anything but her. "Nope," he said. "Let's get out of here." He offered her his arm, and she took it, and he felt like the most fortunate man in the world.

He glanced over his shoulder at Long John and Willie. They were both grinning and fist-bumping and thumbs-upping him. Because of course, they were trying to push him and Kayla together. Matchmaking. He should have realized it before.

He just hoped the two older men knew what they were doing. Because Finn felt like he was diving into a sea of risks, and he couldn't predict the outcome.

When they walked into the Cold Creek Inn, Kayla's breath caught.

The dining room was full of well-dressed people, mostly couples. Waitstaff in white jackets hovered and smiled and carried trays high on one hand—a feat she'd only ever seen in movies. The decor was that of a hunting lodge, with rough-hewn wooden rafters overhead, a pine plank floor and wall hangings depicting hunting scenes.

But most impressive of all was the view. The whole front of the restaurant was glass, a floor-to-ceiling window, and it looked out over the valley. As the sun sank, pink and orange and gold filled the sky, and lights flickered on across the valley.

Breathtaking.

Kayla had read about places like this, had seen them on television, but she had never been. It was way out of her league, and a wave of anxiety washed over her. Would she know how to act, what silverware to use? Would she spill a glass of water or not know how to ask for the right food?

She was holding Finn's arm, his muscles strong beneath her fingers, and she must have tightened her grip because he looked down at her and patted her sleeve. "Pretty highfalutin for a couple of ranch hands," he said. "But let's just enjoy ourselves, okay?"

As the maître d' led them to a table by the window,

she tried to walk with assurance. The man helped her into her seat while Finn took the chair across from hers and thanked him.

Even if she could handle this place, even if she didn't make a fool of herself, she still felt shaky about Finn. Had he really wanted to ask her out? Or was he just using up a gift card?

Regardless, he looked confident and sophisticated in his suit, his shoulders straining a bit at the fabric, his boots making him even taller than usual. Finn dressed up was just plain devastating. And she needed to pull herself together. She focused on the fact that it was a side of him that she hadn't seen before.

"Wait a minute," she said, pleased that she was able to sound light and casual. "I just realized I don't know much about your background before the ranch."

Some of the carefree light went out of his face. *Oh*. She hadn't meant to stir up the bad part of his past. "Did you live in LA or New York or something?" she added hastily. "Did you do client dinners at places like this?"

He laughed. "Far from it," he said. "My family's from Virginia. After the service, I got into agricultural sales. Fertilizer, seeds, stuff like that." He grinned. "At most, I'd take my clients to the town diner."

"But you seem so comfortable here."

He nodded. "My mom saw to it that we all knew not to slurp our soup or reach all the way across the table. Maybe once or twice a year, she'd grill us on our manners and then get Dad to take us to a fancy restaurant as a kind of test."

"That's so nice."

"I was fortunate," he said. "I had a great childhood."

She sensed he was about to ask her about her childhood, and that, she didn't want to talk about. "What does your dad do?" she asked, to forestall him.

"Small-town cop," he said. "Everybody loves him. One of my brothers is a cop in the same department, and the other's a firefighter."

"Back in Virginia."

He nodded.

"Then...why do you live all the way out here?"

He looked out over the valley, now shadowed, with stars starting to appear above. "I'd been out here a few times for work," he said. "Liked the wide-open spaces. And when... Well, I needed a fresh start. Felt like I couldn't breathe, back East."

"I know what you mean," she said.

He looked at her sharply, but seemed to discern that she didn't want to talk about the negatives in her past. So he made her laugh mispronouncing various dishes, and joking about the particularly large trophy moose head that loomed on the wall behind her.

He was trying to make her feel comfortable, and she liked him even better for it.

Through the appetizers he ordered for them, the pheasant dish he recommended, the too-frequent refills of their water glasses by their overzealous waiter, he kept the conversation going. And Kayla was both pleased and dismayed to realize that she liked this side of Finn, too. She hadn't known he had a background that would lend itself to a place this classy, but it was nice to relax, knowing that he could handle everything.

"Dessert?" the waiter asked.

"Oh, I couldn't," Kayla said. She was full, and besides, they'd surely used up the gift card now. The prices on the menu had been scandalously high.

Finn looked at her with an assessing gaze. "Maybe we could take a look at the dessert tray."

"Of course, sir." And the waiter hurried away.

"Finn!" She laughed at him. "How are we going to eat dessert?"

A moment later, their waiter returned with a mouth-watering tray of cheesecakes, pastries, cakes and pies.

"That's how," Finn said.

She studied the treats. She'd never before experienced food that literally made her mouth water.

"Change your mind about being too full for dessert?" Finn asked, his voice teasing.

She smiled across the table at him. "Oh, yeah," she said. "I want that one." She pointed at a slice of chocolate cake that was layered with a raspberry filling, with extra chocolate sauce and whipped cream over the top of it.

"Good choice," Finn said. "I'll take the apple pie à la mode."

Of course they had to share their desserts. And of course their hands brushed as they did. Their tones grew lower as the sky outside turned black and candles were lit at each table. They seemed to be embedded in their own little world, a world of smiling and soft laughter and expressive glances miles away from their daily lives at the kennel and the ranch.

When she put down her fork, too full to eat anymore, Finn reached across the table and took her hand. "Kayla, I..." He trailed off.

"What?" One syllable was all she could get out. Even that was an effort, considering that she couldn't breathe.

He kept hold of her hand. "I don't know what's happening between us, but how would you feel about pursuing it?"

She looked at him and tried to remember all the reasons why she didn't want to. Tried to pull them back together into a coherent, reasoned set of ideas. But her doubts had scattered with the same wind that was making the moonlit pine branches below wave gently in the twilight.

It didn't seem like he would do anything to hurt her and Leo. It didn't seem like he would prioritize his military brothers over her. Could she trust him with her story? Was she strong enough to take care of herself and her child if things went south with Finn?

Most of all, could he really want to be with her?

Normally, in the past, she wouldn't have been able to believe it. The years of being unwanted were deeply embedded, so much that they seemed to always be a part of her.

But through her work at the ranch and the spiritual development she was gaining here, she was starting to have a different feeling about herself. A feeling that maybe, possibly, things might go well for her. People might want to be her friend. She might have found a place to belong.

Maybe Finn was a part of all that.

She looked at him and opened her mouth to try to put some of what she was feeling into words. But her phone buzzed with a text, and the waiter brought the check, and the moment was over.

Maybe it was just as well, but she couldn't help regretting it as she reluctantly pulled out her phone and studied the lock screen. "The marshmallow roast is over," she said to Finn. "Leo's ready to go home."

"Of course." He signed the check and stood. Came

around the table to pull out her chair for her. "Let's go get him. It's late."

It *was* late. But Kayla's heart was full of promise as they left the restaurant, Finn's hand barely resting on her lower back.

He was a good person, a person she could trust. A person who understood about Leo's needs, and maybe about hers, as well.

Maybe even a person she could build a future with.

After they'd picked up a very sleepy Leo and put him in the booster seat they'd transferred from Kayla's car earlier, Finn drove carefully down the winding mountain road.

A strange warmth surrounded his heart. He'd felt something a little similar with his wife, but way different in degree, like the difference between a candle and a roaring fire.

What he felt for Kayla was explosive, powerful, hot. He didn't want to go back to the friendly coworkers they'd been. He didn't want this night to end.

He heard Kayla murmuring over her shoulder, and Leo said something almost indistinguishable, and then Kayla spoke back.

"Music okay?" he asked, and when she nodded, he turned on the radio and found some quiet jazz.

It was always good to keep a kid calm right before bed. He remembered having arguments with Deirdre about that, when Derek was just Leo's age. Finn had liked to come home and play with Derek, but the excitement had meant the boy didn't want to go to sleep anytime soon. It had annoyed Deirdre, and now, from a more mature perspective, he could see why.

He'd been young, inconsiderate, all about his own desire to have fun with his son on his own terms.

If he had it to do over again…

He glanced over at Kayla. *Might* he have the chance to do it all over again?

He didn't want to be disloyal to Derek and Deirdre by having a good life when they'd been denied the chance. But his conversations with Pastor Carson over the past weeks had him thinking that maybe, just maybe, he didn't have to pay the price of his sin forever. Maybe the accident hadn't been entirely his fault. Maybe not even very much his fault, and though he'd always blame himself, at least to some degree, light and hope were slowly seeping back into his life. He was starting to live again. And Kayla was the reason why.

Thinking of the dinner they'd just had, he smiled. It wasn't the normal thing they would do together, wasn't something to be repeated often, but they'd made the most of it and they'd had a blast. He wanted that to be the case again, in other contexts. How would she like a rafting trip? A museum? A specialty food tasting? Marge's sled dog show?

He had the feeling that, with Kayla, anything would be fun.

"Leo's out," Kayla said and settled more deeply into her seat, facing forward. "He was exhausted. Thank you again for stopping to pick him up."

"I enjoyed it. I enjoyed the whole evening."

"So did I."

The words seemed to hang in the air between them, floating on soft notes of music. They hadn't gotten to discuss what he'd wanted to—whether she wanted to explore the connection they were feeling—but he'd read interest, at least, in her eyes.

He reached out and squeezed her hand, and the petite size of it in contrast to his own big paw, the mix of soft skin and tough calluses, moved him and made him want to explore her contrasts further.

They had a lot of ground to cover, a lot of background to reveal. He needed to tell her about what had happened with Derek and Deirdre. And he needed to know more about what had happened in her past, what had caused the bruises on her arms when she'd first arrived, what made her jumpy.

Needed her to know that he'd protect her from harm like that in the future.

He eased the truck through a narrow part of the road and came out onto a broad, flat stretch lit by moonlight. Pines loomed on either side of the road, casting shadows in the silvery light.

"It's beautiful," she said softly. "I've never been in a place so beautiful."

"I love Colorado. I wouldn't want to live anywhere else." Then he realized that sounded inflexible. "Though, I guess, for the right reasons—"

"No," she said, putting a hand on his arm. "You fit with this land, and that's a good thing. You're an important part of this community. You belong here."

She got that about him? He drew in a breath and thought he caught a whiff of the flowery scent of her hair. He wanted more than that, though; he wanted to bury his face in its softness, the softness she'd revealed tonight.

Be careful, some part of his mind warned his heart.

They were coming into a section of driveways and

houses now, not exactly heavy population, but heavy for this area. Automatically, he slowed.

Suddenly, from a driveway, a car backed out in front of him. *Right* in front of him, going fast.

He slammed on the brake and veered left. He had to avoid the hit at any cost, because if they collided with another car...

Crash.

It was a slight crash, but it made a loud, metal-on-metal impact, and as the car rebounded back and started to rotate, he heard a scream behind him. Leo. Then it was joined by a higher-pitch female scream as the car hit a patch of loose gravel on the road and spun faster.

He kept steering into the spin, his instincts carrying him as his heart and mind freaked out.

It's happening again.

They're going to die.

It's your fault.

He pulled his mind out of that abyss and back into the present. He saw the cliff's edge coming at them fast, and with superhuman effort, he steered the car away. Time slowed down. They were just a few feet from the edge.

Inches.

Millimeters.

A hair's breadth from the drop-off, the car stopped.

Kayla unsnapped her seat belt and turned to the back seat, basically crawled right over. "Leo. Baby. Baby, it's okay."

She was speaking coherently, so that was one difference.

But Leo's sobs...

He couldn't look back to see what was happening to Leo. Had happened.

There was a knocking sound beside his head, but he couldn't turn to look at it.

He was somewhere else, in another car on another road at another time.

More knocking, then shouting. "Sir! Sir, are you all right?"

"Man, I'm so sorry... Oh, no, Dad, there's a kid in there." Some disassociated part of him heard the hysteria in the adolescent boy's tone.

There were noises. Someone opening the back car door. Voices: Kayla's. A stranger's.

In the distance, the sound of a siren.

His heart was still thudding hard in his chest. Sweat dripped down the middle of his back, soaked his palms that still clenched the steering wheel in a death grip.

With a giant sigh, he let his hands and his shoulders go loose. And then he couldn't hold himself up, or together, anymore.

Finn put his head down on the steering wheel and surrendered to the darkness.

Nine

The next morning, Kayla walked out onto her cabin's porch, coffee in hand, watching the sun break through a bank of clouds and cast its rays over the valley. Gratitude filled her heart.

They were okay. They were all okay.

Leo had a temporary cast on his wrist, and Kayla had a painful, colorful bruise across her shoulder and chest where the seat belt had dug in. She'd been terrified, of course, all through the ambulance ride to the hospital, until the doctors had reassured her that Leo had suffered no ill effects.

As for her resilient son, he'd loved the ambulance ride, the lights and the sirens. Future fireman or EMT, one of the guys had said, laughing as Leo begged to be allowed to sit up front and look at all the buttons and switches.

Finn seemed fine, physically, although he'd made himself scarce at the hospital, after a brusque question about whether she and Leo were all right. But that made sense. Delayed shock reaction, most likely. She couldn't wait to see him today, to talk to him about what had happened. During the car accident, but also beforehand, at the restaurant.

She wrapped her arms around herself, unable to restrain the big smile that spread across her face.

He liked her.

Finn, a real, honorable man, wanted to—how had he put it?—pursue a relationship. With her!

They had a lot to talk about. She was going to have to tell him the history with Mitch, let him know why she'd initially been so guarded. Now that she knew him better, she was pretty sure he would understand.

Behind her, she heard Leo call out, "Mom!" Footsteps pattered and then Shoney's tail thumped. She barked a happy greeting to her boy.

So the day was starting, Kayla would get Leo's breakfast and then help the ranch put on an amazing open house. There was so much to do, and she'd normally have been stressed out about it, but the events of last night had put it all in perspective.

She lifted her face to the sun's warmth and said a silent prayer of thanks: for their safety last night, and their freedom from Mitch, and for the fact that she and her son had found a home.

The day was a whirl of activity. They had almost double the number of visitors as they'd expected, due in part to their social-media sharing and in part to the word that had gotten out after the presentation last night. Everyone had to pitch in. Willie noticed that supplies of hotdog buns and cola were running low, and took off in the truck to buy more. At the kennel tour, Long John talked up the dogs so positively that people started asking about adopting them. So Kayla set him up at a table with forms to handle that unexpected bit of new business.

Kayla led tours of the ranch, and Finn talked about the veterans' side of it. Penny, who'd just arrived back in town late last night, explained the organizational structure. They all pitched in to keep the free food and drinks coming.

The whole time, people kept coming up to Kayla and hugging her and telling her they'd heard about the accident, and were glad that she and Leo were safe.

When she got a free moment, she asked Missy how everyone knew about the accident.

"Small town," Missy explained. "And Hank Phillips kept telling everyone over and over about it."

She nodded. "He felt awful, and so did his son." The boy, backing out of the driveway on a new learner's permit, had stepped on the gas instead of the brakes, and the car had shot into the road right in front of them. He'd apologized over and over, and had barely managed to restrain tears. "The outcome could have been so much worse. I hope that poor kid doesn't stop driving forever."

"You're such a sweetheart, Kayla," Missy said, hugging her. "A lot of people would be angry. You're really generous, being so understanding."

Kayla waved away the praise, but she felt it. Felt like she and Missy might become friends.

Leo spent much of the day running around with his buddies from camp and church, making siren sounds and crashing into each other, reenacting the car accident. After a few efforts, she stopped trying to keep him still. Play was his way of processing what had happened, and even though he was fine, it had been a scary thing for all of them.

She hoped for an opportunity to talk with Finn about it, but every time she got a free moment, he was busy. And her own free moments were few, because in between tours, she was creating live videos and posting them.

When people finally started leaving, Penny beckoned her into the offices. "Check it out," she crowed, clicking into the crowdfunding page on the old desktop computer. She spread her hands, pointing them toward the full-to-the-top fund-raising meter. "Ta-da! We have enough to pay the back taxes and more!"

They hugged and did a little jig, taking it out into the driveway, where Leo and other kids saw and laughed and joined in. Then they all escorted the few remaining visitors toward the parking area.

Finally, Finn walked up to her and she started to open her arms. Everyone was hugging, right? But something in his face stopped her.

"Can we talk?" he asked.

"Um, sure." Some of her excitement seeped away as her inner danger alert sprang to attention. "We made a good amount fund-raising. Plenty to pay the taxes."

"Good. Let's walk." His voice was flat, his face without emotion.

She watched as he started away from her, leaning heavily on his cane. Something was different about him. His usual calm now covered over an intense energy.

"Did you get the response you hoped for from the veterans in the group?" she asked his departing back. Hurrying after him, she kept talking. "There were more of them than I expected. All different ages, too."

As soon as they were out of earshot of the others, he turned to her. "Look, it's not going to work between us."

She tilted her head to one side as her heart turned to a stone in her chest. "I don't understand."

He didn't look at her. "It's not complicated. I thought about it and I realized that this—" he waved his hand back and forth between the two of them, still without looking at her "—that this isn't what I want."

The old interior voices started talking. Of course, a man like Finn wouldn't want to be with a woman like her. It had been too much to expect.

But, she reminded herself, she *wasn't* that unwanted girl. She wasn't ugly. She wasn't bland and boring. People in Esperanza Springs liked her. People here at the ranch, too: Penny, and Long John, and Willie.

Finn still wasn't looking at her. Why wouldn't he meet her eyes? "Talk to me," she urged him. "Let's try to work it out, whatever happened."

He shook his head and looked off to the side. Like he didn't even want to see her face. "No."

Confusion bloomed inside. She couldn't understand what had caused him to erect this sudden wall, to refuse to share what he was feeling even though they'd been getting closer and closer these past weeks and especially last night. "Why are you being like this?"

"I'm telling you, it's not going to work."

She put her hands on her hips. "We have something, Finn! What we felt at the restaurant last night, what we've been feeling for a while now, it's worth exploring. You're a good man—"

He held up a hand like a stop sign. "It's *not* real."

"Did someone say something today? One of the visitors?" She couldn't imagine what might have been said, nor that Finn would be so sensitive about hearing it.

"No. The guests were fine." He drew himself up,

wincing slightly as he straightened his bad leg. "Look, you did a good job helping with the open house. We worked together, probably more than we should have, and it led us to think we had feelings for each other. That's to be expected."

Tears pressed at her eyelids as she tried to recognize the man she cared about in the squared jaw, the rigidly set shoulders. "Why are you doing this?" she choked out.

"Mr. Finn!" Leo came running up and stopped himself by crashing into Kayla, then bouncing off her to Finn. "Look at my cast!"

Finn closed his eyes for the briefest moment. "I don't want to look at it." He turned and started to walk away, his limp pronounced.

Leo ran a few steps after him. "But, Mr. Finn, I want you to sign it."

"No!" He thundered out the word.

Leo stared after him and then looked back at her, his face sorrowful. "Why is he mad at me, Mommy?"

Kayla sucked in her breath and tamped down the loss that threatened to drown her. "It's okay. Come here." She knelt and opened her arms, and Leo was enough of a little boy that he came running and buried his face in her shoulder. Her bruised, aching shoulder, but never mind. She clung to him fiercely.

Finn had seemed to be different from other men, but apparently, he wasn't. In the end he didn't care enough. The abrupt way he'd pulled back stabbed her like a dull knife to the chest. She might not have believed him, might have thought he was covering something up, except he'd been mean to Leo.

That wasn't the Finn she knew. But maybe she hadn't really known him at all.

She didn't understand it, but she was a person who accepted reality when it stared her in the face. She'd never believed in fairy tales, like some of the girls she'd known in school, imagining knight-like boyfriends who'd sweep them off their feet, visualizing wonderful, romantic wedding days.

But Finn was romantic and wonderful last night, a sad little voice cried from deep inside her heart. *He wanted to pursue a relationship. What happened to that?*

She shook off the weak, pathetic questions so she could focus on the real one: how to go on from here. Should she stay in the best community she'd ever known? The community where Leo had relaxed out of his hypervigilant ways and learned to be a kid again? The place where she'd started to feel at home for the first time in her life?

Could she stay, seeing Finn every day and knowing the brief flame of their relationship was doused for good?

Two days later, Finn still hadn't gotten over the awful feeling of rejecting Kayla and Leo. Pushing Leo away had been like kicking a puppy. Pushing Kayla away... that had just about ripped out his heart.

But that pain didn't even compare to what he'd felt when the car had spun out of control, when he'd heard Kayla's gasps and Leo's screams.

He'd spent the past two days driving himself hard, getting the kennels cleaned before Kayla got back from dropping Leo off at his camp. When she was around, he made himself scarce by painting a couple of rooms at the main house, mowing grass, even exercising the two horses.

His leg was so bad he couldn't walk without an obvious limp, but he couldn't stop moving. The shame of what he'd started to do—the way he'd almost put another family at risk—just kept eating at him.

Now, near sunset on Monday, he felt a mild panic. Two hours of daylight left and he was out of chores. His leg was throbbing, and he should rest it, but to stop moving would let the thoughts in.

He noticed the old shed behind the main house. They needed to pull it down, build something new on the slab.

He would do that now.

He got his chain saw and carried it around the shed, planning his work. It wasn't hard to see the symbolism: *you're real good at ripping things down, breaking things apart.*

And that's all you're good at.

He destroyed everything he touched.

The last person he wanted to see was Carson Blair, the pastor, but here he came in his truck, down from the direction of Kayla's cottage. Jealousy burned in Finn. Had she replaced him so quickly, so easily?

"Need some help?" Carson climbed out of his truck and Finn saw he was dressed in work boots and carrying a pair of gloves.

"No. I got this." He revved the chain saw.

"That's not what I heard." Carson crossed his arms and watched Finn as if he could see into his very soul. He probably could. Wasn't that in the job description of a pastor?

Finn started on the posts that held up the shed, taking satisfaction in the harsh vibration as he cut through them. Once he'd gotten through one side, he pushed at the shed with his foot.

"Hey, Finn!" It was Penny, calling from the back door

of the main house. "I want some of that wood," she continued as she walked down toward Finn, the pastor and the shed. "It's weathered real nice. Got some things I could make out of it come winter."

"As a matter of fact, I know someone who'd like that door," Carson said. "Mind if I pull it off?"

Finn's intended task, a solitary demolition, was turning into a community event. Fine. He started pulling off some of the boards that were in good shape. "I'll get these cleaned up and bring them over," he said to Penny, hoping she would leave.

She didn't. "What's going on with you and Kayla?" She had her hands on her hips. Vertical lines stood between her brows.

"Nothing that needs to concern you."

"It does concern me," she said, "because they're thinking about leaving."

His head jerked around at that. He wanted to ask, *When? Why? Where will they go?* He wanted a way to patch the hole that her remark had torn in his heart.

But wouldn't it be best if they left?

"Finn," Penny said, "I like you. And I've put up with you and your darkness. The Good Lord knows we all have it. But the way you've treated her beats all." She grabbed a couple of boards and headed toward the house.

Finn glared after her. Maybe he'd been cruel, but it was kindly meant. Kayla and Leo would be better off without him.

He glanced over at the pastor. The man was removing the door from the shed, focused on the task, but Finn had a feeling he'd heard every word.

That impression was reinforced when the pastor

spoke. "Anything you want to talk about?" He asked the question without looking at Finn.

"No." Finn walked over to his truck, started it and backed it up to the shed. He found a rope in the back. Tied one end to the truck hitch and the other to a side support of the shed. "Gonna pull it down. Watch out."

He put the truck into gear and gunned it a little, watching his rearview mirror. With a scraping, ripping sound, the shed tilted and then collapsed, boards jumping and bouncing before they settled, the metal roof clanking down.

It wasn't as satisfying as he'd expected it to be.

He stopped the truck, climbed out and limped over to the wreckage. His doctor was going to have his hide for working like this without a rest, messing up his leg worse than it already was. He tugged at the aluminum roof.

Without speaking, the pastor went to the other side and helped him lift the roof off and carry it out of the way.

"Thanks," Finn grunted.

"Why'd you hurt her like that?" Carson went back to the demolished shed and pulled out a couple of jagged pieces of brick.

"To not hurt her." Finn ripped at the corner of the shed that was still standing. The rough wood tore his hands. Good.

"What do you mean?" Carson tossed the bricks into a pile of debris.

"I was driving when my wife and son were killed!"

Carson didn't speak, and when Finn managed to look at his face, there was no judgment there. But, of course, Carson was a pastor. He had to listen to all kinds of horror with a straight face.

Carson came over to help Finn tug at the stubborn corner post. "Does every person who's driving have total control over every circumstance on the road?"

Finn felt like he was choking. The pastor's words were bringing it all back, clear as if he were looking at a movie. He could hear his own voice, yelling at his wife. Her anger, the way she'd shoved at him.

He'd wanted to pull off the road. Why hadn't he pulled off the road?

Because it was a narrow mountain road. There was no place to pull off.

No place to escape the bobtail truck that had come barreling around the curve at a faster speed than it should have.

Just before impact, he'd caught a glimpse of the driver's face. He knew, now, that the driver hadn't died; that after being acquitted of any wrongdoing—although Finn seemed to remember something about a warning from the judge—the man had moved out of state.

The moments after the truck had rammed into them, he couldn't bear to relive. It was bad enough to have experienced the edge of it again when they'd had the near accident with Kayla and Leo.

"Well?" Carson gave the post a final tug and it came loose of its moorings with a scraping sound. He caught his balance and started tugging it toward the pile of debris. When he'd let it fall, he walked back toward Finn. "What do you say? Do you have total control?"

"No, but I should have." He tried to pick up a couple of loose boards, but his leg nearly gave out from under him. With a groan he couldn't restrain, he sat down on a stump. "I should have protected them." The lump in his throat wouldn't let him say more.

"I'm guessing you did the best you could at that moment." The pastor looked at him. "We aren't God."

Finn cleared his throat. "Why did God let that happen?" The words came out way too loud.

Carson looked at him steadily. "Talk to me about it."

"Me, Deirdre, that I can understand. We were fighting, and... But Derek was a kid. An innocent. He didn't deserve to die before he got to live!" Finn heard the anger and harshness in his voice. Anger felt better than raw grief, but not by much.

He hadn't known how angry he was at God until just this moment.

Carson wiped his forehead on the sleeve of his shirt and sat down on a pile of boards, a couple of yards away from Finn, not looking at him. Instead, he stared out toward the mountains. "I wish I had an easy answer, but I don't. Some things, we'll never know, not in this life. But your son is with Him, and I have to believe your wife is, too." He clipped off the words and looked away. "Some things we have to try to believe."

In the midst of his own raw feelings, Finn wondered about the pastor. He was a widower. How much had Carson worked through about his own wife's death?

Because he really couldn't stand on his leg anymore, Finn stayed where he was. He picked up a board, took the hammer from his belt and started pulling out nails.

Carson carried load after load of wood pieces over to the debris pile. When he almost had it cleaned up, he stopped right in front of Finn. "You don't have to suffer forever, you know. Maybe there was some sin in there on your part. There usually is. No one's perfect, but we *are* forgiven."

Forgiven. "Yeah, right."

"It's at the center of the Christian gospel. You know that."

A high-pitched sound came their way. It was laughter, Carson's girls. They ran toward the pastor, Leo right behind them. But when Leo saw Finn, he came to an abrupt stop. He looked at Finn a moment, both fear and reproach in his eyes.

Finn's throat closed up entirely. He busied himself with kneeling down—and man, did that hurt—to pick up some nails. Didn't want the kids to step on them.

"Daddy, come on! We caught a frog and a crawdad, and we wanted to keep them, but Miss Kayla said we better let them stay in the pond. But we took pictures, and Miss Kayla sent them to Miss Penny on her phone. Come see!"

A twin clinging to each leg, Carson looked over his shoulder at Finn. "Catch you later—maybe at the men's Bible study. We deal with some tough questions. Thursday nights." He lifted his hand in a salute-like movement and then followed his girls toward the car.

No way was Finn going to a men's Bible study. Bunch of brainiacs analyzing the deep hidden meaning of some verse of Scripture that no one cared about.

Although come to think of it…now that he was getting to know Carson, Finn realized it wasn't likely to be completely irrelevant.

It was only when he turned to head for his house that he noticed Leo was still standing where Carson's SUV had already pulled away. Looking directly at Finn. His face held sadness and longing and hunger. "Mr. Finn," he called.

That face and that voice made Finn want to run to the boy and scoop him up and hug him, tell him he *was* loved and that men—some of them, at least—could be protective father figures.

Except he wasn't one of those men.

With what felt like superhuman effort, he turned away from Leo and started walking toward his house.

A sound made him look back over his shoulder. Something like a sob. If Leo was crying...

"C'mere, buddy." Kayla knelt near Penny's place. Her voice sounded husky as she spread her arms wide.

Leo ran into them and she held him against her. Over the boy's shaking shoulder, she leveled a glare at Finn. And then her face twisted like she was about to cry herself.

Everything in him wanted to run to them, to hold them, to explain. To ask if they could try again, have another chance.

But that wouldn't be right, because for Finn, there couldn't be another chance. He couldn't *take* another chance.

He turned away and started walking.

It was the hardest thing he'd ever done. It felt like he was ripping his heart out of his chest and leaving it there on the ground, there with Kayla and Leo. But he was doing it for them, even though they didn't know it.

Kayla tried to brace herself for the task at hand. Straightened her spine and made herself move briskly, cleaning the dinner dishes off the table. It was now or never, though; she needed to pack tonight and leave early the next morning.

She drew in a deep breath. "Come sit by Mom, honey," she said to Leo. "We need to talk."

Leo had seemed dejected throughout dinner, and now,

as he plodded over to where she was sitting on the couch, he looked resigned. Kids could sense trouble, and it was pretty obvious things had changed here at the ranch. Leo knew: something bad was going to happen.

It was only now she realized he hadn't looked like that in a while. Redemption Ranch had been good for him.

But no more.

"Honey," she said, putting an arm around him, "we have to move away."

She felt him flinch. He was so little to already understand what that meant.

He stared down at his knees. "Why?" His voice sounded whispery.

Because I can't stand being around Finn, loving him, not able to have him. Because I can't stand to see you get your heart broken over and over.

"We need to find a place where we can live full-time," she said. "This job was just for the summer."

"It's still the summer," he said in a very small voice.

"I know."

Was she doing the right thing? There was no question that tearing Leo out of this life would be hard on him. Staying would be hard, too. She was just trying to find the thing that would be the least painful for him. The way he had been getting attached to Finn, the constant rejection was hurting him. He needed to be around men who wouldn't reject him.

And Finn. The conversation she'd had with Penny had cinched her decision. "Don't judge him too harshly," Penny had said. "You and Leo remind him of his losses." She'd hesitated, then added, "His son was just Leo's age."

Penny's words had shaken her, put everything she

knew about Finn into a different perspective. Even though she was furious at him for rejecting her and Leo, the deep shadows under his eyes spoke to her, tugged at her heartstrings.

If she and Leo caused Finn pain, it wasn't right for him to have to keep avoiding them. He had been here first. It was his place. He was the veteran. He was the one with the real skills.

"We're going to find another good place," she said to Leo.

"But I like this place," he said. "I like my friends."

"I know you do. You've gotten so good at making friends. You'll be able to make other ones." She tried to force confidence into her voice.

This was killing her.

He shrugged away from her and slid down to the floor. He lay down next to Shoney, who, as usual, was at their feet. The shaggy black dog rolled back into Leo, exposing her belly for a rub. "Shoney doesn't want to move." Leo rubbed the dog's belly and nuzzled her neck.

This was the worst part. "Shoney can't come."

"What do you mean?" Leo stared up at her, his eyes huge. Beside him, Shoney seemed to stare reproachfully, too.

"We're going to be driving a long time, and we'll stay overnight at some places that don't allow dogs." Kayla wasn't sure where they were going, but she'd found a couple of promising job possibilities online. "Once we find a new place to live, we'll have a lot of settling in to do. It wouldn't be fair to Shoney to take her to a brand-new place and leave her alone a lot, even if we were allowed to have a dog wherever we end up."

Kayla made herself watch as Leo started to understand. His eyes filled, brimmed over. She slid down to sit on the floor beside him.

"No, Mom!" Leo wrapped his arms around the dog, who obligingly nuzzled back into her son. "Shoney needed a home and we gave her one. We can't put her back in the kennel."

Kayla cleared her throat and swallowed hard. "We're going to take Shoney to Long John and Willie to look after."

"But Mr. Finn said they can't have another dog. He said it would be too much for them."

"Willie can keep her for a little while. Maybe after we get settled, we can get her back."

Leo buried his face in Shoney's fur. "We'll *never* get her back."

Kayla couldn't even make herself argue, because she knew it was probably true. And how sad that a little boy would have that realistic of an outlook, that he wouldn't be able to be comforted by kind platitudes.

She was kicking herself for letting them settle in this much. Why had she agreed to take Shoney? Of course Leo had gotten attached to her; they both had. But she should have thought ahead enough to know the job wasn't permanent.

To know things probably wouldn't work out, with the job or with Finn.

"I can help more." Leo sat up. "I can take her for more walks. I can feed her and clean up after her. You won't even know she's with us."

Kayla's heart felt like someone was squeezing it, twisting, wringing. She shook her head. "You've been the best helper. But we still can't take her."

Leo buried his head in the dog's side and wailed.

Best to do this fast now. She stood and knelt beside him, rubbing circles on his back. "Do you want to come with me? Help me bring Shoney's stuff up to Willie's place?"

"No! No! I won't go!" He flung his arm to get her away from him, catching her cheekbone with his little fist. Pain spiraled out from the spot. That would be a bruise.

Leo's upset escalated almost instantly into a full-fledged tantrum, and she couldn't blame him. She felt like lying right down on the floor and kicking and screaming alongside him.

But she was the grown-up. Like a robot, she found her phone and called Penny over Leo's screams and sobs. "Can you come up and look after Leo for half an hour?"

"You're really going through with this."

"I have to, Penny."

Kayla loved the older woman for not arguing with her, for just saying, "I'm on my way."

By the time Penny arrived ten minutes later, Kayla had gathered all Shoney's things in a big box. Leo's crying had settled down into brokenhearted sobs, and he wouldn't let Kayla touch or comfort him. He just hung on to Shoney, who, bless her, allowed what amounted to pretty rough treatment without so much as a growl or nip.

"Have you tried to talk to him?" Penny asked, pulling Kayla into the kitchen area, where Leo couldn't hear them.

"He's too upset. He just keeps crying."

"I mean Finn," Penny said. "He's going around looking like someone shot his best friend. If the two of you could hash it all out, you might have a chance."

Kayla hated thinking of Finn being miserable. But he'd get over it, probably just as soon as she and Leo left the area. She shook her head. "The surprise was that he started to act like he liked me," she said. "He's an amazing man. He could have any woman he wanted."

Penny dipped her chin and gave Kayla a pointed stare. "Doesn't seem like he wants just any woman. What if he wants you?"

"He doesn't. He told me." Kayla shook her head. "And anyway, that just doesn't happen for me."

"Kayla. You've got to work on—"

Kayla held up a hand. "I know. I'm a good person. Working here, getting away from…" She waved a hand in the general direction of the east. "From what was going on back in Arkansas, it's done so much for me. I appreciate your giving me a chance. I know you're the one who talked him into it in the first place."

"Do you know what happened with his wife and child?"

Kayla shook her head. "I don't need to know all that." She was curious, but knowing more details about Finn was likely to just add to her misery.

"You're making a mistake."

"Look, I've just got to take Shoney down to Willie's place before Leo and I both fall apart." She turned away from Penny, clenched her teeth together and walked over to Leo. "Come on, buddy. Let go of Shoney."

"No, Mommy. Please." He looked up at her, his face swollen and red. "Please."

She pressed her lips together to hold back the sobs and wrapped Leo in a hug. This time, his need for comfort overcame his anger and he collapsed into her arms, sobbing. They stayed that way for a couple of minutes. Shoney whined beside them and Kayla cried a little, too.

Be strong for him.

She drew in a gasping breath, then another. "Shoney will be okay. She'll miss us, but she'll be okay." She stood, staggering under Leo's weight as he clung to her.

Penny came over and reached out. "C'mere, buddy. We've got to let Mom go for a little bit."

Blinking hard against the tears, trying to breathe, Kayla took Shoney's leash off the hook by the door and attached it to the dog's collar. True to form, Shoney jumped and barked and tugged. She loved her walks.

Penny turned away, holding Leo tight. And Kayla walked an eager Shoney out the door.

At the bottom of Willie's porch steps, she knelt down and wrapped her arms around the shaggy black dog. "You've been a good dog," she said, rubbing Shoney's ears and the spots where her collar scratched her neck. Shoney collapsed down on her back, ecstatic with the attention, and Kayla tried to put all the love she felt into this last little bit of doggy affection.

The door of Willie's house opened and he came out onto the porch, backlit by the light from inside. Shoney sensed Willie's presence and jumped up, always ready for the next adventure.

Willie came down, rubbed the dog's head, and then picked up the box of Shoney's belongings and carried them up the steps.

Kayla buried her face in Shoney's coat, so soft and silky.

Shoney couldn't see, and she couldn't hear very well, but she made up for that in an ability to sense emotions. She licked Kayla's face and pressed closer into her arms.

Get it over with.

She picked up the dog, carried her up the porch steps and set her down, handing the end of her leash to Willie. "Thank you," she whispered.

Willie nodded, his weathered face kind. "I'll take care of her. She'll be all right."

Kayla nodded, turned and walked toward her cabin, her eyes almost too blurred to see. She couldn't go back and help Leo when she was a wreck herself. She stopped in the cool night air and drew in big breaths, trying to pull herself together.

Down at the main house, she saw a few lights. Penny had come in a hurry, leaving the place lit up.

And there was a single light on in Finn's place. The front room. She pictured him there in his recliner, reading. He liked old Westerns and Western history books. Rarely watched TV. They had that in common.

So, yeah, he was probably reading.

But she'd never know what.

The thought of that—that she'd never get to tell him a silly little thing like that she'd finished the Louis L'Amour book he'd lent her—made her shoulders cave in. The loss in her stomach and chest hurt too much. She wrapped her arms around herself.

She'd thought since they had all those weird things in common that they might have something. She'd imagined sharing books and listening to country music together, on into the future.

But it wasn't only about that.

It was about the caring in his eyes. The respect she had for him as a man. The way they both worked hard at life, and tried to overcome past challenges with an upbeat attitude.

In the end, they *hadn't* overcome. She shouldn't be surprised, but she was. Like a fool, she'd gotten her hopes up.

She looked up at the stars and tried to pray, but God seemed as distant as they were.

She drew in a deep breath and let it out slowly. Then another. Good—she was steadier. She turned and marched toward her cabin.

Through the screen door, she heard Leo sobbing. Her heart gave another great twist.

"I don't know if I can do this, Father," she said to the cold, glittering stars.

But she had to. No choice, when you were a mom. She squared her shoulders and headed into the cabin.

Ten

The men's Bible study, which consisted of a circle of nine or ten men at Willie's house, was breaking up. Men stood, talked, helped Willie to clear away the refreshments he and Long John had made.

It was pretty obvious to Finn that Willie hadn't needed any extra help tonight. Calling Finn and saying he did had been a ruse, probably done in cahoots with the pastor.

Finn didn't really mind. Because one, he had nothing else to do; and two, he'd gotten thought-provoking ideas out of it.

Something bumped against his leg, and he looked down and saw Shoney. A bad feeling came over him. "What's she doing here?" he asked Willie.

"Kayla's leaving tomorrow, and she felt like she couldn't take Shoney along. She doesn't know where they'll land, what kind of place they'll live in or where they might have to stop along the way." He paused. "I put Rockette back in the kennel for now, but I can't leave her there."

That made him sigh, and he knelt and rubbed Shoney's sides, causing her to pant and smile.

She was okay now, with Willie. She was a resilient dog. But going back into the kennel, with her disabilities, wouldn't be a good thing.

And what must it have been like for Kayla and Leo to let Shoney go? They'd gotten so attached. Her blindness and deafness hadn't been any kind of barrier to them; they'd accepted her as she was, and they loved her.

It must have just about killed them to leave Shoney behind. The thought of it put a lump in Finn's throat.

The father of the boy who'd nearly hit their car came over and clapped Finn on the shoulder. "Glad to see you here tonight, because I wanted to thank you again," he said. "Without your driving chops, that accident could have gone a lot worse. If we had to collide with someone, I'm glad it was you."

Finn clenched his teeth to keep himself from snarling at the man. Finn wasn't glad it had been him, because it had broken him apart from Kayla and Leo.

But that was a good thing, right? Because it kept them safe. Safe from the unsafe Finn.

Who this man was saying was actually extra safe. That didn't compute at all.

"My son, man, he's still beating himself up about it," the man continued, oblivious to Finn's inner turmoil. "I wish he'd been here tonight to hear what the pastor had to say. We're none of us in control, not really, are we? Once something's past, you can't keep beating yourself up for it, I told him. You've got to move on."

"Right," he said as the man moved on to talk with someone else.

All the words he'd said swarmed in Finn's head and he didn't know how to process them.

We're none of us in control.

But he wanted to be in control. Wanted to be able to protect anyone on his watch.

He was the man of the family. He was supposed to be able to protect women and children. Back in the Middle East, his was one of the few units that hadn't had a failure in that regard. He hadn't killed any civilians, and neither had any of his men.

He supposed he'd come back cocky, thinking he was superhuman.

The punishment for that arrogance had come real fast.

He folded up the extra chairs and stacked them on the porch to carry down to the main house, then went back inside to see if Willie and Long John needed anything else.

They didn't, of course; they were fine. "Glad you could come," Long John said. "Mighty sad about that gal and her boy leaving us. Sure you can't talk 'em into staying?"

Long John's voice sounded plaintive, and Finn realized that these two old men had grown attached to Kayla and Leo, too. She'd listened to their stories, laughed at their jokes and appreciated their efforts to father her. And Leo had become a grandson to both of them.

"Sure am going to miss them," Willie said.

Everyone liked Kayla and Leo. No one wanted them to leave.

An idea of stopping at her place started to grow in the back of his head. She wasn't likely to forgive him for being so mean to her and Leo, but at least he could explain. Apologize. Pave the way for her to be able to come back for a visit, at least, see the old guys and Penny.

He hoisted the chairs to his shoulder, said goodbye to the last couple of men who were coming out of the cabin.

"Want me to drive those down the hill?" Bowie Briscol asked. "That's what I usually do when we meet here. No need for you to kill yourself hauling them."

Finn started to refuse and then thought, *Why not?* Obviously, Willie and Long John had manufactured the excuse to get him to come, but they'd had a good thought in doing so. They were doing their best to take care of him.

That was what Redemption Ranch was all about. People taking care of each other. And, he realized, he wanted Kayla and Leo to have the chance to be taken care of a little bit, too.

He couldn't repair the fragile thing he and Kayla had started to build, but could he maybe get her to agree to stay on? It had to be safer for her, better for Leo. They needed security and stability. Redemption Ranch could provide that.

He helped load the chairs into the back of Bowie's pickup, waved off the offer of a ride for himself and then strode toward Kayla's cabin, feeling more energized than he had since their falling-out.

There was a car outside Kayla's cabin. Not her old beater, but a late-model, city-style sedan.

Finn stopped and took a few steps back. Under veil of twilight, he watched as a tall, broad-shouldered man in a suit walked up to the door, opened it and went inside.

Heat rushed up Finn's neck. She'd gotten together with another guy this quickly? He'd been having all these *feelings* for her, and she was basically cheating on him?

Like Deirdre?

And with some suit in a fancy car, who probably had enough money to give her the life of luxury she didn't need, but probably wouldn't mind having?

His fists clenched and he hit the road to his place, making it home in record time.

When he got home, he went in the bedroom closet and started digging through boxes, frantic as a loon. He knew what he wanted to find and why.

It was a box of photographs of the years with Deirdre and, later, Derek. He'd hidden them away because it hurt too much to look at them, but he needed to now. Needed to remind himself what it felt like to live with a cheater. To remind himself that women couldn't be trusted.

He pulled out the wedding album, flipped through it and stuffed it back in the box. When those pictures were taken, they'd been happy, of course. Deirdre had been faithful to him, before the wedding and at least through the first year.

It was when he'd gone to the Middle East that she'd changed. He could track it in the pictures she'd sent, that he'd pasted up around his bunk like a fool, showed off to the other guys. She'd lost weight and done up her hair fancy, started wearing high heels.

She'd looked great.

Only when he'd come back had he realized she wasn't doing it for him—not for him alone, anyway.

They'd fought, separated, almost broken up, but then she'd gotten pregnant. It had infuriated her that he'd insisted on a paternity test, but given how much she was running around, it had only made sense to him. When Derek had turned out to be his baby for sure, he'd thought they could mend things between them.

And they had, for a while. The first couple of years of

parenthood had been hard, but happy. But when Derek had entered his terrible twos, Deirdre had had her own rebellion.

She'd had issues, obviously. And Finn, young and immature and haughty, hadn't dealt with them well.

He shoved the photos back in the box and leaned against the bed, straightening out his leg, flexing it. The idea that he'd fallen for another cheater...

But even as he had the thought, he was comparing what he'd seen with the reality he knew.

Kayla wasn't the type who'd go into town and pick up some new guy in a bar, just because she'd had a fight with Finn. She just wasn't. And no, he and Kayla hadn't had a relationship, not really, but they'd had the beginnings of one. She'd felt it. She'd said it herself: *we have something here.*

And a woman like Kayla, feeling like that, wouldn't go looking for love somewhere else—not so soon, at least.

There had to be another explanation. A friend, cousin, brother. It would make sense if she'd called someone to help her out, and he should be glad she had a little male protection.

He didn't *feel* glad, but he knew he should.

As a matter of fact, he should call his detective friend and tell him there wasn't anything more to search for. Whatever secrets hid in her past, he didn't need to know them. Because through all that had happened, he'd actually learned to trust Kayla.

That was some kind of progress, at least.

He walked outside for some air, scrolling through his contacts to make the call, when the familiar, rattly sound of Kayla's car came along the road. It made him smile. He was always glad to hear it, glad she and Leo and that beater of a car had made it back to the ranch in one piece.

No sooner had he thought it than worry tugged at him. When she left the ranch, where would she go? Who would be there to notice she'd made it safely home? To worry if she hadn't?

He'd give her a call later, see if they could talk a little. In preparation for that, he lifted his hand in a wave.

She stared back but didn't wave in response. Her face was set, rigid. She gunned the bad motor and continued up the hill.

Well. Maybe talking to Kayla wouldn't quickly mend the broken bridges between them.

But at least he could call off his watchdog.

He found his friend's name and clicked the number.

Kayla drove the rest of the way up the dirt road that led to her cabin, confused. Why had Finn waved?

She was *not* going to get excited because the man had waved.

Leo, depressed about it being his last day of camp and about Shoney, had finally fallen asleep in the back seat. Fortunately, he hadn't seen Finn's semi-friendly expression. No use getting his hopes up again.

No use getting hers up, either.

Today had been her last day of work, too, and that had been hard; saying goodbye to all the dogs, working alongside Penny because Finn was AWOL.

Her heart was shredded and she had a million things to do and he *waved*?

She glanced back at Leo, his face sweet and relaxed in sleep as it hadn't been since she'd let him know they were leaving. The day-camp group had given him a little goodbye party today, which was sweet. But not surprising. That was the way Esperanza Springs was.

She pulled up to the cabin and stopped the car. When she leaned into the back seat and tried to pull the still-sleeping Leo out, she could barely manage it. Asleep, he seemed to weigh a ton.

It had been so great when Finn had carried him to bed.

She shifted, getting her feet under her, getting him adjusted on her shoulder. She wouldn't have Finn helping her anymore. And guess what: she didn't need him. Her muscles were far stronger now than they'd been six weeks before, when she'd started at Redemption Ranch. And it wasn't only her muscles that were stronger. So was her mind and her confidence.

She shouldered open the front door. It was good to be home. Despite all the turmoil, she'd sleep well tonight.

She took another step and froze, just inches inside.

Why had the door been partly open? She always locked the door when she left.

Even as she reviewed the moments when she'd left the house, she stepped back. One step. Two.

The door swung the rest of the way open. And there, inside, stood Mitch.

She jerked back and Leo stirred, so she forced her body into stillness. How had Mitch found her? How had he gotten into her house? Where was his car? Sweat broke out on her face and back. "What are you doing here?" she asked around a stone of terror that seemed to have lodged in her throat. "Where's your car? How did you find us?"

"I pulled the car around back." He leaned against the

door frame and crossed his arms, and his presence in this place felt like a violation. "Oh, and by the way, that was a real cute photo of my son on one of the Eighty-second sites."

Kayla sucked in a breath. Had *Finn* posted a picture? Surely not, but…

"Nice how the name of the town was right there in the picture," Mitch said, his voice and stance casual, his eyes anything but. "Esperanza Springs Community Days. What kind of a town did you bring him to? It's not even American!"

"The Fourth of July." Kayla closed her eyes, just for a second. That soldier Leo had mistaken for Mitch. Kayla had gotten the man's wife to delete the photos with Leo, but several other people had been around. One of them must have taken a photo and posted it. Probably thinking a closed group website was safe.

No time to wonder why Mitch had been browsing through a random Eighty-second site. No time to wish she'd been more diligent about keeping cameras away from Leo.

They'd been found. Now she had to find a way to keep her son safe, against all odds.

Seeing Mitch brought back the last time, his big boots kicking her as she'd lain on the floor, trying to breathe, trying not to wake up Leo, gauging the distance to the door, escape, safety even as she'd known she could never leave her son in the house alone with his father, not even for a minute.

She backed to the edge of the porch. The worst thing she could do would be to go inside with him. Out here, with the stars starting to twinkle overhead and the cool, piney breeze from the mountains, she had freedom and a chance.

"Get in here." It wasn't a suggestion, but an order. "Want to talk to you."

Despite his casual posture, his hands were fists and his eyes burned beneath a furrowed forehead. If she ran for it, holding Leo, she'd only make it a few steps before Mitch caught them. Leo would wake up and be afraid.

If Mitch had to fight her and drag her inside, his rage would boil over. If she went inside as he'd asked, it might placate him for a moment.

She nodded and walked through the door and tried not to feel doomed when he closed it behind her. Despair and hopelessness wouldn't save her son. "Let me put Leo down."

Maybe Leo wouldn't have to see this and get traumatized again. Maybe she could talk Mitch down, make promises of seeing him tomorrow, get him to leave tonight. And then she could call Penny and Finn and the pastor and anyone else she could think of to get her out of this bind, because, yeah, she was independent, but she had people to help her now. She wasn't alone.

Mitch stood in front of her, blocking her way, and her stomach twisted. She'd forgotten how big he was. He could knock her out with one blow from his hamlike hand.

She knew. Knew, because he'd done it.

She straightened her spine. "Let me pass. I want to put him down so I can focus on you." *And get you out of here.*

His eyebrows drew together and he looked at her, suspicious, assessing. "Fine." He stepped to the side, not far.

She had to walk within a couple of inches, close enough to smell his sweat. Her stomach heaved.

Keep it together. She'd thought to put Leo on his bed in the sleeping loft, but then he'd be a sitting duck, trapped. She didn't want him that far away from her. So she grabbed a blanket off the back of the couch, wrapped it around him and took him into the bathroom. She slid Leo onto the floor and put a towel under his head for a pillow. Thankfully he was a good sleeper.

She turned on the bathroom light, in case he woke up and was scared. *Please, God, whatever happens to me, protect him.*

Mitch stood in the doorway, emanating hostility she could feel like radiant heat. She turned, patting for her cell phone. Good—it was in her back pocket. She'd be able to get to it if he turned his back.

Which, from the hawk-like way he was watching her, didn't seem all that likely.

She walked right up to where he stood in the doorway, knowing that to show weakness would be fatal. "Come sit down," she said, feigning confidence and hospitality.

When he moved out of her way, she closed the bathroom door behind her. Anything to increase the chances that Leo would sleep through this, that he wouldn't get set back from all the progress he'd made.

"Would you like something to drink?" *Would you like to turn your back long enough for me to call for help?*

"Get me a beer," he ordered.

"Don't have any. Soda?"

He snorted in obvious disgust. "Fine." But he followed her to the refrigerator and stood too close, so she dispensed with the idea of a glass and handed him the can. Grabbed one for herself, too. It might come in handy. Lemon-lime carbonated beverage, square in the face, could sting, and a can could work as a missile, too.

She gestured him toward the sitting area and he plopped down on the couch. "Come sit by me."

Um, no. "I'll sit over here," she said, keeping her voice level as she felt for the stand-alone chair and sat down.

"Why are you acting so cold?" He banged his soda down on the end table.

Was he kidding? Hot anger surged inside her, washing away her fear. "You're an uninvited guest. You broke into my cabin. You expect me to roll out the red carpet?" And then she bit her lip. She had to stay calm in order to keep Mitch calm. It was tempting to scream out all the rage she felt at him, but she had to be wise as a serpent here, pretend a gentleness she didn't feel.

"You sure it's not to do with the big guy?"

"What big guy?" she asked, although she knew he must mean Finn.

How did he know about Finn?

"The one that lives right down the road and spends a lot of time with you," he said. "Finn Gallagher."

The surprise must have shown on her face, because he laughed, a high, nasty sound. "Oh, I've been watching you for days now. I know exactly what you've been doing."

She couldn't restrain a shudder. "What do you want with us?"

"You're my wife." His voice rose. "And he's my son. You left me. I have every right to bring you home."

She couldn't let this escalate. Something she'd read in a publication about dealing with aggressive dogs flashed into her mind. She relaxed her muscles and lowered her voice. "Mitch. I'm not your wife. We're divorced."

He glared. Apparently, what worked on dogs wasn't going to work on Mitch. And then his head tilted to one side as he shook it back and forth, and the whites of his eyes showed, and everything inside Kayla froze.

Mitch didn't look stable or sane. He barely looked human.

Every other time he'd been rough with her, he'd seemed angry—enraged, even—but he'd had his senses and he'd known exactly what he was doing.

His expression now made it seem like he'd lost it.

He stood and walked toward her, hands out. "I want you back."

"No, Mitch. Don't touch me."

He kept coming.

She jumped up and away from him and pointed at the door. "Go on. Get out of here or I'll call the police."

He seemed to get bigger, throwing back his head and shoulders and breathing hard. Heavy and threatening, he came at her.

She spun away. "I mean it. I have no problem calling 911."

"What're you going to call with, this?" He reached for the cell phone in her back pocket. She jerked away from his hand and heard her pocket rip.

He had the phone.

Miserable, hopeless thoughts from the past tried to push in: *You deserve whatever he does to you. This is the only kind of man who'll like you. No way can you escape him.*

But she was stronger now. Wasn't she? She *didn't* deserve Mitch's abuse. She wasn't alone; she had friends. She'd even, for a little while, drawn the attention of a good man.

Finn respected her. Finn thought she was a good mother. A good person.

So did Long John and Willie and Penny.

She had to try to get Leo and run. Or maybe she could barricade them in the bathroom. She made a break for it, dodging Mitch, but he grabbed her arm and pulled it, hard. Pain ricocheted from her wrist to her shoulder, and she couldn't restrain a cry.

He took a pair of handcuffs—*handcuffs?*—out of his suit jacket and clicked one side to her wrist, the other to one of the wooden kitchen chairs, forcing her to sit. "Just in case you get any ideas," he said with a sadistic grin.

She tugged, but the cuffs held. And he'd cuffed the arm he'd hurt, so every effort shot pain from her wrist to her shoulder.

"Mommy?" The plaintive voice from the bathroom doorway made them both freeze. "Daddy!" There was an undertone of happiness there, but fear, too.

"Get back in the bathroom," Mitch snarled.

"But…"

"Go!"

Leo edged, instead, toward Kayla. She could see the sweat beaded on his upper lip, the vertical lines between his eyebrows, the shiny tears in his eyes.

"It's okay, honey," she said, trying to put reassurance into her voice and eyes, her free arm reaching for him without her being able to stop it. "It's going to be okay."

Leo took a step toward her and Mitch stepped between. "You pay attention to me, not her!"

He grabbed Leo's shoulder and walked him back into the bathroom, none too gently. Leo started to cry.

There was a swatting sound, and Leo cried harder.

She exploded out of her chair and headed toward the bathroom, dragging the chair behind her.

Mitch emerged, slamming the bathroom door behind him. From the other side, Leo sobbed.

"Stop right there!" Mitch dug in a black case against the wall and turned toward her with an automatic rifle in one hand and a hunting knife in the other.

Kayla froze, then sank back onto the chair. He'd truly gone over the edge. He'd always liked weapons, but he'd restricted their use to shooting ranges or country roads. He'd never pointed one at her, and he wasn't doing that now, but the threat was palpable. Not only to her, but to Leo, because a gun like that could make a wooden door into splinters in a matter of seconds.

A stray thought broke through her terror: not one of the vets she'd met at this ranch—Long John, Willie or Finn—would flaunt weapons so casually. Mitch wasn't a typical vet.

She looked around desperately, wondering how to escape or what to do, aware that if she made a wrong move, it might be her last.

On the counter was the big travel coffee mug Finn had given her when he'd noticed her rinsing and reusing a Styrofoam cup. He was a man of few words, but his actions said it all. He paid attention and tried to make her life a little easier, a little better.

She could trust him because of how he'd treated her. She should have told Finn the truth. Airborne or not, Finn would never have betrayed her to someone like her ex.

Mitch came closer and again she smelled his perspiration, tense and sour. He loomed over her. "You left me and took my son. You can't get away with that. You're going to pay."

He didn't care about Leo, had never been even an okay father, but she didn't dare to say it, not with him this volatile. She pressed her lips together.

Why had she made such a stupid mistake? Maybe if she'd been honest and up front with Finn, he wouldn't have dumped her.

Leo's cries were louder now, breaking her heart. "Let me go to him," she pleaded. "Just let me talk to him a minute."

Mitch turned toward the bathroom. "Shut up!" he thundered.

But Leo's crying only got louder.

A desperate plan formed in her head, and without a moment's hesitation, she put it into action. "Give him my phone," she said. "He likes to play games on it. He'll quiet right down." And maybe, God willing, he'd use his five-year-old technology skills to call for help. She'd taught him how to use the phone to call 911, and he knew how to call Penny, too.

Mitch hesitated. Leo's wails broke her heart, but they obviously grated on Mitch. He pulled her phone out of his pocket and headed toward the bathroom.

Please, God.

He hesitated at the door and looked back. She tried not to betray anything on her face.

"You're trying to get him to call for help!" He kicked the bathroom door. "You shut up in there, kid, or I'll hurt Mommy."

Leo's cries got quieter. From his gulps and nose-blowing, it was obvious he was trying to stop.

Poor kid. If they could get out of this alive…

Mitch came back over and squatted in front of her. "Suppose you tell me what you thought you were going to gain from leaving Arkansas." He glared at her. "Go on—talk. This ought to be good."

Discouragement pressed down on Kayla.

"Talk!" he yelled, shaking the leg of the chair so that she nearly fell off.

From somewhere inside her, outrage formed and grew. There had been a time when she'd thought she deserved bad treatment, that it was the best she was going to get, but she knew differently now. "I left because I wanted a fresh start for me and Leo," she said, chin up, glaring at him. "I refuse to live a life hiding from you and terrorized by you."

Mitch looked...startled? Was that worry on his face? She'd never stood up to him before.

"You unlock these handcuffs and go back where you came from," she ordered, sweat dripping down her back.

He raised a hand. He was going to punch her.

"Don't. You. Dare." She put every bit of courage and confidence she had into the words.

Mitch stepped back and looked around. "What was that?"

"What?" Was he seriously going to pretend he'd heard something to avoid a confrontation with her? Hope swelled. "You didn't hear anything. Unlock these cuffs!"

"I heard something." He lowered his weapon and moved to the window of the cabin like a cop in a TV movie. A bad movie.

If she could just get to her phone, which he'd left sitting on the chair...

She tried to scoot, quietly, while he leaped around the room, pointing his weapon into every corner. She got within a yard of the phone. If she could move a few inches closer…

"Aha!" he yelled as he leveled the rifle at her.

And Kayla realized two things.

No matter how weak Mitch ultimately turned out to be, he was holding a deadly weapon.

And he *really* didn't act a bit like the veterans she'd gotten to know over the past two months. "Were you ever even in the Eighty-second Airborne?" she blurted out before she could think better of it.

He roared something indistinguishable and came at her.

Eleven

Finn had been wrestling with God, and God was winning.

Guilt about his past mistakes with his wife, he was realizing, had made him into a worse person. Maybe that was why God forgave mistakes. Because to spend time punishing yourself for all your past sins meant you weren't much good to anybody in the present moment.

Further, he realized that he did want to be involved with people. He wanted to be a husband and father again and do it right this time.

He'd never entirely get over what had happened with Deirdre and Derek. He'd always wonder whether he might have been able to save their lives if only his reflexes had been faster, his speed lower, his focus more intent.

But he wanted to go on living. And that had a lot to do with Kayla and Leo.

His phone buzzed, and he was relieved to escape his own thoughts. He clicked onto the call. "About time you called me back," he said to his friend.

"I have very little to report," Raakib said. "Believe me, my friend, I tried, but I haven't found anything against Kayla. From all accounts, though, her ex-husband, Mitch, is bad news. Quite volatile."

It was nothing more than what he'd expected. He knew Kayla was good. Even without someone vouching for her, he knew it.

Crunching gravel outside the window marked Penny's arrival at her place. Unlike Kayla's car, Penny's had a quiet, well-maintained sound.

Kayla's car. Worry edged into his awareness.

When Finn had been getting jealous of the man in the suit, Kayla hadn't even been in her cabin. So what was the guy doing there? "What does her ex look like?" he asked Raakib.

"Sharp dresser," Raakib said. "Tall, about six-two. Large, because apparently he's obsessed with lifting weights. Though not as large as—"

"Gotta go," Finn said. "I think he's here."

He clicked off the call and grabbed his gun and ran outside. Penny was getting out of her car with a load of groceries.

"Drive me up to Kayla's," he barked. "I think her ex might be here."

Penny's face hardened. She dropped the bags and got back into the car. Finn got into the passenger side, and she gunned the gas the moment he was in.

The car he'd seen before was gone. But Kayla's was there.

So maybe it had just been a friend of hers, who'd visited and left, and Finn would be making an idiot of himself. But he wasn't going to take that risk. Not with Kayla and Leo.

"Whoa—wait," Penny said as she pulled in beside Kayla. "Look at that."

Finn looked in the direction she was pointing. Willie was coming up the road at a pace that was almost a run. Behind him, Long John limped as fast as Finn had ever seen him go, Leo beside him, holding his hand.

It would have looked comical, except for the intent, angry, scared expressions on all three faces.

And the fact that both Long John and Willie had weapons at the ready.

Finn had to salute their courage, but mostly, he had to get to Kayla before they did. "Keep them back," he said to Penny and ran to the cabin door.

Finn walked in on chaos. The man in the suit was on the ground, on top of Kayla. But Kayla was scrambling out from under him. A chair fell and knocked into the man—Kayla almost seemed to be jerking the chair around—and she punctuated that blow with a kick in the man's face.

She might even be winning the fight, but Finn couldn't wait for that to happen, especially with the automatic weapon on the floor near the man.

The man was going for it.

No.

No way. Finn moved faster than he ever had in his life, leaping onto the man just as his arm reached for the weapon.

The man was strong, burly. He landed a good punch on Finn's face.

"Get the weapon," Finn yelled, and Kayla rolled and stretched her arm and grabbed it.

The door banged open just as Finn started to get the

jerk under control. "Sorry," Penny called, "I couldn't hold them back. Leo, wait!"

"Mom!" Leo ran to Kayla.

Finn got the guy into a full nelson. He saw that Penny had secured the gun. Kayla was laughing and crying, one arm wrapped around Leo. "How did you get out?"

Leo puffed out his chest and grinned.

"Kid climbed out the bathroom window," Willie said, shaking his head in obvious admiration. "Came running down and got us."

Finn's prisoner—who had to be Mitch, Kayla's ex—started to struggle.

"I could use a hand here," Finn said, breathing hard. "We need to tie him up."

"I've got some handcuffs," Kayla called, "if you can take them off me and get them onto him."

Only then did Finn realize that Kayla had been fighting this fight while handcuffed to a wooden chair.

Her hair was coming out of its braid, her face red and scratched, the sleeve of her shirt ripped. He had never seen anyone so beautiful.

"Key to the handcuffs," Penny barked at the man, who stopped struggling and actually looked a little cowed. He nodded toward his side pocket.

"I'd get it," Penny said, "but I don't think I can stand to touch him."

Willie extracted the key from the man's pocket, none too gently. Penny freed Kayla and handed the key back to Willie and Long John along with the handcuffs. A moment later Mitch was sitting in the chair, his hands cuffed behind him.

"Those military pins you're wearing," Long John said. "What unit were you in?"

"Eighty-second Airborne," he mumbled.

Finn's head jerked around at that. "Seriously? Dates of service?" This guy did *not* seem like any paratrooper Finn had ever met. More like one of the wannabes that sometimes hung around veterans' events acting way too aggressive and boastful. "I think we're gonna check on that."

"What's your full name?" Long John, who prided himself on keeping up with the latest technology, had his phone out and was clicking on it.

"It's Mitchell Raymond White," Kayla said.

"Friend in veterans affairs owes me a favor," Willie said. "Think I'll give him a call."

"Where were you stationed?" Finn asked. "And I didn't hear you say your dates of service."

Mitch looked away. "I was on special assignment."

Right. Finn looked over at Kayla and Leo. Kayla met his eyes, her own wide and concerned. But Leo was talking excitedly, explaining how he had climbed out the bathroom window.

Good. The boy wasn't listening. He didn't need to learn about his father's deception this way.

Willie clicked off his phone. "They never heard of him."

"He's not in this record, either," Long John said, scrolling through his phone's screen.

Finn glared at the lowlife cuffed in the chair. "Stolen valor is a pretty serious offense."

"Especially when you've been getting veterans benefits for years," Kayla said from the corner, her voice indignant.

Willie drew himself up to his full height—about five-five—and glowered at Mitch. "Between that crime and what you tried to do to this woman and child, young man, you're going to be behind bars for a good long time."

Penny fussed over Kayla while Willie called the police and Long John tended to some scratches Leo had gotten jumping out the bathroom window.

As for Finn, he sat off to the side, against the wall, his mind reeling.

Something terrible had almost happened, and together, they'd managed to stop it. Kayla and Leo were safe. And he made a decision: he wasn't going to waste another moment.

Whatever Kayla felt, he knew his own heart.

But when he turned and really studied her, he noticed she was holding her arm tight to her side. "Do we need an ambulance?" he asked Penny, who was kneeling beside Kayla, running her hand over her shoulder, arm and wrist.

"Not for me," Kayla answered promptly.

"Maybe a quick visit to the ER or the Urgent Care," Penny said. "I don't think your arm is broken, but it's definitely sprained. Here, let it loose."

As Penny held Kayla's arm straight to examine it more carefully, Leo watched with a little too much concern in his eyes. "Hey, Leo," Finn called softly, and the boy looked his way. "You did a real good job today."

A smile tugged at Leo's mouth. And then he ran and jumped into Finn's open arms.

Finn's heart swelled almost to bursting as he held the wiggly little boy, then put him down to hear, again, the story of how Leo had screwed up his courage and climbed out through the window to find help for his mom.

Leo was hungry for praise; well, Finn was glad to

give it to him, because what he'd done had been more than praiseworthy.

Finn had a hungry heart, too, and talking to the little boy, commending his quick thinking and agility, seemed to fill it up a little.

He and Leo might be good for each other, he reflected. And as he distracted Leo from the distressing sight of his father being led away in handcuffs, as he talked about ways Leo could help his mom while her arm healed, he felt like he'd been given a second chance.

If only he could convince Kayla to take a chance with him.

A week later, Kayla strolled the midway of the county fair, with Leo holding her hand and Finn beside her.

She wondered what to do.

Rather than packing up the car and moving away, she and Leo had stayed around, at first to give evidence against Mitch, and then to let her arm heal a bit, and now...

Now it was decision time. Tomorrow would be the back-to-school information day. All the kids at Leo's camp were talking about it—the start of first grade was a big deal—and Leo wanted to know: Would he go to school here, or were they moving somewhere else?

She didn't know the answer.

They'd fallen back into their routine here. Leo had been attending camp. Kayla had helped with the dogs as best she could, given her wrenched arm. Shoney had come back, first for a visit, and then an overnight to sleep in Leo's bed, and now somehow she was back to living with them again, her old accepting, ecstatic self.

Finn had been friendly and helpful, but a little

guarded. They hadn't really had the chance to talk in depth, because Leo, understandably, was sticking pretty close to Kayla's side.

Mitch had gone to jail, then gone before the judge, and then somehow managed to post bail. With no contacts in Colorado, and forbidden to see Kayla or Leo, he'd gotten permission from the court to go back to his job in Arkansas. Kayla suspected he would also try to destroy evidence of his fraudulent claims of military service, but the likelihood was that he'd be charged with a federal crime. That was because he'd received benefits and discounts he wasn't entitled to.

She still worried about him, and would until he was behind bars. But with Finn, Penny, Long John and Willie on high alert—and friends back in Arkansas reassuring her daily that Mitch was there, going about his routines—she found she was able to relax.

She wouldn't go back there, but she might move on. She liked mountain living, but there were plenty of places, especially here in the West, where she could have it.

The problem was, Finn wouldn't be there.

Penny had talked to her about taking on some additional duties as they worked to expand the ranch. They'd need cleaning and cooking help if they were to open the old bunkhouse.

Everything in Kayla longed to stay in this community where she'd made friends and felt valued, where Leo was happy and social, where the mountains loomed good-heartedly over the flat bowl of the valley, reminding her on a daily basis to look up to God.

But if staying meant watching Finn move on, take up

with other women, become a distant friend, she didn't know if she could bear it.

Too much thinking. She squeezed Leo's hand and inhaled the fragrances of cotton candy and fry bread.

"Mom! There's Skye and Sunny!" Leo tugged at her hand. "Can I go see them, please?"

"I'll come with you," she said and then looked questioningly at Finn. "Want to come along?" They'd basically ended up together at the fair by accident, and she didn't want to assume he intended to stay with her and Leo.

But he smiled amiably. "Whatever you two want," he said and followed along.

That was how he'd been acting. Like he wanted to do things with her and Leo; like he cared. But there was a slight distance. They hadn't talked about why he'd pushed her away before, and it kept a wall between them.

"Leo!" Skye called as they approached. "We're going to go do the pony rides. Can you come?" She clapped a hand over her mouth and looked up at her father. "Oops. I'm s'posed to ask first. Daddy, can Leo come with us?"

Carson fist-bumped her. "Good job remembering, kiddo. And of course Leo can come."

"Can I, Mom?"

Not can *we* go, but can *I* go. He was growing in independence and she was glad and sad all at the same time.

"I'll watch over him," Carson said. "It's run by folks in our church and it's supersafe."

"Sure," she said, and instantly the three children ran toward the other side of the fairgrounds, Carson jogging after them, calling for them to wait.

That left her and Finn, standing together. It felt awkward to Kayla, so she looked out across the valley. The sun was low in the sky, just starting to paint the tips of the mountains red. God's reminder that He lingered with them, even in the dark of night.

"Do you want to ride the Ferris wheel?" Finn asked abruptly. "Over there," he added, gesturing toward the little midway.

How did she respond to that? *Yes, I want to do that because it seems incredibly romantic*? *No, because I don't want to get closer right before we go away*?

"Scared?" he asked, his eyes twinkling down at her. "I'll hold your hand."

That sent a shiver through her. She wanted him to hold her hand, not just now but into the future. He was looking at her funny, and she almost wondered whether he was having the same thought.

But then, as they headed toward it, he kept looking at his watch. Was he bored? Eager to get back to the ranch?

"The line's kind of long," she said, giving him an out in case.

"That'll give us the chance to talk."

Oh. He wanted to talk. Kayla tried to ignore the tremor in her core.

As soon as they got in line, he turned away from the loud family group in front of them. "Why didn't you tell me about Mitch?" he asked quietly.

She looked up at him. "I asked myself the same question, when I thought he'd got us trapped for good. I...I should have. But Airborne Rangers are so loyal, and I'd bought into his story."

Finn's mouth twisted. "Beneath contempt. All of it."

"I know. I still can't believe he maintained that lie for so long. And I feel like a fool for buying into it."

"You had no way of knowing." He shook his head.

"Those guys…they're good at concealing what they're doing. He'll pay for it. But, Kayla." He put his hands on her shoulders. "Even if he *had* been a military brother, I would never choose someone else over you."

Kayla's throat tightened and she felt the tears glitter as she looked up into Finn's eyes. He was being sweet; he was being kind.

But she couldn't quite trust his kindness. "Why'd you push me and Leo away, Finn? That really hurt."

He nodded, studying her face. "Do you have some time?"

A half smile tugged at the corner of her mouth. "The line's moving pretty slow." The group ahead of them was playing a guessing game now, Mom and Dad obviously trying to keep their young kids occupied. Behind them, a pair of teenagers stood twined together, clearly focused only on each other.

Finn drew in a deep, slow breath. "You know my family died in a car accident."

She nodded.

"Well, I…I was driving."

"Oh, Finn." She stared at his troubled eyes as the implications of that sank in.

No wonder he was so mired in it—tortured, even. How would you recover from something like that? She took his hands and squeezed them. "I'm so sorry. How awful that must've been."

He nodded. "I was officially exonerated, but…" He shook his head slowly, meeting her eyes briefly, then looking away. "I've lived ashamed for a long time."

His dark sadness, the way he drove himself, all of it made more sense now. Of course Finn would beat himself up, even over an accident that wasn't his fault. He was a protector to the core, and to not be able to protect his family, to have been driving when they were killed… Wow. She put an arm around his waist and squeezed, because she couldn't find anything sufficient to say.

"Next!" The attendant barked out the words.

Finn helped Kayla climb into the narrow-seated cart, and then turned back and spoke to the attendant in a low voice. The attendant looked at him, looked at Kayla and then shook his head.

Finn moved and reached for his wallet. She couldn't see what he was doing. Paying the attendant? They hadn't gotten tickets, but she'd thought rides came with the price of admission.

"Let's get a move on," somebody yelled from the line, the voice good-natured.

Finn climbed into the seat beside her and fastened the bar over them, carefully testing it for security.

"Were you giving that guy a hard time?" Kayla asked.

Color climbed Finn's neck. "You could say that."

As the Ferris wheel slowly filled up, and their car climbed incrementally higher, Kayla looked out over the fair, the town and the broad plain, sparkling with a few lights from far-flung homes and ranches. Her heart gave a painful squeeze.

She loved this place. She loved the land and the people and the discoveries she'd made here, the strength she'd found.

The trouble was, she loved Finn, too. And to stay here loving him… Well, that would be hard and painful. Not just for her, but for Leo, who had also come to care for the big, quiet soldier.

Most likely she *couldn't* stay, but that made her reckless. "Tell me about the accident," she said. "What happened?"

He took a breath and looked around as the Ferris wheel jolted them to the next level. "You really want to know?"

Something told her that for him to tell it was important, was maybe a key to his healing. If she couldn't be with him, she could at least do that much for him. Be a true friend. She reached for his hand and squeezed it. "I want to know."

He looked down at their interlaced hands. "So I was driving, and we were having a fight. What it was about doesn't matter now."

She nodded, sensing that he needed to tell it his own way, at his own pace. The twilight, the small passenger car, the separation from the noise of the fair, made it seem as if they were alone in the world.

"She took Derek out of his car seat."

"While you were driving?" She stared at him. "What mother would do that?"

"She wanted to get out, wanted me to stop. But it wasn't safe, because there was no shoulder to the road. So I kept driving. I was yelling at her to buckle him in again, to fasten her own seat belt, but instead, she grabbed the steering wheel and jerked it."

"And that's what…" She looked at his square, set jaw, the way he stared unseeingly out across the plain, and knew he was reliving what must've been the worst moment of his life.

He cleared his throat. "We went straight into a semi-truck bobtail."

"And they were both killed." She said the last word

steadily, because she sensed that it all needed to come out into the open.

"Instantly." He hesitated, then met her eyes. "I was buckled in. I came out of it with barely a scratch."

"Wow." She'd been holding his hand through the whole recitation, but now she brought her other hand around to grip it, to hold his hand in both of hers. "That must have been so, so awful."

"I wished I had died. So many times. What kind of a man lets his family be killed while he walks around healthy and whole?"

She hesitated, looking up at his face. Around them, the noise and lights seemed to dim. "I don't want to speak ill of someone I don't know, someone who's dead, but it does sound like she caused the accident."

He nodded. "That's what the police report concluded, and I know that in my head. In fact, I'm still angry at her for taking Derek out of his car seat. If he had been buckled in, most likely..." He looked away, his throat working.

"Yeah." She remembered how she'd felt when Mitch had upset Leo, how she'd worried that the hurting would become physical. That was really what had prompted her to leave. But to have a partner actually cause your child's death... Her own throat tightened, and she cleared it. "Nothing I can say can make that better, but I am so sorry."

"It doesn't make you hate me?" He sounded like he really thought she might.

"Of course not!" To see this big, experienced soldier look so insecure, so torn apart... All she could do was put both arms around him. Not as a romantic thing, but for comfort. Friend comfort. It was a short hug, and then

The Soldier's Redemption

she let him go so she could meet his eyes. "If we were blamed for all the awful things that happened to us, nobody would escape unscathed. Look, I know I'm not to blame for being abused by Mitch. At the same time, I made a bad choice in marrying him. Maybe you made some bad choices, too." She reached up and ran a finger along his square jaw, feeling the roughness of his whiskers. "You're human, Finn. Just like everyone else."

He closed his eyes, nodded slowly and then looked at her. "I've started to make my peace with it."

"The men's Bible study?"

"That, and the pastor, and some thinking and reading I've been doing."

"I'm working on making my peace about Mitch, too." Finn would understand that. He would know that resolving such big issues in your past didn't happen all at once. It was a process, one that would never be fully completed, not in this world.

She'd barely noticed that the Ferris wheel had filled up and that they were moving fast now. But as they went over the top and sank down, her stomach dropped and quivered. She wasn't sure if it was the Ferris wheel or the company, but she squeezed Finn's hand and giggled when it happened again.

He put an arm around her. "You *are* scared," he said. "Chicken!"

"I'm not!" she said with mock indignation. "Look at this." She lifted her arms high in the air.

"Whoa!" He grasped her hands and put them back firmly on the bar in front of them. "Don't do that to me."

So she put her head on his shoulder as the ride continued, then slowed and finished. The cars jerked as people exited the Ferris wheel, but when it was their turn, the operator skipped past them.

"Hey, you missed us," she called back to him, but he didn't seem to be listening.

Oh, well. She didn't mind being here with Finn for a little longer. She looked up at him and noticed beads of sweat on his upper lip. Was *he* the one afraid of the Ferris wheel? Somehow, with his life experiences, she didn't think so.

Now they were back at the top of the Ferris wheel, and it creaked to a stop. She leaned over the edge and looked down. The whole wheel was empty except for them. "Hey," she yelled down. "You forgot us!"

"Kayla."

She jerked around to look at Finn, because there was something strange in his voice.

"Kayla," he said quietly as he took her hand, lifted it to his lips and kissed it. "Kayla, I'm no good at this, but I…I…"

She cocked her head to one side, staring at him. "What? Finn, what is it?"

"It's not a spot to get down on one knee, and anyway, I can't do that too well, not with my bad leg. But…" He reached into his pocket and pulled out a small box. Opened it and then looked into her eyes. "Kayla, I don't want you and Leo to leave. I want you to stay, and not just stay as a coworker. I know it's fast, and I know a lot has been happening in your and Leo's life, but…"

Kayla couldn't breathe.

"So I know it might take you a little time, but for me, I'm more sure about this than I've ever been about anything in my life. I love you, Kayla. I want to marry you. I want to make a family with you and Leo. And if you say yes—even if you say you'll consider it—I promise to protect you and care for you for the rest of my life."

It was more words than she had heard from Finn, all at once, since she'd met him. Warmth, even a banked fire, shone in his eyes. He was holding her hands so gently.

She felt tongue-tied.

"At least look at the ring?"

"Oh!" She looked down and saw a simple square diamond on a white gold band. She reached out and touched it with one finger, and the sharp hardness of it made her realize that this wasn't a dream, that this was real. The most real thing she'd ever experienced, and the best.

And yes, she should wait and think and make sure. But no way. "Nothing would make me happier than to marry you. And Leo, well, I know he'd be completely thrilled to have you as a dad."

He clasped her to him and held her, and the swelling emotion in her chest made her dizzy. "I want to be a dad to him," he said. "But if he needs to stay in touch with Mitch, I understand that and I will help to make that happen."

Her heart melted at his words. She suspected that Finn could be jealous and possessive, but he was willing to work with Mitch to make things good for Leo. That was selflessness.

He touched her chin, and when she looked up at him, his face was framed by stars. "Did you really say yes?"

She smiled. "Yes! Yes, I said yes!"

He let out a quiet exclamation and lowered his lips to hers.

As he kissed her with a restrained intensity that warmed her all the way to her toes, she felt like her shoulders were loosening, her chest was opening, and she was free. Free of that feeling of being unwanted. Free of having other people think she was a mistake.

He lifted his head and smiled at her. From the ground, she heard the sound of cheering.

"Do people know what you're doing?" Suddenly it all came together for her. "Did you plan this? Did you tell the attendant?"

A sheepish expression came onto his face. "I'm sorry, but I did have to get a few people involved. Carson knows. That's why he brought the twins by, to help get Leo out of the way."

From below, she heard a shout. "Mom! Did you say yes?"

"Leo knows?"

Finn rolled his eyes and shook his head. "He wasn't supposed to. But I guess Carson let it slip to the girls. That or the ride attendant or the jeweler spilled the news. It's a small town." Then he leaned over the edge of the cart and waved. "Hey, Leo. She said yes. That okay with you?"

Kayla might have been the only one who heard the uncertainty in his voice.

"Yes! Yay!" Leo cheered, and others were talking and laughing and cheering, too. The Ferris wheel slowly rotated their car to the ground and stopped, and there were all the people she cared about: Penny, and Long John and Willie, and Carson and the twins. And of course, Leo. When the attendant opened the bar, Leo ran to them. She opened her arms, and Finn opened his, and Leo leaped into them.

"Want to go for a quick spin as a family?" the ride attendant asked, his eyes crinkling at the corners.

"Yeah!" Leo yelled.

And as they both hugged him, then tucked him carefully in between them, talking and laughing—and in Kayla's case, crying—the warmth and rightness of it overwhelmed her. She looked up at the sky, and the stars seemed a canvas on which God had written His plan. "Thank You," she murmured. "Oh, Father God, thank You."

Epilogue

Four months later

Finn stood at the front of the little church, and even though his fancy tie was half choking him, he couldn't be happier.

"I can't stand weddings," Finn's veterinarian friend Jack DeMoise said from his position behind Finn.

"That's no way to talk, young man," Willie said. It had been a toss-up for Finn which of the two older men should be his best man, but Long John had insisted he didn't want the honor; he had other plans for the wedding. Plans, as it turned out, to walk Kayla down the aisle.

So it was Willie and Jack who stood up with Finn, and Carson who was doing the ceremony. Finn knew what it was to have a band of brothers, but this group wasn't bonded just by fighting; they were bonded by life. They were family.

The changes that being with Kayla and Leo were already working in him felt like a gift from God. He'd been closed in, hurting, before, such that joy couldn't gain a foothold. Now he felt joy every day.

Kayla, too, was changing and growing. She and Leo had been seeing a counselor, trying to deal with Mitch and what he'd done. Both of them seemed to stand taller, as if burdens they'd been carrying had been lifted from their shoulders.

The music changed, and he looked down the church's short aisle. There was Leo, a cute little man in a suit and new cowboy boots, standing straight and serious with his responsibility of carrying the rings. He walked forward slowly, biting his lip, and then he looked up at Finn. Finn gave him an encouraging nod and smile, and Leo started to speed up. Soon, he was running full speed, clutching the satin ring pillow in his fist.

What could Finn do but kneel down and open his arms to the little boy who already seemed like his own son?

He got Leo straightened out and standing in the right place, and looked up in time to see Penny, already halfway down the aisle. Her dress was simple, her hair loose, and behind him, he heard Willie suck in a breath.

Poor Willie. If only everyone in the world could be as happy as Finn was.

Next came Kayla's friend Janice from back in Arkansas. She'd come for the wedding and basically fallen in love with the place, and Finn wouldn't be surprised if she moved out here sometime soon.

And then he lost focus on everything else because there was Kayla. Her classic wedding dress, sleeveless and ivory and fitted, looked incredible. Rather than a veil, she wore a wreath of flowers.

She had a lightness in her steps, a lift to her face that

was completely different from when she had arrived at Redemption Ranch. She was radiant, and it wasn't just a figure of speech. She glowed.

She held Long John's arm and Finn wasn't sure who was supporting whom, but they both looked happy.

Kayla caught his eye as she got closer, and love shone out from her eyes, as deep blue as a Colorado sky. This time, he was the one who sucked in a breath.

"You're a blessed man," Carson said, and Finn looked sharply at him.

"It's the simple truth," Jack said from behind him. "You know me and Carson wish you all the happiness in the world." There was a hunger in his voice. Neither Carson nor Jack thought they could have this kind of happiness. They had talked about it a lot in the men's Bible study.

Of course, a year ago, Finn would have never guessed he could have this kind of happiness, either.

As the music swelled, Long John delivered Kayla to Finn. He was taking his fatherly role seriously. "You better be good to this woman," he said to Finn, his voice stern.

"I intend to." Finn watched as Long John sat down and then centered his full attention to Kayla.

Kayla, soon to be his wife.

His heart soared as the pastor began the simple ceremony. Against all his expectations, he'd been given a second chance. With a woman so well suited that they seemed to have been made for each other.

They had both had their share of grief and tribulation. But maybe that just made this happy time all the sweeter.

"I love you," he said to his bride, keeping his voice low.

But not low enough. "You're getting ahead of your-self," Carson said, and the congregation laughed.

"I'm okay with that," Kayla said. "I love him, too."

"Then can we be done and go have cake?" Leo asked.

"Just a few minutes, buddy," Finn said, rubbing Leo's hair.

So Carson made quick work of the ceremony. And then came the cake and congratulations, toasts and dancing. It felt good to be surrounded by their friends, old and new.

But after a couple of hours, Finn pulled Kayla aside. "You had enough of all this?" he asked.

She nodded up at him, her eyes shining. "I can't wait until we're alone together."

He put a hand on either side of her face, leaned down and kissed her lightly. "We're the bride and groom, so we don't have to wait," he said. "What do you say we take off?"

Her eyebrows shot up. "Can we?" she asked. "Without saying goodbye?"

"We have to go through the hall to do it. Should we try?"

Of course, they didn't make it, because Carson and Jack had their eyes open for just such a move. While Finn and Kayla found Leo and said goodbye to him—he was staying with Penny, but had plans for daily visits with Carson and the twins—the news that they were leaving spread through the crowd.

When they made a run for the borrowed old Cadillac they were taking to their brief mountain honeymoon, they were pelted with birdseed. And sometime while the reception had been going on, the car had been decorated with signs, tin cans and shaving cream.

But that was all fitting, because they were starting their lives together as part of a community. A nosy, interfering community, but one that wanted the best for every member, where neighbors were quick to extend a hand.

Once in the car, Finn leaned over and gave Kayla the thorough kiss he'd been longing to give all evening, earning catcalls and cheers. He looked into her eyes. "Are you ready?" he asked.

She nodded, her eyes locked with his. "I'm so ready," she said. "Let's go."

* * * * *